The Decomposer
Part 1
Fallow

By C. Sonberg Larson

DOUBLE HELIX
PUBLISHING

Copy editor: Carol J. Amato
Cover Design: Jeffrey Vogel
Interior Design: C. Sonberg Larson and Jeffrey Vogel

Published in the United States by Double Helix Publishing.
ISBN-13: 978-0692334935
ISBN-10: 0692334939

I dedicate this book to my 3rd grade teacher, Gloria Orozco—the one who saw the writer.

PART I
SYMPATRY

ONE

In a wood of pines in the Angeles forest, Auster stood, as silent and still as the trees around him, letting his mind travel. He registered the myriad signals sent from around the globe, all unintentional.

Such a waste. Humans could be so alive, yet they dwell in their minds, reliving instead of living.

Spreading out his long fingers in front of him, he analyzed his crepe-like skin. *This body has served me well, but it has grown frail. Time to renew.*

His black trench coat snapped in the wind, giving it a cloak-like feel as it whipped around his spare frame.

A cough interrupted Auster's trance. He followed the sound to see an expensively dressed man approaching. He took a step forward. "You chose an interesting place to meet, Rawson. This is where you were born."

"Yes, it was." Rawson gazed at the tall canopy above. "These trees were mere saplings when you brought me back." He held out both arms. "Look at them now—robust giants, life force strong and true."

Auster closed his eyes and felt the energy of the trees. "Acknowledged." He turned his attention back to Rawson. "You've been a good Hand. Your decision to be destroyed is unfortunate."

"Being a member of your legion of slave killers is not a life."

"It seems to have suited you well." Auster gestured toward Rawson. "You're well-coiffed, multilingual, have wealth and advanced degrees—a far cry from the angry half-wit in torn and bloodied clothes I met years ago." He tipped his head as he recalled. "Long, stringy hair, gaunt from inadequate nutrition, filthy, living in squalor, barely able to articulate a thought. You were quite a sight."

Rawson stared at the ground, an undeniable look of shame flooding his face. "I'd be a liar if I didn't admit to relishing the attributes of being a Hand. Evolution has its perks without a doubt, but over time…" He peeled his gaze from the forest floor and stared at Auster. "As you know, being able to see without the use of rods and cones can be as much of a punishment as a gift."

Auster huffed. "Only a human would believe that."

"I wouldn't know." Rawson shook his head. "I'm glad I'm not one of your Sentries. For years, I coveted their power, their immortality."

"The unique characteristics that make a Sentry come around once in several hundred years, sometimes longer."

"It was a blessing in disguise." Rawson smiled. "I'm allowed to go. They're not."

"True," Auster said. "Sentries must remain. Still, Hands rarely request to leave."

"I'm tired." Rawson leaned against the trunk of a pine as the coo of a mourning dove cut through the trees. "The path is lonely. For over a hundred years, I've traveled the world for you."

He looked Auster up and down. "Fought your war, yet I still don't know what the hell you are."

Auster smiled. "What you are is more fascinating. A serial killer who wants out because he's tired of killing. Ironic."

"Ironic or not, find another to aid you in your quest. I've done my part to bring hell to this place. You agreed to let me go if I asked. I'm asking. And make it quick."

"Fair enough. Be assured there is another ready to replace you at this very moment. In case you haven't noticed, your world is fertile ground for those like you to flourish." Auster raised a hand. A light shone from each of his fingertips.

"I've noticed." Rawson stood up straight, squared his shoulders, and lifted his chin. "Do it."

A ray of white light shot from Auster's palm into Rawson's body. Within seconds, the ashes that were Rawson spilled across the blanket of pine needles.

As the last bit of residue drifted through the trees, Auster lifted his head to the sky, closed his eyes, and inhaled the clean, mountain air. "So many with potential. So, so many. Who will call to me first?"

Auster focused, as though listening to some unheard message. Then his eyes snapped open. "Could it be?" He turned toward the west, his black coat billowing in the breeze.

He smiled.

TWO

Jonathan Thornton Flynn clutched the phone to his ear and stared at the computer. "Those figures include the foreign sales?"

"Yes."

"That's three months in a row, Wilks."

"I know, sir."

Johnny leaned closer to the computer screen. "Maybe we're at the mercy of the fluctuating economy. Run the East Coast numbers again, wholesale and retail. I also want to see if we can push foreign sales." He ran his fingers through his hair. "Trends show the affluent haven't cut down on luxury spending, so let's also look closely at production costs. We may need to send more work overseas."

There was a moment's pause. Johnny knew the numbers would reveal nothing new. Profits were slimming down because Vander Broek Corporation, Flynn's main competitor, was playing dirty. Johnny was aware that Jan Wilkinson, his vice president, knew this as well, but Wilks, loyal from the start, wouldn't question another look.

"The report will be on your desk in the morning, sir," Wilks said in his Dutch accent. "Would you hold for a moment while I send the query?"

"Sure." Johnny stood up and gazed out at the city through the glass wall of his office. By the age of forty-three, J. T. Flynn Diamond Corporation had made him a billionaire. He'd bought the high-rise the previous year after the company acquired two multi-million-dollar competitors.

"I'll admit, Wilks. I didn't think they could squeeze me out at this point."

"Those in the diamond business do have an annoying fealty."

"No shit. Their antiquated thinking really shakes my tree. I'm still paying for last year. How was I supposed to know the fucking old-timer Hallisford would keel over and die?"

"He couldn't handle learning that the business he'd started thirty-five years ago was being absorbed," Wilks said.

"Apparently." Johnny punched the desk. "I may as well wear a fucking black hat."

"No need, sir. The competition is painting it on just fine. You know there's always buck-back after the acquisitions."

Johnny clicked on the business section of the web. "I take it you've read the news today?"

"About Hector Dennington?" Wilks asked.

"Yeah. It doesn't look good when we crush Owen Corp and their CEO is immediately appointed to the board of directors at Vander Broek."

"No, it doesn't."

Johnny thought for a moment. "Dennington's long-time connections give Vander Broek that sentimental boost that reeks of old money, and the rich love their own."

"True. They didn't welcome you when you were a young go-getter, and they hate you even more now. We'll talk more after reading the reports again. Anything else?"

"Not now. Give me time to think on it."

Johnny ended the call and shut down the computer. Anger surged through him as he felt the stress. "Second place is as good as last," he muttered to himself. "This just won't do."

He stepped close to the window, staring at the flame-orange glow of the horizon and contemplating his next move. He placed his palm against the cool glass. *I know what I have to do.* He sucked in air until his lungs were full. *I never thought I'd have to go there again.* He checked his watch. *If I take off now, I'll be able to set up the meeting for tomorrow.*

Johnny left the office, hopped into his jet-black Lamborghini Diablo, and squealed out of the parking lot. He raced along the winding coastal road, glancing at the pink sky as the ocean swallowed the sun. Twenty minutes later, he drove through the large electric gates that guarded his vast estate. He pushed open the heavy front door, finding the house dim and silent.

"Hey," Danielle's soft voice echoed in the foyer as she entered from the living room. Her smile faded when she saw Johnny's expression. "Bad day?"

Johnny loosened his tie. "Yeah."

She stroked his hair and kissed him. "You'll get through it, strongman. You gonna keep working in your office?"

He looked around. "Where are the kids?"

"Michael's at band practice and Maya's at track." Danielle sighed. "I told you all this yesterday."

Johnny crossed his arms. "I can't keep all of their extra-curricular shit straight, Dani. When do they actually sit in class and learn, for Christ sake? They're gonna to go into high school next year fucking illiterate."

Danielle chuckled. "Listen to you, grump."

"Sorry." Johnny paused. "We've taken another loss."

"Really? That's three months in a row."

"I know." Johnny placed his hands on Danielle's shoulders. "It's not that I don't care about the kids. I just have a lot on my mind."

"It's okay." She leaned forward and pecked him on the cheek. "Go into your office and I'll bring you some tea."

Johnny's gaze followed Danielle as she walked toward the kitchen. He exhaled, allowing the peace of home to surround him, then headed to his office. He flicked on the light, slid onto his desk chair, and sat motionless for a moment, feeling the anger rise again like boiling milk. "I've worked too hard to have a bunch of nostalgic fucks wreck everything I've built."

He reached forward and logged onto the computer.

"It's not my fault that old shit dropped dead. He should have known his limits and retired rich. If you choose to play, don't cry when you lose."

Johnny scanned his on-line contact list, found who he was looking for, and typed the email. "Well, Vander Broek, here's a little something to feed your fucking nostalgia. Right where you *live*, motherfucker!" He pressed send, then sat back and inhaled deeply.

The door cracked open and Danielle walked in, stopping abruptly before reaching the desk. "Oh, my god! Are you ok?" She took a half-step back.

"Yeah, what?" Johnny sat up a little.

"Your face, it looks strange. Are you feeling sick?"

Johnny stood up and peered at the mirror on the wall. His skin looked raw and seemed to close in over his eyes, making them look small and beady. "Weird." He ran his hands across his cheeks. "I can't feel it. Probably allergies. Maybe something I ate."

"I think you should finish up soon and come to bed early." Danielle turned and walked toward the door. "If you still look like that tomorrow, go see the doctor. I've never seen you like this and it worries me." She turned, one hand on the jamb. "You sure you feel okay?"

"Yeah, bed sounds good." Johnny shut down the computer.

∞∞∞∞∞∞

Johnny sat in the kitchen sipping the day's first cup of coffee. He smiled when he heard the familiar rumbling above, followed by the thunderous descent of the twins down the stairs.

"'Sup, Dad," Michael chirped as he burst into the kitchen and flung the refrigerator door open.

"Not much," Johnny answered. "How was the field trip yesterday?"

"Fine."

"What did you do?"

"Nothin'. Just walked around."

Johnny turned to Maya. "Did you do nothin', too?"

Maya smiled. "We went to the natural history museum. We did do a lot of walking around." She turned toward Michael and raised her voice. "Although someone may have made out with Wendy Simmons in the North American Mammals room."

"Shut up!" Michael spun away from the fridge and threw a bag of lettuce at her.

Maya dodged it. "HEY!"

Johnny tried to keep a straight face. "No food fights!" He pointed at Michael. "Pick it up!"

Michael trotted across the kitchen. His glasses slid off as he bent down to swipe up the bag.

Johnny leaned toward him. "Is Wendy hot?"

Michael grinned. "Smokin'."

"Hey, Dad!" Maya crossed her arms. "Would you ask me that if I made out in the museum?"

"No way," Johnny said. "I'd track the bastard down and tell him to keep his lips off you or I'll cut 'em off!"

"Not fair!" Maya tried to look mad as she dropped a protein drink into her bag, but Johnny knew his and Michael's laughter made it impossible.

Paula Strathmore, the family nanny and housekeeper, strolled into the kitchen, humming a tune and smiling as she tied an apron around her waist. "Good morning to you, Mr. Flynn."

"Morning, Paula."

Paula looked at the twins. "What's all the laughin' about?"

"Nothing," they answered in unison.

Paula planted her fists on her round hips, her gaze narrowing as everyone cracked up again.

She turned to Johnny. "Do I want to know what thirteen-year-olds would be chucklin' about this early, Mr. Flynn?"

"Probably not," Johnny answered with a laugh.

"All right, then." Paula checked her watch. "Off to the car with you both or you'll be late for school." She turned to Johnny. "I'm making stew for dinner if that sounds good, sir."

"Sounds great."

"I'll stop at the market after I drop off the children. Text me if there's anything else."

"Okay. Thanks."

"Bye, Dad," Maya said.

"Have a good day, Petal."

Michael smiled as he high-fived Johnny. "Later, Pops."

"Later, Casanova."

Michael nodded up and snickered.

Danielle came in from her morning jog as the kids were leaving. She took Johnny's face in her hands. "You're back to normal. No swelling or anything."

"Probably just stress."

Danielle grabbed a coffee cup. "I knew my strongman would make it through."

Johnny smiled and flexed. "Strongman off to meeting now." He stood up, patted her bottom, and refilled his coffee to-go mug.

Not wanting to be too conspicuous, he elected to drive the Porsche to his morning meeting. He headed northeast toward a little coffee house in Pasadena. He reached toward the glove box for a pack of smokes only to remember he'd quit a decade ago.

Johnny recited one of his father's mantras. "Payback's a bitch." He gripped the steering wheel.

"But this isn't just payback, Daddy," Johnny said aloud as he clicked on the radio to a classic rock station and steered onto the freeway. "They're trying to kill your boy. This is a reckoning."

THREE

A uster soared above a small cluster of huts nestled amongst the trees thirty miles off the South American coast. He focused, reading the energy below. The familiar pattern radiated.

The life source is present.

He changed form, appearing only as dust and mist, and dove down.

The sun was setting and people bustled about, finishing the day's work. Women set down baskets overflowing with ripe fruit and gathered palm fronds to be woven. Men returned with fresh fish to be cooked for the evening meal and smoked for later use.

Auster glided from hut to hut, reading each life force. *Each dwelling seems to have a presence.*

He swooped into the hut of a man and woman who had married the night before. As tradition stated, they were expected to forgo work the day following the ceremony for the purpose of coupling. Conceiving the day after marriage was a sign that the child would be born strong and bring luck to the village.

The sweaty bodies pumped and thrust. The blood stains on the woven mat beneath their hips was also a positive sign.

Auster felt the energy. *Both of them have it.* He sent forth the light. In an instant, the couple disintegrated.

He drifted outside, where the air felt heavy and moist. As storm clouds raced in from the low horizon, the adults called to their children. Strong, brown legs churned, bringing a score of laughing youngsters toward their homes. They peeled off in the direction of their families' huts, plowed through the doors, closed the flaps, and settled down on thick rugs of woven reeds. Silence fell upon the village as the cadence of the downpour swelled.

Auster glided into the hut closest to the trees and materialized. The family inside backed against the far wall. The mother, eyes wide with fear, moved to stand in front of her two children. Auster raised a hand and in an instant, all three were gone. The father fell to the ground, speechless and bewildered.

Auster visited each hut, and before night fell, he drifted toward the coast, leaving only twelve broken and confused survivors to contemplate what had just happened.

FOUR

Johnny spotted Ming on the patio of the little coffeehouse in Pasadena, sipping his espresso and smoking a cigarette. The Asian man looked much younger than his age, blending in quite well with the hookah-smoking college kids wearing overpriced jeans made to look like they were straight from the local thrift store.

Ming made eye contact and flagged Johnny over. "It's been a couple of years," he said as Johnny sat down.

"Yeah, it has been a while." Johnny eyed the jagged scar on Ming's left cheek, which had faded over the decades, but was still pronounced. He then motioned toward the pack of cigarettes. "Bum a smoke?" *So much for quitting.*

Ming lit a new cigarette for himself with the old one and then tossed Johnny the pack. "I read business is going well. You've become quite the corporate badass."

"Not so much lately," Johnny said. "The tide has turned. The old fucks are trying to make me *persona non grata* of the diamond industry." He took a drag, forcefully blew out the smoke, then gritted his teeth. "And that just won't do, my friend."

"I see." Ming ashed on the ground. "So, what did you have in mind?"

"We're going a little larger this time." Johnny leaned forward and laid out the plan.

Just before the clock struck noon, Johnny walked back to his car, a pot of coffee churning in his stomach and his mind reeling with what he just put into play.

I'm two million dollars poorer. Ming will get the other three million when the job is done. Let's hope this is the last time.

∞∞∞∞∞∞

A week later, Johnny flipped on the morning news and heard the report.

> "Last night, a robbery occurred during the annual Vander Broek Diamond Celebration, leaving five dead."

Johnny cracked a smile. *Hope Ming made sure the old fuck, Dennington, was among them.*

> "Over ten million dollars' worth of diamonds were stolen. The annual black tie event is a favorite among the rich and famous, but last night's tragedy may change that. The police currently have no suspects."

The broadcast hadn't finished when Johnny dialed Wilks.

"What's up, J.T.?" Wilks asked.

"Flip on the TV." He paused while Wilks watched the report.

"Jesus me," Wilks said. "*Five* dead?"

Johnny spoke slowly. "Listen carefully, Wilks. How we handle this is paramount." He gave the instructions.

Johnny called a news conference after the event. The press clamored around him as he made his announcement.

"What happened to Vander Broek on that horrible night is nothing more than an act of pure evil. My company is like family to me, and I cannot imagine the heartbreak that Mr. Vander Broek and the other victims are experiencing right now. I am offering a million-dollar reward to anyone who supplies information that could lead the police to the monsters who did this."

A reporter stood up. "Why are you doing this, Mr. Flynn? Isn't Vander Broek your main competitor?"

"He is." Johnny took a deep breath, gazed up at the sky, then directed his attention back toward the crowd of reporters. "My children are twins. When they were born, my son, Michael, weighed just over two pounds and had a hole in his heart. For several days, my wife and I thought we were going to lose him. Those were the longest days of my life. After going through that, and losing my father four years ago, I feel overwhelming sympathy for Vander Broek's loss. I also happen to believe that it's inhumane to capitalize on another's tragedy. I'm a businessman, not a monster."

∞∞∞∞∞∞

"Keeping a low profile has served you well over the past year," Wilks said as he sat across the desk from Johnny.

Johnny stared at his computer screen. "Do these figures include the foreign sales?"

"Yes, sir."

Johnny smiled. "That's three months in a row."

"It is, J. T. This is very good news."

Johnny grinned. "Looks like J.T. Flynn Diamond Corporation is no longer in second place."

"No, sir, and we've evidence to prove it."

Johnny pulled out the newspaper. The front page featured Johnny and Danielle at a charity event. "*Diamond Mogul Has A Heart of Gold*," he read aloud. "Seems Johnny Flynn is no longer the bad guy, either, Wilks."

"There's no denying that, sir. As a matter of fact, I brought something to celebrate our return to the top." Wilks reached into his briefcase and pulled out a bottle. "Single malt, small batch, forty years old."

"You shouldn't have." Johnny got up. "But I'm fucking glad you did." He strode over to the small bar on the east wall and retrieved two crystal snifters.

"Excellent." Wilks opened the bottle and poured a dram for each of them, the only sound in the room was the silky glug of the amber liquid slipping into each glass.

Wilks set down the bottle. "Remember the whiskey-tasting tour in Scotland?"

"Oh, God," Johnny took the glass and warmed it in his hands. "Never thought I'd drink again."

Wilks laughed. "It kind of snuck up on us, didn't it?"

"Yes, it did." Johnny let the scotch warm a bit longer and then raised it up and tilted the glass, watching the whiskey cling to the sides. He lifted it to his nose and inhaled. "Mmmm, rich, leathery, a bit of smoke."

"You were always far better at that," Wilks said. "I've never been able to train my nose."

"Well, you were a little distracted on that trip." Johnny winked at him.

Wilks smiled. "That I was. She was quite a beauty...curvy, raven-haired." He tipped his glass to one side. "Angie, I think her name was." He eyed Johnny. "You've never strayed, have you?"

"No." Johnny shrugged. "Young, pretty, a dime a dozen."

"A million a dozen, really." Wilks laughed.

"True," Johnny chuckled. "Nah, Dani's too important. What we have," he gazed at the whiskey. "It's too solid. I'd never risk it."

"To each his own." Wilks raised his drink. "To success."

"And to those who make it happen." Johnny angled his glass toward Wilks.

Two refills later, Wilks sauntered toward Johnny's office door. "Glad I'm not driving." He turned back. "Perhaps you should let the limo take you home, too."

"That's a good idea." Johnny stood, reached toward the coat hanger, and pulled the keys from his jacket pocket. He tossed them to Wilks. "Have them lock it up. I'll be ready to go in a few."

"Will do."

Johnny watched the door close behind Wilks, then glanced at the bottle and two empty glasses in the desk. His mind drifted back to coffeehouse meeting he'd had with Ming eleven months prior.

It was worth it. I couldn't let them take everything away.

Johnny glanced at the picture of his father on the wall. "My fields will never be fallow, Daddy. I promise you that."

FIVE

Auster entered the Gypsum Ridge Medical Center using a key card he'd swiped from a janitor in the parking lot.

Time for a new body.

He'd consumed several rodents and a wolf the previous day, which had molded his form into a grotesque blob with lupine-esque hind legs and short, rodent-like forearms. His hunched torso was thick and globular, taking most of the tissue he'd created and forcing his skin to stretch thin like a sausage casing. If he didn't build a more suitable body soon, within a day or two, parts of him would spill onto the ground like jelly.

Despite his disfigurement, Auster roused no suspicion. Eyes passed over him as though he were invisible. A black burqa covered him from head to toe, even his formless face. His awkward, methodical movements were reminiscent of someone very old, making him even less likely to get attention.

Lumbering through the hospital corridors, Auster searched for life force ready to leave its host. He waited until the nurses had completed their rounds, then crept into the burn unit and stood at the foot of the first bed.

He stared down at an unfortunate soul in a drug-induced coma. The patient's charred flesh left tender nerves exposed over much of his body.

He doesn't have long, but I can't use him.

The next stop was the emergency ward. The closest bed squeaked beneath a crack addict who rocked back and forth, wringing her hands and picking at her scabbed skin.

Not a chance.

The bed next to the addict had the privacy drapes pulled. Auster peeked past to see a six-year-old child, delirious with fever, his parents flanking his bedside.

Death won't find him tonight.

The next bed held a young man wrapped in bandages from head to toe. Blood seeped through the dressing around his chest. Auster read the chart. *Car accident.* He smiled until he read the age.

Forty-nine. Too old. Perhaps the trauma unit will yield results. It's always a good bet.

He shuffled into a room where a teenage boy lay, IVs snaking from both arms and a breathing tube plunged into his trachea. Auster lifted the clipboard from the end of the bed.

Football player, twenty-one-years-old, spinal cord and head trauma.

He glanced at the flashing lights. *The machines are trapping the life force. Perfect.*

Auster read the heart monitor: 73 BPM. He raised a rodent-like claw to the respirator, and it stopped pumping. The pulse reading on the monitor began to fall. 68, 60, 55, 49, 42, 33, 21, 12.

The ECG flatlined.

Auster faded into the hallway as the alarms sounded.

Code blue.

SIX

Dr. Anisha Patel rushed into the room, followed by five members of the code blue team. "Get the paddles!" she barked at the nurse behind her.

The nurse pushed a small cart next to the bed, removed the defibrillator paddles, and handed them to Anisha.

"Clear!" the doctor called.

The boy arced off the bed as the paddles bolted electric current into his chest.

Anisha checked the monitor. *Flatline.* "Again! CLEAR!"

No change.

Anisha tried several more times, but it was no use.

All were still for a moment, and then Ben, the nurse assigned to the room, picked up the boy's chart and spoke as he wrote, "Time of death, 2:57 a.m."

Anisha squeezed her eyes shut. "So young."

"Yeah." Ben replaced the clipboard, gazed at the departed, then smoothed the sheets and adjusted the tossed body so the boy appeared to be sleeping. He turned to Anisha. "His family's in the waiting room."

Anisha took a deep breath. "Okay, I'll tell them." She paused. "It's the third time this week I've had to deliver this kind of news."

Ben reached over and squeezed her shoulder. "I'm sorry, Ani."

"I've done this one hundred and four times, and it still sickens me every single time."

Ben looked at the boy. "Who could ever be ready to hear it?"

"No one, ever." Anisha walked into the hallway, fighting the urge to scream.

"You'll adjust, Anisha," the other doctors had told her when she was in her residency. "It's a reality of the job. Know that you've done your best. If you wrestle with it and blame yourself, you won't last."

But even after working for years in both the ER and trauma units, Anisha Patel still hadn't found the combination that unlocked the place in her mind where this kind of thing could be shelved.

The waiting room seemed to rush toward her. She reached the doorway, paused for a moment to collect herself, then stepped into the room.

Three people snapped to attention, eyes searching hers.

Anisha looked at the middle-aged couple holding hands, and the teen-aged girl sitting next to them. "Mr. and Mrs. Gerville?"

The family stood up.

"How is he?" the mother asked.

Anisha looked the woman in the eye, having learned not doing so caused people to think she was being dishonest or that something shady had happened. Anisha tried to soften her own gaze to add comfort. "We did everything we could—"

"NO!" The mother turned to her husband. "NO! Billy's not dead! Billy's not dead!"

The young girl collapsed onto the floor into a crying heap.

Billy Gerville's mother fell into her husband's arms. "No, no. My baby!"

Mr. Gerville trembled with grief.

Anisha stood quietly for a moment. "I'm very sorry. We did everything we could."

"I want to see him!" Mrs. Gerville sobbed. "Please, let me see him before..."

"Yes, of course. Please follow me."

Anisha ushered the family down the hall. Unlike the trip to the waiting room, the trek back to Billy's deathbed seemed miles long. Mr. Gerville had to practically carry his wife, and the younger sister trailed far behind, her unrestrained wails reverberating off the walls.

Upon reaching Billy's room, Mrs. Gerville screamed and pushed Anisha against the door frame as she rushed inside and fell over her son's dead body. Billy's father wrapped both arms around his daughter, sobbing as they approached.

Ben stood in the back of the room.

Anisha raised her chin toward him.

Ben nodded back. *I got this.*

Anisha mouthed, "Thank you," and quietly shut the door.

Mind racing, she strode to the nurses' station and plunked down in a chair, oblivious to the flurry of activity around her. She forced herself to be still and tried to calm her thoughts. She thought of the Gerville family, about their irreversible sorrow and grief. She reran Billy's care, step by step, through her head. *There was nothing more we could do.* She replayed the moment the family heard the news.

Nothing will ever be the same for them.

A memory rushed forward, the same one that always plagued Anisha when she was in emotional pain. She forced out a breath.

Why? Why always this?

Anisha closed her eyes and, once again, relived the first time she had delivered life-changing news—seven years earlier.

Anisha could still picture the salmon-colored sofa with big flowers where her mother sat, she could still feel the thick-pile carpet beneath her bare feet and smell the steaming *dhokla* wafting from the kitchen. She remembered how the light from above pooled around her, making her feel like she was on a stage.

She recalled how she had fought to keep from trembling as she spoke. "Frank asked me to marry him, Mother."

Mother, as still as a statue, gave nothing.

"I said yes." Anisha forced herself to smile. "I'm going to become Mrs. Corby." She held out her left hand for Mother to see the two-carat solitaire.

Mother's demeanor stiffened even more, her eyes scrutinizing Anisha's hand as though it had dog shit on it. "You would do this thing? You would do this to your family?"

Anisha felt her body go limp. "Mother, we've been together for two years. I've told you how I felt. We love each other. Frank and I are meant to be together."

Mother looked as though Anisha had told her she was selling her body on the boulevard. "This boy doesn't know you. He doesn't understand who we are."

"He *does* know me, Mother. We share a passion for healing, the arts, and so many other things. We understand each other better than anyone else and love each other very much. We *are* getting married next June. Please, Mother, give us your blessing."

Mother stood up. "You will break your father's heart." Eyes averted, she marched past Anisha and flipped off the light, leaving her to stand alone in the dark.

The wedding was lavish but cold. It turned out Frank Corby's parents were no fonder of their son marrying *the brown girl* than Anisha's were of her union with *the white boy*. Anisha's saving grace was her younger sister, Anjali, whose unbridled enthusiasm eclipsed the cloud of ugliness looming on both sides.

Then there was Frank, whose unwavering support through the storm had proven to her how much he really did love her.

After Anisha had broken the news of her engagement to her mother, she had never visited the home she grew up in without leaving in tears, and, unless there was a word that couldn't be translated, Anisha's mother had never spoken English in her presence again. She spoke in Gujarati, forcing Anisha to translate if Frank was present.

Things had never been the same.

Anisha shivered as she pulled her thoughts out of the past. She took a deep breath and checked her watch.

I need to get out of here.

She got up and strode toward the hospital exit, desperate for fresh air. In the distance, an old woman in a black burqa lumbered down the hallway. Anisha dismissed it at first, then a strange, prickling feeling flooded her body, a sensation that would kick in once in a while for as far back as she could remember.

Something's not right.

The woman stopped and turned. The eyes behind the black screen blinked. The two stared at one another for a few moments.

The thought flashed through Anisha's mind again, stronger this time. *Something feels very wrong. It's like a disruptive force, but I can't identify it.*

The old woman turned away and continued down the hall.

Anisha forced herself to look away. She cut left, toward the cafeteria, her gait lengthening as she neared the neon EXIT sign.

SEVEN

Auster entered the pathology department and ducked into the morgue. He disrobed and stowed the burqa in an empty cadaver drawer. He transformed into mist and hid under a metal autopsy table as his prize was wheeled in, transferred into another drawer, and closed away.

Auster waited until the room was clear, then moved with haste. The body needed to be consumed while it was still warm, just after the life energy vacated, so the tissue would be responsive to new life force. When the tissue died, it was useless. He might as well be trying on a steak. Organ transplants in medicine functioned the same way, but Auster took the process a little further than exchanging an organ or two. He absorbed the entire being.

He pulled out the drawer, peeled away everything covering the corpse, and spread his naked form over it. Skin on skin contact was necessary. Within seconds, a glowing light emanated from Auster's abdomen, sending white rays of light into the cadaver. The skin began to melt, and then the sinew and bone beneath it. When the tissue turned to liquid, Auster drew it up into himself.

Within minutes, only one form remained, breathing through freshly created lungs.

Auster climbed out of the drawer, retrieved the burqa, and dressed. He waited until the coast was clear and left. His posture was already straightening, his walk that of a healthier person, but he was mindful to keep a modest pace.

He turned the corner to move toward the lobby and ran into a large male nurse heading the opposite direction.

The nurse grasped Auster's arm to prevent him from falling. "Pardon me, madam. I'm so very sorry. Are you all right?"

Auster nodded but said nothing. He glanced up at the man's name badge.

Benjamin Emerson. You exude a very familiar energy signature, and a powerful one as well.

Regaining his composure, Auster hobbled past the nurse, feeling the man's stare on his back.

Another one. First, the female doctor and now this man. Their kind is abundant here.

Auster wound through the labyrinth of hallways toward the public entrance. He tossed the key card into a waste basket, crossed the lobby, and headed toward the double doors leading to the outside.

The air was brisk and the sun had lifted the veil of darkness, revealing a faint gray sliver of light on the eastern horizon.

Time to rest and settle in.

Auster looked north, where the mountains rose from the LA basin, to the place where Rawson had left the Earth. He focused on his destination, commanded his body to draw toward it, and began to change.

Onlookers would have seen something out of a science fiction movie: A person fading from sight, becoming translucent, then changing into what appeared to be a hovering cloud of mist. The particles rose, stretching into a serpentine blur, then shot north like they were blown by Santa Ana winds.

Auster had learned over time that he didn't need to hide when changing states. No man had ever admitted to seeing it, at least publicly.

A few moments later, Auster wove through the trees in the Angeles National Forest, searching for a quiet place to fuse his new tissue, rest, and allow his new body to settle into place.

I will enjoy the form of a young man again. I hope I'm handsome this time. Things are easier for humans who are fair-of-face.

EIGHT

Johnny pulled into the school parking lot to pick up the kids from their freshman camping trip. *I still can't believe they're in high school already.*

Detecting the faint smell of cigarettes on his windbreaker, he peeled it off and stuffed it into the trunk before walking on campus.

I've gotta quit smoking. Again.

Inside the gates, tired-looking teenagers sitting on the ground or on rolled up sleeping bags lined the hallways. Johnny scanned the group of young faces and finally spotted Michael and Maya at the end of the hall.

Maya glanced up and a smile spread across her face. "Daddy!"

Michael, who sat atop his sleeping bag with arms crossed, startled. He looked at Johnny and gave a half-smile.

Johnny knew something was up. *Uh-oh.*

"Mr. Flynn?" A tall, brunette teacher strode toward him.

"Yes?"

The woman held out her hand. "I'm Ms. Sanders, one of the teachers supervising the camping trip. May I speak with you?"

"Sure."

Sanders led Johnny into the first room down the hallway, which appeared to be some sort of computer lab with laptops sitting side-by-side around the perimeter of the room. Three larger tables sat in the center of a space.

Sanders swung an open hand toward one of the chairs. "Please, have a seat."

"All right." Johnny lowered himself into one.

Sanders sat across from Johnny and took a deep breath before starting. "I hate to have to start your weekend with a negative report, but Michael did something during this trip that warrants discussion."

Johnny laced his fingers together and placed them on the table. "What did he do?"

"This morning, we had our last hike before lunch. The trail on this particular hike involved trekking up a hill. One of the boys is, well, heavier, and he was having great difficulty with it." She paused and took another breath. "Several other boys chuckled at him as he struggled to climb the hill. I took them aside and spoke with them about it. The mood changed, shortly after, and students actually started cheering the boy on, chanting, 'You can do it.' It was great to see the students supporting him."

The teacher smiled. "When the boy reached the top, students—even the ones I had to speak to—high-fived him and patted him on the back. The kid was beaming. It was quite a moment for him. I've been working with him all year on self-esteem and on not being afraid to try, so you can imagine the level of pride he must have felt."

"Yes, of course," Johnny said. "Good for him."

Sanders' smile faded. "The group took a minute to have some water before continuing, and that's when Michael pushed the boy back down the hill."

"What? He *pushed* him?" Johnny felt the blood drain from his face.

"Yes, Mr. Flynn. Other students reported that Michael had said, 'Okay, Fatass, let's see you do it again.'"

Johnny shook his head. "I can't believe it. Are you *sure* it was Michael who did it?"

Sanders nodded. "I heard the word fatass." She crossed her arms. "Everyone heard that, and I spun around just in time to see another teacher running toward the edge of the hill as the boy toppled back down." She crossed her legs. "If this had happened earlier, we would have expelled Michael from camp and had you come to get him, but we were a meal away from getting on the bus. So, here we are."

Johnny shifted in the little chair.

"The principal was informed of the incident. Freshman camp is a school function and all of the same conduct rules apply. As a result of his choice, Michael has been suspended from school for three days."

Johnny stared down at his hands. "I don't even know what to say, Ms. Sanders. I didn't raise my son to be a bully. I'm ashamed of his behavior. I'll discuss this with him right away."

"Good. Please do."

"It just seems so out of the blue." Johnny raised his head to meet the teacher's gaze.

Sanders shrugged at this. "Michael's never pushed or hit as far as I know, but he has said things to other kids that I've had to call home and speak with Mrs. Flynn about. The last time was about three weeks ago when he called a girl a slobby slut."

Johnny thought for a moment. He placed his palm against his forehead as he recalled the incident. "I do remember that. He lost the use of all his electronics for a week over it."

She shrugged again. "Apparently Michael hasn't learned his lesson yet, Mr. Flynn. Not only is he continuing to bully, he's gone from verbal to physical."

"Clearly, I'm going to deal with this, Ms. Sanders," Johnny said as he stood up. "I promise you that. Once again, I'm sorry."

"Okay, then. The suspension begins on Monday, so we'll see Michael back at school next Thursday."

Johnny held out his hand. "All right."

Sanders shook it. "Thank you, Mr. Flynn."

Johnny headed toward the door, then stopped and turned around. "The boy Michael pushed, is he okay?"

Sanders stopped in her tracks and glanced toward the ceiling. "The look on his face at the bottom of the incline will stay with me for a long time." Her eyes glazed over. "It was complete heartbreak."

She swallowed hard. "Several kids ran down the hill and helped him climb back up. Others told Michael off. The students' support seemed to help the boy's spirits immensely. I sat with him during lunch and many students praised him for climbing the hill twice." Sanders pressed her palms together. "I'm hoping that positive energy will prevail over the negative in this situation."

"Me, too," Johnny said. "Is the boy still here? I'd like to—"

Sanders shook her head. "His parents picked him up before you arrived. We spoke with them about the incident and they were upset, but Frederi— the boy was more interested in telling his parents about how he climbed the hill *twice* than he was about telling them about being pushed." She sighed. "He'll be okay."

"I'm glad to hear that," Johnny said.

The crowd had thinned out quite a bit by the time Johnny and Ms. Sanders emerged from the classroom. Michael and Maya sat in the same spots down the hall. Maya stood up as soon as Johnny stepped into the hallway. She tapped Michael, who sat slumped with his arms crossed. He stood without looking in his father's direction.

The kids trailed behind Johnny to the car.

Johnny opened the passenger door for Maya, then looked at Michael. "In the back."

Johnny started the engine and a voice belted through the speakers. He had been listening to the news on the radio on the way over. He let the station play as he pulled out of the parking lot. No one spoke for several minutes. The blathering of the newscast kept complete silence at bay.

> "Police are still investigating the disappearance of a body from the morgue at Gypsum Ridge Hospital. Officials say a key card had been found in a trash receptacle in the hospital, but the employee to whom the key card belongs has not been able to be contacted.
>
> In other news, Colton Lee Haddix, also known as the Campfire Butcher, is set to be put to death by lethal injection at San Quentin in three days. Appeals have been made to the governor, and the prison will be standing by if he elects to call off the execution.
>
> Colton Lee Haddix was sentenced to death eleven years ago for murdering three families, dismembering their bodies, then rearranging them around a campfire."

"What a monster." Johnny spat as he flicked off the radio. "The world is an evil place. What the hell's gotten into people?"

"It can be a nice place, too, right, Daddy?" Maya asked. "Not everyone is evil."

Johnny exhaled and patted her hand. "You're right, Petal. There are good people."

He glanced in the rearview mirror at Michael and thought about how to handle this effectively. He wanted to teach his son, to guide him, as his own father had done for him.

Johnny ran his discussion with Ms. Sanders through his head several more times, then the words busted out in a loud bellow. "What in the hell were you thinking? What kind of person pushes a boy down a hill, especially a boy who—" Johnny shook his head. "Why would you do such a thing?"

Michael stared down at his lap.

Johnny waited for a response, then he blew his top. "Why? Say SOMETHING!"

Michael shrugged his shoulders and pushed his glasses up.

"That's all you got? You victimize another kid, and when you're asked why, all you can do is shrug your damn shoulders like you're being asked why you picked cake for dessert?"

Michael shrugged again.

Johnny gritted his teeth. "Another shrug. Okay. So that's how it's gonna be. Now you listen, Michael J. Flynn. You're thin and able-bodied because you were born that way, not because of some superior talent you have that the poor, heavy kid doesn't."

"Able-bodied?" Michael spat. "I'm the freaking slowest kid on the soccer field because of my damn heart." He pulled off his glasses and held them up. "And my eyes suck!" He slid his glasses back on and crossed his arms. "I'm pathetic."

Johnny sighed. "You're slow, so you pick on a kid who's slower than you?"

"It's not like that."

"Then what is it like? What made you think you had the right to push that kid?"

Michael lifted his shoulders again and looked away.

"I think I know why," Johnny said. "You're slow on the field and your eyesight isn't as good as others'. You've accepted those limitations. That kid you bullied is heavy. He's not supposed to be able to climb that hill, but he *didn't* accept it. He pushed himself and he climbed it, and that made you mad."

Michael looked out the window.

Johnny eyed his son. "I've got a newsflash for ya, spoiled brat."

Michael's eyes widened in shock.

"I've met many millionaires and billionaires. Some handle wealth with dignity and responsibility. They work hard, give to charity, and never forget what it was like to *not* have wealth."

"Others," he glanced in the mirror at Michael, "usually those who are *born* into wealth, *like you* act as though they're *entitled* to what they have and like they're *better* than everyone else." Johnny stared daggers at him.

Michael stared down at his lap again.

"And do you know what those spiritless, wealthy-born pricks hate more than anything?" He glanced back at Michael, who didn't look up. "You know what really pisses them off?"

The back seat was silent.

Johnny shook his head. "Never mind."

"What?" Maya whispered from the passenger's seat. "What angers them, Daddy?"

Johnny turned to see Maya, calm and curious. He sighed deeply. "Someone who reaches their status through hard work, Petal. It reminds those lazy bastards that they *didn't* work to get what they have. It reminds them of how weak they really are."

Maya nodded and fiddled with a bracelet on her wrist.

Johnny directed his attention to the rearview again. "It took *character* for that boy to climb the hill, Michael. Something inside you didn't like that. Perhaps you saw a quality in him that you *don't* possess and it made you angry, or jealous, so you punished him for it."

"*Jealous*? Yeah, right." Michael scoffed. "Jealous of *Frederick Olmstead*."

Johnny wrapped his fingers around the steering wheel. "Grounding and removing privileges isn't enough this time, Michael. You have no character." He moved his gaze back to the road ahead. "But I'm gonna see to it that you build some. Be damned, you're gonna build some."

NINE

Auster walked toward the entrance of a little sports bar in Pasadena, California. He caught sight of his own reflection in the window. He glanced at his arms, lean muscles rippled under firm, tanned skin. His blond hair fell to his neck and his eyes were light green.

My form has settled into something quite handsome. Somewhat close to the body I acquired— older, of course. He glanced at his long fingers. *And there are always residual properties of the others before it.*

He wore loose-fitting jeans and a black t-shirt that featured an airbrushed scene of a scantily-clad, buxom Latina female draped over a lowered purple Chevy with red flames on the hood. The words *Brown Pride* were scrawled in cursive above the scene.

Auster scanned the televisions suspended around the place. Most of the TVs featured sports programs, but his attention was drawn to one that had a news channel going.

He couldn't help but smile when the reporter in front of Gypsum Ridge Hospital gave an update of the "body snatcher" case. Then the face of Colton Lee Haddix flashed on the screen and another newscaster standing in front of San Quentin spoke of the upcoming execution.

He smiled again. *A few more days.*

A blonde server wearing a miniskirt was at Auster's table as soon as he sat down.

"What can I get you?"

Auster couldn't help but appreciate the young woman's oversized breasts, since they were exactly eye-level.

"A pint of your house brew," he answered, finally making eye contact.

She walked away from the table and his gaze followed her. His attention drifted to the patio outside, where an Asian man with a scar across his left cheek and a cigarette in hand sat at a table. He seemed to be watching the news as well. Auster honed in on the man's energy. *He would be a magnificent catch. But his candidacy won't be up for a while. I'll focus on the other one. His time is near.*

The server brought Auster his beer and rushed off. It was Friday night and the place was packed. The energy permeating the place exuded sex, and Auster watched in interest as the young men and women circled each other like sharks in the ocean. Women passing by did double-takes, sometimes triple-takes, at Auster. He smiled in return.

A few beers later, three women sauntered through the door. They immediately noticed Auster as they walked to the bar, giggling among themselves. A minute hadn't passed when one of them, a tall brunette wearing a white top and cut-off shorts, approached.

She placed one hand on the table where Auster sat. "Hi, you a body builder?"

Auster's smile widened as he thought about the young man he had to consume. "Yes, I think you could call me that."

The brunette looked Auster up and down. "I'm Lena. My friends and I are working to keep up the buzz we caught at the tavern around the corner. You want to come party with us?" She gestured toward the other two, who stared back, grinning.

Auster rose from his seat. "I'd love to meet your friends."

Lena smiled and took his arm. "Great."

Auster followed her over to a booth and sat down with the three young women. He felt his nether-regions harden like a rock. *A fine welcome back, indeed.*

"This is Laura." Lena pointed to a blonde wearing a tight, red checkered shirt. "And this is Rhonda."

Rhonda smiled. "Hey, sexy."

"Nice to meet you." Auster gestured to the busty waitress. "Can we get the ladies some drinks?"

The server gave a half-smile and walked over to take their order.

The girls hung all over Auster like rag dolls, slurring and laughing. Auster felt the impact of the alcohol as well, but it was minimal.

Lena wrapped her arms around Auster's neck. "What time is it?"

Auster glanced around, searching for a clock.

"It's time to get outta here," Rhonda said, then she leaned over and kissed Lena on the mouth. The two made out while Lena still clung around Auster's neck.

The crowd around them cheered.

Auster glanced around at the onlookers. *I don't understand this.*

The third girl, Laura, leaned in and shouted to Auster. "Do you want to come home with us?"

"Sure."

The small flat the girls shared was walking distance from the bar. After Lena fumbled with the key in the lock for a full minute, the three stumbled through the door and immediately began tearing their clothes off. Auster followed, taking in the scene.

Laura peeled off her panties. "Allow me."

Auster raised his arms and she pulled off his shirt. The other two hopped onto the bed and beckoned him to join.

"Ready for the ride of your life?" Laura asked as she pulled Auster toward the bed.

Ride of my life?

The three women slithered around, giggling, licking each other, licking him, putting their fingers inside each other, putting his fingers inside of them.

Auster attempted to participate several times, only to have one of them say, "Not like that, baby. I'll show you how it's done."

After several minutes of trying to figure out what they wanted him to do, he found it easier to take directions.

Per their requests, he rode them.

This is familiar.

He spanked them.

That's an odd thing to ask for.

He watched them probe and grind on top of each other.

Should I leave now?

And each sucked him off.

This does feel nice.

The women moaned and came over and over.

Perhaps this is a contest between them.

After they'd squealed themselves hoarse in delight, the three draped their sweaty bodies around Auster for a coming-down-from-a-buzz, post-cum slumber.

Rhonda kissed Auster on the cheek. "I'll bet that was the best fuck you've ever had in your life, huh, baby?"

Auster decided to tell the complete truth, knowing, in their inebriated state, what he said would be forgotten, anyway. "I've participated in sexual demonstrations as a form of art, joined many cultures in their kinesthetic illustrations of the flowering of spring, and was bestowed the gift of virginity by women more times than I can count. This, however, was unlike anything I have previously experienced. I would classify it as *odd*."

All three women twisted from their curled-up positions to glare at him in disgust.

Auster was taken aback. He looked from woman to woman. "I've angered you?"

"*Odd*?" Laura slurred. "What the fuck are you talking about?"

Lena sat up, teetering back and forth. "Every guy in that bar would have *loved* to come home with us!"

Rhonda mumbled. "Not... one..."—she slapped the mattress between each word—"...fucking... bitch can do what *we* do!"

Oh, I see.

"I apologize," Auster said. "I wasn't aware that you were competing sexually with every woman in the bar last evening, as well as every woman I've been intimate with in the past."

They stared daggers at him.

My apology wasn't effective. Although what just occurred required no skill, let's try this. "If you would like, I'll make sure to report that you were *amazing* and *unlike any other*, which would be true, to some extent. Would that please you?"

Laura pointed toward the door. "Get out!"

Auster glanced at the other two, who sat with arms crossed.

"Out, now!" Lena added.

Auster slipped off the bed. "Before I leave, I must make sure that none of you have conceived."

"We're on the pill, asshole!" Laura said.

Auster stood for a moment.

"That means we can't get pregnant!" Rhonda slurred.

"Not *can't*," Auster said. "The pill is only 99% effective."

"*Only* 99%? Geez." Lena shook her head and lay back on the bed. "You're definitely *not* from around here,"

"That's why he's acting so fucking weird," Laura said.

Auster pointed to the shower. "I must—"

"Just do it quick and get the fuck out." Rhonda fell back, her head making a soft *thump* on the pillow. "You're still hot, though." She chuckled.

The other two giggled with her.

Auster stared at the naked women, who curled up together on the bed like a litter of puppies, then stepped into the bathroom and showered off the night's residue. He went back into the bedroom to retrieve his clothes and saw that all three were passed out cold.

I'd better make sure.

Auster moved forward and stood over them, placing a hand over Rhonda's abdomen first, and sent forth a weak ray of light.

Rhonda brought her hands slowly to her middle, cradled her womb and mumbled, "Ummmfff, cramps."

Auster repeated the process with the other two, then dressed and left them sleeping.

Time to move north. Another Hand will be on the table soon.

TEN

Johnny wrapped his arms around Danielle before they walked downstairs Sunday morning. "I hope this does something to help Michael."

"Me, too." Danielle said. "I contacted Bridget right after you told me about what happened at camp. She assured me there are lessons to be learned at the shelter." She kissed Johnny. "Don't worry, handsome, our boy will come around."

"Let's hope we don't hit traffic," Johnny said as the Flynn family piled into the car, readying for the forty-five minute drive to the Thousand Wells Homeless Shelter. "What time are they expecting us?" he asked Danielle.

"I told them we'd be there at eleven."

"Good." Johnny shot Michael a look.

The ride was tense. Not a word was spoken, and music did little to lift the mood.

Johnny knew they were close to their destination when he saw groups of tired-looking, disheveled people congregating in small groups along the sidewalks and in the two parks they passed. Many looked high or drunk.

"There it is." Danielle pointed to a large, white building with peeling paint.

Johnny glanced along the street. "Nowhere looks safe to park, so I guess I'll just park in front."

"Okay," Danielle said.

Getting out, he took her hand and led the way up the steps to the shelter. "I think this is a good idea, Dani," Johnny said as he opened the door.

Danielle glanced back at a sour-faced Michael, who slogged several steps behind. "Let's hope this gives him a little humility."

Johnny turned to Maya, who had caught up with them. "You didn't have to come, Petal, but I'm sure glad you did."

"Me, too," Maya said. "I want to help out."

Johnny wrapped an arm around her. "That's my girl."

A tall woman with long, gray hair twisted up in a bun approached Danielle. "Mrs. Flynn?"

Danielle held out her hand. "Yes. This is my husband, John, and my daughter, Maya. Are you Bridget?"

The woman shook Danielle's hand. "Yes." She shook hands with Johnny and Maya. "Pleased to meet you both." Bridget leaned to the side to see behind Danielle. "You must be Michael."

Michael nodded without looking at her.

Bridget took a step forward and held out her hand. "Pleased to meet you."

Michael dropped a limp hand into hers, his gaze still fixed on some point off to the right.

Bridget shook Michael's hand, seeming to pay no heed his attitude. "All right, then, let me give you the grand tour."

She led them into a small dining area set up cafeteria-style with tables and benches. Behind the glass sneeze guards, two women and a man in aprons bustled back and forth, clinking pots and running water.

Bridgett held out her arms. "This is the chow room. It seats sixty. We serve breakfast, lunch, and dinner every day of the year." She peered around at the tables. "Lately, it's been packed during every meal. There are lots of hungry people out there."

She moved beyond the dining room and down a hallway that led to a huge open room lined with fold-out cots, each equipped with a thin mattress, a small pillow, and a dark-gray blanket. The room was empty but for one woman on a cot at the far end, who sat nursing a tiny infant. At her feet sat a small boy, occupying himself by rolling a toy truck back and forth in a crescent-shaped pattern around his crossed legs.

"This is the women and children's dormitory," Bridgett said. "The men's is down the hall. The homeless are permitted to sleep here only at night. Part of the terms of their stay is that they look for work and permanent residences during the day." She nodded toward the woman. "We made an exception for Rachel because her newborn is ill, and Rachel is still recovering from giving birth."

Maya caught up to Bridget. "Where's the kids' father?"

Bridget shrugged. "He left when she was pregnant."

"That's so sad," Johnny heard Maya whisper to Michael as the group moved back down the hall.

Michael glanced back at the woman, who focused on the newborn. "Yeah."

Bridget stopped in the middle of the hallway and opened a door on the left. Inside was a public bathroom similar to one found at a truck stop, equipped with several private toilets and three showers. "This is the women's bathroom. The men's is on the opposite side. As you could probably guess, it can get pretty crowded here—and pretty filthy."

Bridget closed the door and turned to the Flynns. "Well, that's it."

"It's quite something," Danielle said. "It's so wonderful that a place like this is here to take care of people who need help."

Bridget nodded. "We depend on volunteers to keep things going. As you can see, there are many tasks completed each day in order to provide these services. Meals must be cooked and served, the kitchen and dining areas require constant cleaning, bedding needs laundering, and bathrooms have to be stocked and scrubbed."

"That's why we're here," Johnny said. "Where can we start?"

Bridget checked her watch. "Well, lunch will be served in about an hour, so Mrs. Flynn, why don't you and Maya help out in the kitchen? People will need plates, silverware, napkins, and a clean place to sit. Go back into the dining room and ask for Lupita."

"You got it." Danielle turned to Maya. "Ready?"

"Yep. Let's do it."

Bridget watched the girls march off toward the dining room, then faced Johnny and Michael. "Though the bathrooms need a good cleaning, I don't want your first day to be tending to them. You may never return. So how do you feel about doing laundry?"

"We're up to it," Johnny said. "Tell us where to go."

"We have one washer and dryer, which are located in the back of the building. Gladys should be out in a moment. She's already done two loads of sheets today."

Johnny turned to Michael. "How about you? Ready to help?"

Staring off to the side, Michael shrugged.

Johnny leaned down "Look at me."

Michael did.

Johnny held out a finger. "Do your job and be polite. There are people here clinging to survival. No one here wants to deal with your teenage 'I'm mad at Daddy' crap." He turned back to Bridget and forced a smile. "We're ready."

Bridget stared down at Michael, who had returned his fixed gaze to the wall. She whispered to Johnny, "I have three grown children, two boys and a girl." She winked and added, "I know where you're coming from. It'll pass." She took one last look at Michael and added, "Hopefully sooner than later."

Johnny smiled at her. "Yes. Let's hope for sooner."

"Ah, finally," Bridget said as a young woman approached.

"Yes, yes. Here I am."

Bridget wrapped an arm around her waist. "Gentlemen, I'd like you to meet Gladys. She's my number-one volunteer and one of the best people in the world."

Gladys was curvy with big, brown eyes and apple cheeks. She wore a flower in her jet-black hair and her toothy smile was genuine, almost infectious. She had a spring in her step that only hope and youth could inspire.

Johnny and Gladys shook hands. "Pleased to meet you."

"Same here." Gladys turned to Michael. "And you are?"

"Michael." He held out his hand, and for the first time in days, his frown disappeared.

Johnny turned to Bridget, who flicked her eyebrows like she'd planned the whole thing.

"Well, off to the laundry with you," Bridget said. "After lunch, we'll see how things are going."

"Okay," Gladys said. "Let's go."

Gladys walked alongside Michael. Johnny couldn't help but grin as he listened in on their conversation.

"How old are you?" Michael asked her.

"Twenty-six. How about you?"

"Fourteen. What made you decide to volunteer?"

"I came here when I was seven years old."

"You volunteered when you were seven?"

Gladys smiled. "No, silly. We were homeless."

"Oh," Michael said. "Wow. I didn't, I mean—"

"It's okay. My dad left and my mom lost her job. We had nothing. If it wasn't for this place, I don't know what my mom would have done."

"How long were you here?"

"About a month. Bridget had just started volunteering back then. I promised her that when I grew up, I would come back and help." She pointed at herself. "And *this girl* keeps her promises."

"Wow, you're twenty-six and you're keeping a promise you made at *seven*." Michael sounded surprised.

"You bet. I come here on weekends and after work twice a week."

"Where do you work?"

"I just started my nursing career at Thousand Wells Hospital." She stopped and pointed to a small washer and dryer. "Okay, so here's where we do the wash…"

Johnny barely heard Gladys' instructions as he watched Michael transfer sheets into the dryer and put detergent into the washing machine.

∞∞∞∞∞∞

The ride home was just as silent as the ride to the shelter. Johnny glanced back at Michael, who wore a placid smile as he lay his head back and closed his eyes. Maya dozed off as well. Johnny reached over, took Danielle's hand, and kissed it as he whispered, "Thank you, my love."

She exhaled a cleansing breath. "I'm relieved. Hopefully it sticks."

∞∞∞∞∞∞

"How was your day?" Paula asked as she served dinner.

"It was great," Danielle answered.

"Very enlightening," Johnny added.

"There are some really neat people who volunteer at the shelter," Maya said. She turned to Michael. "What did you think?"

"Yeah, Gladys was pretty cool."

Johnny fought the urge to slap him on the back. *He's still in trouble. Don't warm up too quickly.*

Michael couldn't help but crack a smile.

"I didn't realize so many people need food," Maya said. She turned to Johnny. "Are we going back?"

"That's the plan, Petal."

They traded stories of the day's events over chicken croquettes and chocolate mousse pie. Michael spoke up and shared his experiences as much as Maya did.

Johnny glanced across the table at Danielle. Their eyes met and her nod was almost unnoticeable, but Johnny knew what she was telling him. *We did it.* Johnny flicked his eyebrows at her.

Her smile widened.

After dinner, they settled in the movie room for a flick, where both Michael and Maya crashed out.

After everyone called it a night, Johnny slipped into bed beside Danielle and let out a great sigh.

She turned toward him and laid her arm across his chest. "How are you feeling, strongman?"

Johnny looked down at her. "I feel a thousand pounds lighter." He rolled over and slipped an arm around her waist. "Dani, you're a genius. I've never seen him work that hard, and he didn't mind it."

"I had a hunch," Danielle said. "He's a good person. He's just a confused kid."

Johnny thought about the day. "That young girl, Gladys, really influenced Michael. She's adorable, and she's a nurse at Thousand Wells Hospital."

"Adorable and smart. I'm getting a little jealous."

"Yeah, right. She's almost young enough to be our kid, but Michael's smitten, that's for sure." Johnny leaned over and kissed her. "She wears flowers in her hair, like you used to."

Danielle smiled. "I haven't done that for a while."

He raised an arm. "I vote for the reintroduction of flowers in your hair."

Danielle slid her hand below the sheets. "I vote for my husband reintroducing himself to my flower."

Johnny reached down. "Tsk, tsk. Naughty girl. I will gladly tend to your garden."

Danielle chuckled as he pulled off her nightgown.

ELEVEN

Auster stood outside the gates of San Quentin Correctional Facility. It was execution day for Colton Lee Haddix, the notorious Campfire Butcher.

The media had descended on the place several days earlier. Guards lined the fences as both death penalty supporters and protestors filled the streets, pumping signs in the air and clamoring for a spot in front of the news cameras for the chance to spew their points of view to the world.

Auster stood amidst a large group of people chanting, "Murder is murder by friend or by foe. Murder is murder wherever you go." Others shouted, "They say death row. We say hell no!"

"We're not a third-world country!" the woman standing next to Auster shouted. She glanced over and paused to check him out. "Can you believe this? I mean, they have to list *homicide* as the cause when they write the death certificate! I can't even process why this occurs in America."

"I can," Auster replied, making eye contact with the woman. "Humans have advanced intelligence, but barbarism still permeates their world."

She seemed to process Auster's comment and decided he was siding with her. "Yeah, no shit!" She gave a stern nod and turned away to resume chanting with the crowd.

Auster moved toward the fringes to get a better view of the door that led to the place where Colton Lee Haddix was condemned to die at midnight.

Ten feet away from the no-kill crowd stood another line of guards herding in the death penalty advocates, also known as the *death squad*. They clustered together, fists pumping in the air, chanting, "Let him die! Let him die!" Auster moved into their ranks, inching forward to get a clearer view of the door to the east block.

A tall, bottle-blonde woman wearing an American flag t-shirt chanted along with the crowd, adding, "The needle's too kind for that bastard!" Auster bumped into her and she glared at him, then softened her gaze after looking him up and down.

"Pardon me," Auster said.

"It's fine." The woman nodded toward the no-kill crowd. "Can you believe those hippy bastards? They think The Campfire Butcher deserves to live. The sick bastard chopped entire families into pieces and reassembled their bodies around a campfire, and those idiots think he should be spared!" She gritted her teeth. "The image of the man with that little girl's severed head on his shoulders will haunt me forever. Haddix is a monster. How many people does someone have to hack up before enough is enough?"

"Haddix will never be of service to humankind," Auster said. *But he will serve me well.*

The woman gave Auster a half-smile and checked her watch. "It's six o'clock!" she hollered to the crowd. "They're probably moving him to the holding cell right now!"

Cheers erupted and then shouts of, "Kill him! Kill him!"

The other group continued to belt out, "Death row, hell no!"

The energy intensified. Someone from the kill-him group threw a bottle at the no-kills. It smashed against the side of a guy's head, shredding his scalp just above the left ear, which seemed to send him off the edge. Blood poured from his scalp into his ear as he ran through both security lines and clocked a kill-'em guy in the face. The mobs clashed and the guards couldn't hold the masses back.

"This world is shit because of you people!" the blonde woman screamed at the no-kills.

A bottle sailed toward her head. "Bitch!" A voice yelled.

"Ach!" she yelped as she deflected it. "Fuckers! They should give you assholes the needle, too!" She gripped Auster's arm. "Let's kick the shit out of these tree-huggers!"

Auster stood amidst the mayhem, feeling the energy that only hate can generate. He eyed the door to the cell block, channeled his energy, and changed form, braking apart into millions of particles. Then, like dust kicked up by a gust of wind, he drifted toward the cell block.

Auster saw the blonde turn to look for him. "Can you believe these—" She stood for a moment, mouth agape, then rubbed her eyes. "I'm losing my shit," she said to the woman standing next to her. "That hot guy was just here."

Auster watched the crowd close in where he once stood, and when an officer entered the east block, he seized the opportunity, moving as wisp of dust through the closing door.

∞∞∞∞∞∞∞

Per standard protocol, San Quentin had been on lockdown since the day before the execution and would remain so for one day after. Extra guards were stationed throughout the prison, each manning his post with rigid tension. The uncertainty and awkwardness were excellent tools that fed seamlessly into Auster's plan.

He floated through the east block, familiarizing himself with the layout of the place. Auster located the lethal injection room and marveled at the cross-shaped gurney—*sea-foam green of all colors*—with thick, black straps to restrain the condemned. He glided down the corridor and through the bars of the holding cell where Colton Lee Haddix sat, waiting to die.

Haddix was a small man, frail and weak. His thin, black hair was greasy and plastered to his sweaty, leathery scalp. His sunken eyes stared dully from a pocked, unshaven face as he rocked back and forth on the bench, wringing his hands and mumbling to himself. Several of his teeth were missing and those remaining were broken and decayed.

Auster glided between the bars and swirled above Haddix, spreading his mass thin so that guards outside the cell wouldn't notice. He swooped next to Haddix's head and whispered, "Tonight you will die, but I will bring you back."

"Who's that? Who's there?" Haddix jerked his head in all directions.

"Ssshhhhhh! Look up."

Haddix did as he was told, eyes widening as Auster condensed his mass enough to give a glimpse of his face.

"You're not real," Haddix said. "They drugged me earlier so I wouldn't freak out."

Auster swirled above the condemned man's head. "Your senses may be impaired, but I am very real. And if you do as you are told, you will walk outside tonight."

Haddix glanced through the bars into the corridor, where two guards stood. He nodded quickly. "Okay, okay," he whispered. "What do you want me to do?"

"You will wake with a body over yours. Stay still or stay dead. Do you understand?"

Haddix nodded. "Yes. Yes, I do. Stay still or stay dead."

"Good. I will tell you when it is safe to move."

"Okay okay. You tell me." Haddix squeezed his hands together. "You tell me when to move."

"See you in seven hours." Auster rose to the ceiling and slipped through the bars.

Haddix stood and crossed to the edge of his cell, watching the thin wisp of fog drift down the hall.

One of the guards strolled up to him. "Supper will be up soon, Haddix."

Haddix smiled. "Thank you, sir."

∞∞∞∞∞∞

Auster emerged as people jostled their way into their private rooms to view the execution. To avoid suspicion, he changed back to human form low to the ground, his mass solidifying in a hunched-over position.

A man plowed into him. "Sorry," he said. "I didn't see you."

Auster stood. "I picked the wrong place to tie my shoe." He reached into his pocket and clipped on the press badge he'd taken from a young man he'd met in a coffee shop thirty miles out that morning.

Uneasy silence filled the room. The press and official witnesses took their seats facing the lethal injection room. Auster noticed that people avoided eye contact. His gaze drifted from person to person. *I don't understand. This is what these people want. Why the shame?*

The grim audience stared at the closed curtains behind the windows. The minutes crept by—the tension palpable. Finally, at 11:52 p.m., shadows moved behind the curtain. Periodically, light shining through the space where the curtains met went dark as someone passed behind it. *He's being strapped down.*

Others seem to have noticed because several people shifted uncomfortably in their seats. Finally, the curtains opened, revealing Colton Lee Haddix strapped to the gurney with IV catheters plunged into both arms. He appeared more doped up than when Auster saw him earlier.

I hope he remembers his instructions.

The attendants turned Haddix so he faced the audience. "Any final words?"

Haddix trembled, and in his apparent fear, couldn't keep his voice steady as he muttered, "See ya in a while."

The press scratched the last words onto their little pads as Haddix lay back his head and closed his eyes. The sound of the speaker clicking off silenced the room.

Auster glanced at the clock. 11:59 p.m.

The room was still.

12:00 a.m. The execution began.

Haddix lay silent. His head and extremities didn't move, but his mid-section appeared to suck in and roll.

The witnesses waited as the vitals were monitored every few minutes.

12:09 a.m. No heartbeat. The attending physician pronounced Haddix dead.

The crowd stood, still avoiding eye contact, and filtered out of the room.

The man who had sat next to Auster during the event looked to the side and said, "Could you even—?"

But Auster was already floating above him.

The young man glanced around, seeming confused, then shook his head and said, "This whole thing is surreal."

TWELVE

Ryan Lindberg and his new partner, Peter Brightman, of the Marin County Coroner's Office, waited in the doorway of San Quentin's east block as the nurses pushed the gurney holding Haddix's body toward them. The two men nodded silently at the nurses as they took possession of Haddix and wheeled him out to the van.

Lindberg heard shouts from the distant crowd but couldn't make out what they were saying as he swung open the double doors in the back of the van. He shielded his face as a sudden gust of wind brought in a bunch of dust. "Ack! Where did this come from?"

"Dunno," Brightman answered from behind. "It's like dirt and fog mixed together."

"Let's get 'im in quick," Lindberg said. "On three." He grasped one end of gurney. "One! Two! Three!"

The two pushed Haddix inside and Brightman climbed in to secure the body.

Lindberg trotted around to the driver's side, pulled open the door, and slid onto the seat. He waited until Brightman was at the passenger window before starting the engine. "Let's go."

"Yeah. Let's get outta here." Brightman shut the door and dusted off his curly, red hair. "That was weird as fuck. Sandy crap just whipped all inside the van. We're gonna have to sweep it out when we get back."

"Great." Lindberg's sour tone echoed in the cab as he stared at the road ahead, trying to ignore the peering faces as the van passed by the crowds. He glanced to the side. Brightman's glazed-over stare registered the same discomfort. Lindberg pressed harder on the accelerator and the van plowed forward.

Lindberg had shuttled cons who died of old age, illness, or violence too many times to count. The route from the prison to the morgue was less than six miles, about ten minutes depending on traffic. Most of the route was along a residential stretch of Highway 101. But a tiny patch of freeway just before the turnoff leading to the coroner's office was nothing but darkness and trees.

Driving through that half-mile stretch at night had creeped out Lindberg for as long as he could remember. He even set the trip meter in his own car when he drove through it to monitor his progress through 'the dark patch' as he referred to it. Lindberg thought his fear must be rooted in some buried childhood memory, so he usually laughed at himself when he automatically pushed the button of the trip meter as the trees approached.

On execution night, driving through the area with the corpse of a monster amplified Lindberg's trepidation to the point where he couldn't laugh it away.

After they'd driven about three miles, Lindberg visualized the darkness that would soon surround them after the highway bent left, just beyond the houses. Clouds blocked the moon, leaving the sky black and drivers dependent on hazy pools of light from the intermittent street lamps lining the highway.

Lindberg did the math in his head, swallowed hard, and slowly reached forward to push the trip meter. In a mile, they'd reach the trees, the darkness. In about 1.6 miles, they'd be through it.

In an effort to keep his mind off of this childish nonsense, Lindberg glanced at Brightman, who slumped in the seat next to him, staring blankly out the window. "This is your first rodeo, isn't it?"

Brightman nodded. "Yep. First time doing an execution haul for the county. I was a medic before. I've seen lots of shit. Patched up some, couldn't patch up others. At least this one's not squirming around screaming as I try to compress an artery."

"True," Lindberg said. "They're pretty still when we get 'em."

Brightman chuckled. "Gotta admit, though, there's a level of angst I didn't anticipate." He patted his tummy. "Insulin pump's hit me more than usual today."

"Diabetes?"

"Yeah, since I was a kid."

The van lurched to the side.

Brightman glanced out the window. "What the fuck was that? Did we hit something?"

Lindberg examined the street in the rearview mirror. "Doesn't look like it."

The van lurched again.

Brightman twisted around in his seat. "That felt like it came from the back of the van."

Another jolt.

"You're right," Lindberg said. "It does feel like—"

The van rocked hard.

Brightman slammed his fist against the armrest. "FUCK! I didn't secure the body well enough. Pull over so we don't arrive with the fucker's arms and legs broken."

Lindberg shook his head. "It doesn't matter. They're going to throw him into the furnace as soon as we get there."

Brightman shook his head. "Bullshit. You know they'll check him out first. Like you said, it's my first rodeo. I don't want to lose my job or get my balls busted for the next twenty years because I didn't secure The Campfire Butcher."

The back of the van jerked to the side again.

"What! Is he fucking *dancing* back there?" Brightman turned to Lindberg. "Pull over!"

Lindberg flicked the turn signal and veered to the right. He glanced ahead, then in the rearview mirror. Darkness and trees surrounded the van as it slowed to a stop. The blood drained from his face. He didn't need the trip meter to know where he was.

The dark patch. Fuck me.

THIRTEEN

Auster hovered inside of the van. His acquisition was losing the ability to regenerate minute by minute and he couldn't risk letting the van reach the coroner's office. He had to slam Haddix against the side of the van several times before the driver finally pulled over.

The passenger side door opened and closed. Footsteps echoed outside, leading to the back of the van. There was a click, then the back doors swung open.

Brightman climbed in and froze. "What the hell?"

Haddix's naked body, which had been removed from the body bag, lay face up on the gurney.

"How in the fuck did this—"

Auster swooped down and picked up Brightman by the neck. "*I'm* how."

Brightman gurgled as Auster squeezed.

Snap.

Auster stripped Brightman of his clothing and laid the body on top of Haddix's, making sure their faces were pressed together. He held both of his hands above Haddix and rays of light pulsed from them into the corpse. Haddix's body vibrated and his fingers began to move. He sucked in a breath.

"Stay still!" Auster spat.

Brightman's body quavered, rippled, and began to melt into Haddix's. Auster directed the light toward the two faces, melding them into one.

Haddix squealed in pain.

"Hey, rookie!" the driver shouted from up front. "Why the fuck are you taking so long? Is everything cool?"

Auster dug his fingertips through Haddix's new red hair. "Shut up and don't move!"

Haddix whimpered and trembled as Auster finished the process and peeled away the glob of flesh that was Brightman moments earlier.

Auster scrutinized his new creation. "Be still, and breathe. Your new body will form soon." *Wonder what this goon will resemble when the flesh settles?*

Auster scooped what was left of Brightman into the body bag and zipped it closed.

Haddix lay still, malformed, hideous, but alive.

Auster leaned forward. "We need to get away from here. You're going to have to get up now."

With trembling arms, Haddix managed to roll over and push himself up. Auster pulled him out of the van.

Haddix opened his mouth and tried to speak. "Shank yooooooo."

Auster grabbed Haddix by the arm and dragged him away from the vehicle, changing back into vapor as he held his grip around Haddix's arm.

∞∞∞∞∞∞

Lindberg checked his watch. *It's been almost five minutes. Where in the hell is Brightman?* He peered outside at the trees. *God, don't make me get out of the van. Not here.*

He slammed the dashboard with his palm. "Brightman, hurry your ass up!"

Another minute passed.

Fuck me.

Lindberg got out of the van, slammed the door, and marched toward the rear. "Brightman! You're being a prick. Just put the body—"

Through the gaping back doors, he could see the body bag resting inside, but Brightman was nowhere in sight.

Lindberg let out a sigh of relief, planted his hands on his hips, and shook his head. "You picked a helluva place to take a piss!" he called out toward the trees. "We're only a few minutes away, for Christ's sake!"

Lindberg walked toward the trees and froze. Between the van and the forest ten feet away, a cloud-shaped creature held a naked, deformed man by the arm. The man could barely stand. His red, curly hair framed a face that looked like lumps of clay around dark, beady eyes.

The form holding the wretched thing hovered slightly above the ground, and although Lindberg could see right through the creature, it was obviously strong enough to heft the weight of the naked guy.

The form raised the other arm and pointed at Lindberg. A deep voice bellowed, "Your clothes or you die."

This can't be fucking real.

Lindberg could feel his teeth chattering as he unbuttoned his shirt as fast as he could. He tore the last few apart before throwing the shirt at them. He pulled off his shoes and tossed them forward, unbuckled his belt, pulled down his pants, and kicked them away. He could see his breath as he fought to keep his composure.

The cloud let go of Haddix's arm. "Dress yourself."

The man-like beast collapsed to the ground and fumbled on his hands and knees toward the clothing.

The form faced Lindberg and pointed to the van. "Get in."

Lindberg scrambled back to the van and climbed inside. The body bag next to him wasn't scary any more.

∞∞∞∞∞∞

Auster slammed the doors, waited until Haddix was dressed, then took him by the arm again. "Close your eyes and don't open them until I tell you to. We're going to fly very, very fast."

Haddix nodded and shut his eyes.

Auster focused on his destination, let his mass orient, and whisked through the trees with Haddix in tow. In the distance, he heard a scream from inside the van.

Shouldn't have unzipped the body bag.

FOURTEEN

Johnny sat in his office wearing a placid smile as he read the monthly sales figures on the computer screen. He clicked to the local news and scrolled down to the social events page. He smiled when he saw his photo at the homeless shelter under the head line.

FLYNN GIVES BACK TO THE COMMUNITY

Johnny glanced at the framed poem on the far wall, his father's favorite by Alfred Lord Tennyson. He'd memorized it long ago, but Johnny's eyes couldn't resist scanning the elegant text.

With many a curve my banks I fret
By many a field and fallow,
And many a fairy foreland set
With willow-weed and mallow.

I chatter, chatter, as I flow
To join the brimming river,
For men may come and men may go,
But I go on forever.

Johnny remembered the look of pride in his father's eyes when he broke the news that he had made his first million. Remembering his own sense of pride, Johnny reached out and picked up the photo on his desk of the two of them, taken five years earlier, shortly after his father's diagnosis. They'd traveled the world together the following six months until it was no longer possible.

Roland Flynn had died a painful death, drowning in the fluid in his own lungs and weighing less than one hundred pounds. Johnny could only stand by and watch, helpless and powerless. Three days after the burial, Johnny bought the optical company that had exposed his father to asbestos and liquidated it.

"I'm *The Brook*, Daddy," Johnny said to the photo, eyes stinging with tears. "Never will my fields lay fallow. Competitors will try to destroy me, but J.T. Flynn will go on forever."

Johnny checked an email from his travel agent, reviewing the itinerary for his upcoming trip with Danielle to the French Riviera. Danielle had fallen in love with the place after taking a trip with Johnny a few years before the kids were born.

"Twenty years," Johnny said aloud. "Hard to believe it's been that long, Dani."

With the trip only a week away, Danielle was bustling about, making arrangements for the kids, shopping for a new wardrobe, and texting Johnny non-stop.

Johnny checked his phone for any new messages from her. "Nothing today. My girl must be out and about." He turned his attention back to work. "Stay focused, gotta get shit done here."

He blew out a breath, grabbed his coffee mug, winced as he slurped the dredges from the bottom of the cup, and settled in. "Okay, quarterly report, don't fucking let me down."

Wilks burst into Johnny's office, a wide-eyed look of horror on his face. "It's Danielle!"

Johnny leapt out of his chair. "What the hell are you talking about?"

Wilks paused.

"WHAT?" Johnny screamed.

Wilks spoke in rapid spurts. "She was shopping. Two men wrestled her down. Threw her into a van."

"NO!" Johnny screamed. He pointed to Wilks. "Pull the kids from school, NOW!"

FIFTEEN

Officer Richard Brickford sat at his kitchen table, munching on a grilled-cheese sandwich, sipping green tea, and reading the latest news online. He stopped on the picture of Colton Lee Haddix. "Glad that fucker's gone." He scanned the text, his brows knitting together when he reached the last paragraph.

> If the drama surrounding the execution of Colton Lee Haddix wasn't enough, the Marin County Coroner is dealing with more criticism after the van carrying Haddix's body broke down during the short trip back from San Quentin.
>
> Sheriffs arrived to find one of the employees had fled the scene and the other was severely distraught. Officials won't reveal details of the event, but an unnamed source reported that the employee, upon checking the body of Colton Lee Haddix, discovered that it had sustained what the coroner's office is calling *unexplainable chemical decomposition*.

> The coroner's office is attributing this to the body sitting in the van for an extended period of time.

Brickford shook his head. "That's some fucked up shit."

He took a bite of his sandwich. *Not bad. This no booze, vegetarian thing four days-a-week doesn't suck as much as I thought.* He took a swig of his green tea and put a hand on his gut. *A day at a time. A pound at a time.*

He scrolled farther down the news page and found the article he'd been searching for about the case he was working. "Fuck." He sighed deeply as he read the short article.

> Police still have no one in custody for the Gypsum Ridge Hospital body-snatching case. Police are searching for a custodian who has not been seen since the day of the incident.
>
> Hospital officials and the police are working together to find out how such a breach of security occurred.
>
> The family who has lost the remains of their loved one hopes the police find some answers so they can have closure.

Brickford shook his head and took another bite. "What the fuck am I supposed to do?" he said to the computer around a mouthful. "I interviewed twenty employees."

He reached into his pocket and pulled out his notepad to review his notes. *I interviewed everyone in the ER, trauma unit, nurses, orderlies, custodians. It has to be the missing janitor.*

He closed the notepad. *I'll call in and tell them I'm going back to the morgue again. Maybe there's something I overlooked.*

He'd just finished up his grilled cheese when the phone in his pocket rang. He answered it. "Brickford." He listened. "Right. Kidnapping. Some billionaire's wife. High priority. Where are they now?"

He grabbed his notepad, picked up a pen, and scribbled down the information. "And what about the hospital case? Who's going to—? Okay, got it. I'll be there within the hour."

Brickford ended the call, gulped the tea, added the dirty dishes to the pile in the sink, and tucked the notepad in his back pocket. He reached the entry and glanced in the mirror, noticing a greasy blop of cheese on his shirt.

"Damn it!"

He trotted back to the bedroom and slid open the closet door. Six uniforms from his rookie days hung neatly on one side.

Couldn't get my right leg into those now.

He pulled out a clean, white, button-down shirt and a red-and-blue-striped tie that Maddie had given him last Father's Day. He peeled off the dirty shirt and turned to face the full-length mirror as he buttoned up the fresh one. He cinched up the tie, reached into to the chest of drawers, and pulled a baby wipe to mop the sweat from his bald head.

He briefly recalled the days when he once had a cap of wavy, blonde hair. *Where have eleven years gone?*

"You're an out-of-shape fuck!" he said to the mirror as he tightened his buckle. "But not for long."

He marched toward the front door and reached for his keys on the entry table. His gaze fell on the picture of himself with Helen and Maddie. The divorce had been finalized four months ago, but the photo still hung in the same place it had when they were married. Pictures of a growing Maddie surrounded it.

Brickford kissed his finger and placed it on the most recent picture of Maddie wearing a cheeky grin as she knelt in the front row of her softball team. "Love you, kid."

He let the door slam behind him, then slid into the car the PD issued him. He glanced at the crack in the dashboard and shook his head. "Piece of Shit."

"Bullshit." He turned the key in the ignition and reached into the glove box to pull out his smokes. "Bullshit leaves crimes unsolved and gets people killed. It's first thing I learned on the job." He lit a cigarette. "This billionaire kidnapping reeks of it already, even through the phone when I took the call."

He turned on the speaker in the car and pressed the speed dial.

"Hello?"

Brickford cleared his throat. "Hey, Helen. It's me."

There was a brief pause. "Hey, Dick."

"How's it going?"

"Fine, I guess. You?"

"Good. I'm doing that no-booze, vegetarian four times-a-week thing you were talking about."

"Really?" Helen's voice brightened. "That's great, Dick. How do you like it?"

"It's my third week."

"Your *third* week? That's great."

"Yeah, I've started jogging, too. Granted, it's only a mile or so, but it's a start."

"Dick, I'm so prou—" She paused. "That's just great."

Brickford could tell by Helen's voice that she was smiling, which made him smile, until she added, "Are you still smoking?"

He eyed the cigarette in his hand. "Baby steps, Helen. One thing at a time."

"Right." There were a few silent moments before she asked, "How's work? That hospital thing is getting a lot of press."

"We're pretty sure it was the custodian, but they just pulled me off the case and put me on a new kidnapping."

Another pause. "Well, you're good at *those*, right? When the cops need to find out who took someone, they can always rely on *Dick the Brick*."

Brickford winced. "Yeah, I guess I'm the guy you call when there's a kidnapping. *Although one case cost me you and almost my fucking job.*

Helen sighed on the other end. "You want to talk to Maddie?"

"Yeah, she's there, right? Isn't it minimum day today?"

"Yep. Let me get her."

Brickford waited. He smiled when he heard the phone change hands.

"Hi, Daddy."

"Hey, baby girl. How's it going?"

"Good."

"How's softball?"

"It ended last week. I'm in dance now."

"Oh, dance. Is it ballet, or jazz—?"

"It's hip-hop."

"Oh, hip-hop. That's great. Let me know when you perform so I can come watch."

"Okay, Daddy, I will. I gotta go."

"Okay, baby girl. I love you."

"I love you, too, Daddy."

The phone clicked dead.

Brickford's smile faded. He rolled down the window and took a drag off his smoke, enjoying the forty-minute drive before he would have to hurl himself into the middle of the shitstorm.

SIXTEEN

Johnny paced back and forth. "Where the fuck are the cops?" he snapped at Wilks.

"They'll be here any minute."

Johnny's thought of Danielle. *Please, baby, be okay.*

Paula sat on the couch with her arms around the kids. Maya sobbed, her eyes nearly swollen shut from crying. Michael's face was buried in his hands.

The doorbell rang.

"Finally!" Johnny stormed across the foyer and threw the door open. Outside stood a chunky, bald man wearing a red-and-blue tie. "It's about time! Get in here!"

The cop walked in and checked his watch. "It hasn't even been an hour."

"An hour's a long fucking time!" Johnny spat.

The detective squared his jaw. "For your information, Mr. Flynn, police responded to the *crime scene* in minutes. Officers are still at the scene now, investigating where the kidnapping occurred before the area becomes contaminated." He extended his hand. "I'm Dick Brickford, lead investigator on your case."

Johnny ran his fingers through his hair. "Yeah, of course. That makes sense."

Two black-and-whites pulled up just as Johnny was about to close the door.

Brickford jerked his head in the direction of the police cars. "Those officers will be bringing some equipment into the house that will help track down who took your wife if the person tries to contact you."

"Right." Johnny waited while four officers carried in boxes of electronic equipment. He ushered everyone inside and the police got to work setting up radios, microphones, headsets, and recording devices.

Brickford noticed the kids and walked over, kneeling down so that he was eye-level with them. "I'm Detective Brickford. I promise, I'll do everything I can to get your mom back, okay?"

They both nodded, then Michael buried his head back in his hands and Maya started crying again.

Brickford turned to Johnny. "Is there a quiet place we can talk?"

He nodded and gestured toward two chairs sitting by the fireplace at the other end of the spacious great room. "They won't be able to hear us over there."

Brickford eyed the destination, then muttered, "This room's the size of my entire place."

They settled in, trying to ignore the sound of the officers behind them. Brickford took out a notepad. "I need to ask you a series of questions, Mr. Flynn. These questions are not tailored to you personally. They're standard protocol, so don't be offended."

"Okay," Johnny said. "Go ahead."

"Is there any reason someone would want to harm you or your family?" His eyes drilled into Johnny's.

Johnny's gaze met his. "Yeah. Shitloads. I soak up companies. If you want a list of 'em, just pull out the *Wall Street Journal* over the last three fucking years."

Brickford leaned back. "All right, let's start there." He motioned to a thin, young cop behind him. "Keesler, I need a list of employees for each of the companies Flynn's taken down. Start with the most recent and keep going back."

"I'm on it, boss."

Brickford turned to Johnny. "When we get the list, I'll give you a copy and you can tell me if any names ring a bell."

"Okay." Johnny thought of Ming. *No one knew about the Vander Broek shootings. I didn't even involve Wilks that time, though I'm pretty sure he's guessed. Could Dani's kidnapping be revenge? Should I say something and risk dying in prison?*

Johnny pinched the bridge of his nose, and then looked up. "I'll pay any ransom."

"Okay." Brickford flipped through his notepad. "Do you trust everyone who works for you?"

"With my life," Johnny said.

"The VP of your corporation is a Mr. Jan Wilkinson?" He pronounced *Jan* the same as the female name.

"Yes, and it's pronounced *Yän*. The man's like family. He's known Dani almost as long as he's known me. We spend holidays together. When my dad died...." he paused and hung his head.

"It's okay," Brickford said. "Take your time."

Johnny stared down at the floor. "When my dad died, Wilks was my rock. He handled everything while I carried out my father's final wishes. He went to my kids' sporting events, kept Dani informed about business. Hell, he kept the company going for almost a month because I was a wreck. He was there for my family at a time I couldn't be. For that, I'm forever in his debt."

Johnny watched Brickford scratch down some notes. "Can you really keep track of everything in that little pad? They have electronic notepads, even Dictaphones, you know."

Brickford looked up. "The police department's pretty cheap. They don't see the purpose of dropping any extra money on a cop when pen and paper cost next to nothin'."

Johnny raised his eyebrows. "I see."

Brickford finished writing and then looked up. "Besides, this is the way I've been doing things for eleven years. The scribbles and sidebars I add to my notes, which would be omitted had I dictated them, have often proved helpful. Mind you, I do go home and transcribe them afterward, but I always keep the notepad close by."

"Fair enough," Johnny said.

Brickford flipped a page. "Okay, about your wife, Danielle. How long have you been married?"

"Twenty years in June."

Brickford wrote it down. "Has she ever been unfaithful to you?"

Johnny shook his head. "No."

"Have you ever been unfaithful to her?"

"No."

"Was there any marital strife or problems in the family recently?"

Johnny shrugged. "Well, my son got in trouble at school—"

"For what?" Brickford interrupted.

Johnny stared at him. "For pushing a kid." His stomach lurched as Brickford wrote it down. "I don't think that has anything to do with—"

"Probably not, Mr. Flynn. As I said before, these questions are standard protocol."

Johnny glanced over at Michael, grateful that the conversation was out of earshot.

"Okay, I think that'll do for now, Mr. Flynn. I'm going to need to speak with Mr. Wilkinson and your housekeeper—" He checked his notes—"Ms. Strathmore, then we'll talk further."

Johnny stood up. "Yeah, okay."

Brickford strolled toward the entry, reading his notepad, then, to Johnny's surprise, he pulled out an electronic dictation device, clicked it on, and started talking into it.

Why didn't he use that during our interview? What kind of hack is this guy?

∞∞∞∞∞∞∞∞

Brickford looked back to see Jonathan Flynn staring at him with a look of shock. He turned around and held the recorder close to his mouth. "Jonathan Flynn interview yielded no solid leads. Corporate competitors will be investigated based on the nature of Flynn's work. Flynn claims no marital strife, though the fidelity claim will need to be further investigated given the nature of his status. No billionaire I've ever known of has been faithful to his wife."

Brickford clicked off the recorder and glanced back into the living room. Flynn had moved over to the couch to sit with his kids.

He clicked the device back on. "Flynn's clearly dismayed over the event. I don't really think he's in on it at this time, but I need more info before pulling him off as the primary suspect. Flynn has unwavering trust for employees. Will interview VP and full-time housekeeper next."

Brickford stepped outside to have a smoke. He lit up and glanced around at the Flynn estate and the stretch of the Pacific coast that it overlooked.

So much money, he thought, as he strolled forward to see more of the beach. *Why can't these rich fucks just enjoy it? If I had a small fraction of what they have, I'd quit my job and take Helen and Maddie around the world.*

He lingered as he finished his cigarette, then dropped the butt on the ground and kicked dirt over it. "Okay, *Yän*, let's see what you have to say."

SEVENTEEN

B rickford walked back inside the Flynn residence and found Jonathan Flynn talking with Capra about the equipment on the table. "I'd like to speak with Jan Wilkinson next, please."

"Yeah, sure." Flynn went to retrieve Wilkinson as Brickford moved into the great room and settled into the same seat where he'd interviewed Flynn. A hefty, white-haired man with a beard and mustache approached and sat down opposite him.

My God, it's Santa Claus meets Colonel Sanders.

Brickford looked down to avoid staring and pulled out his notepad.

"Don't you have an electronic dictation device?" Wilkinson asked.

"I do, but I don't use it for this."

Wilkinson regarded the tiny pad. "Why not?"

"Why do you fly thousands of miles to view diamonds in person when you can see them clearly over a computer screen?"

Wilkinson leaned back. "Touché."

Brickford clicked his pen. "How long have you been working for Mr. Flynn?"

"Twenty-two years. Since the beginning."

"Were you in the diamond business prior to teaming up with Mr. Flynn?"

"I worked for a small company in the Netherlands, where I'm from, then in Antwerp."

Brickford scratched the notes onto his pad, then flipped several pages back. "Flynn's main competitor, Schuyler Vander Broek, is also from the Netherlands. Do you know him?"

"Yes."

"Ever work with him?"

"Yes."

Brickford waited, but Wilkinson didn't offer anything more.

"Where and when did you work with him?"

"Many years ago."

"Back in the Netherlands?"

"Yes."

Brickford set the pen down. "Look, these short answers are getting us nowhere fast. I get that you're uncomfortable about this, but I'm going to find out the nature of your relationship with Mr. Vander Broek whether *you* tell me or someone else does. So you may as well tell the story now. Complete sentences would be nice." He picked up the pen again. "Please, just start at the beginning."

Wilkinson licked his teeth. "The Netherlands is a hub of the diamond industry. When I was fourteen years old, after I wanted to study lapidary work—that's the cutting and polishing of gems. It was then I worked with Schuyler. I was his understudy."

"Okay." Brickford scribbled wildly.

"He had been in business for about ten years and was building quite a name for himself in the local community. He gave me my first job."

"How long did you work for him?"

"Two years."

"Why did you leave?"

"I left of my own accord."

"Why?"

Wilkinson shifted his weight. "I realized I couldn't in good conscience work for someone who was that unscrupulous."

"How did you come to believe Vander Broek was unscrup—"

"NOT believe—*know*," Wilkinson shifted in his seat. "Schuyler lied, cheated, cut dirty deals. He shut down honest companies and strong-armed others into selling to him. I know sometimes in business corners are cut, but Schuyler's entire corporation was built on a pile of deception and destruction."

Brickford looked up from the notepad. "I don't mean to be offensive, but hasn't Flynn Corporation shut down many companies?"

"The acquisitions J.T. Flynn Corporation has made were all above board, not using mob-style bullying. It's not the same at all."

Brickford flipped another page. "Okay."

Wilkinson glared at the pad in Brickford's hand. "After two years of watching Schuyler hurt the community where I grew up, I left and went to Belgium."

"Antwerp?"

"Yes."

"Antwerp is also one of the diamond capitals of the world, is that correct?"

"It is," Wilkinson said.

"Were you successful there?"

"I was. I met my wife there, we had a son, and I was very happy."

"Where did you meet Mr. Flynn?"

"There, in Antwerp. He was just starting out at the time. I saw the fire in his eyes and knew he was going to be someone special. We hit it off immediately. At first, we saw each other twice or three times a year at social affairs. Later on, he came to my house for meals and to play with my son, Karel. He brought Danielle with him several times. He'd always say to me, 'When I make my first million, I'm bringing you aboard, Wilks.'"

Brickford wrote furiously. "And he kept his promise?"

"He did," Wilkinson smiled as he recalled the incident. "He actually brought a *bank statement* over to my house, spread it on the kitchen table, and said, 'Let's turn this million into a billion, Wilks!'"

Brickford looked up. "Really?"

"Yes." Wilkinson smiled. "I had my family on a plane the next week."

"And you've made your billion."

Wilkinson leaned back. "We have."

"I'll bet Mr. Vander Broek isn't happy knowing a former employee built a company that is now his biggest competitor."

"No, he's not happy about it. Schuyler moved to the States shortly after I did. We've seen each other at social events since I've joined Mr. Flynn."

"Did he threaten you?"

Wilkinson shook his head. "Schuyler doesn't threaten, but I do remember him paying back competitors who he felt needed a lesson when I worked for him in the Netherlands."

Brickman wrote, *no direct threats.* "And what happened with the people he *paid back,* as you put it?"

"Someone usually had an accident. Mind you, it was never the person Schuyler spoke with." He sighed and looked down.

"If not them, who?"

"It was always an innocent." Wilkinson said, his voice even and deliberate. "Someone they cared deeply for, like their child, or a grandmother—"

Brickford stopped writing and looked up. "Or wife?"

Wilkinson nodded. "Yes. So, now you see why I could never work for such a man."

"Could Schuyler Vander Broek have something to do with Mrs. Flynn's kidnapping?"

Wilkinson's expression turned to stone. "Back when Schuyler was clawing his way the top, there was nothing outside the realm of possibility."

"But not now?"

Wilkinson shrugged. "Schuyler's old and bathing in money. No one can touch him. I don't think he would do something like this, especially after J.T. went outside of bounds to honor his company after the shootings last year."

"I remember that," Brickford wrote something down, and then stood up and called out to the other cops. "Keesler! I'll need all the details on the Vander Broek shooting. Let's make sure they're not related."

"Got it."

Wilkinson then leaned forward and whispered, "Yes, do look into it, Officer Brickford. Just to be sure. Throwing someone's wife in a van and taking her isn't Schuyler's style, but you never know. Danielle is like a daughter to me. It would break my heart if..." He leaned back. "You know, something terrible happens."

"I will, Mr. Wilkinson." Brickford closed the pad. "I think that's all for now. Thanks for your time."

Wilkinson got up and smoothed his pants. "I need some fresh air."

Brickford followed him into the front yard and split in the opposite direction. He lit another cigarette and pulled out his recorder. "Wilkinson interview yielded interesting info. Check into Schuyler Vander Broek, everything from far in the past to recent, and run plates of all cars. While you're at it, run the plates of all cars registered to Flynn Corp. as well. Wilkinson seems genuinely concerned."

He clicked off the recorder and took another hit. The sun was fast approaching the horizon, painting the clouds fiery pink.

Time to see what Paula Strathmore has to say.

∞∞∞∞∞∞∞

Can I get you a cup of coffee before we talk, Mr. Brickford?"

Thank god. "Yes, that would be great."

A few minutes later, Paula returned with two cups filled to the brim and steaming.

"Thank you very much," Brickford said as Paula sat opposite him. "How long have you been working for the Flynns?"

"Since the children were babies. Prior to that, they had a housekeeper who primarily did cleaning and such."

"So you take care of—"

"Cooking, cleaning, shopping, picking up and dropping off the children at school and team practices. Things of that sort."

Brickford paused. "Wow. I might still be married if I had someone who—" Brickford felt his face get hot. "Sorry, shouldn't have said that."

"It's quite all right. Mrs. Flynn often says she's aware of how fortunate they are."

"Paula, I'll risk to say you know the Flynns better than most?"

"I think so. I've been with them for almost fifteen years. I love those kids as if they were my own."

"Do you know of *anyone* who would want to hurt the family? Have you seen or heard anything suspicious lately?"

"No, sir."

"Are you familiar with Schuyler Vander Broek?"

"Certainly. He's Mr. Flynn's biggest competitor."

Brickford jotted something down. "Has Mr. Flynn mentioned anything about Vander Broek—"

Paula shook her head before he could finish. "I don't know anything about Mr. Vander Broek other than that his company competes with Mr. Flynn's. I deal with the day-to-day running of the household."

"Okay, let's stick with that, then. Has the family been under any strain?"

Paula tipped her head to one side as though trying to remember. "No. They've actually been pretty happy since Mr.

Flynn's business has picked up again. There was the incident with Michael being suspended that caused quite a stir, but I imagine lots of families have anxiety when their children misbehave and have to be disciplined."

"Did Mr. and Mrs. Flynn fight over that?"

"Quite the opposite. They were united. They wanted to teach Michael a lesson, so they took him with them to a homeless shelter, and they've been volunteering there ever since."

Oh, shit. Brickford looked up. "When was this?"

"A couple of months back. At first, the whole family went along to help, but for the last several weeks, it's only been Mrs. Flynn and Michael. The boy must volunteer for three months before Mr. and Mrs. Flynn give him his privileges back. The experience has really had an impact on the child." Paula seemed to sense Brickford's concern. "You don't think someone at—"

"It's something I'll need to investigate."

Paula became visibly upset. "But, Mrs. Flynn goes there to *help* those people. How could they possibly—"

"People who are desperate do desperate things."

Paula leaned forward and placed a hand on the detective's arm. "You're going to find her, aren't you, Detective Brickford?"

"I'm going to do everything I can, Ms. Strathmore."

"Have you handled...these types of things before?"

"Several times."

Paula wiped a tear from her cheek. "Did they hurt them?"

At this question, Brickford closed his eyes. *Fight it, Dick. Don't go there again.* He opened his eyes, met Paula's gaze, and answered, "Once."

Paula's expression glazed over. She stared beyond Brickford out the window. "What do you think the kidnappers want with Mrs. Flynn?"

"Money," Brickford said. "That's been my experience."

Paula clicked her tongue and folded her hands in her lap. "Of course."

EIGHTEEN

Auster sat crossed-legged on a bed in a shabby hotel room, staring at Colton Lee Haddix.

"What the—" Haddix stood in the bathroom, looking back and forth from Auster to his own reflection. "Is that me?"

"It is."

"How come I look different?" He yanked on his locks of curly, red hair.

"It was necessary." Auster rose from the bed and moved behind him. "You needed a new body and the world knows your face."

Haddix stared at his new high cheekbones, thin lips, freckles. He faced Auster. "I'm kinda good lookin."

Auster shrugged. "Anything was an improvement."

Haddix smiled, noting the full set of straight, white teeth.

But the eyes, Auster noticed, were the same—dark and empty.

Haddix ogled his reflection. "We should go get some girls."

"We have work to do."

"Okay, work, then girls?"

"In time."

Haddix walked out of the bathroom. "Okay, tell me what you want me to do."

"First, you must learn to comport yourself. Let's spend this day around others to see how you behave compared to the average citizen. We will begin at the store down the street."

The clerk at the local drug store paid little attention when the bell rang as Auster and Haddix entered the establishment.

Haddix's gazed hungrily around the place. "What are we gettin' here?"

"The necessary sundries you will need to remain hygienic." Auster glanced above at the signs then made his way toward the correct aisle. "It is important to—" He stopped when he realized that Haddix was gone.

Auster spun on his heels and marched across the store, peering down each aisle. He spotted Haddix crouching down at the end of the liquor section and stormed up to him. "You are not to leave my side."

Haddix slowly stood up, both hands over his middle, which looked overstuffed.

Auster felt frustration building. "What are you hiding?"

Haddix lifted his shirt to reveal a bottle of bourbon and two bags of chips.

Auster stood above Haddix. "Thievery is not necessary. If you continue to steal, I will destroy you."

"Okay, no stealing."

After Auster made the purchases, the two walked several blocks to the local shopping mall.

Haddix looked around in awe at the two-story mammoth complex of stores and kiosks teeming with people, then he screamed at the top of his lungs, "Whoooooeeee! I'll bet this is what Disneyland is like!"

Auster grabbed Haddix by the neck and squeezed. "Do *not* howl like an animal."

Haddix trembled. "Okay, no stealing, and no howling."

A simple walk through the mall wasn't an easy task. Haddix ran up to a group of shoppers and peered into their bags, shouting, "What'd you get, huh?"

Then Haddix spotted two pretty girls carrying pink bags out of a lingerie store. He made a start toward them, but Auster kicked forward and tripped him.

"Argh!" Haddix yelped as he careened to the tile floor.

Auster pulled Haddix up as the girls passed by. "Look around you. People do not behave this way."

Haddix looked almost childish, as though his feelings had been hurt. "I'm sorry. I just've never been to a place like this."

"Shut up, walk, and watch."

They continued on, Auster scrutinizing Haddix's every move.

I suspected he may be challenging, but this is extreme. If I don't see a change today, I will destroy him and move on.

They came to the end of the first level and stepped onto the escalator.

"Whoa," Haddix said as they ascended.

At the top level, they came upon a chocolate store. The smell of caramel wafted out into the open walkway.

Haddix's eyes grew as big as candy coins. He turned to Auster. "Can we go in there?"

"Sure."

Haddix trotted inside and spun around in circles. "Would ya look at this place."

In the far corner of the store, a man in a red apron stood over a large pot, stirring the warm caramel. The glass counters lining the perimeter contained every type of confection imaginable.

A portly woman with gray hair wrapped in a bun stood behind the counter holding a silver tray of samples. She smiled at Auster and Haddix. "Would you gentlemen like to try our new cocoa mint crisp today?"

Haddix looked up at Auster.

Last chance.

Haddix slowly walked up to the woman and took one sample. "Thank you very much."

"You're very welcome."

Haddix popped the chocolate into his mouth. "This is really good."

"Isn't it?" The woman smiled and helped another customer.

"Good," Auster said.

You have no idea how close you came.

During lunch at the food court, Auster gained some insight into human behavior control. Sitting across from them was a woman with two children. One child, who Auster figured to be about six years of age, sat calmly and ate his food.

The other child, who looked to be about four, did not behave…at first. He reminded Auster a great deal of Haddix. He began the meal by running around the tables, bothering other patrons, screaming, even attempting to take their food.

Auster watched with great interest as the mother scooped up the child from the ground and plunked him in the chair next to his brother. Auster focused his sense of hearing to discern what the mother was telling the child, whose eyes widened in fear as his mother pointed a finger in his face and spoke.

"You'd better listen when I say the words, or I'll spank you all the way out to the car and we'll never come back here again!"

From that point forward, when the child spoke too loudly, the mother would simply point and say, "Inside voice," which rendered him silent.

The child got up and ran from the table again. The mother scooped him up, pulled his chair away from the table and food, and said, "Time out. Three minutes. If you sit nice, you'll get to finish your hamburger."

The child sat quietly as the woman updated him on the time remaining. "Two minutes left. One minute left. Thirty seconds. Okay." She picked up the chair with the boy in it and sat him in front of his meal. "Eat and be quiet. No more chances."

The boy finished eating without bothering anyone.

I like this method of training.

Auster made a point to smile at the woman as she and the children got up to leave.

The woman looked at Auster, smiled warmly, and led her boys out of the food court.

From then on, if Haddix made a public display of himself, Auster simply said, "Time out," focused his gaze, and squeezed Haddix's trachea.

Haddix's eyes would widen as he pleaded and whimpered.

If Haddix spoke loudly, Auster would say, "Inside voice," and cause his tongue to swell so much that he gagged and choked.

With this new method of training, Haddix's behaviors mimicked that of an average citizen in just over a week. To celebrate the success of the training, Auster purchased Haddix a more suitable wardrobe.

"Where do you get all your money from?" Haddix asked Auster as they arrived back in their shabby hotel room.

Auster reached into his pocket and pulled out a card. "I've amassed wealth over time from many sources."

"Hmm." Haddix assessed the clothes he'd just laid on the bed. "I've never had such nice stuff."

"You'll need them where you're going."

"Where's that?"

"Chad."

"Huh? I'm going to see a guy named Chad?"

Auster stood for a moment. "No, Chad is a country in Africa." He looked Haddix up and down. "It's time to equip you with more skills."

"Skills like what?" Haddix said.

"More cognitive ability, for one thing. You'll need to problem-solve on your own. You must also read and speak French."

Haddix looked worried. "I can't even read English."

"I'm able to give that knowledge to you."

"Oh, okay."

Auster placed his hand on Haddix's head. "Hold still—I'm told this hurts."

The light came through Auster's palms, enveloping Haddix's head in a glowing aura. Haddix cried out, squealed, and jerked back.

Auster grabbed a fistful of hair. "Be still. Not much longer."

The light intensified, then, with one final flash, was gone.

Haddix crumbled to the floor, blood spewing from his nose, ears, and mouth.

Auster glanced down at him. *He'll sleep for a while. I have time to check on a few of the others.*

∞∞∞∞∞∞

Auster nudged Haddix with his shoe. Haddix opened his eyes and stared at the ceiling.

"*Bonjour,*" Auster said.

Haddix sat up. "*Bonjour.*"

Auster stood. "*Parlez. Dis quelque chose en français.*"

A look of astonishment flooded Haddix' face. "*Je comprends. Je comprends ce que vous dites.*"

"Of course you understand," Auster said.

"Can I read as well?"

Auster pulled the Bible from the nightstand and threw it down next to him. "See for yourself. It's written in English."

Haddix let the Bible fall open and ran a finger along the text, tracking the words. He looked up with an expression of shock. "I'm able to read!"

"You're prepared," Auster said. Now get dressed."

Haddix pushed himself up from the floor. Rubbing his head, he took a few steps toward the bathroom. Then he stopped and glanced back at Auster. "You know, I have no desire whatsoever to behave like an idiot. Why didn't you give me intelligence *before* behavioral training?"

"I've learned that intelligence fades first," Auster answered. "Animals resort to primal behaviors in times of stress and when cognitive ability is depleted. Your primal behaviors needed to be modified or you would be useless."

"Makes sense." Haddix walked into the bathroom and glanced into the mirror. He leaned forward, assessed the caked blood on his face, and ran his fingers through his hair. "Boy, I'm a mess."

His gaze met Auster's in the mirror's reflection. "Know where a gent can get a hair cut around here?"

∞∞∞∞∞∞

Two days later, a well-dressed and well-manicured Haddix accompanied Auster to Los Angeles International Airport.

"I've never been to an airport, much less flown on a plane," Haddix said as they examined the list of departing flights.

"It's the safest way for humans to travel. Fewest number of incidents per capita and fewest reported deaths."

"Interesting. I didn't know that." Haddix glanced at his plane ticket and opened his passport. "I'll have to get used to being called *Thomas Hasler*."

"You will." Auster leaned to the side and glanced at the photo. He smiled when he noticed that Haddix's—or *Hasler's*—dark eyes registered more intelligence.

Hasler tucked the passport in an inside pocket of his jacket. "Should I contact you when I arrive?"

"No. You have your instructions. Do your work and return in five days. Do not stay to watch the effects of it."

Hasler nodded, though impassively.

"I can be where you are going in a matter of hours." Auster took a step closer. "If you flee—" he pointed to his own head and then Hasler's—"I will find you. We are connected. I can just as easily take away what I have given you."

Hasler's eyes flickered with fear as Auster pointed a finger an inch from his face.

"Your appearance and your intelligence were both acquired through me. The body I gave you breaks down differently from the one you were born with. Your attributes do not last the duration of a human life, or even a half-life. You'll perceive subtle differences as the years pass. Eventually, you will need a new body."

"All right. When I arrive back I'll call—"

"No need to call," Auster said. "When you are about to land, all you need to do is think back to when we first met. Do you remember?"

Hasler thought for a moment, a dark expression flooding his face. "In the cell before…"

"Yes, before the execution. Just recall the memory and I will be there to pick you up when you land."

"What will you do while I'm gone?"

"There is much to do. While you've slept, I traveled around the world to make contact and update assignments."

Hasler looked interested. "It would be enlightening to talk with like-minded…people like me. Will I ever meet them?"

Auster smiled. "If you do, it means one of you has been assigned to kill the other."

Hasler's smiled faded. "I'll see you in five days."

"Yes, you will. And one last thing."

"What?"

"Do not allow any photographs or video footage to be taken of you. If, by chance, your likeness is captured, destroy the device. Do you understand?"

"Sure, no pictures. Got it."

"Off with you then."

Hasler walked toward the gate, glancing at his boarding pass then to the overhead display. An attractive flight attendant stopped to help him. He said something to cause her to laugh, and she pointed him in the right direction.

Auster watched his new creation depart. *I'll be watching you.*

Hasler stepped onto the moving walkway beside the flight attendant and said something to make her laugh again. He glanced back at Auster, flicked his eyebrows, and cracked a huge smile.

NINETEEN

Johnny was about to jump out of his skin by the time Detective Brickford finally gathered everyone together in the great room.

"Okay, I'm going to fill you in on the steps we're taking to get Mrs. Flynn back home." He gestured toward two cops, male and female, seated next to the equipment at the table. "These are officers Burnham and Capra. They'll be tracking all communications. If the kidnappers contact you here, we'll be on it. Officer Keesler, whom you met earlier today, is investigating the possibility the kidnappers might be linked to a company Mr. Flynn put out of business."

"Any leads other than those having to do with my business?" Johnny asked.

"Yes. I also have a car going out to the homeless shelter where Mrs. Flynn volunteered."

Michael seemed shocked to hear this. "It could be somebody from *there*?"

"We're investigating all leads, son," Brickford said.

"What can we do?" Johnny asked. "Is there anything at all? I hate just sitting here."

Brickford shook his head. "These cases are a waiting game. If the criminals wanted your wife dead, they would have already killed her. Instead, they made a public display of her kidnapping."

"Okay," Johnny said. "So you think this is about ransom?"

"I do," Brickford answered. "I think they want you to know she's been kidnapped and they expect you to wait by the phone so they can contact you with their demands."

Maya stood. "They're gonna know cops are here!" she said between sobs. "They're not stupid." She covered her face. "That could hurt Mom!"

"Hold on, honey." Brickford held his hands up. "Kidnappers always know the police are involved."

"They should have called by now!" Maya screamed. "Mom's been gone too long."

"You listen now." Paula pulled Maya back down to the couch and wrapped her arms around her. "We're all very upset, love. Let Detective Brickford finish. He knows what he's doing. We have to trust him."

Brickford turned to Johnny. "They usually make demands that involve one person from the family going to a very public place, usually a large, open space, with the ransom they demand."

"So we're going to sit here and wait?" Wilks appeared agitated.

"Yes. We wait, while my officers investigate the leads I've just discussed."

Paula checked her watch. "It's almost six o'clock. Mrs. Flynn was taken almost seven hours ago. Is that a long time? When can we expect—"

"Some have contacted us two hours after the kidnapping, others as long as ten days after." Brickford leaned back. "What was the record, Capra?"

"I believe it was eleven days, sir."

"So, we just wait." Johnny felt a wave of anger wash over him.

Brickford gestured toward the phone. "We have no other choice, Mr. Flynn."

TWENTY

Anisha Patel Corby sat on the back porch of her home in the hills just outside of Gypsum Ridge. She inhaled a cleansing breath as she took in the glittering lights of the city below. The hospital stood like a giant glowing cube amidst a sea of skyscrapers. A helicopter landed on the emergency pad and she thought of the person inside fighting for life.

Hope you are saved tonight.

The sky was clear, and cloudless. Anisha glanced up at the full moon and thought of her sister, Anjali. *I'll call her tomorrow.*

Frank slid open the screen door. A moment later, he emerged carrying two steaming cups of green tea. "So, you finally had a good day. You needed one of those."

"That's for sure. The police have finally grown tired of asking me about the Gerville boy. I've lost count of how many times I've repeated the same sad story."

"They've determined it was the janitor, Lewis, then?" Frank sat down and slid his glasses further up on his nose.

"Everyone thinks so. The underground market for organs is stronger than ever; lots of rich people are willing to pay big money to avoid dying while waiting for an organ. Lewis's wife is from Mexico. Many doctors perform the surgeries there."

Frank ran a finger along the rim of his cup. "It all makes sense. I mean, the body stolen belonged to a healthy young man who had an untimely accident."

"Yep. Police have witnesses who claimed to have seen a refrigeration van in the area on the night the body was taken, and several people have come forward to report seeing a guy who looks like Lewis traveling south of the border. He won't need his keycard in Mexico."

"There ya go. It's pretty obvious. Case of body stolen from hospital morgue—closed."

Anisha raised her cup. "Yes, it is. So the police have backed off, and today was a *very* good day. How was yours?"

"Well, let me see. Hmmmm, how should I put this?" Frank tried to look serious.

Anisha smiled. "You're bad at deception, my husband. What are you hiding?"

Frank reached over and took his wife's hand. "I'm up for it. I'm on the short list."

Anisha squeezed his hand. "Chief surgeon?"

"Yep. Can you believe it?"

"Yes, I can! You're brilliant and you've worked your tail off. No one deserves this as much as you."

"Thank you, love."

"Finally, the recognition you deserve." Anisha leaned back and sipped her tea. "It's so peaceful here."

"I like it, too." Frank turned to her. "Hey, you haven't told me about *your* day. What made it *very* good?"

Anisha took a deep breath. "Well, two things, actually. First, Ben and Jacob are getting married."

"Wow," Frank nodded. "That's great. When?"

"Next summer sometime. And knowing Ben, this thing is going to be over the top."

"I can totally see that." Frank laughed. "I mean, after his fortieth birthday party—"

"Oh, my, yes," Anisha cut in, covering her face with both hands. "I think the whole city came to that party, and I ate enough Hawaiian cuisine to—"

"I don't think I've had any since," Frank added with a laugh. "Yes, your best friend has made it clear over the years that he loves grand affairs. Did he ask you to be in the wedding?"

"Of course." Anisha whipped her head around. "I will be Ben's *best woman*, with flowers in my hair."

"You'll be beautiful." Frank lifted his cup.

Anisha gazed at her husband. "Don't know about beautiful. I'll try to pull off cute, since I'll be very round."

Frank nearly choked. "What?"

"That's the second bit of news that made today very good, my love." Anisha put her hands on her tummy.

"You're –?"

"Pregnant," she beamed.

"Really, Ani?"

"Really. About four weeks along."

Frank leapt up and lifted Anisha from her chair. "I can't believe it. This is incredible."

"Yes, it is," Anisha held him tightly. "Your job, Ben's marriage, and our baby. It's a trifecta of joy."

Frank put Anisha down and took hold of her shoulders. "This *is* a trifecta of joy." He glanced up at the full moon. "We should mark the calendar."

"I already have," Anisha said. "But I have to add your news to it."

Frank sat back down. "Have you told Anjali?"

"No, silly." Anisha took Frank's hand. "I had to tell you first. I wanted tonight to be just about us, about our budding family. I'll call her tomorrow. You'll know I've called when you hear the cheer from across town."

"No doubt." Frank looked around. "Think this place is big enough?"

"Plenty," Anisha said. "I love it here."

"Me, too." Frank finished his tea. "There's no way I can go to bed now." He held up his empty cup. "Another round?"

"Yes, please."

They stayed up until three in the morning discussing career plans, Ben's wedding, and baby names. Anisha made a point to savor every moment of it. She felt, happy, successful, like a grown-up, beautiful. But once in a while, she felt her smile fade slightly. She dared not mention the thoughts that caused this. It was too perfect a night, a sacred night.

But underneath it all, buried deep inside, was the dull ache. That word that could usurp the joy and replace it with angst. The brick in the pool that pilfers the chlorine and leaves the water cloudy.

Mother.

TWENTY-ONE

On the second night after Danielle Flynn's kidnapping, Johnny sat with his family and the police waiting for a call. Wilks elected to stay as well. Paula had to force the kids to go to bed at 1:00 a.m. At three o'clock, a tiny cop named Trillson and a very tall, freckle-faced man named Gingham had replaced Burnham and Capra.

Once Gingham had all of the updates, he gave Johnny the details of each lead. Then he took the time to show Johnny how the equipment tracked incoming calls.

"We'll get 'em, Mr. Flynn," Gingham said after the lesson. He nodded toward Brickford, who had drifted off in one of the chairs next to the fireplace. "Brick's the best at this type of case, and he's got a lot of guys on it."

Dawn broke and Johnny hadn't slept a wink. He went to the kitchen. Paula was up and a full pot of coffee sat on the counter.

"Did you sleep at all?" Johnny asked her as he opened the cupboard.

"No, Mr. Flynn. Did you?"

He shook his head.

He poured two cups of the strong brew, one for himself and another for Brickford. He walked into the living room to find the officer had roused from his slumber.

Johnny handed him the cup.

"Thanks," Brickford took a gulp. "That's good." He stood up, looked at his watch, and addressed the officers. "Any blips?"

"Nothing, sir."

He turned back and regarded Johnny. "Did you get any rest?"

"Not a chance. I can't sleep knowing she's out there, terrified and helpless."

"That's not going to help." Brickford took a breath. "Look, I know this is difficult, but as I told you yesterday, if you lose yourself, it could hurt the objective. When the call comes in, you won't be able to function if you're a tired, starving mess." He pointed to Johnny's trembling hand. "You need to stay strong—for your children and your wife."

Johnny closed his eyes and nodded once. "Okay. I get it."

Brickford checked his watch again. "It's six o'clock. I'm going to jet home, have a meal, take a shower, and change clothes. I suggest you do the same. I'll be back in three hours. Then we'll meet and see if the investigators found anything new. They've been combing all of the databases non-stop since this happened, so we should have more information. Sound good?"

Johnny conceded. "Sounds like a plan."

∞∞∞∞∞∞

Brickford peeled onto the main road, desperate to put as much space between himself and that pit of negative energy. He'd forgotten what that felt like and it made his stomach churn.

He reached for his phone to dial Helen but thought better of it when he remembered the time.

They're getting ready to leave for school.

He caught a whiff of himself. *I stink to high heaven. A shower will feel good.*

Brickford resisted the temptation to pull into the drive-through and order something greasy and meaty. *If I break my program on the first day of a new kidnapping case, Helen will think it was all...* He shook his head and stayed the course.

He got to the front door and it did its usual sticking business. He twisted and pushed, forcing the warped wood to let go at the base. It gave a loud creak as it swung open. He tossed his keys onto the entry table, kissed his finger, and tapped Maggie's photo. "Morning, kid." He was heading toward the kitchen when his phone rang. He pressed the call button. "Yep."

"Hi, Boss. Keesler here."

"Hold on." Brickford put the phone on speaker, and pulled the notepad from his back pocket. "Okay, whatcha got?"

"There are eight companies that J.T. Flynn Corporation has absorbed or put out of business over the last five years. We've tracked down the CEOs and some former employees. Most hate Flynn and have no problem going into detail about it, but no one stood out as having what it takes to plot revenge, except for one."

"I'm listening."

"Owen Corporation was sent packing by Flynn about two-and-a-half years ago. The company had a final dinner for all of its employees the week before they closed their doors. Former employees reported that Roderick Dennington, Owen's VP, stood up and toasted the company's history and progress, and then swore that he was going to make Flynn pay for ripping apart what his father had spent his life building."

"No shit?" Brickford wrote furiously.

"Yeah, he may be our guy, Chief. They said that Roderick, who is usually reserved and quiet, delivered the speech with such rage that even his own father became uncomfortable."

"Damn. That's intense."

"It is. Now, get this. Hector Dennington was a long-respected businessman in the community and ended up on the board of directors at Vander Broek Corporation."

"Really? That's a coincidence."

"And here's where it gets sticky, chief. Hector Dennington was one of the people shot dead at the Vander Broek incident last year."

Brickford dropped his pen. "Holy shit."

"Now, everyone knows Jonathan Flynn was hailed as a hero during that time, you know, pulling out all the stops to help catch the shooter."

"How could I forget?" Brickford scooped up the pen and jotted down another note. "The press wouldn't leave it the fuck alone."

"I don't think Roderick Dennington felt the same way. If he hated Flynn before his father was shot dead, you can imagine how he feels about him now. He's a cool character, Chief. Forty-one years old, well-connected, and rich as hell."

"That's motive and means any way you cut it."

"We haven't been able to reach Dennington, but apparently there's video footage out there of that speech. I'm on it now and I'll let you know what I find."

"Great. Good job, Keesler."

"Thanks, boss."

Brickford sat back and took a deep breath. He plugged his phone in to the wall to juice it back up. "Well, Mr. Flynn, looks like we'll have something to talk about when I come back."

He stood and stretched. Bright morning light poured in through the window. Brickford placed a hand on the red-checked tablecloth. *Warm already.*

He went to the sink, filled a cup, and watered the small ivy plant on the window sill that Helen had decided to leave behind. He placed the long tendrils along the ledge.

I'll be damned if I'm going to let you die, little fella.

He checked his watch. "Shit, where'd the time go?" He dashed over to the stove to rustle up an egg-and-cheese sandwich.

TWENTY-TWO

Paula gazed at Johnny as she entered the kitchen. "You look much, much better, Mr. Flynn."

Per Brickford's request, he'd had a meal and a shower, and it did make a difference. "I hope we hear something today, Paula. I don't think I can stand this for much longer. Are the kids asleep?"

"Finally, yes. Neither fell asleep until it was light outside, so I think they'll be down for a while. Goodness knows they need the rest. Michael's plagued with guilt. He thinks this is his fault."

"*His* fault?" Johnny felt as though he'd been punched in the stomach. "Why on Earth would he think that?"

Paula leaned against the counter. "It started when he found out that the police are researching the homeless shelter for possible suspects. He thinks that if he hadn't gotten in trouble, Mrs. Flynn would've never have volunteered there."

Johnny pinched the bridge of his nose. The renewed feeling he had after the shower bled out like gas out of a punctured tank. "For Christ's sake, Paula, it's not the boy's fault."

"I know that." She took a step toward Johnny and crossed her arms. "I told him and retold him that very thing. Maya said it, as well. But the child refuses to believe anything else. It's making him sick, Mr. Flynn."

"I'll talk to him as soon as he gets up." He looked at Paula, eyes ringed red from lack of sleep. "How about you? How are you holding up?"

"I'm fine."

"Have you slept at all?"

"A little, after the children fell asleep."

"Listen, Paula, you need to take care of yourself right now, too. Bathe, change, eat, rest. I don't want you cooking and cleaning. Like Brickford told me, we're not any good for the kids or anyone else if we're running on empty."

She glanced down at her hands.

"Call around and have meals brought in." He nodded toward the living room. "Make sure there's enough for the cops, too."

"I'll do that, Mr. Flynn."

"Okay." He put his hands on her shoulders. "You're like family. I don't know what I'd do if you weren't here."

Tears spilled down Paula's cheeks. "Thank you. This family means so much—"

Johnny leaned forward and wrapped both arms around her. He felt himself tremble as he thought of his wedding day, the kids' birth, his father's death.

"Mr. Flynn?" someone called from the entry.

Johnny let go of Paula. "That's Brickford. Let's go."

Johnny walked into the living room to see Brickford talking with Gingham. He had his little notepad out and was reading from it as Gingham typed something on the laptop.

Johnny approached. "Any news?"

Brickford nodded. "Ever heard of Roderick Dennington?"

"Hector Dennington's son. Sure, I've heard of him."

"Well, he's heard of you, too. Apparently he wasn't very happy about you taking down Owen Corp. Here, see for yourself." Brickford turned the computer screen toward Johnny.

A tall, thin man with slick, blond hair stood at a podium delivering a speech at a black tie event in a hotel ballroom.

> "That monster, Flynn, and his devil V.P Wilkinson will stop at nothing, NOTHING, to acquire anyone who they believe stands between them and a monopoly. They are the epitome of evil. They killed something beautiful when they forced us to close our doors. And they will someday pay for this..."

Dennington continued, railing Johnny and Wilks with such vitriol that the little hairs on the back of Johnny's neck pricked up and he got goose pimples. Johnny exhaled loudly. "Jesus."

"That's one pissed-off dude," Gingham said.

"Imagine how he felt when his father was gunned down at Vander Broek's party," Brickford added.

The memories flooded back. *Ming, make sure you get that fuck, Dennington.*

"So, you think *he's* the one who took Danielle?" Johnny's fear turned to anger.

"He's our number one suspect, but that could change at a moment's notice. Just because he's enraged doesn't mean he'd be willing to kidnap your wife. And we have no evidence to link him to the crime."

"Well, what did he have to say? Have you spoken with him?"

"He's unreachable right now."

I need to contact Ming, but the cops are monitoring all of my communications. Johnny glanced toward the ceiling. *Shit, I wish I hadn't thrown away the phone from—* the thought came again— *the shooting.* Johnny pushed it back.

"I'll let you know when we reach Dennington, Mr. Flynn."

Johnny thought of Michael. "Did you find anything out about the homeless shelter?"

Brickford turned a few pages in his notepad. "Officers spoke with a Ms. Bridget Fitzworth and a Ms. Gladys Reyes. Neither had heard any talk or noticed any unusual activity. They were both very upset when they heard what happened to Mrs. Flynn, as were some of the homeless she had helped." Brickford closed the notepad. "Our guy's not from there."

"Okay," Johnny said. "Michael will feel better knowing that."

∞∞∞∞∞∞

Two hours later, Michael and Maya stumbled into the room, each with a fresh change of clothes and combed hair.

"Hi," Maya said as they both plopped on the couch.

Johnny was relieved to see them both looking more rested. "Hi there. Did you both eat? Paula had sandwiches brought in."

"Yeah," Maya glanced around the room at the officers. "Have they found Mom?"

"They think they know who might have taken her, Petal."

Michael looked into Johnny's eyes. "Who?"

"A man from a competing company." He leaned forward and put a hand on Michael's shoulder. "No one from the shelter is involved. Police are certain of that."

Michael looked like a giant weight had been lifted from him. "So they think they can find her?"

"We're hoping so. We just have to—"

The shrill ring of Johnny's phone erupted on the table.

Everyone froze. Brickford pointed to Gingham, who ran over and stared at the computer screen. "It's coming from Danielle Flynn's phone."

"Mom!" Maya shrieked.

Johnny swallowed hard.

Brickford glanced at the other officers, who gave him a thumbs-up.

Gingham nodded to Johnny. "We're ready, Mr. Flynn."

Johnny lifted the phone and pushed the button. "Hello?"

The voice on the other end was deep and electronic, as though it was being filtered through a distortion device. "Deliver twenty million in small, unmarked bills to Gypsum Ridge Park at 9:00 p.m. Drop the money on the bench at the one-and-a-half mile mark on the running trail. Your wife will be close by waiting for you."

"Okay." Johnny's hand was trembling.

"We know your house is full of cops. We're monitoring the park now and will be until the time of the meeting. You come alone—no plants, no tail, no ghetto birds—or she gets a bullet in the head."

Click. The phone went dead.

TWENTY-THREE

Auster stood along a walkway at Los Angeles International Airport, watching passengers arriving from incoming flights. Over the previous four days, Hasler had signaled Auster hundreds of times, though he probably didn't know it. *Humans refuse to live in the present. I've never seen anything like it.*

Auster leaned against the window, his muscular arms crossed over his chest. His hair was pulled into a ponytail. He noticed the attention that women—and men— paid him as they walked by. The paparazzi, rushing around LAX as they tried to catch a celebrity in transit, also showed interest.

A pretty brunette wearing glasses ran up to him. "Here, Greg!" she shouted to the cameraman tailing her.

Auster was taken aback by the two closing in on him. He stood up straight, uncrossed his arms, and fought the initial urge to destroy them.

The woman glanced back. "Ready?"

"Got it," the cameraman said.

She tipped a microphone toward Auster. "Hi, there. What film were you in again?"

Auster's gaze darted from the microphone to the camera, and then back to the woman.

She blushed.

"I haven't been in any films." Auster focused on the camera and it began to smoke.

"Holy shit!" The cameraman backed the lens away from his face.

The reporter's eyes widened. "What the hell? Didn't you check that thing out before we left?"

The cameraman looked visibly annoyed. "Yes, I checked the damn thing!"

She stomped her foot and punched the air with the hand that clasped the microphone. "Damn it! We've lost everything we shot today."

"It's not my fault!" he spat as they marched away, bickering and cursing.

A security officer approached them, saying something in his walkie-talkie and pointing at the smoking camera.

Auster redirected his attention to a figure in the distance.

Hasler was just as clean and well-groomed as when he'd left. He wore a button-down shirt with slacks and pulled a small rolling suitcase behind him. He was in deep conversation with an African man wearing a traditional, fire-colored boubou.

Hasler noticed Auster and his expression shifted from exuberant to sober.

The African man nodded at Hasler. "*Au revoir.*"

Hasler gave him a half-smile. "*Au revoir.*"

They peeled off in different directions.

Auster watched the African walk away. "I see you're making friends."

"I am," Hasler grinned. "And I'm learning much about this great world of ours."

"Perhaps you can enlighten me while reporting the events of your trip." Auster gestured toward the exit.

Auster had actually checked on Hasler twice in that five-day period, as he did all of his Hands during their fledgling journeys.

Let's see if he tells the truth.

They sat outdoors at a bar and grill on the outskirts of Los Angeles. Auster was pleased that Hasler's reports of the events that occurred were factual.

Hasler finished his second beer and sat back. "I've read three books since I left."

"Exercising your intelligence. Good."

"You know what really blows my mind about all of this?" Hasler gazed at the setting sun.

Auster's brows knit together. "Blows your mind?"

Hasler stared blankly at him. "*Blows my mind* means something similar to 'surprises', or 'shatters a preset belief.'"

Auster thought then nodded. "Understood. Go on."

"What blows my mind is that I never knew people lived this way. That *I* could live this way."

"Live *what* way?"

"Flying around the world, reading books." He pointed to his glass. "Going out for beer, speaking French." He shook his head. "It's just so..."

Auster felt the signal. *He's going back in time.*

Hasler's expression darkened as he reached into the suitcase, pulled out a newspaper, and tossed it onto the table. "I bought this while waiting for the connecting flight from New York."

Auster glanced at the front page, which displayed the now infamous mug shot of Colton Lee Haddix. The headline read, *The Monster is Dead.*

Hasler peered down at the paper. "I read it all. About the execution, what I did." He looked up at Auster. "I remember doing it. I remember the way I thought back then."

Auster lifted his pint glass. "Your point?"

"I lived like an animal. I lived in the woods, waited for people, and..."

Auster felt the signal strengthen.

Hasler glanced from side to side to make sure no one was listening, then he leaned forward. "There were more than the families around the fires. I just did that for display. There were many before that."

"I know." Auster drained his glass and set it down.

Hasler leaned back. "You know? *How* do you know? How *could* you know?"

"I own your memories." Auster tapped his head. "*All* of them."

"You *own* my memories?"

"When I brought you back, I absorbed all of your memories, from birth until death. I know everything about you, perhaps even things you've forgotten."

Hasler looked sick. "I haven't forgotten. I *was* an animal." He glanced at the front page. "I'm glad that I'm gone as well." He snatched the paper off the table, got up, and tore it in two before tossing it into the trash. Then he sank down onto his chair.

A server walked by and Hasler held up a finger. "I'd like another beer."

The server pointed to Auster's glass, then up at him. A flirty smile played at the corners of her mouth. "You want another, too?"

"Sure." Auster directed his attention back to Hasler. "Humans are interesting."

"How so?"

"Colton Lee Haddix murdered twenty-three people."

Hasler looked surprised. "Is *that* how many there were?"

"Yes." He paused as the server set two beers on the table in front of them. "Colton Lee Haddix was unkempt, inarticulate, and uneducated," he said, watching her walk away. "He murdered twenty-three people and was thought of as a monster by fellow humans."

Hasler tipped his glass back and took a gulp. "I *was* a monster."

Auster continued. "*Thomas Hasler*," he gestured toward him, "is presentable in appearance, seemingly educated, multilingual, and articulate. Society accepts him."

Hasler sighed with relief.

"And he's just returned from a trip to Chad where he executed a government representative and innocent citizens. He also murdered the official's family and any household staff in his employ."

Hasler looked like he was going to puke.

Auster took a sip of his beer. "*Thomas Hasler* murdered seventeen people in five days." He leaned back. "Even your improved, *intelligent* mind can acknowledge that speaking French, bathing, and killing with a gun instead of an axe can hardly be considered evolution in progress."

Hasler looked dumbstruck.

"You're still a monster, *Haddix*." Auster leaned forward. "You're just *my* monster now. Did you happen to hack up any of those people like you did during your old life? Perhaps a man who fought back when the gunshot didn't kill him?"

Hasler swallowed hard.

"Of course you did, you animal." Auster leaned back and gestured toward the luggage. "I'm aware that you're thinking of fleeing."

"No, I wasn't." Hasler looked panic-stricken. "I just—"

"All of my Hands do at first." Auster shrugged. "It's only natural, I suppose, when one acquires intelligence and the means to navigate around the world, the mind begins to wander." Auster thrust a finger at Hasler's face. "*I* created you. You don't have that choice."

Hasler's hand trembled as he raised his glass to his mouth.

Auster eyed him. "Mind you, if you try to leave, I *won't* kill you. That would be too kind, considering the work I've put into you. But I *will* find you. The way you humans use your minds makes hiding impossible. I'll lay a hand on you and make the change. You'll watch as your brain returns to the equivalent of a scared rodent's and your body degenerates into something hideous."

Hasler looked ill.

Auster leaned closer. "So if you want to continue to travel around the world in expensive clothes, speak French, read books, and pretend like you're a member of the civilized world, do what you're told. Or you will once again be repulsive to humanity."

TWENTY-FOUR

Johnny stood with Brickford's team around the dining room table, staring at a map of Gypsum Park.

Brickford traced the perimeter with his finger. "All right, as we speak, seven undercover officers have trickled in around the fringes and are making their way toward various points within sight of the running trail. Flynn will walk it like they asked."

Johnny waved both hands like a ref signaling an incomplete pass. "Hold on. They said no cops. If there are people walking along the path at night, these guys will know what's up. They're not stupid."

Brickford shook his head. "They went in as homeless starting about an hour after we got the call. They'll be tucked away in the bushes. The park's a big place. That's why the kidnappers picked it, but we can use it to our advantage as much as they can." He turned to Johnny. "We're lucky that they wanted you to keep your phone. We'll be able to signal you if something changes or if there's a problem."

Johnny pointed toward the door. "I need a break. I'll be back in five."

"Mind if I join you?" Brickford reached into his pocket for his pack of smokes.

Johnny eyed the cigarettes. "Not at all."

They strolled across the front lawn to the edge of the property that overlooked the city.

Johnny checked back and saw they were alone. "Can I bum one?"

"You bet." Brickford shook out a cigarette and handed it to Johnny then pulled one out for himself. "Listen, Mr. Flynn, I can tell that you're flustered by all of this."

"It's just a lot of details." Johnny lit his smoke. "I can't fuck this up, man. Dani's life is on the line."

"You won't fuck it up. The kidnappers want you to do all of the leg work because they know you're emotionally involved and will be off-balance. I know this is a lot of responsibility, but try to stay clear-headed. Deliver the money and you'll get your wife back."

Johnny took a drag. "I hope you're right." He nodded toward Brickford. "You married?"

The detective exhaled a stream of smoke. "I want to say yes but have to say no. The divorce was final four months ago."

"Sorry to hear that. Any kids?"

"One girl. Eight." He watched the smoke curl away and then looked at Johnny. "She's somethin' else, I tell ya. I love her to death."

"Dani and I have been together for twenty-two years." Johnny took another drag. "I remember the moment I first laid eyes on her. It was at a party at my friend Robert Corby's house on the beach. His little brother, Frank, had just graduated from high school and was going off to study pre-med at Harvard."

Johnny flicked ash on the ground. "I had just started up the business and wasn't even thinking about women, but all that changed when I saw Dani."

"Yeah?" Brickford smiled.

"Yep. I had just finished congratulating Frank and I grabbed a beer to take outside. Then I saw her: tall, tan and shapely, wearing a little pink Hawaiian-print dress. She had long, blonde hair with a pink flower in it." He glanced over at Brickford. "I was—"

"Done." Brickford finished.

Johnny chuckled and jabbed a finger in the air "Done! So true."

"Bet you were. That's a great story."

They finished their smokes and walked toward the house.

Before they reached the door, Johnny turned to Brickford. "I just want to thank you for everything. I know you're working your ass off." He held out his hand.

Brickford shook it. "I want you to *both* thank me, when she comes home."

∞∞∞∞∞∞

Johnny watched the police close the suitcases full of stacked bills. He tried to keep from shaking because Michael and Maya stood on each side of him, but it was impossible.

Brickford put in the earpiece he'd use to listen in on the wire and walked over to Johnny. "You ready?"

"Ready as I'll ever be. I hope this works."

Brickford patted Johnny on the shoulder. "It's just the money they're after. Do as they ask and it'll work."

"Be careful, Daddy." Maya, eyes swollen from crying, wrapped her arms around his waist.

"I will, Petal." Johnny's voice broke. He turned to Michael. "I'll get your mom back, Bud."

"Okay." Michael embraced Johnny.

Everyone watched the cops load the suitcases into the trunk.

Wilks placed a hand on Johnny's back. "Be strong for her. She needs you right now."

"You'll never know how much I appreciate what you've done over the years, old friend."

Wilks held Johnny by the shoulders and looked him in the eye. "Return shortly with your wife."

Johnny hugged and kissed the kids and walked to the car, where Brickford was bent over, checking out the interior.

"Okay, let's do this."

Brickford looked back. "Do you keep a piece in here?" When Johnny didn't immediately respond, he stood up. "Where?"

"I have a thirty-eight hidden in the spare compartment."

"Leave it there. You may have to deal with them up close and get patted down, or they may have you drop the suitcases from a distance and walk away. Either way, remember my instructions."

"Right. Wait until I see Dani, although you didn't need to tell me that. I'd never leave without her."

"Good." Brickford looked down, toed the concrete for a moment, then propped his arm on the open car door. "Look, Mr. Flynn, these situations are touchy. Whether these guys are cool, collected pros, or scared-shitless novices, they're still under a great deal of strain, so *nothing* is predictable. If they feel threatened, or think their plan isn't working, someone could get hurt, so it's important they feel their plan *is* working. If there's a problem, say the word, and the guys in the bushes will be on it."

"I will."

Brickford moved aside to let Johnny slip into the driver's seat. "Questions?"

Johnny thought for a moment. "No. I think I've got it all."

"All right then, you'd better jet. Punctuality is important." He closed the door and took a step back. "Keep your phone close."

Johnny tossed his phone on the passenger seat and started the car.

Brickford spoke through the window. "We're tracking the car and your phone, so you're not alone. Good luck, Mr. Flynn."

"Thanks." Johnny shifted the car into drive and rolled down the path toward the street. In the rearview mirror, he saw the kids huddled together, watching him go.

Please, let this go as planned.

The trip to the south side was the longest drive Johnny had ever taken. Every red light bled his heart, every slowing of traffic sent his stomach up and into his throat.

"Dani," he repeated, over and over. "Hang on, baby, just a little longer." He drove on, yet he felt like he wasn't moving.

Finally, up ahead, he saw a sign for Gypsum Ridge Community Park. He sighed.

Okay, baby, I'm almost there.

His phone rang. "Hello?"

"Change of plans," the electronic voice said. "Our meeting point is now the pier next to the abandoned glass factory off of Seaport Drive. Know where it is?"

"Yes."

"The time is the same. 9:30. You're late, she's dead."

"What? The pier's almost twenty miles away!"

But the voice was gone.

Johnny peeled off the highway, threw the car into a turn, and punched it going the opposite direction.

"Please, Brickford, be on this."

∞∞∞∞∞∞

Brickford was sitting in the same chair by the fireplace when the message came though. "Holy Shit!" He sprang up. "The pier! They changed it to the pier! Find out who's close by and get them there, now! Call the hospital, I want emergency vehicles there."

Gingham picked up a phone and started dialing. "I'm on it, Brick."

"Call CHP and PD first. Clear the roads so Flynn can fly." Brickford checked his watch. "Jesus, he's only got twenty minutes. Drive like a motherfucker, Flynn."

∞∞∞∞∞∞

Johnny's sweaty palms gripped the steering wheel. He'd been going well over a hundred the entire trip and the roads were surprisingly clear of traffic. He glanced down at a freeway onramp that had been blocked by cops.

Thanks, Brickford.

After what seemed like eternity, Johnny exited at Seaport Boulevard and glanced at the time: 9:24. *It's a fucking miracle I made it.* He turned right at the exit, drove about a quarter mile, then hung a left onto the service street that led to the factories.

The road was poorly-lit along the dilapidated wooden piers. Johnny passed by the huge, deserted factories with boarded-up windows. He spotted some kind of light casting shadows on the side of one of the crumbling edifices.

Dani!

He punched the accelerator and halted between two buildings. A group of junkies shooting up around a fire set in a trash can glanced up at him, eyes hollow and empty. Johnny drove on.

The glass factory was the largest structure at the end of the street. Johnny pulled up beside it and looked around for other cars. There were none.

Where are they?

He glanced at the clock again: 9:28.

The phone rang. Johnny grabbed it. "Hello. I'm here."

"Carry the suitcases down the last pier."

Johnny pushed the button to pop the trunk and got out of the car. Though the air was chilly, sweat tricked down his back.

Please, let this work. Be okay, baby.

He hauled out the suitcases and started walking. The decaying wood creaked under each footstep as Johnny plodded forward. He cringed at the acrid smell of urine, salty air, and fish. In the distance, yellow light from a lamp above pooled around two individuals, one standing, the other kneeling.

As he moved closer, the scene became clear.

"Dani!"

Her hands were tied above her head to one of the dock posts. A masked man stood beside her, holding a gun to her head.

Johnny dropped the suitcases, put his hands up and walked toward his wife. Halfway down the pier, his eyes met Danielle's.

"No!" she shrieked. "You shouldn't have come. Go back, Johnny. They never planned to let me go. They want to kill us both!"

He heard footsteps behind him, then the pop of a gun. Pain ripped through his backside, driving him face first onto the pier. *I'm hit!*

He lifted his head to see another masked man, standing beside the first. Johnny reached toward Danielle.

"You shouldn't have come," she cried.

"I love you, Dani," Johnny shouted. "I'll never leave you."

They locked gazes.

"The kids," Danielle trembled. "Tell them—"

The masked man above her pulled the trigger.

Johnny screamed from the bottom of his soul.

He saw the blur of the gunmen moving away from Danielle and jumping over him.

Danielle's limp form hung from the ropes that bound her to the pier.

Johnny dragged himself toward her. *Please, kill me, too.*

Johnny heard another pop. Pain seared though his back and more blood splattered on the deck around him. He heard the sirens and kept crawling forward. When he reached Danielle, his vision blurred. Her hand was warm when he took it.

He gazed at her, pleading. "Dani. It wasn't supposed to be this way."

Dark blood trickled from her blonde hair onto the splintered wood.

"Your beautiful face." Johnny gazed into the vacant eyes of his wife and vomited.

Everything faded to black.

TWENTY-FIVE

Brickford hunched over in a chair in the middle of the living room, the phone six inches away from his ear.

Gingham looked up at him. "There's no way we could have known."

"What is it?" Wilks spat.

Brickford drew in a deep breath and faced him. "There's been a shooting. They're on the way to the hospital now."

Maya screamed. "No!"

"Oh, no, please say it's not true." Paula grabbed the hands of each child. "Into the car. We're going now."

"How could you allow this to happen?" Wilks stormed toward Brickford, arms stiff at his sides, hands fisted. "How?"

Brickford felt like he'd been punched in the face. "This had to be their plan all along. Whatever just took place wasn't about money."

TWENTY-SIX

A uster and Thomas Hasler sat outside at a coffee house in Santa Barbara, California, their attention glued to a map Hasler had called up on his laptop.

Auster pointed to the screen. "So, you've cleared this area?"

"I have."

"Good, let's move." Auster got up.

Two young women wearing flirty, summer dresses sauntered up the sidewalk. One noticed Auster, smiled, and whispered something to her friend, who, in turn, checked out Auster and flipped her hair back.

Auster watched the women strut past, then fell in behind them and led Hasler along the crowded walkway. "I find that this body is more alluring than any I've had before. It also prefers beer and meat more than anything else."

"*This* body? You've had other bodies?"

"I've had thousands."

"Thousands? How long have you been—"

"Longer than recorded time."

"How long will I live?"

"If you prove yourself worthy, I will replenish your energy with another body when the one you're using wanes to incompetence."

"Which is how long? You said this body won't last the length of a normal life."

"It's hard to predict in your case. The body you absorbed had a deficiency."

"Deficiency? What do you mean?"

"The energy of the man you absorbed was abnormal, but we were short on time and it had to do. Normally, a Hand can live up to fifty years, depending on the age at first death and the age of the body absorbed."

"A *Hand*? Is that what I am?"

"Yes."

Hasler looked insulted. "That's basically a minion, right?"

"More or less."

"How many *Hands* do you have?"

"Hundreds. And there are Sentries who have the ability to create them as well."

"Are the Sentries like you?"

"No, but I have granted them the power to wield light. They can rebuild themselves and create Hands as they see fit. I have bequeathed the power of light to very few humans. Each had a unique energy source that called to me as their time was about to expire."

"So the most I can hope for is to be granted *renewal* over and over?"

Auster tipped his head and looked at Hasler. "Would you have preferred to remain dead on that green cross in San Quentin?"

"No." Hasler pulled his gaze away.

Auster scoffed. "Humans relish their fortunes for such a short time before the desire for more sets in— more wealth, more power. Avarice seems to be hard-wired into your psyches. The angst it creates drains your life energy. You need not worry. From what I'm told, the life of a Hand is often rich and good."

"Are there female Hands?"

"Yes."

"Female Sentries?"

"Yes."

Auster regarded Hasler. "You've performed several tasks successfully without straying from your directives. I believe it's time I give you the final tool that a Hand needs to become autonomous."

"Right now?"

"No. Tonight." Auster pointed up the mountainside. "There's a trailhead a mile north of here. When the sun sets, take it to the top and find a clearing. Do not eat or drink anything but water for the rest of the day."

Hasler froze. "This is going to hurt, isn't it?"

"I've heard that it does."

A moment later, Auster was gone.

∞∞∞∞∞∞

The moon shone bright in the cloudless sky. Auster sat beside Hasler in a small treeless patch high above the city lights. A gallon of water rested in front of him.

Hasler regarded the jug. "What's the water for?"

"You."

"Are you going to set me on fire?" Fear plagued Hasler's face.

"No, but you'll need water to replenish."

"So, there's some kind of physical activity I have to perform? Like running from some nocturnal predator?"

"No."

"Then why here?" Hasler held out both arms. "At night? And why couldn't I eat after lunch? Couldn't we have done this in the hotel like when you gave me intelligence?"

"No. This characteristic drastically opens the mind. Ambient and man-made energy sources can distort and interfere with the newly created aperture."

"*Aperture*?" Hasler scooted away from Auster. "What the hell do you mean? You're going to put a hole in my head?"

"Not literally. Consider it more of a portal in the mind."

"That's not any more comforting." Hasler swallowed hard. "What's about to happen?"

"Each life force has a unique signature that is derived from the source energy and the DNA that initially encased it as a life form. I'm about to give you the ability to read a very specific life signature. Mine."

Hasler looked confused. "I'll be able to read yours and no one else's?"

"When the aperture is receiving information, you will detect millions of life sources, but you will be able to recognize mine."

Auster rose, walked behind Hasler, and placed both hands on top of his head. "There are two parts to this acquisition of skill. First, we open."

He sent the light into Hasler's skull, which caused him to vibrate like he was sitting in the electric chair. Auster sent forth the surge for five seconds...ten... fifteen.

Hasler coughed and made choking sounds as blood oozed from his ears and nose.

Auster pulled back the light and Hasler crumpled to the ground like a rag doll.

An hour passed.

Hasler stirred. "Arrggh. I feel like my brain is on fire." He squirmed on the ground, then sat up.

Auster thrust the gallon jug into Hasler's chest. "Drink."

Hasler drank like his insides were ablaze. He finished the water and dropped the jug, inhaling a deep sigh of relief. "That's much better."

"Look around you," Auster said.

As soon as Hasler gazed up, he froze. "Oh, my. This can't be." He rubbed his eyes and turned toward Auster. "Whoa, you're glowing!"

"You can see the energy. That's good. Be still for a time while everything else comes into focus."

Hasler sat quietly as he adjusted to his new sight. Then his jaw slackened. "Amazing, there's light all around!" He stood up. "Every tree, every blade of grass—" he pointed toward the sky— every small insect—he turned around and pointed toward a bush, "every rodent that scurries in the brush, every living thing exudes light."

"Good. The opening is effective."

Hasler pointed to two squirrels in a distant tree that were invisible moments ago. "Why is the light at different strengths?"

"The larger squirrel is much older. The fainter glow denotes waning in that case. But size matters as well. Larger animals require more energy to subsist."

Hasler turned to Auster. "You're brighter than everything, and you're ancient."

"I burn brightly because I require far more energy than any animal."

"So, I *do* have the gift of light," Hasler said, craining his neck in all directions.

"In a way. You can see it, even recognize it, but you cannot control it. The intensity will settle to a point where it isn't distracting. Now you understand why this place was ideal."

Hasler sank down beside Auster again.

"Are you beginning to notice the subtle differences in each life source?"

"Yes, but I can't describe it." Hasler pointed to the bushes. "Like those two squirrels, but the light's different in other ways."

"Good. You can recognize varying sources. You will become more adept as you continue your observations over time."

Auster then reached into the inside pocket of his jacket and brought out a pocket knife. "Now for the second part of the acquisition."

Hasler crawled back. "Oh, no. Please don't—"

"I'm not going to cut *you*." Auster raised his own shirt and drove the knife into his abdomen. Blood oozed from the wound as he carved a circle the size of a fifty-cent piece, then twisted the knife in and scooped out a hunk of flesh.

Hasler gagged at the sight.

"Here, you must eat this." Auster held out the dripping chunk of skin, fat, and muscle.

"Eat it?" Hasler held up both hands. "I don't—"

"You must. Take it!"

Hasler recoiled.

Auster grabbed Hasler by the hair and shoved the flesh into his mouth. "Do not swallow it like a pill. You must chew it and have your awakened senses read all of the information."

Hasler chewed twice and gagged.

"If you vomit, we'll have to do it again, but not before I beat you senseless."

Hasler closed his mouth and chewed quickly. He forced back multiple gags, but continued to chew. He swallowed once, chewed some more, swallowed one final time, and exhaled. "Okay, okay. I did it."

"Good. You can now read my signature in any life form. If someone is descended from me, you'll recognize it."

Hasler wiped blood from his chin. "Are there more beings like you?"

"Yes, there are more of my kind."

"Where?"

Auster gazed into the starry night sky. "Beyond the scope and reach of all life here." He stood up. "Your final assessment will be soon. If you pass, I will grant you autonomy."

Hasler brought his knees up to his chest and wrapped his arms around them. "Lucky me."

TWENTY-SEVEN

Anisha Patel Corby's phone vibrated. "Patel. Okay, I'll be there when they arrive."

She ran down the hallway toward the ER, following a procession of doctors called to handle the shootout at the pier.

Anisha passed Ben, who backed against the wall to allow the emergency staff through. Their eyes met briefly. *Pray my patients make it to see you in the ICU, my friend.*

Ben held up a hand in understanding.

She bolted out the door and had just enough time to catch her breath alongside another doctor. "I'll take the first," she said.

"You got it."

The whining of distant sirens grew loud and within moments, the ambulance careened through the parking lot and screeched to a stop at the entrance. Paramedics threw open the doors and rolled out a gurney.

Anisha ran to it. "Status?"

"Male, mid-forties, two gunshots to the back, one penetrated the right lung and the other appears to have shattered his left hip. Pulse dropping fast. BP 60/30. Lots of blood loss."

Anisha glanced back. "Where's the other one? The call-in said there were two."

"The guy's wife was DOA!" The paramedic shouted.

The man on the gurney moaned and struggled to breathe.

Anisha rolled her eyes. *Fool. He can hear you. You needed only to shake your head.*

They thrust the gurney through the doors and Anisha took over. "He needs blood! No time to cross-match. Compress the wounds and prep him for surgery. We need to get those bullets out."

The man drifted in and out of consciousness, mumbling and shifting.

She leaned close to his face. "You're going to be okay. You're in good hands here."

∞∞∞∞∞∞

Johnny opened his eyes. Everything lay hidden in mist, then a scene came into focus: white room, curtains, figures standing above him. Each breath he took felt as though a thousand needles pierced his chest. He shifted his weight and his right side burned like acid had been poured over it.

Johnny turned his head to see Michael curled into a fetal position in a chair and covered with a blanket. Paula and Maya lay together on the couch by the window.

Johnny opened his mouth. It felt dry and sticky. He forced the word out. "Petal."

Maya's eyes snapped open. "Daddy!" She leapt off the couch and ran to his side, calling out the door, "Ben, my dad's awake!"

Michael pushed the blanket aside. "Dad."

A tall, muscular man entered the room. "Glad to see you're awake, Mr. Flynn. I'm Ben and I'll be your nurse this evening."

"How long was I out?" Johnny asked, still groggy.

"You faded in and out for about two days. You're very lucky to be alive."

Johnny thought of Danielle. "Where's my wife? I want to see her."

The nurse didn't move.

Oh, no! "I want to see my wife!"

Maya fell to her knees and sobbed, "Oh, Mommy!"

Paula covered her face with her hands and rushed over to Maya.

"No!" Johnny cried out.

Ben took a small step back. "Let me get the doctor, Mr. Flynn."

Paula bent down and lifted up Maya. "You have to get up, honey."

Michael fell onto the chair and pulled the blanket back over his head.

An Indian woman entered a minute later. "Hello, Mr. Flynn. I am Doctor Patel."

"Where's my wife? Where's Dani?"

The doctor stood with her hands at her sides. "When the paramedics arrived at the scene, your wife was already gone, Mr. Flynn. Nothing could be done for her. I am so very sorry."

A flash of memory swept through Johnny: the pier, Dani, the man holding the gun, the shot. " No." His voice broke. "This can't be real. Tell me she's not dead." He trembled.

Wilks walked in. His rumpled clothes looked as though he'd slept-in them and his eyes were bloodshot. The faint smell of alcohol trailed behind him as he crossed the room to stand at Johnny's bedside.

"Wilks." Johnny pointed to the doctor. "Tell them! Tell them Dani's not dead!"

Wilks leaned down. "I wish I could, but I can't, son." He pressed his palm against his forehead. "I can't. She's gone."

"No! Dani!" Johnny strained to sit up.

"Calm down, Mr. Flynn. You'll tear your stitches."

Johnny grasped the side rails of the bed and attempted to lift himself. "Get me the fuck out of here!" He tugged at his IVs.

The doctor turned to Ben. "Sedate him."

"You need to rest, Mr. Flynn." Ben took a syringe and pushed its contents into Johnny's IV.

Johnny tried to fight it, but the room became misty again.

Dani, this is my fault. All my fault.

TWENTY-EIGHT

Auster navigated through the bustling streets of Buenos Aires alongside Thomas Hasler. He gestured toward the crowded sidewalks. "Your final test is to identify the people with my life signature."

Hasler gazed around, eyes wide with concern. "How many are there?"

"No more information will be provided. Start walking."

They threaded through throngs of people: shoppers, diners, tourists, and hotel guests. Hasler appeared anxious.

"Give it time," Auster said.

Twenty minutes after they'd begun, Hasler pointed to a woman entering a bookstore. "Her."

Auster nodded. "Yes."

Five minutes later, they came upon an outdoor café.

Hasler stopped and nodded toward a family eating lunch. "Them—the man and children. Not the wife."

"Correct."

Nearly an hour passed before an older gentleman, briefcase in hand, exited the hotel across the center.

Hasler turned to Auster. "His signature is stronger than the others."

Auster considered the man. "Closer descendant."

"Oh."

"I'm pleased. You've made no mistakes."

Hasler smiled. "So, I'm autonomous?"

"You are."

"Yes!" Hasler halted. "What does that mean exactly?"

"It means that you are to go out into your assigned region and locate those with my signature."

"So, I'm like the protector of your bloodline?" Hasler gazed at his own reflection in the glass.

"I said nothing about protecting them."

A look of confusion swept across Hasler's face. "Then what do you want me to do?"

Auster turned up both palms. "What did you do in life before I brought you back?"

Hasler froze for a moment, his gaze locked with Auster's. "You want me to *kill* your descendants?"

"Yes."

"You're kidding, right? This is part of the test, to see if I would actually hurt one of your relatives?"

"You've passed the final test," Auster said. "You can read my signature without failure. This is why you need to read it."

"Can't you do it?"

"Of course. The ones you've identified thus far will not see tomorrow. There are many more, though. Many, many more. I can't be everywhere at once."

Hasler thought back. "So, my first assignment in Chad—"

"Contained my descendants."

"*Everyone* in those villages?"

"No, which brings me to the next parameter of your role. You are not to harm *anyone* who does not have my life signature. For example, I will visit the family you identified at the café, but I will only take the lives of the father and children. The mother will live."

"Why?"

"It is not necessary to destroy her. Unnecessary death is not part of this."

Hasler looked confused. "So the innocents in Chad—"

"Casualties of your training. You couldn't read the signature yet and I wanted to ensure you were capable of doing what you were told."

They resumed walking. Hasler identified another descendant.

"Good," Auster said.

Hasler gestured toward the man he just identified. "So, for the rest of my life, I'm to stay within a given area, search for people with your signature, and murder them."

"Yes."

Hasler looked perplexed.

"You look displeased," Auster said. "This is what you did before, wasn't it? It shouldn't be so difficult."

Hasler frowned. "Right. I take it all of the Hands are former killers as well?"

"Each and every one. It wouldn't make sense to bring back someone who wasn't comfortable with killing."

"And the Sentries? Were they murderers, too?"

"Yes," Auster answered.

Hasler pointed to a woman. "Her, the tall redhead. She's one."

"Correct. You're doing well."

"Yes!" Hasler punched the air.

Hasler's reaction reminded Auster of a child filled with joy at pleasing its father.

"So, where is my assigned region?" Hasler gestured toward the crowded streets.

"Here," Auster answered. "South America. You're to begin by sweeping the villages along the Orinoco River first, then span out to larger cities and eventually head down to Brazil."

"But I don't speak Spanish or Portuguese."

Auster grabbed Hasler by the hair, pulled him around the side of the building and into a vacant alley. He threw Hasler to the ground, placed his hand on his head, and sent forth the light.

Hasler squealed in pain.

Auster pulled back his hand. "Now you speak Spanish and Portuguese. Get up."

Hasler pushed himself from the ground and, with the back of his hand, wiped the blood that oozed from his nose.

Auster reached into his pocket and pulled out a credit card. He handed it to Hasler. "This will get cash from any machine in the world."

Hasler took the card. "It has my name on it."

"It does. Along with your passport, this should get you anything, anywhere. All of the Hands draw from this source. It has unlimited funds."

Hasler's eyes widened. "Unlimited?"

"Yes. You may purchase what you need: accommodations, clothes, meals, even a vehicle when necessary, but there are restrictions."

"Okay, what?" Hasler gripped the card, eyes hungry with excitement.

"You may not be so exorbitant that you draw attention to yourself. You are to fly coach, drive used vehicles, and stay in temporary housing or hotels. Do you understand?"

"Yes."

"Good," Auster pointed at Hasler. "You are to be *invisible* to society. No one should want to know who you are. An occasional pricey meal is acceptable. A six-hundred dollar bottle of single malt whiskey is not. Be untraceable, nomadic, and forgettable. Is that clear?"

"Yes. It's clear."

"Which brings me to the final parameter of being a Hand."

"What's that?"

"Drugs and alcohol are permitted. But be advised, if you abuse them, if you become addicted, or reside in a constant state of intoxication, you will be terminated."

"That makes sense." Hasler paced back and forth in the alley. "I assume we're to keep in touch?"

"You check in by using your memory, like you have each time before."

Hasler stopped and hung his head. "Right. The day of the execution."

Auster squinched his nose. "You think of that day very often. I constantly have to disregard the signal. I want you to use a more benign memory, one that you would have to make a cognitive effort to recall."

Hasler thought for a moment. "I suppose I could think of..." A long pause followed. "How about the day old Mr. Babbs gave me free licorice at the town store?"

"Okay, stay on the memory for a moment."

Hasler focused.

The signal registered with Auster. "That will work. You're to check in with me every four weeks to start, then we go for longer periods. I check on the progress of my Hands about once a year, although there are several Hands who have been with me for ages. They go the entire duration of their absorbed lives before checking in."

"So, you're going to leave me here?" Hasler gazed around at the empty alley.

"Yes. Tomorrow you will journey toward the Orinoco River."

"All right. Um, just one more thing." Hasler said. "Is there a certain quota you're expecting with regard to, you know?"

"No. Those with my signature are spread throughout the population. There are over a million around the world. You shouldn't have any trouble finding them. Four weeks from now, recall the memory we discussed. I will be wherever you are before the day's end."

"Auster?"

"Yes?"

Hasler took a step toward him. *"¿Por que? ¿Por que quieres matar a su propia familia?"*

"I don't *want* to kill them." Auster walked to the end of the alley. "I have to."

He turned to dust and blew away.

PART II
POLYMORPHY

TWENTY-NINE

Auster stared down the white cliffs lining the English coast. Next to him, stood a tall, sinewy man with shoulder-length, black hair and eyes the color of aquamarine.

Auster raised his chin and inhaled the crisp ocean breeze. "There has been progress, Torphis. I've felt a minor, very minor shift."

Torphis glanced out at the horizon. "We have made strides, Auster. Many are gone."

"True." Auster exhaled an audible breath. "But not at the rate I had hoped."

"The new Hand?"

"He will do for now," Auster said. "But he is little more than a feral animal. I had to implant cognitive ability, and we've seen how that's worked out in the past."

"Oh, yes," Torphis said. "Their efficacy fades quickly. If the man is not competent of mind, you've done little more than train a sophisticated bovine." He turned to Auster. "A physical visit is rare. The last time was over one hundred years ago. What brings you here?"

"Custom," Auster answered. "I feel an energy building that is reminiscent of what came from you and the others."

"Another Sentry?" Torphis smiled.

"Yes." Auster faced him. "I've come to tell you that you will stand as a *dayyanum* to determine if he is worthy."

Torphis closed his eyes. "An honor." Then he asked, "Who will be the other *dayyani*?"

"Fokazi and Boke Gal."

Torphis smiled. "When?"

Auster rose into the air. "Soon. When the time is close, I will call to you."

THIRTY

On the morning of Danielle Flynn's funeral, traffic had to be diverted to allow the half-mile procession of black limousines. News vans lined the entrance of Gypsum Ridge Cemetery, reporters giving a play-by-play as each car that was believed to contain someone of public relevance passed though the massive iron gates.

Johnny stared at the lush, green landscape, spanning five acres with views overlooking the Pacific Ocean. The thought that it was a noted place of interest sickened him. *Why would people want to visit dead celebrities, luminaries, and athletes?*

He shifted uncomfortably in the back seat of his ride, grateful for the blackout tint of the windows as cameras on the other side loomed inches from his face.

A week had passed since Johnny woke up to hear that Dani was dead. The emotional pain combined with the physical was too much to bear. There were the surgeries, the new hip, the punctured lung, and the pain that coursed through his body from the moment he opened his eyes in the morning to when he closed them at night.

Dr. Patel said Johnny was to stay in the hospital for at least three weeks but gave him special permission to attend Danielle's funeral, providing that Ben, the nurse who oversaw his care during the day, attended as well. Johnny was expected to return to the hospital as soon as it was over.

Johnny sat next to Ben, who wore green nurse's scrubs. Michael and Maya sat across from them, stone-faced and silent beside Paula, who clutched a handkerchief in a gloved hand.

Johnny peered across the vast sea of headstones.

So many.

He remembered how a group of billionaire land developers he'd golfed with occasionally had bitched about the inaccessibility of this prime piece of real estate.

"Those fuckers would unearth the dead if they could," he had told Danielle.

"Anything for profit, I guess," she had said.

"I'm no hero by a long shot," he had told her, "but I'd let the dead rest in peace."

He remembered how Dani had stretched out on the bed and held out her arms. "I think it's bad luck to build on a cemetery. Come here, strongman. Why don't we wake the dead right now?"

Johnny glanced down at his new hip, wrapped tightly beneath his slacks and throbbing with every subtle gesture.

I deserve it. He moved his leg to bring on the pain and cringed as it jolted through him. *All of this is my fault. I'm the reason Dani's dead. My kids' lives are ruined because they have no mother.*

Ben held a hand over Johnny's leg. "Be careful, Mr. Flynn."

Johnny's gaze drifted back out the window. On a distant hill, he spotted a white canopy where several men were opening and arranging folding chairs.

That's where they're going to put Dani in the ground.

The car pulled up in front of the massive, gothic-style chapel, reminiscent of the large abbeys seen in the United Kingdom. When Ben brought the wheelchair around, Johnny stepped out of the car and lowered himself into it. He spotted Wilks and asked Ben to wait up for him.

Wilks leaned down. "Everything is as you wish. How is the pain?"

"Everywhere." Johnny glanced at Paula and the kids. "This wasn't supposed to happen."

"I know." Wilks placed his hand on Johnny's. "We'll just have to get through it moment by moment."

Ben pushed Johnny up the ramp and though the front doors. The chapel was alight with candles and the scent of flowers floated in the air. It almost looked like a wedding was about to take place. Then Johnny saw the blue casket, resting on a pedestal below the stained glass windows at the front of the room. He felt sick. *The funeral director insisted that the casket be closed. Insisted. I'll never see her face again.*

Johnny proceeded toward the front pew, feeling the stares as he passed each row. His mind was fuzzy, partially due to the pain medication, partially due to the pain. He noticed a row of Danielle's friends. A few rows forward sat Schuyler Vander Broek, who nodded solemnly and whispered, "I'm so sorry, son."

He passed a section of volunteers from the homeless shelter. Gladys sat next to Bridget, dabbing her eyes. There were no flowers in Gladys' hair, and for some reason, Johnny appreciated that.

He spotted Danielle's family. Her parents appeared tiny and frail, trembling in each other's arms. They glanced at his broken body with expressions that reflected the same shock and confusion that he felt inside.

Ben stopped the wheelchair next to the front pew, assisted Johnny onto the bench, and then took a seat behind him.

Johnny placed his arm along the back of the pew and stared at the casket. *Blue, your favorite color. I wish I could run up there, pull the lid off that thing, and take you to the Riviera. But I can't even walk, and you can't...*

A man in a black suit walked to a podium to the left of the casket. Whispers and muffled conversations dwindled to silence.

Johnny and Danielle weren't fans of organized religion, so he had asked that Danielle's service be conducted by someone non-denominational. The last thing he wanted to hear was some agenda-filled preacher raging on about sin and what befalls people who stray from God. He had insisted on someone who would conduct a tasteful service that respected all beliefs.

The man began by talking about Danielle's contribution to the community. He spoke of her recent work in the homeless shelter, as well as other projects and committees where she'd served. The talk then moved to her role as a family member: a daughter, a sister, an aunt, a wife, and a mother.

The time then came for people to come up and speak about Danielle. Johnny was slated to go first, and he had argued about having to do it, but Paula said the children needed to hear him speak about their mother. Wilks agreed, so he conceded.

Ben wheeled Johnny up to the front, helped him push himself up from the wheelchair and grasp both sides of the podium, then faded back into the shadows.

Johnny scanned the sea of black and gray that filled the massive chapel. Women wearing elaborate hats sat up straight, as though straining to be seen, and tugged at their tight skirts.

The reality of this being a social event set in. Attendees would seek the paparazzi to be photographed for the social pages and business deals would be made. Briefly, Johnny recalled forwarding his own business relations at funerals in the past. Rage set in. He gritted his teeth, trembling. *You fucking vultures. This is Dani's funeral. The mother of my children.*

Attempting to stuff the anger, Johnny focused on Michael and Maya. He tried to take a deep breath, stopping suddenly because of the pain, then leaned forward and spoke. "There's no way I can sum up in a few words, or even a million, what Dani meant to me. She was the love of my life. She loved me when

I was just a young man with a dream. We had no money, but we had a heck of a good time." His voice broke. "She was there when times were tough and she believed in me when no one else did. I couldn't ask for a more wonderful, and beautiful, wife and mother for my children."

Johnny glanced down at Michael and Maya, their upturned faces wet with tears. "Petal and Bud, your mom loved you both *very* much, and I know she'll always be looking down on you. *Always*."

Johnny gazed back out at the crowd. Muffled cries and sniffling echoed in the silence. He caught sight of a woman dabbing her eyes, the feather in her expensive hat swaying as she tilted her head. Johnny opened his mouth, then paused. "I can't do this." He pushed away from the podium and fell back into the chair.

Ben emerged from the fringes and guided Johnny's wheelchair back to the pew.

Danielle's father spoke next, followed by her siblings, her friends, and teachers and other parents from the kids' school. Bridget from the homeless shelter also came up and shared.

Johnny absorbed very little of it. The smell of the flowers was becoming noxious and the pain medication was wearing off. He hadn't eaten, and his stomach was a churning cauldron of acid and meds. Water, he thought. I need water.

After what seemed like an eternity, the pastor returned to the podium. "The Flynn family has put together a video presentation they would like to share."

With Paula's help, and the cooperation of Danielle's family, Johnny had assembled a collection of photos that spanned from Danielle's infancy to the month before her death. Johnny wanted it for the kids and he wanted it for himself.

The lights dimmed as a large screen unfurled from the ceiling.

Johnny watched as two people held a pretty baby in a bonnet on their knees. More pictures of Danielle's childhood flashed before the silent room followed by pictures of her in her teens—a spunky cheerleader laughing with friends, then driving her first car, and finally, high school graduation. Johnny started appearing in the pictures of Danielle in her twenties, her long, blonde hair adorned with flowers in almost every shot.

Johnny stared up at the screen. *This is how I will always remember you.*

Wedding pictures followed, and then the trips to Europe, Africa, Asia, and South America. Pictures flashed on the screen of the newborn twins coming home from the hospital, their first birthday, first steps, and subsequent birthdays. On the kids' third birthday, Danielle's hair had been cut to the shoulder-length style she would wear for the rest of her life.

For a brief moment, Johnny forgot that Danielle was gone. He smiled at the picture taken the previous winter during a day trip to the local mountains where Michael fell into the wet California snow and was drenched. Johnny glanced to the side.

Michael watched intently but didn't smile.

After the presentation ended, the pastor approached the podium. He stood for a moment before saying, "What a magnificent celebration of such a beautiful woman."

Johnny watched the screen roll up into the ceiling, wishing it would come back down so he could see the video again. He glanced at the coffin. *This can't be real. She was right there.*

The pastor thanked everyone for taking time to remember Danielle and reminded the mourners how she wanted only the best for others.

"Danielle was the light of many lives," the pastor said. "And on this day, I want her light, through this new day, to shine on each of you."

The pastor gestured to someone off stage and the shade covering the window rose. Bright sunlight cut through the darkness, traveling across the chapel floor to bathe the space in obscene, blinding light.

The effect was as if someone had turned on the radio full blast. Johnny shielded his eyes against the vulgar assault that seemed to blaspheme the solemnity of the occasion. He glanced down at Michael and Maya to see them bent forward, crying in their hands.

Fuck this new day bullshit.

When everyone had quieted after the battering of light, the pastor raised a hand. "For those of you who wish to join the family, the ceremony where Danielle will be laid to rest will take place in approximately twenty minutes,"

The room emptied and Johnny remained with the kids and Paula. He watched as the pallbearers—Danielle's father, her two brothers, her uncle, her sister's husband, and Wilks—approached the front of the room.

I don't even have the strength to carry you one last time.

The pastor gave instructions, and on someone's count, the six men lifted the coffin and carried it outside.

Johnny was last to get into the car after Ben, Paula and the kids, hanging back to watch the coffin—*Dani*—be moved into the hearse for the drive up the hill.

This can't be happening.

Johnny fought against crying out in pain as he lowered himself into the car. With a trembling hand, he reached for the water bottle in the cup holder.

Ben pulled out the pain medication and gave Johnny another dose. "Here, Mr. Flynn."

Johnny exhaled. "Thank you, Ben"

"You're welcome."

The car rolled forward, the canopy shading Danielle's final resting place moving closer and closer.

Johnny peered again at the myriad stones peppering the endless blanket of green. *How many tears have been shed here? Such a horrible, horrible place.*

THIRTY-ONE

Dick Brickford rang the doorbell. He shifted back and forth and checked his watch to make sure he'd timed it right. He heard the sound of footsteps and wiped his sweaty palms on his jeans. The door opened.

"Dick?"

"Hi, Helen. I know you have to go pick up Maddie at dance class soon. I was wondering if I could have a minute."

Helen swiped a stray blonde hair away from her face. "Sure, come on in." She stepped back and swung the door wider. "Can I get you something to drink?"

"Water'd be fine." He followed her into the kitchen, glancing around. "The place looks great."

"Thanks," Helen filled a glass with ice and held it under the tap. "I have more time to keep it up since I don't have to commute so far." She placed the water on the counter.

Brickford sat on the stool and took the glass, recalling that it belonged to the first set of dishes they bought together after they were married.

"You need to talk about the case?" Helen asked.

"No, I've spent enough time talking about that."

"I'll bet. The news hasn't left it alone."

Brickford gulped the water. "Tell me about it."

Helen leaned forward, resting her elbows on the countertop. "I tried to call you several times."

"I know. I completely failed." Brickford looked away. "I just didn't have much to say."

"You didn't fail, Dick."

"The hostage's head was blown off!" He threw his hands up. "A beautiful woman with two young children—dead. Flynn was practically shot in half. It's a miracle he lived at all." He gazed up at her. "I looked the man in the eye, Helen. I told him things were going to work out if he followed *my* directions. I made a promise and—"

"I'm so sorry, Dick." She reached forward and took his hand.

Brickford felt his eyes well up. "I'm the one who should be sorry."

"You did everything you could. You don't need to be—"

"I'm sorry about everything—about Mrs. Flynn getting killed, about Franklin being killed the last time." He drew a nervous breath. "I'm sorry about our marriage. That time. I just—"

"Dick, don't do this. Punishing yourself isn't going to help."

He leaned forward. "I need to say this, Helen. I came here to say this to you."

She pulled her hand away. "Okay. Go ahead."

"Two years ago, when Franklin was shot down, it was the first time I really felt responsible for a case turning bad. I can't begin to explain how it feels when someone is dead because of a decision you made."

"I can't imagine."

"When I went to that bar…"

Helen stiffened.

He hung his head. "I was so drunk. I don't even remember it. I didn't even know her—"

"We've gone over this, Dick. It's about trust. You broke a vow and—"

"I regret it every day. Every. Single. Day. And I came here to say I'm sorry." His eyes met hers. "They're transferring me to Thousand Wells."

"Thousand Wells?" Helen gasped. "That place is horrifying. Gang activity, drugs, lots of homeless. Is this a demotion?"

"Technically, no, but my hopes of a promotion any time soon have been shot in the ass. The Flynn kidnapping is a pretty high-profile case. A billionaire's wife was executed and he was shot to pieces, all under my watch. PD needs to show they're doing something to compensate."

Helen pressed her lips together and closed her eyes. "It doesn't seem fair. What could you have done differently?"

"I dunno." Brickford pinched the bridge of his nose and shook his head. "The Thousand Wells department is an hour's drive longer than I have right now. I'll probably have to move."

Tears welled in Helen's eyes. "Maddie will be crushed."

"She's not the only one." Brickford took a shallow breath and added, "I had a dream, Helen. I had a dream that I would make Captain and earn enough so that you would be able to quit your teaching job and finish your book." He leaned forward and took her hand. "You're *such* a good writer."

Helen swiped away a tear.

"I dreamed of coming home one day and saying. *Quit your job! I got us, baby. You're a full-time writer now. Grab Maddie and let's celebrate.*"

Helen covered her face. "Oh, Dick."

"I dreamed of taking Maddie to your first book signing and saying, "There's your mommy. She's a writer. See, you can be whatever you want when you grow up, just like she did."

Helen cried openly.

"But Franklin got killed, then I killed our marriage." Brickford stared off into space, letting the memories flood his mind as a tear slipped down his cheek. "Now a woman is dead, her husband is maimed, and I've murdered my career. I'm so sorry, Helen. For *everything*."

Helen grabbed a towel on the counter and wiped her eyes. "All this time, I never knew about the dream you just described."

"I was raised to believe that a man provides for his family. In a way, coming home and telling you to quit your job was as much about me becoming a man as you becoming a writer." He gazed into her eyes. "Have you worked on the book at all?"

"Teaching takes it out of me." She sighed. "I have nothing left at the end of the day."

"Yeah, I hear ya." His gaze drifted to the clock on the wall and he sighed. "You have to get Maddie now."

Helen glanced down. "Yeah."

"I still have to figure out the logistics of the transfer," Brickford said as he stood up. "I'll keep you posted as I figure things out."

"Okay."

He walked down the hall and reached for the doorknob.

"Dick?"

He turned around.

Helen stood in the hallway. "Would you like to go pick her up with me?"

"You mean it?"

Helen gave a faint smile. "She'd love it. It would surprise the heck out of her."

"I'd really like that." He pointed at his tear-streaked face, "if you don't mind riding with a pussy who cries."

Helen chuckled and touched his shoulder. "You're not a pussy, Dick."

They locked gazes then burst out laughing.

"Haven't heard that one in a while." Brickford continued chuckling.

Helen pressed her hand against her forehead. "I never thought I'd laugh again."

Brickford opened the door. "I can't remember the last time I did, either." He let out a cleansing breath. "It does feel good, doesn't it? He turned to her. "Maybe we can swing by that pizza place on the way back, the one with all the games that Maddie loves?"

Helen stroked her hair. "But I look so terrible. I've been crying and—"

"You look beautiful, Helen." He placed his hand on the side of her face. "You always look beautiful."

THIRTY-TWO

Three weeks after Danielle's funeral, Johnny was discharged from the hospital. Dr. Patel had said that more time in would benefit his recovery, but Johnny insisted he'd be better off with his kids. So, with the promise of weekly returns for physical therapy and counseling, he was given the okay to leave.

He was much more ambulatory than he had been at the funeral but needed the help of a cane. He'd elected to stop shaving and sported a wild, mountain-man-style mustache and beard.

The media descended as soon as Paula pulled up to the curb. Pictures of Johnny being wheeled out to the car with a blanket over his head went viral almost immediately.

Paula followed as Johnny pushed open the front door and stepped into the foyer. It was a school day, so the house was quiet. Johnny thought it was important for the kids to return to school to instill some sense of normalcy back into their lives, provided they were guarded by security every moment they were out of his sight. Johnny stood in the entry, unsure where to go first.

Paula closed the door. "I'll be picking up the children from school in about an hour, Mr. Flynn. Dinner will be at six." She must have sensed Johnny's indecisiveness, because she added, "If you'd like to set up in your office, I'll bring you some tea."

"Not now. I'll be there in a while. I'd like to walk around first."

"I'll get started on dinner, then."

Johnny spent the next hour walking through each room of the house, paying particular attention to the scent in the air, knowing when it faded, it would never return.

His office, the only room without Dani's scent, was cold and dark. The blinds had been drawn, and when Johnny opened them, light from the outside poured through the slats. He squinted at the glare, unable to stop memories of the funeral from flooding his thoughts.

He retreated down the hallway and limped toward their bedroom. He placed his hand on the door, paused to breathe, and then pushed it open. He stared at their bed, neatly made and stacked high with pillows, and at the picture of him and Danielle on the nightstand. A lump formed in his throat as he forced himself to enter and gimp past the bed to Danielle's massive walk-in closet. He pulled open the double doors and the automatic lighting clicked on, displaying her extensive wardrobe.

Johnny walked around the large space, his hand grazing each soft garment. He leaned forward to inhale the fragrance that wafted off a silk dress. He glanced up at the collection of handbags that lined a shelf above and caught sight of a green beaded clutch. Reaching up for it, he placed too much weight on his bad hip and fell forward, slamming his hand into the clutch and tumbling it to the floor.

Johnny regained his balance, bent down, and picked up the bag. The top opened and out fell a tube of lipstick, a pen, and a napkin. He picked up the napkin and slowly unfolded it, knowing exactly what to expect. It was a note, like the many he and Danielle secretly passed back and forth during social events and fancy dinners with business associates. Some notes would be silly, some a bit naughty, others just proclaiming utter boredom.

Johnny looked at his wife's handwriting:

Do you love me, Mr. Flynn?

Then his own scrawl:

YES

Then hers again:

Wanna get lucky later?

To which he responded:

WHY, YES MRS FLYNN. LET'S TAKE OFF AFTER
THIS SLEEPING PILL IS FINISHED YAMMERING.

Johnny held the note to his lips and collapsed, yelping in pain as his new hip hit the floor. He curled into a fetal position, clutched the napkin to his chest, and heaved through the searing pain in his back.

He stayed on the floor of the closet for the rest of the afternoon. He vaguely remembered Paula struggling to help him up and forcing him to take his meds and crawl into bed, which seemed large and empty. Johnny wrestled with his thoughts as he tossed and turned in a drug-induced fog.

Finally, sleep allowed him to escape.

∞∞∞∞∞∞

Johnny had breakfast with Paula and the kids the following morning and tried his best to catch up on what'd had been going on in their lives.

"I'm sorry I didn't see you yesterday when you got home from school."

"It's okay, Daddy," Maya said. "Paula told us that the meds kept you asleep. Does it still hurt a lot?"

"Yeah, Petal. It does, but I'll heal. You just focus on school and getting back into the routine."

"I'm still not used to the beard and mustache," Michael said.

When Paula took them to school, Johnny settled in his office, steering his thoughts toward the one thing that kept him going the previous three weeks.

Who killed Dani?

Who did this to us?

I will find them and make them suffer.

Paula pushed the door open with the tray she was holding. "Here's some tea for you, Mr. Flynn."

"Thank you." Johnny logged onto the computer, queried a phone number, and dialed.

"Gypsum Ridge Police Department."

"Hello, my name is Jonathan Flynn. I'd like to speak with Dick Brickford, please."

"Hold on please, Mr. Flynn."

Johnny waited.

A new voice came on the line. "Mr. Flynn?"

"Yes."

"My name is Alex Yore. I'm lead detective in your case."

"What happened to Brickford?"

"He's been transferred to another division."

"What! Where?"

There was a pause. "Mr. Brickford now works out of Thousand Wells."

Johnny ran his fingers though his hair and thought for a moment.

"Mr. Flynn?"

"I'm here. Look, I got home from the hospital yesterday. I want an update on my wife's murderers."

"We're working on the leads we have."

"Is Dennington still a suspect?"

"He's one."

"Well, what are you—"

"Mr. Flynn," Yore interrupted. "I can assure you that we've been working on your case non-stop. If I learn anything, you'll be the first person I call. Let me give you my cell number."

Johnny took out a pad of paper and a pen. "Okay, I'm ready." He took down the number. "Right, thanks. Look, I'd like you to call me with updates. When can I look forward to hearing from you tomorrow?"

Johnny heard the officer exhale on the other end of the phone, then pause before answering, "Well, I suppose we could arrange a weekly call to touch base."

"Weekly? No. Call me every day. If you're working the case the way you say, there should be new information daily. My request isn't unreasonable." Johnny tapped his pen on the pad.

"All right, Mr. Flynn. I'll call you tomorrow and inform you of our progress."

"Good." Johnny hung up and drummed his fingers on the desk.

I need to get ahold of Ming.

He glanced at the computer. *I can't risk email.*

He looked at his cell phone. *An untraceable phone is how we communicated before, but how can I get to a convenience store?*

Johnny sat for a moment, then several thoughts came together as a plan. He sat forward and read the time. *Yes, this can work.*

∞∞∞∞∞∞

"This is crazy, Mr. Flynn," Paula said as Johnny scootched down next to Michael in the black sedan the following morning.

Maya twisted around in the passenger seat to get a look at Johnny. "This is kinda weird, Daddy."

"Yeah." Michael patted Johnny's shoulder. "I don't know if it's a good idea."

Paula scoffed, then drove down the winding drive, through the iron gates, and onto the main road. A few paparazzi were out, but paid no heed to the daily caravan of Paula and the hired security taking the kids to school.

Johnny waited a few minutes before sitting up. "Did you call the shop, Paula?"

"Yes, Mr. Flynn. The car's ready to be picked up. We'll swing by after dropping off the kids."

"Good."

"So, you're just going to drive around, and then come home?" Maya asked.

"Yeah, Petal. Daddy needs some think time."

Paula glanced in the rearview mirror. "I don't think the doctor would approve of this, Mr. Flynn."

"She doesn't have to know. It's not like I'm doing anything physical. I just want to get in a car and drive so I can get my mind right. I haven't had a moment alone in a very long time. I need that right now."

Paula dropped the kids off at school and drove to the auto shop where the Flynns had their cars serviced. Johnny stepped out of the car and hobbled over to a low wall to sit and wait as Paula made arrangements. He'd dressed in the old, paint-stained clothes he'd always worn when he built models with Michael and also donned a baseball cap and glasses.

About five minutes later, Paula pulled up next to Johnny and handed him a set of keys and the gate opener. "It's the blue Toyota sedan over there, Mr. Flynn."

Johnny peered at the shop. "Did they have any questions?"

"No. I simply told them we hired temporary help who needed the extra car to run errands. It's not a problem." She looked at Johnny. "You're certainly incognito, Mr. Flynn. With all of that facial hair, if you would have walked up to me, I wouldn't have known it was you at all."

"Good. I just need some privacy for a day."

"I understand. Should we expect you back for dinner?"

"Probably. I have my phone if you need to reach me."

"Okay," Paula waited until Johnny got into the Toyota then waved and pulled out onto the road.

Johnny rolled down the window as he drove onto the highway. Being on the open road felt liberating. Johnny glanced at the cars as he passed them and smiled when other drivers barely acknowledged him.

I'm invisible. Mission accomplished.

He drove about twenty miles before exiting and pulling into the parking lot of a dingy convenience store. He elected to leave his cane in the car for the short walk inside, where he used cash to purchase three prepaid cell phones, a bag of chips, and a soda. He noticed the cigarettes behind the counter and gestured toward them, then stopped and cursed his damaged lung.

He limped back to the car, ripped the package off one of the phones, and dialed.

"Ming. It's me. We need to meet."

Three minutes later, the blue Toyota merged back onto the highway heading east. Johnny turned on the radio and settled in for the hour-long drive.

All right, Ming, let's see what we can do.

THIRTY-THREE

Johnny cruised through the broken city of Thousand Wells. *I can't believe this is the same place I visited as a kid.*

Growing up, Johnny's father had told him many stories about the city. His favorite was the legend of the city's namesake, Thousand Wells, a shaman with the ability to call down rain. Legend stated that Thousand Wells saved his tribe several times from drought, and once he even spared his people from a savage attack by calling on the clouds to deliver a rainstorm *so* fierce that it washed out the invaders.

Some locals believed that Thousand Wells still watched over the people who lived there and shielded them from harm. As a gesture of loyalty, surviving tribe members left bouquets of wildflowers at the base of ancient trees, in doorways to sacred places, and other places where they believed Thousand Wells watched over them.

Johnny's thoughts returned to the task at hand when he spotted the homeless shelter where his family volunteered. He slowed when he drove by.

The last time I was there was with Dani.

Johnny parked and walked through Town Center Square, where the historic Thousand Wells Fountain stood at its center. He scanned the towering stone water feature that used to leave him awestruck as a boy: the stone-carved creation of mountains and fauna, the coyote standing atop the highest peak, the three waterfalls, the legendary shaman standing at the base of the north cascade, rain stick in hand.

Johnny felt a prick of sadness as he glanced up at the stone giant. Once was the city's crown jewel, the fountain now looked old and worn, streaked with calcium deposits and caked in bird crap. Then his gaze fell on a bouquet of fresh flowers at the shaman's feet.

They still believe that Thousand Wells will help them.

Johnny took a deep breath and pressed on toward a little café where an Asian man with a scar on his left cheek sat alone on the patio, smoking like a chimney.

THIRTY-FOUR

Anisha Patel Corby sat in the passenger seat while Frank drove them home. She wept openly, allowing every emotion to come forth unfiltered.

Frank put a hand on her thigh. "It's all right, Ani. Everything is going to be fine."

"ABCD," she responded through sobs. "I cannot believe that my own Mother referred to her future grandchild as "ABCD."

Frank kept his eyes on the road. "You still haven't told me what that means."

"It means American-Born-Confused-Desi."

"*Desi*?"

"*Desi* means *of the homeland*," Anisha said between sobs. "Trust me. It's a slam."

Frank shook his head. "I'm not one bit surprised she said that. Are you?"

Anisha sniffed loudly. "I shouldn't be. My rational mind knows how she is and that she will never accept me, or you, or our child."

"That's right," Frank said. "She never will. No matter what you do, she won't accept you. She's made that clear time and time again. Crying won't change that."

Anisha took a deep breath. "You're right." She wiped her eyes. "You're absolutely right, Frank Corby. We should enjoy this sacred time. The crying stops now."

They rode in silence for a minute.

Anisha sniffed again and placed her hands on her tummy. "I'm getting a little bump, I think."

"Really?" Frank reached over and felt it. "Nah, that's gas."

Anisha chuckled. "Hey, I know how we can top off the evening right."

"How, sweetheart?"

"Let's drive to *your* parents' house and tell them the news!"

"Good idea," Frank said. "They can call the kid a coconut, and that should make the evening perfect."

They cracked up.

Frank added, "We can go find an old Cher album and blast the song *Half-Breed* from the stereo as we pull into their driveway—you know, sort of like a warning."

By this time Anisha was bent over laughing. "Stop talking! Stop it or I'll pee!"

"Or—" Frank leaned toward her—"we can go get ice cream."

"Ice...cream!" Anisha spat between laughs. "Yes, let's do that instead. I'd love a dipped cone. Large, of course."

"Done. A large dipped cone for my beautiful wife and baby." Frank merged onto the highway.

THIRTY-FIVE

Auster felt his muscles loosen as the sun drenched his skin. He sat in the solarium of Fokazi's expansive home in KwaZulu-Natal. A glass of wine rested on the table before each of them.

"The numbers are diminishing," Fokazi said. "There has been progress here."

"That is good." Auster looked Fokazi up and down. "Is there a reason you're clinging to that body? You need rebuilding. You appear old and frail."

The large African man sitting across from him ran a hand along his own deeply creviced neck then looked at his fingers, bent from years of arthritis. "I *am* old, Auster. Granted, not as old as the other Sentries." He looked down at himself. "I've enjoyed this particular body. I hope the subsequent one will bring as many positive experiences. The next time we meet, I will be renewed."

Fokazi regarded Auster. "Your new form is very Americanized. I don't think you've ever appeared so—how should I put it—aesthetically pleasing."

Auster recalled his tryst with the three women. "Humans are reacting to this form in ways I never would have imagined."

"Humans are visually driven," Fokazi said. "With regard to our business, I came across another group in Kenya. They're gone now, but the work seems endless."

"Which is why I am here," Auster said. "I can feel the energy of one who has the strength to wield the light, similar to what I felt when I came upon you and all of the others."

"You mean another Sentry?"

Auster nodded.

"You're here in person to tell me that?"

"I'm here to tell you that you will stand as a *dayyanum* to determine if the candidate is worthy, along with Torphis and Boke Gal."

Fokazi sat up straight. "I will use my best judgment. When will this happen?"

"It won't be long," Auster gazed out of the glass wall to the setting sun. "The universe has started the process of calling his energy back."

THIRTY-SIX

Ming watched with raised eyebrows as Johnny set his cane against the side of the table. "I didn't even recognize you."

"That's the point." Johnny stroked his beard and sat down.

"I get that." Ming paused for a few beats, then added, "I'm sorry about Danielle."

Johnny didn't respond.

"You all right?"

"I'll live, unfortunately."

"You being tailed?"

"Not a chance."

Ming lit another cigarette with the first. "The spouse is always the number one suspect. Especially a couple with your status." He gestured to the pack. "Smoke?"

"Not with one lung."

Ming flicked his ash on the ground. "Plan on having the cops tail you for a while."

"The cops do what they do. I have nothing to hide." Johnny leaned forward. "Do you know anything about who did this? Based on what the cops say, everything points to Dennington."

Ming blew out a puff of smoke. "It's not Dennington."

"How do you know for sure? The cops haven't even found him."

"Yes, they have." Ming took another drag. "Roderick Dennington's been on a coke-infused fuck-fest for the past two months on a yacht that's cruising the French Riviera. He's hooked up with some married contessa and a dozen naked ladies-in-waiting."

"Why haven't they brought him in?"

"Why should they? They know he didn't do it and he's off the grid. It's easier on the police if they steer the public toward thinking the suspect is known and out there hiding."

"True," Johnny said. "They'll let people assume he's the guy while they search for the real killers."

"You got it. If the ticking clock runs out and push-comes-to-shove, they can drag him in and charge him, but Dennington's lawyers will tear the asshole out of the case and he'll walk."

A waitress, donning full-sleeve tattoos on both arms, ambled up to the table. "More coffee?" she asked Ming.

"Please."

She turned to Johnny. "Would you like a menu?"

Johnny scanned the ink on her arm before answering, "Coffee's fine for me, too." He waited until the waitress left, then said, "I honestly thought it was Dennington. Did you see his rant at the farewell dinner?"

"Yeah." Ming crushed the butt into the ashtray. "The video went viral. It's the wind in the sails of the cops' case. But it's not even close to proof."

"How do you know all of this?"

They paused when the waitress bustled back to the table with Johnny's coffee.

"As you know, I have several moles inside the PD." Ming lit another cigarette. "Come on, Johnny. You can't tell me it's not staring you in the face."

"You know who did it?"

Ming shook his head in disbelief. "You *don't*? You have no idea who would stage a kidnap/ransom/murder to ruin someone? Do you think it's an *accident* you're alive? Honestly, how many pros shoot you at close range and only manage to hit you in the ass?"

Johnny's eyes widened. "Vander Broek?"

"The man himself."

"But he's old and—"

"Hard and unforgiving," Ming finished. "I've heard about the shit he's done in the past. He always went after the family and left the guy knowing he caused tragedy to his own kin." He looked at Johnny. "Sounds like what you're going through, doesn't it?"

Johnny glanced at the window of the coffee house and saw his own frail reflection. He was a shell of his former self. Whoever it was, they got him where he *lived*.

"He must know about the last shooting," Ming continued. "It's the only thing that makes sense." He shifted in his seat. "Although, I have no idea how he could have figured it out."

Johnny slumped in his chair. *My greed cost me Dani.* He looked at Ming. "Have any proof?"

"We found the money."

"The ransom money? Do the cops know?"

Ming lit another smoke. "Sort of. My guys on the inside found it before the other cops, so they don't know yet."

"Who?" Johnny's jaw clenched.

"I traced the info on the marked bills after I'd heard about what happened. The shooters sent it through the laundry several times. The guys who do my wash picked it up digitally when several large sums crossed their path. They checked it out. Same scratch."

Johnny leaned back. "No shit."

"Yep. We dug a little deeper, found out who the perps really were behind their aliases, and eventually traced them back to Vander Broek. The police know nothing. I figured you'd want the cops out of this."

Johnny let the information sink in. His expression went from disbelief to rage. "Okay, let's do this. I have one requirement, though." He leaned in toward Ming. "*I* get the fuckers who killed Dani. I want to look them in the eye when I slaughter them."

"You'll risk everything."

"I don't care. Make it happen."

An hour-and-a-half later, Johnny emerged from the coffee house with a fifteen-million-dollar arrangement that would take down Schuyler Vander Broek and his blood-soaked corporation.

THIRTY-SEVEN

Johnny's days were long and painful: drug regimens, tedious trips to the doctor to check on the new hip and the shrinking hole in his back, and endless nights in an empty bed. Danielle's scent faded too, too, fast.

After Danielle's death, Schuyler Vander Broek made a public plea to find the killers. Teeth clenched, Johnny stared at the milky-blue eyes of the ancient man in front of the bouquet of microphones as a news station replayed the press conference.

Vander Broek took in a rattled breath.

> "What has happened to Jonathan Flynn and his lovely wife is a horror."

Flashbulbs lit the old man's pale face.

> "I am offering a million dollars to anyone who could provide information to the police about this terrible crime. My heart goes out to Mr. Flynn and his children."

That sounds familiar, too fucking familiar.
Johnny completely avoided the news after that.

Paula worked tirelessly, keeping the home fires burning to help everyone adjust to life without Danielle. The kids were a welcome distraction, their school stories linking Johnny to some form of reality.

But, despite all efforts, everyone seemed different, more somber. Johnny would often catch Paula or one of the kids crying when they thought no one was looking.

Wilks sent regular updates on the company, which Johnny only half-heartedly read.

∞∞∞∞∞∞

Three-and-a-half months after Johnny's wife died in front of him, he walked into Dr. Patel's office, clean-shaven and without a cane. The nurse weighed him, took his temperature and blood pressure and ushered him into an examination room. She handed him a tie-back smock. "Please undress and put this on, open part facing forward. The doctor will be in to see you shortly."

Draping his clothes across a chair in the corner, Johnny climbed on the examination table. The paper liner crunched as he shifted his weight to adjust the smock. He swung his bare legs and stocking feet while his gaze wandered across the sea-foam green counter. The equipment was standard: a plastic model skull, isopropyl alcohol, hand sanitizer, glass jars of cotton balls and tongue depressors, and a small, steel sink.

Damn. It's cold in here. He wrapped his arms around his middle and glanced up at the framed pictures of the human skeletal and muscular systems.

Someone knocked twice on the door.

"Okay," Johnny said.

Dr. Patel walked in wearing a placid smile that Johnny hadn't noticed before.

His eyes moved down to her swollen belly. "You're expecting!"

"Yes, I am."

"Congratulations, Doctor. How far along?"

"Almost nineteen weeks."

"Is it your first baby?"

Dr. Patel nodded. "Yes. We're having a little girl."

"That's great. I'm very happy for you." Johnny peeled his gaze away from hers. "You know, I've made a LOT of money in my life, but my kids are the greatest thing I've ever made—or helped make. You know what I mean."

"Yes, I do," she answered. "My husband and I are so excited we can hardly keep a consistent thought between us. We're still figuring out the logistics of work since we're both on call and our schedules constantly change."

"Oh, your husband is a doctor, too?"

"Yes, he's head of surgery at Thousand Wells Hospital."

"Thousand Wells, huh?"

Dr. Patel flinched. "I know it's not the best area, but the hospital *is* one of the finest."

"I've heard that," Johnny said. "Thousand Wells used to be a great place once upon a time."

"People have told me that."

"It's true. I used to visit the place with my father. It's quite a commute for your husband, isn't it?"

"We live between here and there right now, but I'm in the process of transferring to Thousand Wells Hospital as well, so we'll be moving. Growing family, bigger place." Patel grinned. "Kids are a lot of work, even before they are born, aren't they?"

"Kids *are* a lot of work," Johnny said. "But they're worth it. Dani…" He paused for a moment. "My wife stopped working when our kids were born."

Dr. Patel's gaze softened. She placed a hand on his shoulder. "I'll bet you and your kids are pulling through this together."

Johnny felt his eyes sting. "I don't know how I'd get through it without them."

"Well, let's see how everything is healing." Dr. Patel said.

"Okay."

She listened to Johnny's heart and lungs. "Sounds good. Now, let's look at the hip. Please step down."

Johnny slipped off the table and Dr. Patel had him pivot back, forth, and around.

"Mobility is increasing. Go ahead and sit."

Dr. Patel checked Johnny's chart and his stats. "You've lost twenty-eight pounds. Normally I would be congratulating my patients, but in your case, the weight loss has put you slightly underweight."

"I haven't been eating much. I've also been sedentary, but I haven't had a choice there."

"That's true. Were you physically active before?"

"I played racquetball and golf."

"I see. Well, many people with artificial hips are able to return to the activities they enjoyed prior to surgery. I don't see why you can't as well. Just give it time, Mr. Flynn. You're not ready for racquetball yet. Start with walking. As for work, I don't see why you couldn't return straight away if you'd like, providing it doesn't add to your stress level."

"I'd like to go back," Johnny said.

"Then, let it be written," Dr. Patel said.

Johnny gave her a weak smile. "Let it be done."

∞∞∞∞∞∞

That night, Johnny lay propped against a pillow with a book in his hands. Reading usually helped him drift off, but the following day weighed on his mind.

He reached for the picture of himself and Danielle that rested on the end table. It was a shot of them taken on their first date after the kids were born. Danielle had a glass of red wine in celebration of weaning the babies off of breast milk.

Danielle had handed her camera to the server at the restaurant, raised her glass, and said, "Here's to no more pumping and no sharp teeth cutting into my nipples!"

"Now, hold on a minute," Johnny replied. "That doesn't include me, does it?"

Danielle giggled and Johnny gave her a peck on the cheek. Then the blushing server took the photo.

Johnny gazed upon her face: her bright eyes, wide smile,—*it was so genuine*—and the glow that seemed to emanate from within her. He traced the outline of her silhouette from the top of her head to her shoulder. "Tomorrow will be the first day I go to work without kissing you goodbye."

He let the frame drop into his lap. "I swear, the fuckers who did this *will* pay." He picked up the photo again and added, "I know who they are, Dani. And we've come up with a plan to put things right in a way that's fucking historic. The echo of revenge will sound from here to the Netherlands and across the globe."

His thoughts drifted to the kids. He glanced across the bed at their school pictures. "You won't even remember her. I was twelve when my grandmother died. I saw her nearly every day, and yet...I can't picture her face clearly."

I don't know if that's good or bad. Dani's their mom.

"They'll be okay, baby," he finally said to Dani's photo. "Kids are resilient. They're moving on, going to school and practices, even laughing." He shook his head. "Not me, though."

He placed the photo back on the end table. "They'll grow up and be happy, and I'll walk around like a fucking ghost for the rest of my life. The only thing that keeps me going is the little meeting with Ming and Vander Broek, and that will happen soon."

THIRTY-EIGHT

Johnny walked through the doors of J.T. Flynn Diamond Corporation for the first time since the kidnapping. Employees lined the entrance of the lobby, their pasted-on smiles failing to hide their obvious shock.

I shouldn't be surprised.

Before the incident, Johnny had jet-black hair and kept in shape. Now he plodded down the hall, broken, weighing almost thirty pounds less, flecks of gray streaking his hair.

"Good morning, Mr. Flynn. We're glad to have you back," the front desk receptionist said. The once-lustful stare the buxom blonde had reserved just for him had been replaced by an expression of pity.

"Thanks, Jackie."

How the mighty have fallen.

Johnny passed through the elevator doors and was grateful when they slid closed.

His office was just as he'd left it, but it felt foreign as he sank into the chair behind his massive oak desk. He glanced at the picture of his father and wondered if he and Dani were enjoying a glass of red in the afterlife. He reread the Tennyson poem on the wall. "My fields are being slashed and burned, Daddy."

There were two knocks at the door.

"Yeah," Johnny called out.

Wilks walked into the office carrying several large files. "G'morning. How are you?"

"As ready as I'll ever be." Johnny felt an ache and shifted his weight.

Wilks placed the files on the desk. "There's a sales meeting at three." He nodded toward the pile. "You'll find the past three months' gross as well as the trajectory for the following three. The other folders contain researched trends, where our competition is advertising, and details of the upcoming Franklin Wren show."

Johnny leaned back, appreciating Wilks' clear attempt at a normal day. He took a deep breath, then played along. "Wren doesn't like me very much. He's made that public many times."

"The man is a braying ass."

Johnny spat out an unexpected chuckle. "I've never heard you use that one."

"It's new—for me at least. Don't see the point of calling Wren's show *exclusive*. He publicizes every bloody moment of it. It seems he's more interested in being in the social column than designing jewelry."

"True," Johnny said. "Because he's a braying ass."

Wilks smiled. "Yes, sir, that he is."

Johnny opened the top file. "Tell sales I'll join you all at three."

"Will do, sir." Wilks walked toward the door. He stopped and spun on his heels. "It's good to have you back, J.T."

"Thanks, Wilks. It's good to be back."

∞∞∞∞∞∞

Johnny trudged through the front door at six 'o clock.

Paula emerged from the kitchen. "Good evening, Mr. Flynn. How was your first day back?"

"Good, but I feel as though I've been hit by a truck."

"Honestly, you do look quite tired. The kids are back from practice. Why don't you change and wash up for dinner? I've made spinach casserole."

"Sounds great," Johnny said as he lumbered up the stairs.

Dinnertime was an adjustment that was still in progress at the Flynn household. Danielle's empty chair at the small table was a blatant reminder of her absence. Paula had even set her place by mistake several times only to say, "Oh, my, I'm so sorry," as she picked the plates back up in haste.

For the most part, mealtime was silent. Johnny would ask the kids how their day was only to receive one-word answers. In the past, they'd always been willing to share their kid-business with him, but after losing Dani it was like pulling teeth to get them to speak. All of the information Johnny received about their lives came from Paula.

But something changed this evening. The kids seemed more animated, more willing to engage. It was as though the entire household took a collective breath when the man of the house returned to his post.

"We got our spring pictures today, Daddy," Maya said.

"I'd better have two on my desk before bed, signed. How was track practice?"

"Good. I'm running the 440 and the 800-meter tomorrow. AND there's a surprise."

"A surprise?" Johnny raised his eyebrows.

"Guess who tried out for football next year?"

Johnny shrugged. "I couldn't begin to guess."

Michael shot his arm into the air.

"Are you serious?" Johnny said. "You tried out for football?"

Michael nodded. "Frederick Olmstead dared me. I told him I would because I owed him from when I pushed him down the hill at freshman camp. I told him he could cheer when they creamed me."

Johnny put down his fork. "I...I don't even know what to say, Bud. I mean, how was it?"

"It was pretty good. They tried me at tight end first, but I'm still effing slow and got tackled every time!"

"Thank you for not saying the actual *word* at the table," Paula said as she brought out a basket of bread.

Michael gave her a thumbs-up. "See, I'm getting better, Paula."

"That you are, my dear." Paula placed the bread in front of him. "Oh, I forgot the parmesan." She bustled back into the kitchen.

Michael turned to Johnny. "Anyway, then they put me at quarterback. And that's when I kicked butt!"

"You did?" Johnny's heart soared.

Michael nodded. "I don't think I'll make first string or anything, but coach says I have an arm."

"Awe, Bud, that's awesome, really awesome."

"Everyone was cheering him on," Maya said.

Paula came back. "You said even Frederick cheered you on."

Michael nodded. "He did. You were right, Dad, Frederick's not so bad. He's actually kinda cool."

"Bud, I'm awestruck. This is such great news. I can't tell you how proud I am. What made you decide to try out?"

Michael's expression turned sober. There was a long pause. "I did it for Mom."

Everyone stopped eating.

Johnny's heart leapt into his throat. "You did?"

"I want her to know that I get it, and that I'm willing to work for what I don't have, like you, and Gladys at the shelter, and Frederick."

Paula dabbed away tears.

Michael looked around the table. "I'm sorry," his voice cracked. "I wasn't trying to make everyone sad."

"Oh, love," Paula said. "You're reading it wrong. We're crying because your mum just showed herself, from inside you." She walked over, leaned down, and planted a big kiss on Michael's cheek.

"Paula's right, Bud," Johnny said. "Your mom would be so proud."

Maya buried her face in her hands.

It was as though a cork had been popped. The admiration and respect Johnny felt for Michael at that moment, combined with his anguish and grief of losing Dani, brought forth a flood of emotions he couldn't contain. He got up from his seat, wrapped his arms around Michael, and lifted him from his chair. "I'm so proud to have you as my son."

∞∞∞∞∞∞

After the meal, the kids plodded off to sit in front of the TV.

Johnny blew out a sigh as he watched them leave the room. "I'm beaming with pride and drowning in grief at the same time," he said to Paula.

"I feel the very same way, Mr. Flynn." She picked up his dish. "How about if I fix you some tea and bring it to your office?"

"That would be great."

Johnny was too tired to work, but he needed to talk to Paula. *I have to tell her my wishes. I have to make sure she knows what to do in case something happens.*

Ten minutes later, Paula walked in with the tray. Beside the teapot lay two signed, wallet-size pictures. "Here are the kids' signed photos." She placed the tray on the adjacent table.

"Excellent." His gaze rested on the faces of his twins. He held up the picture of Maya. "She looks like her mother, doesn't she? A brunette Dani."

Paula smiled at the photo. "She certainly does."

Johnny peeled his gaze away from the photos. "They won't remember her, will they?"

Paula leaned away with a shock-stricken look on her face. "They certainly will, Mr. Flynn. She loved them too much. As you saw tonight, she still affects their lives and decisions. I think she always will."

Johnny nodded. "I hope you're right."

Paula dabbed her eyes with a handkerchief. "Do those men have *any* idea what they did to the children?" She looked into Johnny's eyes. "And to *you*?"

Johnny pursed his lips. *They know what they've done to me.* "Paula, I need to ask you something, something important."

"Of course, Mr. Flynn, you can ask me anything."

He took a deep breath. "Dani's murderers are still out there and, well, there's no easy way to say this. If they end up finishing me—"

Paula looked shocked. "Don't you *dare* say such a thing, Mr. Flynn! The police will find those men and—"

"Shhh, Paula. I hope you're right, but if you're not, and something happens to me, I need you, *and only you*, to retrieve this and follow the directions within." He reached into the filing cabinet and pulled out a ten-by-twelve clasped envelope with the name "Paula" scrawled in black.

Paula frowned. "What is it, Mr. Flynn?"

"If I'm gone, I want Michael and Maya to have a choice. They can live with Dani's parents, her sister's family, or," he swiveled the desk chair so he faced Paula, "they can remain here with you until they turn eighteen and can legally inherit the house."

"Stay with *me*?"

"Yes," Johnny said. "You've raised them with Dani, Paula. You're like another mother to them. But here's the thing. In order for them to have that choice, you need to agree to become their legal guardian."

Paula's lower lip trembled. "Of course I'll agree, Mr. Flynn. I can't even begin to express how touched I am that you would trust me with the most precious people in your life."

"I wouldn't want them with anyone else, Paula. If it were my choice, Dani's family wouldn't have a chance. You're not *like* family, you *are* family, and I thank you for everything you've done for Dani, the kids, and me."

Paula gazed at the photos. "It's an honor, sir. Those little ones captured my heart as soon as I held them. And you and Mrs. Flynn are such wonderful parents."

"This contains documents that bequeath to you the right to legal guardianship, as well as a note to all of Dani's family explaining the kids' decision. It also contains my will." Johnny slipped the envelope back into the filing cabinet, then slapped his thighs. "And there it is."

"Okay, Mr. Flynn," Paula composed herself. "If those are your wishes, I will carry them out." She leaned forward and placed both hands on Johnny's shoulders. "But, please, do everything you can to stay safe. Those children need you."

"I'll do all I can, Paula."

Paula smoothed her apron. "Okay, then. Drink your tea and then it's off to bed with you, Mr. Flynn. You seem to have had an exhausting first day back."

There were two people Johnny took orders from: Dani and Paula. Dani was gone. "Yes, ma'am." He picked up the cup.

Forty minutes later, Johnny lay in bed. He didn't need a book to get to sleep that night. He didn't need to talk to pictures of Dani or use meds to clear his mind. He let his head sink into the cool pillow and closed his eyes as a single thought prevailed.

Everything's in place. Just a few more months to wait.

THIRTY-NINE

Johnny's father had taught him that, in the late spring of each year, the buds of the California jacarandas come into flower, swathing the treetops in veils of pale purple. By late June, pools of lavender cover the green grass below the blooming giants.

In May of 1978, Roland Flynn spoke to Johnny as they walked to school one day.

"See the purple flowers, Johnny?" Roland pointed up at the branches sprinkled with lilac. When they start to fall, the end of school is near."

Johnny craned his head and gazed at the limbs stretching high and wide. "Do they *all* fall to the ground, Daddy?"

"Aye, they do, son. All through the summer, the purple flowers bloom. As fall approaches, the purple flowers go away and we know the new school year is on its way."

From that day forward, Johnny Flynn used the bloom cycle of the jacaranda trees to note the coming of summer. As a teen, he'd smile as he walked under the shady branches on his way to school, knowing the days of hitting the alarm clock were numbered.

When Michael and Maya started school, Johnny shared this tradition with them. He even had the landscapers plant a few jacarandas around the perimeter of his estate so the family could keep track of the time of year without using a calendar.

"It's the way nature does it," Johnny had said to the kids as they drove down the winding drive one morning on the way to school. "Animals don't change their behavior based on a clock or calendar. They respond to the changing seasons."

On this particular day, however, Jonathan Thornton Flynn smiled for a different reason as his limousine sped past the shedding jacarandas.

The wait is over. Tonight, I shall have my revenge.

The long-anticipated wedding of Schuyler Vander Broek's socialite granddaughter, Barbara, was set to be an all-day affair. Aristocrats, celebrities, and politicians sought an invitation to the high-profile, black-tie soirée. A few select members of the press would be allowed inside, and pictures of the affair would, no doubt, end up in social columns around the world for weeks.

Robert Michael Delarusch, the husband-to-be, was a wealthy investment banker who met Barbara Vander Broek when both were vacationing on Fregate Island two years prior. Their courtship was publicly tracked in every social medium and in every who's who column. When the two became engaged, the countdown to the big day began. For the better part of a year, entertainment programs choked the public with daily doses of *Who Will Attend? What will the bride wear?* And *What Will They Eat?*

Schuyler Vander Broek refused to have his granddaughter's wedding in some predictable, five-star spot where wealth was signified by flutes of champagne and platters strewn with escargot and beluga caviar. The day was far too big for that. Instead, the wedding took place at Vander Broek's own sprawling estate, a shining beacon of opulence set upon a three-acre, grassy knoll overlooking the Los Angeles basin.

Invitations went out to four-hundred friends, relatives, business associates, and social acquaintances. Jonathan Flynn and Jan Wilkinson were both on the guest list.

Almost seven months had passed since the shooting, and it would be the first time Johnny appeared at a public event. He took a cleansing breath as the limo ascended the quarter-mile, private drive. When the car pulled up, he was ushered to a massive covered area.

In the shade under the canopies, hundreds of people sat in neat rows of chairs swathed in white with crimson ribbons tied back into perfect, square-knot bows. Johnny took a seat in the last row. He scanned the crowd in front of him and spotted Wilks sitting with his wife about halfway up the aisle.

Johnny had arranged for the kids to be out of town for the entire week at sports camps and had given Paula the week off. He planned to arrive moments before the start of the ceremony to avoid having to socialize. Johnny hadn't even warmed the chair when the wedding music began.

The groom appeared next to the man presiding over the ceremony, hands clasped together in an obvious attempt to keep them from trembling. Johnny hadn't seen the groom in person prior to that day. He was tall and stocky, with dusty brown hair and glasses. Johnny smiled and covered his mouth.

He looks kind of gleepy, actually.

It took a good five minutes for the twelve bridesmaids dressed in crimson couture gowns to stroll down the aisle on the arms of twelve dashing gents in black suits.

Then, finally, amidst a sea of flashing cameras, the bride appeared. The crowd turned to aww and coo as she was led down the aisle by her grandfather. Schuyler Vander Broek beamed as the petite young woman, wearing the mermaid-cut, hand-beaded gown of white silk the media had raved about, hooked her tiny hand around his arm in the slow procession toward the front of the altar.

For the briefest of moments, Johnny felt a twinge of hesitation. *Maybe I shouldn't do this.*

Then he thought of his own wedding, of his beautiful Dani with baby's breath in her hair.

Dani.

Johnny gritted his teeth and steeled his resolve. He stared at the back of Schuyler Vander Broek, shuffling forward next to Barbara as she took the final steps toward her soon-to-be-husband.

You've lived to be old. You've lived to see your grandchildren marry. Dani won't because of you. Tonight you'll eat your last meal, and then I'll send you to Hell.

∞∞∞∞∞∞

Every moment of the Vander Broek wedding day was accounted for, every corner of every space tended-to, every employee well-rehearsed, every need of the guests anticipated. The finest chefs had been flown in to oversee the culinary masterpieces they created specifically for this event.

After the ceremony, the bride, groom, and family posed for a zillion pictures while the guests were treated to hand-crafted hors de oeuvres and cocktails.

Johnny ambled through the crowd with a whiskey glass filled with water. He made nice with those in his path. People were very polite, but seemed uncomfortable and awkward when they spoke to him. Johnny pretended as though he didn't notice.

I don't blame them. What would they say? Hi, sorry that your wife was killed.

At dinner, Johnny sat with Wilks, his wife, Margaret, and a few people from the groom's side. A man named Darby Delarusch, the groom's uncle, monopolized the table discussion with stories of his travels abroad. The man lisped, which was off-putting at first, but he was quite funny and Johnny was relieved that the pressure to be interesting was lifted.

After the meal, the speeches from the best man and maid of honor were followed by the cutting of the five-tier mega-cake surrounded by six two-tier cakes—all white with butter cream frosting topped with a garden of candied flowers.

The dancing began after everyone was stuffed with meat, cake, and booze. That's when Johnny headed to the men's room. He closed the door behind him and retrieved a prepaid phone from his pocket. He pushed the power button, and punched in a number.

"Yep." Ming said.

"On," Johnny said.

"Got ya. Check-out time will be in a little over an hour."

Johnny's hands trembled. "Okay. I'm ready."

Dead silence.

Johnny shook the phone. "Hello?"

"I'm here," Ming said. "Look, you can still pull out and I'll get this done. You don't have to risk being there."

"I want to do it," Johnny said. "I want to look that bastard in the eyes."

"All right. Then the party starts with you. Ring me when you're about to do the deed and my people will spring. Just make sure you take the piece with you and destroy it."

"I will."

"See you in about an hour."

"Yeah, see you soon."

Johnny slipped the phone into his pocket and pulled out a handkerchief to dry his sweaty palms. He exited the bathroom and glanced around at the wait staff tending to the guests, wondering which ones Ming had replaced with his own staff of killers.

His attention went to the middle of the dance floor, where the bride and groom swayed in their first dance as a married couple. The crowd applauded when the number ended, and then Schuyler Vander Broek danced with his granddaughter.

Enjoy your last moments on Earth.

When the expected formalities were over, the ten-million-dollar evening festivities began. Two headlining bands jammed for the younger crowd, while a second stage featured an orchestra for guests more Schuyler's speed, who wanted to sip martinis and dance to the likes of Old Blue-Eyes.

The plan was to make the hit when everyone was boozed up with their guards down. Johnny sauntered through the crowd, ordered whiskey, tossed the contents aside, and then refilled the glass with water. His hip ached, and he exaggerated the limp to give the impression of being tipsy.

Johnny intended to blow Vander Broek's head off in the middle of the event, seeing it as logistically implausible any other way. He had little to no chance of getting the guy in a room alone, and dragging him somewhere private would cause security to step in and the job wouldn't get done. Besides, given the bit of Johnny's plan Ming *didn't* know about, it didn't matter how many people saw it.

Johnny was standing behind the tables set around the orchestra, swaying to their rendition of *Sing, Sing, Sing*, when the unthinkable happened.

The voice came from behind him. "Good evening, Mr. Flynn."

Johnny spun around. "Good Evening, Mr. Vander Broek." Schuyler Vander Broek stood arm-in-arm with a woman who appeared to be not much older than his granddaughter. "You remember my wife, Elizabeth."

"Of course." Johnny shook Elizabeth's hand. "It's a very beautiful wedding. Barbara is lovely. You must be very proud."

Vander Broek chuckled. "Oh, yes. She's been the apple of my eye, as they say, since the day she was born. She truly *is* my pride and joy." He turned to his wife. "Would you excuse us, darling? I'd like to have a word with Mr. Flynn, alone."

Elizabeth nodded and walked away.

Vander Broek turned to Johnny. "Let's go have a drink."

Johnny followed him across the grounds and past the stage where the rock band hammered away. They walked through a massive solarium where people gathered for quiet conversation away from the music and dancing. Vander Broek then ushered Johnny through the grand room where several small groups of guests conversed around an enormous fireplace.

The old man walked into a sizable lounge area where four horseshoe-shaped burgundy sofas encircled small tables lit with candles. A uniformed member of the wait staff stood behind a long, fully-equipped bar. "In here."

I can't believe I got this lucky. Something in the air must have steered the odds in my favor.

Two of the four tables were occupied. At one, two men sat huddled in deep conversation. At another, a couple made out, oblivious to those around them.

"Let's sit at the bar," Vander Broek said.

"Okay." Johnny took the seat next to him.

"I'll have a seven and seven," Vander Broek said to the bartender. He looked at Johnny.

"Same."

They got their drinks and Johnny held up his glass. "To your granddaughter."

"Thank you." Vander Broek took a drink and sighed. "How are you holding up, son?" He sounded genuinely concerned, which Johnny might have fallen for if he hadn't known the bastard was responsible for everything.

"As well as can be expected, I suppose," Johnny answered evenly. His blood boiled, but he kept his composure. "Thank you for asking, and for the public gesture of support."

Vander Broek raised his glass. "I remember that during our tragedy you said business means nothing at times like these—I'm paraphrasing, of course—but you were so right."

Johnny nodded and drank, for real this time. The alcohol warmed him on its way down.

"There are times when life itself becomes the center of importance and all other things fall away." Vander Broek leaned forward. "I think it's time I share something with you, Mr. Flynn."

Johnny's curiosity piqued. "Oh, what's that?"

Vander Broek ran a finger around the rim of his glass. "It's about my son."

"Your *son*? I didn't know you had a son."

"I lost him a long time ago, before coming to this country."

Johnny tipped his head to one side. *Why is he telling me this? Is he comparing his loss to mine? The nerve!*

Vander Broek grasped his glass and drained it. "I was a much younger man. I always assumed my boy would grow up, do good, work hard. I had no idea—"

Johnny gritted his teeth. "Did your son get half his head blown off, like my *wife*?"

Vander Broek froze. "No." He looked Johnny in the eyes. "I hope they find the monsters who did that horrible thing, and justice is done to give you some closure."

"I'm pretty sure there will be closure."

Vander Broek looked surprised. "Yes?"

"I know everything. The money was traceable."

"The money you gave for ransom?" Vander Broek looked genuinely taken aback. "So they've found the men who did this?"

"They found the men who kidnapped my wife and pulled the trigger of the gun that was against her head," Johnny said. "But *they* is not the police. *I* found them. And when I leave here, I'm going to kill them myself. Heard the names Rudman and Leuck?"

"No, I have not."

"Did you honestly think they would *dispose* of twenty million dollars and replace them with *your* non-traceable dollars?"

Johnny reached down and pressed the send button on his phone. "They took your money and tried to launder mine." He growled. "They were in the Caribbean. Two twenty-millionaires."

"You all right, Mr. Vander Broek?"

Johnny turned to see two men in the doorway, jackets pulled back to reveal the guns hooked to their belts.

Ming isn't the only one with people undercover.

Two shots rang out and the guards in the doorway dropped.

Johnny turned back to see the bartender, gun in hand, raise his wrist to his mouth and bark, "Now!"

Johnny stood up and glared at Vander Broek. "Well, you bastard, tonight it comes full circle." He pulled out a revolver and pointed it between the old man's milky, blue eyes.

Vander Broek stared down the barrel of the gun. "God help you, son."

"For Dani," Johnny said. Then he squeezed the trigger.

Blood sprayed as Vander Broek flew backward off the stool.

Johnny bolted from the room, hearing more shots fired behind him. Screams tore through the house and into the garden.

The bartender caught up to Johnny. "Ming gave the go-ahead," he panted. "Let's move."

"Did you kill everyone back there?"

He gave Johnny a strange look. "Of course. There can be no witnesses. You know where to go, right?"

"Yeah."

"You'd better move quickly." The guy veered toward the back of the house.

Johnny backtracked through the solarium, the foyer, and onto the grounds where guests scattered in all directions. As he fled down the lawn toward the circular drive, a chaos of cars screeched away.

"Mr. Flynn!" A man ran forward, pausing when he saw the blood splatter on Johnny's shirt. "My God, you've been hit!"

"No!" Johnny said. "Someone else has. Right in front of me. We need to get a doctor."

"They've already called 911," the man shouted back. "We need to get out of here. Hurry, come with us." He pointed to a black limo, where a panic-stricken woman frantically waved them forward.

Johnny shook his head. "You go."

The guy bolted, jumped into the car, and was still closing the door as it leapt over the curb and fish-tailed onto the drive.

Another limo, engine running and lights off, sat outside the halo of light cast from the driveway lamps. Johnny sprinted toward it. The locks clicked as he reached the back of the car. He wrenched the door open and slammed it closed behind him.

"How was the party?" Ming asked as the car sprang forward.

Johnny sat back. "It's done." He glanced over to see that Ming's shirt and trousers were blood-splattered. Shots still rang out as Ming's black limo weaved down the drive with the other fleeing guests.

"Shit, here come the fucking cops," Ming said as the sound of approaching sirens got closer.

Three police cars, lights flashing, screeched to a halt in front of the drive exit. Officers spilled from the cars and forced all of the people trying to leave out of their limos.

Johnny looked out the window. "We're fucked."

Ming surveyed Johnny's blood-splattered face and clothes. "Lie down across me and act like you're passed out. I got this."

Johnny did as he was told just as a cop rapped on the door.

"Open up!" the cop demanded.

Ming complied. "The ambulance isn't here yet. We've gotta get him to a hospital now, officer. He's been hit!"

Johnny judged by the pause that the cop was looking him over.

"Look," Ming said. "This is Jonathan Flynn. Because the cops fucked up, his wife was murdered and he was nearly killed. Look at us!" Johnny assumed Ming referred to the bloody clothes. "Unless you want to stand in front of the press and tell them that you let Jonathan Flynn bleed to death, you'd better let me get him to a hospital."

The cop shouted. "Vince! Let them through. A guy's been hit." He slapped the roof of the car twice and shouted, "Okay, Go!"

Johnny waited until the car was on the main road before sitting up. "Good. So, did you put the murderers where we agreed?"

Ming nodded. "Yep, Danielle's killers are waiting for you like flies in a web."

FORTY

Johnny settled in for the drive, staring out the window as the car pulled onto the highway. A million thoughts jumbled in his head. *What am I doing? Is this what's best for the kids?*

He wiped the back of his neck and thought of Danielle. *No, I need to do this. It's the only way to be sure.*

A little over an hour later, the car pulled off at the same exit Johnny had seven months prior. The road of broken-down factories was dark, and Johnny's stomach lurched when they reached the last pier where he'd watched his wife die.

"We're here," Ming said.

Johnny reached into his pocket and pulled out the bloody gun he used to kill Vander Broek.

"Don't," Ming handed Johnny another gun. "Ballistics will have a field day if you use same piece."

Johnny took the gun Ming handed him.

The car pulled up in front of the glass factory and Johnny stepped out.

Memories of Danielle's murder flooded Johnny's thoughts as he strode down the pier, the splintered wood creaking under his footsteps. The salty ocean breeze smelled like raw fish and he suddenly felt sick.

The shooters were tied in the same place Danielle was the previous year. Both men knelt, hanging by their bound arms. When they saw Johnny approaching, they snapped to attention, eyes growing wide as he came close.

Johnny stood above the murderers. They were unshaven, their clothes reeked of filth, and dried blood covered their swollen faces. "We meet again. Did you honestly think you'd get away with it?"

One of the men, his face black-and-blue and left eye swollen shut, seemed to register surprise. "Did *you*? You spilled family blood. There could be no turning away from that. Blood for blood."

"*Family* blood?" Johnny said. "Vander Broek's family wasn't touched."

"Several members of Vander Broek's family were also board members. When you decided to shoot up the entire room that night, you should have thought about what you were doing."

"Shut it, Leuck!" Rudman spat.

"No point," Leuck trembled. "We're dead."

"How did he know it was me?" Johnny asked.

"I dunno," Leuck said. "But when you cut into family, count on revenge every time."

"And your assignment was to exact revenge by killing my wife?"

He nodded.

"Were you supposed to kill me?"

"No."

Johnny's gaze drifted across the faces of both men to the wooden planks where they knelt, then noticed the dried blood stains. *Jesus, it's Danielle's. The cops just left it there.*

The image of Danielle's body blurred Johnny's vision as he gritted his teeth, pointed the gun, and fired at Dani's murderers, starting at their balls. The two men screamed in pain, struggling against their restraints as Johnny emptied the gun into them, and then refilled it. When the blood from their lifeless bodies pooled over the stain they'd caused seven months prior, Johnny untied them, let them drop, and kicked them off the end of the pier.

He breathed deeply on his way back to the car. *I'm not shaking anymore. I feel surprisingly calm.*

"Change of plans," Johnny said as he slid onto the back seat.

Ming held up a hand. "If we don't take you to the hospital right now, the cops will know we were lying."

"No worries there. Cops won't wonder about a thing, trust me. Just take me home. I'll destroy the guns and burn my bloody clothes. We've worked too hard to leave a trail."

"Home may not be the best place right now." Ming lit a cigarette.

"Maybe not, but it's necessary. There's one more thing I've gotta to do. Drop me off and you can carry out the rest on your end. I'll take my own car to do mine."

Ming blew out smoke. "Fair enough."

An hour later, Ming dropped Johnny off in front of his house. "Be careful."

Johnny got out of the car. "You, too. And—"

Ming waved him away. "You're welcome."

The limo sped off and Johnny rushed into his garage. He pulled the guns out of his pockets, took them apart, wiped them clean of prints and blood, then stuffed them into a plastic trash bag. He changed out of his bloody clothes and carried them outside, then burned them in the fire pit on the back porch. After dousing the flames, he scooped the carbon remains and dumped them into another trash bag.

Next, the plans I set up with Paula for the kids.

He dashed into the house and rummaged through his office to retrieve the information he had shown Paula months before. He set the large manila folder in the center of his desk. Reaching into another drawer, he pulled out three sealed envelopes, one each for Michael, Maya, and Paula, and placed them next to the folder.

He snatched up the keys to the Diablo, grabbed the bags containing the guns and burned clothes, along with a bottle of vodka, and headed out the door to the garage.

The car screeched onto the driveway. Johnny stopped to gaze back at the empty mansion. *It's just a shell now.* He leaned forward and rested his head on the steering wheel. *When I think of tomorrow, there's no scenario where I'll be okay. None.*

The engine revved, and, taking one last look at the door where he had carried Danielle over the threshold, Johnny sped down the drive and onto the open road toward the freeway. On the way out of town, he made multiple stops to dump parts of each gun. When he had tossed the last of the evidence away, he headed toward Pacific Coast Highway.

As soon as the ocean came into view, Johnny rolled down all of the windows. He drew in a deep breath of moist, salty air as he wound around the curves of the coastal highway.

The last part of the plan.

He thought of the call he'd made to his lawyer weeks before the Vander Broek wedding, making sure his affairs were in order.

Everything is handled. There are no loose ends.

Johnny reached into the glove box, opened a bottle of pain pills Dr. Patel had prescribed, and popped a handful, chasing them down with the vodka.

He'd driven this route enough times to know the best place to do it. On one of the curves ten minutes down the road, a cliff edge dropped a hundred-and-fifty feet to jagged rocks and rough water. There were no houses, no places to stroll along the beach, and no guardrail.

Johnny would be the only casualty.

With the stereo blasting the album he and Danielle used to listen to when they first met, Johnny glanced at himself in the rearview mirror. The face staring back was pale and drawn. *Look at me. I'm dead already.*

He slammed the accelerator to the floor. The curve was in sight. Holding tight to the steering wheel, Johnny closed his eyes. The Diablo launched off the cliff, whining in protest as it left the road and plunged down toward the rocks.

Within seconds, the explosion of glass and metal consumed the silent night. Johnny felt the horrendous jar before he launched through the windshield, his body tearing apart like a rag doll. He heard his back crack as he slammed onto the rocks, then the Diablo crushed his legs and dragged him across the jagged edges.

He couldn't move.

He tasted metal and salt water.

A wave crashed over him, and then the retreating water carried him out to sea. His face sank beneath the surface of the water, the full moon blurred in front of his eyes.

Then a figure appeared above him.

Or was it two?

And he felt the pull.

FORTY-ONE

Amidst seaweed and the half-eaten remains of a dead seal, Auster stood over Jonathan Flynn's lifeless remains. Behind him were three of his Sentries: Torphis, Fokazi, and Boke Gal, present for the advent of their new comrade.

"Can you feel his life source?" Auster asked.

"I can," Torphis answered. "But it is slipping away."

Fokazi leaned forward. "There's not enough flesh to hold life force. He's only strips of meat and bone."

Boke Gal focused. "I can still feel him."

"As do I," Auster said. "He will need to absorb more life to be saved."

Torphis nodded. "I shall go find someone."

"No need. Look closer." Auster said. "There's life all around him."

The three Sentries peered down.

Boke Gal smiled. "Insects. Millions. The sand is teeming with life."

Fokazi bent down. "Yes, their life force is powerful. This will work. Place him where they are most densely populated."

Auster sent a bolt down that threw what remained of Jonathan Flynn onto the dead seal, then raised a hand and bathed the area in intense light.

A million little screams tore through the air as the tiny insects crawling beneath Jonathan Flynn vibrated. The glandular bulbs of the yellow kelp began to burst, one by one. The layers of insects swarming across the seal liquefied and slowly dissolved into their new host.

Flynn's body undulated as the melted creatures assumed the roles of human tissues: fat, flesh, sinew, muscle, organs.

"His form will settle into their state of being, not a human's," Torphis said.

"This is true," Boke Gal said. "He will be an abomination."

"We can meld him with a human casing after adequate life force is absorbed," Auster said. "His source and mind are intact, he still has the makings of a Sentry."

They gazed down at the thousands of wriggling insects squirming beneath the new, squash-colored outer membrane of what once was Jonathan Flynn. The body twitched. The ribcage rose and fell.

Torphis smiled. "He lives."

"Yes," Auster said. "Many of the creatures he's just absorbed go through complete metamorphosis. It is best if he mimics their method of transformation to ensure survival."

Boke Gal scanned Flynn's body. "Based on his size, we will need a large space where he can process tissue for a longer period of time."

Auster leaned forward and placed a hand on Flynn's head. A brief glow emanated from it, then Auster pulled away. Blood oozed from Flynn's ears and nose.

Auster turned to his Sentries. "Take him to the cave." He held up the hand he'd just placed on Flynn. "I will find his offspring and imbue them with his life source."

Fokazi gazed at Flynn. "And then he will be bound to Earth."

FORTY-TWO

Dawn threatened to shatter the darkness as Auster drifted up the San Bernardino Mountains and passed beneath the large, wooden Elkwood Summer Camp sign.

He glided over the cabins spread out over the property, and then slipped though the doors of the massive A-frame building that stood in the center of the complex. The six-foot fireplace was black and cold, the hall surrounding it empty. He floated through the dining room to the cafeteria. A few workers busied themselves, preparing the morning meal.

In a small adjacent room, three camp counselors huddled around a television showing breaking news about a shooting at the Vander Broek wedding. The film cut to a picture of Jonathan Flynn's car, smashed to pieces at the bottom of a cliff.

"How will we tell the children?" a counselor asked the others.

"The police are on their way," another responded. "They know how to handle this."

"Poor kids," the third said. "First, they lose their mother, now this. I hope they're sleeping peacefully. It's the last time they will for a long time."

Auster drifted out of the building and made his way toward the cabins. One by one, he floated through the open windows to read the energy of the sleeping children. Finally, he came across a boy curled into a fetal position.

He is one. Auster scanned the boy.

He's weak. His heart is malformed—but not for long.

Auster hovered above Michael and blanketed him in pale, yellow light.

Michael stirred and then sighed as though he was being comforted.

The light ceased.

Auster rose higher.

Your ailments are gone. You now root a Sentry. May you continue to live so he will.

Auster slipped out of the cabin and wove through several more. Then he came upon Maya.

She is the other.

He scanned her. *You are strong, both physically and in will. Your imbuement will give you strength beyond those of your kind.*

He hovered above and swathed her in light.

Maya roused slightly, stretching both arms above her head. "Whoa…," she mumbled before falling back asleep.

The Sentry is rooted in you now, as well. May you live and be strong.

Auster drifted back outside, where two police cars drove through the camp entrance, shattering the silence as their tires crunched over pine cones on the dirt road.

Sunrise met Auster when he rose into the crisp air and wound through the trees to head back down the mountain.

FORTY-THREE

Anisha stood next to Ben in the break room of Gypsum Ridge Hospital, her attention glued to the television. "I can't believe what I'm seeing."

"Neither can I."

The news coverage cut back and forth between what was being called the "The Vander Broek Wedding Massacre" and footage of Jonathan Flynn's black Lamborghini Diablo, twisted beyond recognition, being hauled up from the rocky coastline.

The camera flashed to a svelte, blonde reporter wearing a yellow suit and bright red lipstick, standing at the entrance to the Vander Broek estate.

> "This is Yvonne Blaire reporting from the estate of diamond mogul Schuyler Vander Broek, where police continue to comb the area searching for clues surrounding the murders of seven people, including Mr. Vander Broek.
>
> "Jonathan Flynn is also reported to have been shot. Officer Trevor Swanson responded to the call and reported sending Flynn to the

hospital after seeing that he'd been hit, but no surrounding hospital has reported that Mr. Flynn was admitted.

"Jonathan Flynn's wife, Danielle, was kidnapped and murdered late last year and Jonathan Flynn was almost fatally wounded when he attempted to exchange ransom for his wife.

"Now let's go to Gypsum Ridge State Beach where Joaquin Santos is there to give you the update. Joaquin?"

The scene cut to a tall, Hispanic male with jet-black hair sprayed so stiff that the coastal breeze lifted the swooping front comb-around off his head in one large piece.

"Thank you, Yvonne. J.T. Flynn drove his Lamborghini Diablo off the cliff behind me late last night after barely escaping death again at the Vander Broek wedding yesterday.

"Envelopes Flynn left behind for family containing letters and final wishes have caused investigators to believe this was a suicide. Police think Flynn made the decision to end his life because he feared for the safety of his children. Jonathan Flynn's body has not yet been recovered."

Anisha ran into the bathroom and threw up her breakfast. *This is horrible, so horrible.*

"You okay?" Ben asked when she returned.

Anisha shrugged. "I can't believe it. I knew Jonathan Flynn, Ben. I *knew* him. He loved his kids more than anything. He doesn't seem like the type of man who would take his own life."

"Look," Ben said. "Flynn's wife was murdered last year and he was almost killed, too. Then he was targeted again last night. He probably figured if he killed himself, his kids will be safe."

Anisha shook her head. "Safe, maybe, but without parents. The Flynns were worth a fortune. The poor things will have relatives fighting over their custody." She hung her head. "No child should go through that."

Ben put his hands on Anisha's shoulders. "Stressing's not good for the baby, Ani. There's nothing you could have done or can do about Jonathan Flynn's decision to launch himself into the sea."

"You're right," Anisha said. "I'll admit I'm glad to be transferring to Thousand Wells right now."

"Me, too," Ben said. "I'm glad you talked me into going with you."

Anisha looped her arm around Ben's. "Let's get away from this television."

"Yeah, fresh air sounds good." Ben led her out of the room and down the hall. "Let's try to focus on something positive, like how you'll look stunning in that lavender dress when you stand as my best woman at the wedding. I can't believe it's next week."

"*Stunning*?" She placed her hands on her swollen belly. "I'm going to look like a purple beach ball."

Ben chuckled. "You're not going to look like a beach ball."

"Okay, an oversized grape, then."

"You're not *that* big, Ani," Ben said. "I'm sure you feel like it, but really, you're not. How's Lamaze?"

"Fine. Frank is still talking *and singing to* my belly because he read that the baby may recognize voices."

Ben bent over to and spoke to Anisha's tummy. "Hey, there, girlfriend, this is your Uncle Ben. I hope you know that you're going to be one decked-out little princess when your Uncle Jacob and I are through with you! AND, just for the record, you're not dating until you're twenty because men are scumbags!"

Anisha chuckled. "Frank will most certainly agree with you on that one."

FORTY-FOUR
FIVE YEARS LATER

Johnny roused enough to notice the pale yellow light. *Am I dead?*

His senses were dull and he couldn't move freely. Parting his lids a smidge, he peered around at the blur. Some sort of milky mucus covered his body. A buzzing sound created a deafening white noise and countless flying and crawling insects skittered on the goo that blanketed him. It smelled of rot. *Oh, god.*

Johnny heard voices, muffled and foreign. As he tried to listen, it occurred to him that he wasn't lying down, but suspended in a fetal position. He managed to open his eyes completely and found himself encased in a rubbery, sheet-like bag. He pressed his face against the flexible fabric, straining to see outside and fighting to stay awake.

The voices grew louder. Johnny could make out two blurry figures several yards away.

"It has been five human years, Auster. He has developed some form, but it does not look human."

Me? Five years? I've been here five years?

Another voice responded. "This is true. He has not taken shape, but he will appear human when the process is complete. Now that his energy had taken root, I will meld him with a vacated human body."

What does that mean? Johnny glanced down at the end of what he thought was his arm. Thousands of tiny insects covered the bulb-shaped flesh in the end of it.

Where's my hand?

Johnny forced himself to turn his neck a bit more. When he saw the rest of his body, he shuddered in disbelief. He was nothing more than lumps of flesh—saddle-like sections of soft tissue clumped together and covered in swarms of minuscule flies, beetles, worms, mites, and ants. He opened his mouth to scream, but no sound came forth.

The voices spoke again.

"It will take a few more sol cycles, Torphis. Two or three should be adequate."

Sol cycles? Years?

Johnny pushed against the sheet, but it barely moved. He glanced down and observed the swirling, insect-infested muck surrounding him. He looked at his deformed body and wondered why he felt no pain.

Shouldn't it hurt?

He felt an insect crawl into his ear. He tried to move but couldn't. He was so, so tired. He drifted back toward oblivion.

I'm dead. That's it. I'm dead, and this is Hell.

FORTY-FIVE

Michael Flynn closed his eyes and moved to the beat as he wove through the crowd at Frederick Olmstead's house.

"There's the guest of honor," Heather Reiser said, taking Michael by the arm and leading him into the living room. She pushed him down on the couch and they made out for a while.

After finishing with Heather, Michael had a brief tryst with Tammy Chandler in the hallway before ambling into the kitchen for a few more shots. He scanned the booze on the center island and snatched up a bottle of scotch.

Frederick stumbled into the kitchen and bellied up to the counter. He cast Michael a sideways glance. "Hey, birthday boy."

"Yep, that's me." Michael grabbed a plastic tumbler. "Me and my sis." He poured a few glugs of the whiskey and eyed the amber liquid. "Wilks said my old man used to love this shit." He held up the drink. "To my old man, who sailed off a fuckin' cliff five years ago." He belted it back.

"Don't go there, man," Frederick said. "Think positive. You only turn nineteen once. Don't fuck it up for yourself. Maya's still at the Olympic trials?"

"Yep, talked to her this morning. She spent our birthday doing timed sprints. And breaking world records." He glanced around. "Shit, I either lost a contact, or it's moved to the back of my eye."

Just then, William Ingelhart strode into the kitchen. "World records, huh?" he said to Michael. "How about you? You going for the world record in number of days drunk off your ass?"

Michael flipped him off and belted back a shot.

Ingelhart chuckled. "Hey, Flynn, let's see if the running thing is familial. How 'bout if we race?"

Michael flipped him off again. "Aren't there a couple of crack whores you can go score with right now?"

Frederick busted up.

"Come on, asswipe!" Ingelhart said to Michael. "If your sister's training for the Olympics, you can at least run around the frickin' block. Let's put twenty on it to make it interesting."

Michael pushed his cup forward and sized up Ingelhart. "Okay, whorefucker, I'll take that bet."

Word spread through the party like wildfire. Five minutes after Michael had agreed to the dare, he stood beside Ingelhart in the middle of the street. Fellow partygoers lined the curbs.

Frederick faced them. "Okay, guys, no red-lighting! Take off when I say 'go.' Got it?"

"Got it!" Ingelhart shouted.

Michael gave a thumbs-up. "Got it!"

"Okay. On your mark, get set..." Frederick stood tall, arms raised. Dropping them, he yelled, "GO!"

Michael and Ingelhart took off down the dark street. The drunken onlookers howled and cheered.

Michael pumped his legs as hard as he could. He looked ahead and focused on the streetlight at the end of the block.

I don't care if my legs fall off, I'm going to beat this fuck.

He didn't slow, didn't stop, didn't relent until he passed the street lamp. Then he turned around and stared behind him.

What the hell?

Ingelhart was so far behind he hadn't even passed the halfway point. Michael put his hand to his chest.

No burn. No pain.

He waited until Ingelhart reached him.

"What the fuck?" Ingelhart doubled over and planted his hands on his knees as he panted. "*You* should be trying out for the Olympics, man. That was fast."

They walked back toward the party together. Michael was stone-cold sober.

I need to call Maya.

∞∞∞∞∞∞

Dr. Harrick held up Michael's X-ray the following week. "It's a miracle. Not only does your heart look normal, but it's functioning the same as a professional athlete's." The doctor swept back the few strands of gray hair he had left. "The scar tissue is gone."

"*Gone*? Are you sure?" Michael glanced at Paula, who sat on a stool in the corner of the exam room.

"Yes." Dr. Harrick seemed bewildered. "But I want to run a few more tests, just to be sure."

"Must be all the great meals you make, Paula," Michael said with a grin.

Paula patted Michael's arm. "Well, you'd better learn how to make some yourself since you're going to live away at school next year. You'll need fuel for all of the required reading."

"Speaking of which," Michael pinched the bridge of his nose. "These new contacts are giving me a headache."

"I'll put in a request for your vision to be checked again while we're at it." The doctor sat down to type notes into Michael's file on the computer. "You may need a weaker prescription, again."

Michael watched the doctor type away for a moment, then glanced up at the X-ray. *How can this be?*

∞∞∞∞∞∞

Four weeks later, Michael finished first overall at the Gypsum Ridge annual summer 10k, running a little under a six-minute pace. *I can't fucking believe this. It didn't even faze me. I've never in my life been able to run for a period of time, much less at this speed.*

He didn't stay to receive his medal or walk through the sponsor tents. He got into his red Lamborghini Diablo and sped home. He had to shower and grab his bag before he, Paula, and Wilks flew overseas to watch Maya compete in the Olympics.

FORTY-SIX

Maya sat in the locker room after her afternoon session on the Olympic track field. She'd broken two more world records the previous day, both of which had been held by men.

Michael's call that morning had sent her mind running as well. "My body's healed itself, Maya!" he had cried in ecstasy. "I don't know how, but doc says my heart is completely normal. And my eyes—I don't need contacts anymore."

Hearing Paula's warm voice made Maya smile. "He's outrunning everyone around here, my dear. There might be another Flynn on the Olympic team at the rate Michael's going."

Maya toed off her shoes and stared at her stocking feet. *What's going on with us?* Her mind drifted back to her own doctor visit during her junior year of high school.

"Read the bottom line," the doctor had requested, pointing to a strip of letters on a square chart.

Maya had covered her left eye and read the line flawlessly then repeated the process covering the right eye.

"From 20/20 to 20/0. That's amazing. If you want to be a sharp shooter, you sure got the orbs, kiddo." He glanced at her chart. "You grew another inch this year. You must be eating your greens. I wish more teens were as fit and healthy as you are."

Maya laughed uncomfortably as the doctor scribbled some notes on her clipboard.

Leaving the clinic, Maya spotted her teammate, Kara, in an exam room across the hall. Maya caught a glimpse of the same eye chart, focused on the bottom line, and could read it perfectly from where she stood, thirty feet away.

Maya was jolted from her memory as she felt someone pat her on the back.

"Miracle Maya!" shouted Coach Tina. "That's what everyone's calling you now. Pretty cool, huh? Go rest up. Tomorrow you have more records to break."

Maya returned to her room and collapsed onto the bed to nap before the evening's festivities. She turned on the television to unwind, but a sense of unease crept through her when she saw a news story of *Miracle Maya's* record-breaking sprints. She flipped though more channels to find her story on almost every newscast. She paused on one station and listened as the reporter listed the number of records she had broken the past year. The news following, however, made Maya's blood run cold.

"Miracle Maya is a fitting name for this young lady. Maya Flynn is the daughter of Diamond King Jonathan Flynn, who, just over five years ago, took his own life by driving off a cliff after fleeing the infamous Vander Broek Wedding Massacre, where seven people, including Schuyler Vander Broek, were shot dead.

"Mr. Flynn left suicide notes stating he feared for the safety of his children, especially after the brutal murder of his wife, Maya's mother, Danielle Flynn, the year prior."

Throughout the news report, photos flashed of Maya during her childhood, with her family, and with friends.

Such vultures. Why do they always focus on life's horrors? And how did those ghouls even get those pictures?

Maya shut off the television and threw the remote across the room, tears welling in her eyes. "The press sucks," she said aloud.

I just want to run. It's what I'm good at, it's what I enjoy. Why don't they just leave me alone?

∞∞∞∞∞∞

The reception for the American Olympic team was held at the United States Embassy. Maya felt out of character as she mingled with other athletes and government officials. As usual, Maya avoided alcohol but decided to indulge in a soda as she circulated through the room. She noticed two men in black suits looking her way. One man was very tall with jet-black hair, the other stockier and balding.

As the evening continued, Maya kept noticing them eyeing her.

Must be security.

Halfway through the event, the men finally approached her.

"Good evening, Ms. Flynn," the taller man said.

"Good evening." Maya glanced from one to the other. "You're guarding us, right?"

"Not exactly," the stocky man answered. "We're here to speak with you."

"With *me*?" She was taken aback. "Are you with the press?"

"No." The tall man chuckled. "We'd like to discuss a possible career for you."

Maya couldn't believe it. "Career? That's not even on my radar right now. I'm kinda busy."

"We realize that," the tall man responded. "Ms. Flynn, you have the ability to break all of the world's running records you're setting out to do. If that is your desire, we wish you all the best."

"Of course it's my desire." Maya felt frustration building. "I've been dreaming about the Olympics since I was ten years old."

"After the games, you will be thrust into the public eye for the rest of your life," the stocky man added. "Your achievements, your history…your family."

Maya thought of the news reports and felt her face get hot. "That's already happening now."

"It'll get worse," the tall man said. "You'll have zero privacy after this. You don't strike us as the type who would be satisfied with a life consisting of photo shoots and cereal endorsements. And you certainly don't need the money."

Maya was offended. "I'm not doing this for fame or money."

"But that's what you'll get." The tall man stepped closer. "There are much better ways to use your unique gifts, Maya Flynn. What if I told you that you could travel the world with a purpose, use your gifts to help in ways you've never thought possible?"

"I don't understand what you mean." Maya took a step back.

"We're saying that your life as an Olympian is finite. Your records will end up in the history books, but your time on the track will end, and you'll spend the rest of your career in front of a television camera and a microphone."

"If you join us," the stocky man added, "you will have a lifetime of experiences. And you may also find answers to some unresolved questions about your family's past."

Maya's mouth suddenly felt dry. "I need some water. Excuse me." She split from the men and strode toward the refreshment table. She filled a glass with cool water, chugged it, and then refilled it.

Okay, this is kinda creepy. Maya took a deep breath and glanced around. Her coaches and teammates clustered in groups around the room, chatting and smiling. She looked at the men, nestled in the crowd and talking to each other. The tall one looked over and smiled at her.

I have to know.

Maya strode back to the men. "Who are you?"

The stocky man gestured toward the United States flag in the corner of the room.

"You work for the government?"

"That's correct. If what we're saying piques your interest at all, meet us in the private lounge of your hotel on the tenth floor at eleven o'clock, and we'll be able to answer any questions you have more openly."

Maya narrowed her eyes. "Why get me alone? Why won't you answer my questions now, with everyone around?"

"Certain departments are more classified than others, Ms. Flynn. We don't discuss what we do in this type of atmosphere. If you need assurance about our status of employ, you may speak with the Ambassador. She has been apprised of our intent to approach you. She'll verify our purpose and support any actions necessary to transfer you to your new position, *if* you accept our offer."

"Your offer?"

"Meet us at eleven and we'll give you the details." The tall man held out his hand. "It was a pleasure meeting you."

"Yeah." Maya shook their hands and watched them walk away.

She scanned the room and saw the ambassador chatting with one of the coaches of the swim team. Maya crossed the room and the ambassador acknowledged her immediately.

"I recognize you," she said. "You've already made quite a name for yourself, Maya Flynn."

"Thank you, Ms. Ambassador," Maya replied. The three engaged in small talk, then the swim coach excused himself for the evening.

"I was hoping I could have a minute of your time, Ms. Ambassador," Maya said when they were alone.

"I figured you would. Why don't we go to my office?"

∞∞∞∞∞∞∞∞

In her room that night, the conversations she'd had at the embassy hummed through Maya's mind at breakneck speed. *The government wants me? And the Ambassador knew? Does Coach know? Should I show up to this meeting at eleven?*

She glanced at her watch: *Ten-thirty.*

Maya flipped on the TV, hoping to unwind and clear her thoughts. She surfed around, stopping on a news channel just in time to see footage of *Miracle Maya's* record breaking 220-yard dash, then a picture of her mother one year before she was killed, and then a shot of Michael drunk at some Hollywood event. Maya gritted her teeth. *Fucking vultures.*

∞∞∞∞∞∞

The tenth-floor lounge was reserved for VIPs who wanted a private moment away from the cameras and microphones. Maya wore plain sweats she'd brought from home and pulled her hoodie forward enough to hide her face.

The lounge was nearly empty, except for the bartender and the two men she'd met earlier, sitting at a table tucked away in a far corner of the room.

Maya reached the table and the two men rose to greet her.

"Thank you for coming, Ms. Flynn," the tall man said. "I'm Daniel." He gestured toward the other man. "This is Mark."

"Hi."

The men ordered mineral water while Maya stuck with a non-carbonated.

Mark laced his fingers together. "So, our proposition intrigued you?"

Maya nodded. "I spoke with the ambassador and I know you work for the government. What exactly do you want with me?"

Daniel wrapped his fingers around his glass. "Let's just say, Ms. Flynn, that instead of returning to American soil with gold medals around your neck, we're hoping you'd be willing to serve your country in a very different way."

"Did you contact my brother as well?"

Daniel shook his head. "Your brother has a constant need for public attention—flashy cars, high-profile events, famous friends. It doesn't suit this type of work Don't you agree?"

Maya thought of Michael. *They're right.*

"He's also not qualified," Mark added. "Only a select few are cut out for what we do. You, on the other hand, first got our attention several years back after state time trials. And now, here we are."

Maya thought for a moment, then picked up her water and leaned back. "Okay, I'm listening."

∞∞∞∞∞∞

During the following morning's workout, surrounded by cameras and news media, Maya ran through a series of practice drills. Each sprint was clocked at world record-breaking time.

"Great!" Coach Tina said. "Two more."

Maya nodded, did a few stretches, then trotted back to the starting line. *Okay. Time's coming soon.*

She crouched to the ready position and waited for the starting gun.

POW.

Maya sprang forward then collapsed to the ground, holding her foot.

Coach ran up. "What is it?"

"My ankle!" Maya cried.

Cameras flashed as reporters tried to get the perfect shot of the stretcher carrying Miracle Maya off of the track.

"It's going to be okay," Coach Tina said as Maya was wheeled to the infirmary.

In the exam room, Maya took deep breaths, steeling her resolve. *This is the right choice. Isn't it?*

When a tall woman with curly black hair walked in, Coach Tina stared at her in shock. "Who are *you*? Where's Dr. Lawrence?"

"He was called away for a family emergency. I'm his supervisor, Dr. Gwendolyn Feronia." She shot Maya a faint smile.

She's in on it, Maya thought.

"Let's see what we have." Dr. Feronia removed the ice pack from the back of Maya's foot. "Can you pivot your foot up and down?"

Maya gritted her teeth in pain. "No. It hurts really bad."

Dr. Feronia examined the foot, but Maya screamed in pain when the doctor reached her ankle.

Dr. Feronia shook her head and pointed to the injured area. "It's not looking good."

Coach Tina's jaw dropped. "You've *got* to be shitting me!"

∞∞∞∞∞∞

The news coverage of *Miracle Maya's* removal from the Olympic Games due to a torn Achilles tendon spread across the globe in record time. Her riches-to-rags tale was the top story nationwide.

To avoid unwanted attention, Maya returned to the States with Michael, Paula, and Wilks before the games began. When she arrived home, she was given a hero's welcome by the press. The mayor of Gypsum Ridge held a small ceremony at City Hall, declaring the day Maya arrived home Maya Flynn Day in honor of her amazing contribution to the Olympic team.

Maya needed Michael's help to make it up to the podium.

She gazed out at the crowd gathered in the auditorium. "Thank you very much for this great honor. If you had asked me where I would be today, I would have answered, 'Running for the Gold.' Maya's voice broke. She paused. "But sometimes life has other plans. I'm grateful for the experience I had with the team, and I will forever support them."

The crowd applauded.

"And when I leave here, I'm going home, turning on the TV, and rooting for the USA!"

The crowd cheered as Maya hobbled from the stage.

That night, Maya popped some corn before the opening ceremonies started on TV. She hopped over the back of the couch and sat with her legs crossed, glancing at her 'bad foot' before she tucked it under her bum. A wave of relief swept over her when the final runner lit the Olympic torch.

The games will eclipse my story of woe.

There were a few blips on her emotional radar during the ceremony, and she wept openly when the USA marched onto the field. But the men were right. Maya was, for the most part, forgotten.

Those who burn bright fade quickly.

∞∞∞∞∞∞

A week later, Maya watched the American flag rise to the top of the arena as her teammate took gold. A twinge of regret turned to tears, as had happened several times before.

That was my dream. What the hell did I do?

Maya reached over and placed a hand on the large clasp envelope which contained the details of her new life. Her mind swirled with all of the information Daniel and Mark had given the evening before she suffered the "career-ending injury." She opened the envelope, pulled out the contents, and reread the first page again. She glanced back up at the television as the American flag rose to the sound of the National Anthem.

A fair trade? Maya's tears slowed. *I think so.*

FORTY-SEVEN

Anisha Patel Corby heard a crash. *Oh, no!* She hurried into the kitchen to find her husband and four-year-old daughter covered in finger paint and laughing hysterically.

"Kathleen Anjali Corby! What did you do?"

Frank grinned. "It was me. We made a teeter-totter with the tins of paint and Katie hit one side really hard."

"It flew and spilled all over me and Daddy," Katie said.

Anisha pressed her lips together to try to keep from smiling, but as she watched blue paint drip from her daughter's long curls, it was no use. She giggled and said, "Just look at you both." She patted her swollen belly. "I'm going to have *three* babies in the house."

"Who, me?" Frank wiped a smatter of green paint from his chin, then stood up and dabbed a dot of it on Anisha's nose. "I'm exposing our daughter to the arts." He gave her a peck on the cheek.

"Mommy's got paint on her nose," Katie sang.

"Well, Mommy had to fit in with you and Daddy." Anisha bent down and took Katie's hand. "Now, miss artist, let's get you in the tub, and then it's nap time. I don't want to eat dinner with a grumpy, tired little girl."

"I don't wanna take a nap," Katie said. "I'm a big girl."

"Yes, you are a very big girl. But how is your baby brother going to learn about naps if you don't teach him?"

"You teach him!"

Frank laughed.

Anisha whispered in his direction, "Don't encourage her!"

Frank got up and took Katie's other hand. "Why don't we make a deal? Pretty soon, you're going to turn five years old and get to go to school, isn't that right, Mommy?" He glanced at Anisha.

She nodded. "Yes. And when you go to school, you won't have to take a nap in the afternoon any more. How does that sound?"

Katie nodded. "Okay."

Anisha gazed at Frank as they ushered Katie to the bathroom. "The arts, huh?"

"Well-rounded exposure."

Anisha raised an eyebrow. "And today was tactile exposure, I take it?"

"Bingo!" Frank flashed a cheeky grin as he edged past her into the bathroom and turned on the tub water.

∞∞∞∞∞∞

Anisha shared Frank's art lesson with Ben and Anjali as they tooled through the local department store the following day.

"I think it's fabulous that Frank's making art fun for her at such an early age," Ben said.

"That man is too funny." Anjali held up a blue quilted handbag. "Country chic?"

Ben mimicked a gag. "More like country bumpkin, honey."

They all chuckled and moved along the aisle. When the children's clothing section came into view, Anjali burst into a trot.

"Hey, I can't do that." Anisha waddled forward.

"What about this for school?" Anjali pulled a dress off the rack and displayed it. "Katie will look darling in it."

"Lovely," Ben marched forward. "I think Uncles Ben and Jacob need to get her something for when the weather cools down."

"You two are buying that little girl more clothes than we have."

"And I'm loving every minute of it." Anjali tossed the dress into the cart.

"As am I." Ben draped two more outfits over the edge of the basket. "You can't know how fun it is to spoil that beautiful little girl. Shall we go get a few things for William Rakesh?"

Anisha glanced down at her tummy. "He's a month away from being born and already he has a full wardrobe."

"And the baby shower is all ready to go," Ben said. "Jacob pulled some strings and the caterer is providing tablescapes and cuisine that are gonna rock your world."

"I can hardly wait." Anisha's smile faded as she turned to her sister. "Mom and Dad are coming, right?"

"Yes." Anjali took over pushing the cart. "And when you announced William's name last week, Father was thrilled that he is getting a namesake."

"Really? I wouldn't know." Anisha's smile disappeared. "I don't really have access to him, do I?"

"Trust me, sister, the man is beside himself with joy. You see how he fawns over Katie every time you visit."

This brought Anisha's smile back. "Yes, *he* does seem to adore her."

"Mother loves her, too, Ani."

"Not like she will love your children. She doesn't even try to hide her looks of disapproval."

"Okay, stop right there." Ben stood in front of the cart. Taking a deep breath, he took hold of Anisha's shoulders. "I've said this before, and I'm saying it again. You must stop trying to work through *why* your mother doesn't approve of you. She doesn't. She won't. Maybe she can't, even."

Anisha swept a tear away.

"Take it from the gay son of ultra-religious parents. The approval you're searching for, that which only a parent can give." He leaned close to Anisha's face. "She'll *never* give it to you. *Ever.* You had the audacity to be the person you really are, instead of who she wanted you to be. In her eyes, that's treason."

"I know." Anisha turned to Anjali. "Sometimes I feel guilty, because you've been thrown in the middle of this."

"I don't blame you, sister." Anjali turned to Ben. "Was it tough when you came out to your parents?"

Ben moved around the cart and wrapped an arm around Anjali. "Little sister, that day is tattooed in my mind forever. It *still* hurts, twenty years later. When I married Jacob, did you see my parents anywhere?"

"No." Anjali leaned into him. "But we were there."

"Yes, you were, and so was Ani, Frank, and little Katie—sort of."

"Oh, she was there all right," Anisha said. "Kicking the heck out of me, I might add."

"Okay, so on to the baby clothes, little sisters." Ben put an arm around Anjali. "See what you get when you go shopping with a woman who's eight months pregnant and a gay guy with emotional baggage?"

"No fooling. It's like we're part of a reality show." Anjali took Anisha's hand. "Come, sister, it's time to continue our retail therapy."

FORTY-EIGHT
THREE YEARS LATER

Johnny woke to the sound of his own breath, heaving in and out and echoing off the walls of what felt like a rubber sheet encasing him. The tepid goo had receded, immersing him only to the calves. His senses were more alert. He noticed a crescent-shaped light source in front of him. He peered down at his body. It seemed normal—thin, but not deformed as before.

He lifted an arm and wiggled his fingers, which responded immediately. He bent his wrist in all directions. Success. He went through the process of moving his feet and shifting his legs, but when he stirred the muck covering them, it sent up a noxious odor, causing him to gag. He tried to twist his body, then froze when he felt himself sway.

I'm dangling in the air. How?

Movement in the yellow glow outside startled him. He recalled the voices he'd heard several times before.

He raised his arms over his head, pushed against the flexible material, and then he heard a tear. *Oh, no.*

Johnny's casing split in two and he plummeted to the ground, slamming onto the rocky soil. A sharp pain ripped up his spine as the slimy substance he had slept in spilled from above, drenching him in liquid foulness that he could only compare to sewage.

He retched, let out a weak squeal, and curled up on the ground in a fetal position, breathing deeply and listening to the rasp of his own breath. The air smelled of damp soil.

I'm supposed to be dead. Why does it hurt if I'm dead?

Johnny sensed movement around him. He lifted his head to see four blurry figures standing farther inside what appeared to be a cave.

A young, muscular blond man stepped forward. "How does your body feel?"

Johnny pushed off with his arms and sat up. "Okay, I guess." He was shocked to hear the deep, guttural voice resonating from his own throat. "Where am I?"

"Try to get up," the blond commanded.

Like an infant, Johnny got to his hands and knees and rocked back and forth, then placed his feet on the ground one at a time. Legs shaking beneath his weight, Johnny slowly went from a front bend to standing straight.

"Your new form suits you," said another man, tall and lean with jet-black hair.

Johnny looked down at his own thin frame; tan-skinned and caked with goo. The slimy mucus covering his body was quickly drying into a dark, clay-like substance. He noticed his genitals and made a gesture to cover them, but the fatigue made him sway and he had to extend both arms to maintain his balance. *Where am I? What's going on? I can't steady my thoughts. I'm tired. So tired.*

"Go ahead and sit down," the blond said.

Johnny obliged.

"What was the last thing you remember?"

"I drove off the cliff. I remember the rocks, the water." he paused. "The kelp, and the smell...the bugs." He glanced around. "Where am I?"

"In South America. I discovered this small alcove under a cliff long ago. I brought you here and you've been—healing for quite some time."

"I thought I was dead."

"You were, but not anymore. I brought you back. You have things to do."

Johnny stared at the blond in disbelief. "You brought me back? What does that mean? Who are you?"

"That will be answered in time." The blond laced his fingers together. "Your attention should be drawn to who *you* are now. It's best if you sleep for a while outside of your chrysalis to get used to the environment. Then you'll be ready to leave."

"My chrysalis?"

Johnny glanced above. What appeared to be a large cocoon, dripping with yellow mucus, hung from the arched top of the cavern. A wave of exhaustion swept through him and he had no choice but to lie down. The blond pointed to the giant case that had held Johnny. A flash of light shot from his hand to the spun strand that connected it to the top of the cave. It splattered to the ground like a soggy blanket.

"Rest now. We will return at next light."

Too tired to protest, Johnny closed his eyes and drifted off to sleep.

∞∞∞∞∞∞

Johnny woke to the sound of rain. His dried cocoon covered him for warmth, but the ground was still cold and hard. He sat up and the dehydrated, vascular material crunched like rice paper as he pushed it away.

He got up with ease and took a few cautious steps. Registering a tickle in his ear, he reached up and felt something inside.

He shook his head violently and three small beetles dropped to the ground, scuttling off in different directions.

Eww.

He trudged to the cave entrance and saw that he was standing under a dome-shaped rock formation set high on a mountainside that overlooked a lush tapestry of green.

"The Amazon is one of nature's great achievements, don't you agree?"

Johnny spun around to see the blond man sitting cross-legged on the cave floor behind him. *How did he get there?*

"You're looking well," he said. "I've found this particular spot to be a great place to rest. It is both inaccessible and relatively invisible to humans."

"Humans?" Johnny walked toward him. "You're not human?"

"No."

"Who, or what, are you, then?"

"I am Auster." He reached behind his back, retrieved a bundle of clothes, and rose. "You look strong. I believe we can begin your training. I'll call to the others." He tossed the bundle toward Johnny. "Seems to be timeless attire."

Johnny unfolded it to reveal a pair of jeans, a white T-shirt, socks, and plain tennis shoes. He felt a wave of anger and confusion flood him as he dressed.

Training? What the fuck is going on?

Johnny bent down to tie his shoes and heard a strange rumbling outside. At first, he dismissed it as thunder, but the constant, wind-like grumble grew louder. He turned to Auster. "What the hell is that?"

"The Sentries are coming."

Johnny took several steps toward the mouth of the cave and froze. "What the…" He shielded his eyes with one hand then planted the other against the cave wall to keep from falling. What appeared to be a colossal gust of soil swept past him into the cavern.

Johnny gaped in amazement as the cloud took the shapes of three men.

"I'm dreaming." Johnny slumped against the cave wall to support himself.

"You are not." Auster gestured toward a tall, svelte, black-haired man with pale skin. "I'd like you to meet Torphis."

Torphis bowed slightly. "Good afternoon."

Sounds like he's from England.

Torphis nodded toward a bald, muscular, African man. "This is Fokazi."

"It is a pleasure," Fokazi said in an accent Johnny couldn't place. Fokazi turned to a fit, Asian man with long, black hair pulled back into a ponytail. "And this is Boke Gal."

The man nodded once and said, "Greetings." Johnny didn't recognize his accent, either. Boke Gal took two steps forward. "Sit. You are about to receive a lot of information."

Johnny sank down and sat cross-legged on the hard ground. Thoughts swirled through his head like a tornado. *Someone—or something—claimed to have brought me back from the dead and I just saw dust turn into men. This can't be real.*

"You have questions, I can tell," Auster said.

"Yes, many."

"I will begin by explaining our purpose, which is now yours."

Johnny listened as Auster explained the steps involved in the creation of Hands and Sentries.

Johnny had to fight to keep his composure. *This is insane.*

Torphis then went on to explain how all of this is done for the purpose of reading Auster's life source in order to exterminate his descendants.

Johnny sat speechless. His gaze drifted across the four faces as Fokazi finished telling him something about light.

This is fucking nuts. He held up a hand. "So, what you're saying is, you brought me back to life using someone else's life energy."

"Many others, in your case," Auster said.

"You are unique, to say the least," Fokazi added.

Johnny ran his fingers through his hair. "I don't understand what you mean by *many others.*"

"It took many life forms to create your new body." Auster stepped forward. "I used what was available—millions of insects."

"Insects?" The thought made Johnny's stomach churn.

"Their life force sustained you," Auster answered. "And when your life force was strong enough, I integrated a human form to give you a normal appearance."

"How in the hell did you do that?"

"I took a freshly deceased body and melded it with the mass created by the other life forms."

Johnny stared forward. "My body was someone else's?"

"Yes. He had lived for thirty-four years."

"How did he die?"

"Motorcycle accident."

Johnny held up his arm and stared at it.

What the fuck?

The muscular, pale forearm Johnny had always known as his own was now tan, sinewy, and hairier. He let it drop to his side. "So, I'm sitting in a cave in South America, you brought me back to life using insects and then stuck me in a dead guy's body, and my new *purpose* is to kill your relatives, who I will locate with some ability you intend to bestow upon me?"

Auster looked at the others, who seemed pleased. "That is correct. But you will be more than just a Hand."

"Hands do the killing?" Johnny asked.

"That's all they do," Torphis said. "They locate and kill. You will be a Sentry. You will wield light."

Johnny pointed to himself. "I'm a Sentry?"

"Not yet," Auster said. "You must prove yourself worthy."

Johnny glanced down at his unfamiliar body. "I realize that this," he held up his arms, "is not what I looked like before the crash. But you have to realize that what you're telling me—"

"Sounds absurd," Auster finished.

"Absurd?" Johnny huffed. "No. It's more like, these-whack-jobs-need-to-be-kept-away-from-the-rest-of-society-crazy! You honestly expect me to believe all of this?"

"We speak the truth." Boke Gal said with a sneer.

Torphis smiled. "We understand that this is a lot to lay upon one frail human psyche. Each of us went through what you are experiencing."

Johnny got up and stumbled forward. "This has to be a crazy dream or something." He coughed and a plume of small insects flew out of his mouth. His jaw dropped as he watched them scurry or fly away.

"I don't understand why the insects still live," Torphis commented.

"Nor do I," Auster said. "They must have continually laid eggs throughout his regeneration."

Johnny gaped at Auster and Torphis and then slapped his own face. "Come on, wake up!" He screamed to himself.

Auster smiled. "What can I do to convince you this is very real and you are *not* dreaming?"

"I wanna see my kids!" Johnny could feel himself shaking.

Boke Gal crossed his arms. "They would not recognize you. You have a different body."

"Eight human years have passed," Torphis added.

"What?" Johnny vaguely recalled the conversation he overheard when he was suspended in the rubber casing filled with goo. "Eight years! No, it can't be."

"It is true," Auster said. "The method you chose to end your life caused a problem with your regeneration. You had virtually no body onto which I could attach a life force. It took much longer to bring you back than any before you."

"Eight years. So my kids are twenty-two?"

"Yes," Auster answered. "Your daughter is in Europe finishing her education, and your son still resides in California."

"That can't be. No fucking way!" Johnny planted his hands down to steady himself.

I'm fuzz-brained. None of this makes sense.

Torphis turned to Auster. "Clearly, he needs to see it for himself. As with every other Sentry, he will have to revisit his past life to learn the truth."

Boke Gal faced the others. "Fellow Sentries, we've cast our eyes upon the new candidate, spoken in unity, and told him of his destiny, as tradition states."

"Yes," Fokazi said. "Shall we read him now?"

Auster regarded his three Sentries. "Yes. I'll join you."

The four faced Johnny.

Torphis held up a hand. "Please stand still."

Johnny felt his skin crawl as the four individuals, standing frozen as a single force, appeared to enter some type of meditative state. They seemed to look right through him. Then, as if some unseen, unheard signal was given, they broke out of the trance and the three Sentries bowed toward Auster.

"We will meet again when it is time to discuss his worthiness to receive the light."

Boke Gal shot Johnny a disapproving glare. "*If* he reaches that stage."

Johnny watched in astonishment as, one by one, the three Sentries dissolved back into floating debris.

Are they mist? Or dust? Smoke, perhaps?

The mass of floating debris rose to the top of the cave and wisped through the opening.

Johnny turned to Auster. "This *is* a nightmare. It has to be."

"I will prove that it is not," Auster said. "You've requested to see your children."

"Yes," Johnny said.

"How about if we go back to the place where you took your own life? There are many familiar things there that will convince you."

"Back to Gypsum Ridge? Yeah, take me there."

"As you wish," Auster said. "Since you cannot change form yet, I will have to take you myself. And you will have to sleep." He raised a hand and sent a ray of light into Johnny's chest.

The light released a warm sensation that radiated into every muscle in Johnny's body. Finding it difficult to stay upright, he teetered over and curled onto his side. *Whoa.*

As he drifted toward sleep, Johnny saw Auster turn to mist, then felt the pull of being lifted from the ground.

FORTY-NINE

Anisha bustled around the kitchen. "Hurry, he'll be home soon! Where are the plates?"

"You put them out already." Anjali said as she cut up tomatoes for the salad. "Katie, why don't you open the party hats?"

"Okay!" Katie rushed from the room.

Anisha checked the oven. "Mostaccioli looks great. Should be ready in about fifteen."

"Still his favorite, huh?" Anjali asked.

"Yep. It was the first thing he cooked for me and he still loves it."

Anjali put her hand on Anisha's tummy. "Well, with baby number three on the way, he's going to be cooking a bit more."

"No doubt, I'll need the help." Anisha looked down at herself. "I think my tummy popped out a lot sooner this time. I feel so big already."

"You look radiant, sister," Anjali said. "And I can hardly wait to hold another baby."

Little William trotted into the room wearing a purple *happy birthday* hat.

"Well, look at you, all ready for the party." Anisha picked him up. "Wow, you're getting heavy."

"Mommy, Daddy coming home to the party?"

"Yes, he'll be home very soon." Anisha kissed his forehead.

"My birthday soon."

"Yes. And how old will you be?"

"Free!"

"Yes," Anisha held up three fingers. "You will be three years old. And we will have a party for you, too, but today is Daddy's birthday, so we're having a party for him."

"And we have cake."

"Yes, let's go look at Daddy's cake."

Anisha put William down, took his hand, and led him into the dining room. She pointed to the tray beside the table where a double chocolate sheet cake with blue piped edges sat. The words *Happy Birthday Daddy* were written across the top. "You see Daddy's cake?"

"I wrote happy birthday daddy," Katie chirped.

"And you did a wonderful job," Anisha said.

William clapped. "Daddy's cake."

Anjali walked in with a stack of salad bowls. "It looks awesome!"

"Courtesy of Ben," Anisha said. "With Katie's embellishments."

"Of course. Are you waiting to put the candles on?"

"I'll put them on now." Anisha turned to Katie. "Want to help?"

"Yes! I'll go get them." Katie ran into the kitchen. "Where are they?"

Anisha turned to Anjali. "Are they still in a bag?"

"I didn't bring any. You don't have any here?"

"Shoot! No." Anisha planted her hands on her hips. "We can't have a birthday cake without candles. I'll run to the store."

"You don't have time," Anjali said. "Frank will be home any minute. I'll go."

"Okay. Don't go all the way to Thousand Wells market. It's quickest to go to the liquor store just inside of town, on the corner of Grand and Amethyst."

"Where? I have no idea—"

"Just let me go." Anisha ran to the entry. "I'll be ten minutes, max."

William ran after Anisha. "I wanna go!"

"No, William, Mommy must hurry. You wait here with Aunty."

"I wanna go with MOMMY!" William screamed. He began to cry.

"Oh, my goodness." Anisha grabbed her purse and keys, then picked up William. "Looks like ten minutes will be closer to fifteen. Take the mostaccioli out when it beeps."

"Got it," Anjali said. "Katie, want to help me finish setting the table? We still have to put out the napkins."

"Yeah!" Katie hopped up and down. "Hurry, Mommy."

"We'll be back in a flash." Anisha rushed through the door with William in her arms. She fastened him into the car seat, belted herself in, and started the engine.

"Ani!" Anjali stood on the porch holding up a cell phone. "You forgot your phone. Ben's calling!"

Anisha waved her off. "Tell him I'll call him back in a few minutes." She threw the car into gear and backed out of the driveway.

FIFTY

Dick Brickford sat behind his desk at the Thousand Wells Police Department, spinning the wedding ring on his finger as he read the next ten pages of Helen's manuscript.

He checked his watch. "Crap. Lunch time's almost over." He marked his page, jumped up, and hurried back into the break room. "Time got away from me."

His new partner, Jason Brady, watched as Brickford opened the fridge and pulled out his container of chicken and broccoli.

"Pussy food!" Brady blurted out.

"No." Brickford patted his flat stomach. "It's food that *gets* ya pussy, rookie!"

"Awe, shut the hell up."

"I'm not kiddin'. I've lost sixty-five pounds by avoiding junk like that!" He lifted his chin toward the fast-food bag sitting in front of Brady.

Brady stood and crumpled his sandwich wrappers into a ball. "So, *Dick the Brick* is now *Dick the Slick*." He chuckled.

"You bet your ass, rookie!" Brickford popped the plastic into the microwave. "Hey, have you heard anything on that shooting the other night at the liquor store? I wanna know if we have the ballistics on it yet."

"You talking about the Glock that put that three-year-old in a coma?"

"Yeah, that's the one."

"The thing's been rubbed clean of serial numbers." Brady glanced at the ceiling. "Freaking animal, shooting a kid while his mother held him. What a monster."

"Yeah," Brickford said. "Which is why I want the damn ballistics."

"Why you so interested? It's just a piece put together by some homeless junkie who knew how to assemble."

Brickford cocked his head. "You know why."

Brady tossed the wrapper into the trash. "Look. There's no way the barrel in that Glock is the same one that put a bullet in Schuyler Vander Broek's head eight years ago. No fucking way."

The microwave dinged and Brickford took out his food. "Ballistics don't lie, rookie." He pulled a fork out of the drawer. "If that's the barrel, I need to know where the junkie got it."

Brady shook his head and held up an index finger. "*First of all*, the junkie won't remember. Dude can't even remember five minutes ago, much less eight years ago." He held up another finger. "*Second*, if you *do* find the location where the barrel was found, so fuckin' what? It could have been moved a hundred times in eight years before ending up in that gun."

Brickford shoveled in a mound of chicken. "Bullshit. The wear from barrel to slide indicates that the gun has been assembled for a while. Even if the junkie didn't put the gun together himself, I might be able to backtrack it to the guy who did and find out where *he* got the barrel."

Brady sat back down and grabbed his soda. "It's a long shot. Honestly, I think you're spinnin' your wheels."

"Maybe, but I have a hunch."

"About the trace on the barrel?"

"Yep." Brickford shoveled in another bite.

"Where do you think it came from?"

He didn't answer.

Brady hit the table with his palm. "Come on, man! You can't do that. You started this!"

Brickford put down his fork and faced him. "I bet the barrel came from somewhere between Jonathan Flynn's old house and that cliff he drove off of."

Brady stared at him for a moment. "No shit. You think he iced the old man and threw it out on his way off the cliff?"

"I do." Brickford picked up his fork.

Brady slumped down in his chair and sat in silence while Brickford finished lunch.

"This has to do with Flynn's wife's kidnapping, huh?" Brady asked when Brickford got up to rinse his dish.

"Yeah, it goes back to that."

"Just can't let it go, huh, Brick?"

Brickford put away the plastic container. "The whole thing just didn't sit right with me. Still doesn't."

"You mean you getting sent down here because of it?"

"Yeah. I followed protocol to the T."

"Yeah, man, but *that* case? They needed to pin fault on someone, and you were the unlucky fuck who was put in charge."

"That's true. Public pressure was a factor, but the haste in which they did it, and the method—it was odd. All my files on the case were pulled and I lost access to the computer."

Brady looked surprised. "You mean they blocked your password so you couldn't even look at the files?"

"Yeah, that's what I mean. It was like IA was investigating us or something."

"Okay, that *is* weird."

"Yep. I've seen guys get sent down many times, but it was never like this case. The entire team who handled the kidnapping was pulled off and dispersed. Trillson and Gingham went back down to the beat, Burnham and Capra were transferred, and I came here. Keesler was the only one who stayed."

"That's some serious house cleaning," Brady said.

"It is. I just want a few minutes with the shooter. I gotta know."

"If I know you, you'll make it happen."

"I already put in a request with the guy's lawyer."

"Well, there ya go." Brady glanced at the clock and held up the car keys. "Time to stop crime. Let's hit the streets."

Brickford wiped his forehead as they traipsed to the car. "Damn, it's hot as hell out here."

Brady swung open the door. "At least you don't have to touch the steering wheel. Damn thing's a thousand degrees."

"I hear ya." Brickford settled in, resisting the urge to smoke.

"How's the car hunt going?" Brady asked.

"Horrible. Maddie wants a red sports car."

"Of course she does," Brady said. "She's a young girl, not an old fart like you."

"Helen and Hank aren't helping. Helen said she wants to borrow it and Hank wants Maddie to pick him up from ball practice in it."

"Wife, daughter, *and* son teaming up against you? You may as well hand over a blank check."

Brickford flipped Brady off. "Stuff it, rookie!" he said over Brady's laughter. "Soon, it'll be you."

"Not for many years! My baby girl's still toddling around."

Brickford stared out the window as they rode in silence for a few minutes.

A call came through. "All units, we have a two-eleven at Town Center Square."

Brady floored it. "So, Brick, if you prove that Jonathan Flynn killed Schuyler Vander Broek, how will it help with the bullshit Gypsum PD pulled during your kidnapping case a year earlier?"

Brickford turned up the air conditioning.

"Another hunch."

FIFTY-ONE

Johnny woke up on the beach with Auster sitting next to him. He scanned the coastline packed with families, then glanced at Auster, bare-chested and leaning back on his elbows.

"What happened there?" Johnny gestured toward several deep gouges on Auster's abdomen that had healed, leaving indentations in what would otherwise be washboard abs.

"You'll find out soon enough."

Two girls in bikinis pranced toward them on the hot sand and waved at Auster.

"Hi," one of them sang out.

"Hello," Auster replied.

"We're about to get a volleyball game started. You two want to join in?"

"No, thank you," Auster said. "We're here on business."

"Business?" The girls glanced back and forth between Auster the Adonis, and Johnny, who felt like a homeless guy who could use a good scrubbing. "Okay, then." They gave each other a strange look before heading back toward the volleyball net.

"So, will I see my son?" Johnny asked.

"He resides in the vicinity."

"In the vicinity? Where?"

"In a penthouse on the coast. Not too far from where you took your life. I don't have an address, but you can find it quite easily."

"What about my house? Does Paula still live there?"

"I don't know anything about your house or the person of whom you speak."

Johnny ran his hands through his hair. *Paula must still live there. I should talk to her first.*

"Okay, so I just leave?"

"Yes," Auster said as they got up. "You are of sound-enough mind to investigate this on your own." He reached into his pocket and pulled out a debit card. "Use this to access funds. The code is on the back. The account is specifically linked to you. Do not overspend and draw attention to yourself."

Johnny took the card. "Thanks."

"You will check in with me in three days' time."

"How? I don't have a phone."

"No, but I have access to all of your memories."

"You *what*? I don't understand."

"When I brought you back, I absorbed all of your memories. Every time you recall an event that took place before you killed yourself"—Auster tapped his own temple—"I know exactly where you are."

"Which is to say, you'll know where I am all the time."

"This is true. Man is the only animal that spends large amounts of cognitive time processing past events. It's a huge waste of life energy for humans, but an easy way for me to keep track of all of my Hands and Sentries."

Johnny's arms fell slack to his sides. "This is unbelievable. My own thoughts aren't mine anymore."

"Your thoughts are yours. I can't read minds," Auster said. "But if your memory drifts back to *any* time before I brought you back, then you've made contact with me and made your location known."

"Fuckin' great." Johnny dug his foot into the sand. "So, in three days, you'll just appear in front of me."

"I would prefer if you selected a specific memory to use as a calling card. It works best if you choose something that doesn't dominate your thoughts—something benign."

Johnny pondered for a moment. The memories were too vast and too many to narrow down at first, then one stood out. Johnny looked up. "The jacarandas. Me walking to school with my father under the trees with purple flowers."

"Focus on it," Auster said.

Johnny did.

"Good. That's specific enough. In three days, call on that memory and I'll be where you are. When we do meet again, you will come with me. Do we agree?"

"I don't have a choice in the matter, do I?"

"No. I'm only granting you this time so you realize that there is no life for you to go back to. Remember, you chose to end your life. I chose to bring you back. You belong to me now."

"What do you want with me?"

"I've explained that."

"I'm no murderer."

"Yes, you are."

"Bullshit," Johnny muttered under his breath. *I'll deal with this later. Right now I have to focus on Michael and Maya.*

Johnny took a few steps toward the parking lot packed with cars. He turned back, "I guess public transport—"

Auster was gone.

Johnny left the beach and snaked through the cars toward the main highway. He passed a large van and froze when he caught a glimpse of himself in the side window.

His once jet-black hair was now a sandy blond. An olive complexion had replaced his ivory skin. His face wasn't his—his nose was thinner and longer, his chin dimpled. His shoulders were as broad as he remembered, but he was lean and sinewy. He bent down and got a closer look at his eyes in the side-view mirror. They were the same piercing green color.

My eyes are all that are left of me. I look like a surfer now. That long-haired Sentry was right. No one would ever believe I'm me.

He got to the highway and stood at the bus stop for a time. He decided to walk the four-mile trek home.

I have to talk to Paula.

He broke into a jog, feeling surprisingly strong and agile. About an hour later, he ascended the road that led to his estate. A small guard shack now stood next to the electronic gates.

A guard emerged. "Can I help you with something?"

"I just wanted to visit," Johnny answered.

"Name?" The guard asked.

It slipped out automatically. "Flynn." *Shit. Shouldn't have said that.*

The guard sighed deeply and shook his head. "Look, wise guy, that's not even funny any more."

Johnny turned as a security vehicle pulled up behind him.

"Is there a problem?" The guy behind the wheel asked.

The guard gestured toward Johnny. "Well, Chad, it seems we have another Flynn here."

"Jesus, they're *still* coming?" Chad gave Johnny the once-over. "The first couple of years after Jonathan Flynn flew off the cliff, every bum who resembled the guy came by to take a shot at claiming the Flynn empire. Those poor kids had to look at the faces of a thousand crooks trying to steal their family's fortune. Must admit you got a lot of balls coming here almost a decade later. And you don't look like Flynn at all."

Johnny suddenly felt sick as he peered through the gates. *I can't believe I put Michael and Maya through that.* He noticed that the landscaping was different than he remembered. *Does Paula even live here anymore?*

"Listen, fella," Chad said. "You can't wander around private property. Why don't I give you a ride back down the hill?"

I have to see Paula. She'll help me.

Johnny bolted toward the iron gates and jumped up the bars. He easily pulled himself over, but his left tricep caught on the sharp end of one of the pointed stakes. His weight pulled him down the other side and he screamed in pain. He tumbled to the ground and grasped his arm. *Shit.* He scrambled to his feet and fled toward his house.

The gate squealed open behind him as he heard one of the guards shout, "We need the PD here! A guy's running toward the house and he seems like a whack job!"

Knowing time was short, Johnny raced on and gaped in awe as the house came into view. An unfamiliar car sat in the drive and what used to be cream-colored trim was now a dark rust color. *The place is different.*

Johnny felt something trickle down his arm. He looked down expecting to see blood, but instead, hundreds of tiny insects poured from under the shirt sleeve onto the cobblestone drive.

What the fuck?

He yanked the sleeve aside and gasped as flies, ants, and worms seeped from the wound in his arm. *Holy shit. I'm not bleeding blood. I'm bleeding fucking bugs!*

"The cops have been called," one of the guards shouted. "Stop where you are!"

Ignoring the warning, Johnny dashed around the property toward the back of the mansion. *The window. Paula grew herbs just outside the kitchen window.* He reached that part of the house and slid to a stop. The flower box on the sill that had held the herbs was gone. He glanced down at his arm again. The stream of insects had dissipated to a trickle and the wound had gone from the size of a dime to nothing more than a pinprick.

What the hell is going on?

"Stop where you are!"

The voice sounded closer.

Johnny stared at the window, his heart aching.

I want to be inside, with Dani, the kids, and Paula, but I can't... His thoughts clouded over as Johnny felt someone take his arm. He turned to the guard. "I'm done here. I'm coming."

Chad ushered Johnny down the drive where a police car waited at the gate.

Johnny recognized the tall freckle-faced officer as soon as he stepped out of the car.

"Gingham."

Gingham stopped. "Have we met?"

"A lifetime ago." Johnny glanced up at his old home. "I just wanted to see the place for myself one more time."

Gingham appeared confused. "Did you used to work here or something?"

"Or something."

"Well, fella, you gave everyone here quite a scare." Gingham gestured toward the black-and-white. "Trespassing is illegal. I'm going to have to take you in, but first I have to frisk you."

Johnny took one last look at the home he shared with Danielle and the children, then closed his eyes and placed his hands on the police car.

"This yours?" Gingham pulled out the credit card in Johnny's pocket.

"My only possession."

"The code is written on the back."

"I know. I forget a lot."

"Right." Gingham opened the rear door of the police car. "Get in."

Johnny slid onto the back seat and glanced at his arm. It had completely healed. Gingham got into the driver's seat and called in the card number.

Gingham swiveled around. "Can you tell me who this card belongs to?"

Shit. Why didn't I look at the name on the damn thing? "Auster."

"An interesting guess, but no." He shut the door and started the engine. "Theft is against the law, too."

"That card is mine."

"Don't push it. You couldn't even tell me who it belongs to."

Now what? Johnny peered out the window as they turned onto the public street. *I've been on my own for a couple of hours. I haven't even had a meal or a bath yet, and now my only source of funds is gone.*

Johnny watched the familiar streets whiz by as they drove in silence through Gypsum Ridge. He thought about asking Gingham where Michael lived, but didn't want to risk it. He inhaled deeply as the car approached the street to the police department, then a shockwave ran through him as Gingham passed the street instead of turning. "Aren't you going to take me in?"

"No."

Shit, he's taking me to the loony bin to have me committed.

Panic struck. Johnny's heart raced. He clasped and unclasped his fists, trying to release the tension surging through him. Then he heard hissing, coming from somewhere around him, or—

Inside of me?

He glanced down at his hands and gasped. The flesh on his fingers had been replaced by thousands of tiny insects, buzzing and spinning in circles.

They're angry. I don't know how I know, but they're angry.

Johnny's mouth felt dry. He peered at the road ahead. "Where are you taking me?"

Gingham peered at him in the rearview. "You'll see."

Fear gripped him. The insects spilled off of him onto the floor, moving forward in thick belts under Gingham's seat.

Holy fuck!

The car slowed and Johnny glanced out the window to see the entrance to the Gypsum Ridge Bus Station. He sighed in relief, then felt a tickling sensation. He glanced down again and had to hold back a scream. All of the insects retreated from the front of the car, back up Johnny's seat, and disappeared into his hands.

Nausea gripped Johnny as he watched the coating of insects meld into skin. Within moments, his hand appeared normal.

Gingham pulled up to the bus station, put the car into park, and swiveled in his seat to face Johnny. "Look, it's obvious you've been through some rough times. I could arrest you right now on two charges, but I'm gonna cut you a deal."

Johnny waited.

Gingham reached into his pocket, pulled out his own wallet, and handed Johnny a bus pass and two twenties through the grate. "There's a bus heading out of town in a few minutes. I'm gonna stay here to make sure you get on it. Get yourself a meal, a night's sleep, and figure your shit out."

"All right."

"Here's the other part of the deal," Gingham continued. "I don't know your name, but I know your face. If I see you in Gypsum Ridge again, I'll arrest you on sight. Do you understand?"

"Yes." Johnny looked through the grate. "Thanks, Gingham. You've always been a really nice guy."

Gingham shot him a funny look. "Right, good luck."

Johnny made it onto the bus just before the doors closed. He handed the driver the bus pass, then trudged down the narrow aisle, finding a seat in the back next to a couple of teens with dyed hair and pierced noses. They sneered and shifted over as Johnny plopped down.

Johnny leaned his head back and took a breath. He examined his hands, turning them over several times.

They look completely fine. What happened in Gingham's car? He settled in, allowing his body to sink into the rhythm of the bus's sways and lulls as it maneuvered through traffic. Then a thought struck him.

I don't even know where I'm going.

Johnny turned to the kid sitting next to him and asked, "Where's the last stop?"

The kid rolled his eyes and gave him a *what an idiot* expression as he answered, "Thousand Wells."

FIFTY-TWO

Dick Brickford spat as he plodded down the driveway of a private residence. "I fucking hate July. Thirty-one merciless days of hot and still." He watched as a gurney carrying a body rolled away from a home toward the coroner's van.

"That was pretty bad." Brady's voice sounded rattled.

"Oh, there'll be more, trust me." Brickford glanced at Brady. "You seem shaken up, rookie. That wasn't the first dead body you've ever seen."

"No, but..."

Brickford stopped. "But what?"

"It's just a fucked up way to go." Brady heaved out a sigh. "His face. I can tell he suffered. Poor old guy." He glanced toward the coroner's van. "That one's gonna stick with me."

"I hear ya." Brickford wiped his brow with the back of his hand. "Fucking heat waves always result in the deaths of those too weak, too sick, or too poor to escape it." He grumbled as his clothes stuck to his skin. "Let's get in the car. I'll drive."

Brickford sucked in a breath as he plunked down in the driver's seat. "It's a fucking oven in here." He pulled out a baby wipe from the center console and mopped his head and the back of his neck. He reached forward and yanked his hands away from the burning steering wheel as soon as he touched it. "Ouch! Damn it."

Brady slid onto the passenger seat. "Where to?"

Brickford sent him a sideways glance. "County. I got time with Jessup. I have to know about that gun." He turned the ignition.

"Let's hope it's worth the trouble," Brady paused, taking a few steady breaths as Brickford pulled onto the street. "Are there any deaths that have stuck with you?"

Brickford kept his eyes on the road as he spoke. "Yeah. First month on the job, a junkie murdered his wife and kid and then hid out at a liquor store. A bunch of units surrounded the place, and the dumb fuck came out shooting." Brickford rubbed his chin. "He was blown to pieces right in front of me."

"Damn," Brady said. "That's harsh."

"Yeah." Brickford leaned forward and blasted the AC. "I'd seen a dead body before that, but that junky was the first person I watched go from being alive to being dead." He shook his head. "I can't explain—"

"No, I get it," Brady said.

"Yeah." Brickford took a swig of his cold coffee. "Now let's see what another junky has to say about an eight year-old gun. It's been a couple of days. Maybe Theodore Jessup's sober memory will be better than when he was high as a kite. Oh, and did I mention that it's hot as fuck? My shoes are gonna melt."

Fifteen minutes later, a wave of cool air swept over Brickford and Brady as they passed through the double doors of the county jail.

Brickford sighed in relief. "Whew, much better."

Outside the interview room, Jessup's lawyer stood alongside an officer. He eyed the report in Brickford's hand. "That the ballistics you were talking about?"

"It is."

"I don't see why a ballistics report is relevant here. My client has already confessed to the crime, so why you're wasting our time is beyond me." He checked his watch.

Brickford held up the report. "Ballistics revealed that the barrel of Theodore Jessup's gun was also used in a homicide that remains unsolved."

"The *barrel* of the gun?" The lawyer smirked. "Just the barrel?"

"Yeah. The striations on the bullet the doctors pulled out of that three-year old child matched those of a bullet used to kill someone else, but the breech markings didn't match."

"So, then it's not the same gun."

"You're right, in a way. Glock parts are interchangeable. So the *exact* gun wasn't used in the previous homicide, but that barrel was, and I'd like to find out where Mr. Jessup acquired it."

"You have ten minutes, that's all. And I'm only allowing it so this shit goes away quick."

"Thanks." Brickford turned to Brady. "See ya in ten."

"Good luck," Brady strolled down the hall. "Where can a man get a cold soda around here?" he hollered.

Brickford stepped inside the interview room and closed the door behind him. "Good morning, Mr. Jessup."

Jessup didn't look up from his slumped-over position on the table. He rested his head on his crossed, tattoo-covered arms. His stringy, brown hair was pulled back into a ponytail.

Brickford stood next to an empty chair across from him. "I'm Officer Dick Brickford. I'd like to ask you a few questions."

"Don't see why. Everyone knows I did it. There's fuckin' video of it and everythin'." He pushed himself away from the table. "I didn't see the fucking woman holding the kid. I just heard a noise and shot toward it!"

"Yeah, I read the report." Brickford sat down. "I'm not here about that. I'd like to know a little more about the gun you used. How long have you had it?"

"'Bout a year or so."

"Did you put it together yourself?"

Jessup grimaced like he'd just heard something crazy. "Nah, I don't do that shit."

"Did the guy you bought it from put it together?"

"He could've. Who knows? It's not rocket science. Just try to find a Glock around here that hasn't been changed around."

"Where'd you buy it?"

Jessup wiped his nose with his sleeve. "Back of a club, you know, a place set up so guys can blow money on drugs, guns, pussy—whatever."

"Where is this club?"

"There's way more than one. Fuck, *you* should know. Cops bust 'em all the time and close 'em down, then the party moves to another place for a while until that one gets busted."

"Do you remember buying the gun?"

"Yeah. Me and my boy, Nicky, had just come across a bunch of cash." He glanced up at Brickford. "Don't fuck with me about how we got it."

Brickford waved him off. "Keep going."

"Nicky said he knew about a club where we could, you know, *celebrate*, so we went."

"Where was this particular club?"

"It's a place over in Granite Shores called Junebug's, next to that big ice factory."

"Yeah, I know it," Brickford said. "Do you remember the name of the guy who sold you the piece?"

"It was something odd, like that old movie guy's." He pressed his hand against his head. "Bur....or...Borm."

"Borgnine? Ernest Borgnine?"

Jessup shook his head. "Like boogie, or bogrite..."

"Bogart? Humphrey Bogart?"

"Yeah, man." Jessup pointed at Brickman. "Bogart. Old Bogey they called him."

"So he was an older man?"

"Yeah, like my dad's age."

"Does this Bogey guy deal primarily in guns?"

"Nah, he's into bigger stuff. Me and Nicky was just partying with him one night and I told 'em I wouldn't mind scoring a new piece. Said he wanted to get rid of the one he was carrying, so he sold it to me."

"When you say Bogart's into bigger stuff, what do you mean?"

"Not sure exactly. Don't think it's drugs. He's hooked up, though. Guys from all scenes talk him up when he's there."

"What does he look like?"

Jessup squinted as he tried to think. "Tall, black guy, gray hair, and green eyes. All the chicks kept making a big fucking deal about his green eyes."

There was a knock on the door. Jessup's lawyer poked his head in and tapped his watch.

Brickford held his hand up. "We're done here."

∞∞∞∞∞∞

"I have to admit," Brady said as they got into the car, "you got way more out of him than I guessed. I didn't think he'd talk at all."

"He's got nothing to lose. The guy's gonna die in prison. And if the three-year-old dies, Jessup's probably headed to the east block at San Quentin."

"So you got a name, but I don't see how you're gonna find out anything from this Bogart guy. He's not gonna cop to anything."

"I hear ya. I'm starting to wonder if I'm chasing my tail," Brickford said. "Finding out the barrel ended up with some dealer who switches guns every month is like watching a polar bear walk into a snowstorm."

"Yeah," Brady said. "Can I ask you something, though?"

"Shoot."

"You told me when you were yanked off the Vander Broek case, all the files were pulled."

"Yeah. They were."

Brady peeled his eyes off the road and looked at him. "So, how do you still have the ballistics report?"

"I kept backups at my place so I could work from home."

"Hmm, kinda forgot to turn those in, huh?"

Brickford smiled. "Completely forgot."

∞∞∞∞∞∞

After several hours in front of a computer screen combing the database for a guy named Bogart who fit Jessup's description, Brickford finally gave up. "Shit." He leaned back in his chair.

Brady, both hands clutching fast-food bags, nudged the office door open with his elbow. "Any hits?" He handed Brickford one of the greasy bags.

"Nothing, not even a traffic ticket for a guy named Bogart." Brickford opened the bag, took out a burger, and held it up. "Thanks. Hope I don't barf this up. Can't remember the last time I had fast food."

"You'll survive," Brady glanced toward the screen. "Maybe Bogart's not his real name."

"That's what I'm thinking. Looks like we're going to have to visit Junebug's."

"To ask about a guy who sold another guy a gun a year ago?" Brady shook his head and grabbed his soda. "I'm calling *goose chase* on that right now."

"Yeah, I hear ya." Brickford reached into the bag and pulled out a handful of fries. "But if this Bogart guy is such a bigwig, someone may know where to find him."

Brady waved a napkin in the air. "Raise the flag and see who salutes it."

FIFTY-THREE

Johnny was one of only three passengers remaining on the bus by the time it reached Thousand Wells. The other two people, an elderly couple, followed him off and tottered toward the gated apartment complex across the street.

Johnny took the sidewalk that bordered a city park, noticing the groups of homeless people clustered together sleeping under the trees to escape the heat. He turned left and headed toward Town Center Square. He felt sweat trickle from the back of his neck down his shirt. *So much for buying a fresh change of clothes and checking into a hotel room so I can take a shower.*

Johnny's stomach growled, which reminded him of how much time had passed. *Damn, if what Auster said is true, I haven't eaten for eight years!*

After rounding another corner, Johnny was surprised to see bulldozers and demolition vehicles blocking Town Center Square. He navigated around the construction area to find the Thousand Wells fountain had been corded off with yellow tape.

A large group of people of all ages stood between the fountain and the demolition equipment, thrusting signs into the air that read, "Don't Take a Wrecking Ball to Our City's History," and "Make the Thousand Wells Fountain a Landmark."

Johnny stared back up at the stone giant: The coyote, the mountains, the waterfalls, and Thousand Wells with his rain stick. His gaze then drifted to the hand-tied bouquets of fresh wildflowers at the shaman's feet.

The locals still believe.

"I hope you win, I really do," Johnny called out as he passed the crowd.

Hunger pangs drove him away from the protesters in the search of food. He scanned the restaurants that peppered the square, but although he felt ravenous, nothing appealed to him— until he spotted a little juice bar nestled between a pizza joint and a Mexican restaurant.

A cold smoothie sounds perfect.

He ducked inside and eyed the menu board on the wall behind the cashier. "I'd like a large strawberry smoothie."

"Okay, that will be five dollars, please."

Johnny pulled out one of the twenties Gingham had given him. *Shit, this forty bucks is gonna go fast.*

He relished being in the cool, air-conditioned little place while he waited. He downed half of the thirty-two-ounce drink within a minute of getting it. *Ooh, shouldn't have done that.* He gripped his stomach, which twisted and churned like a million ants were swirling inside. *Just breathe.* Johnny sucked in deep breaths and the stirrings subsided.

He finished the rest of his smoothie, then made his way toward city hall.

Much better. Now, let's see if the library database has any info on Michael and Maya.

∞∞∞∞∞∞

Inside the Thousand Wells library, Johnny bought two hours of Internet use. He settled into one of the stations, taking in the subtle differences in the interface since he last used a computer. *Wow, these things are paper-thin, but other than that, they don't look too different.*

He logged on and the browser opened to a generic search engine page. He typed in the kids' names and began clicking on the stories one-by-one, his eyes stopping on the date every time.

I still can't believe eight years have passed.

He opened a story from *The Daily Business Review*, where the front page read:

FLYNN HANDING OVER CONTROL OF BILLION-DOLLAR FAMILY CORPORATION.

Johnny's eyes widened when he saw the photo under the headline. *Wilks!*

Jan Wilkinson was a few pounds heavier than the last time Johnny saw him. Standing next to Wilks was a tall young man with Johnny's jaw line and Danielle's eyes.

"Michael!" Johnny said aloud. He read the article.

Michael Flynn, son of diamond mogul Jonathan Thornton Flynn, is relinquishing control of his share of J.T. Flynn Diamond Corporation for an undisclosed sum.

This change feeds the recent buzz in the corporate world that the Flynn Corporation president, Jan Wilkinson, is in talks with Vander Broek Corporation about a possible merger. If this is true, it would be the largest corporation merger in history.

Disbelief swirled though Johnny's mind.

After years of battling with them, and all the filth surrounding it, Wilks is merging with Vander Broek? Of all the companies in the world, how could he do such a thing?

One photo showed Wilks standing in between Michael and a young woman. Johnny stared at his son for a moment. *Wow,*

Bud, you're really an adult now. Then he read the caption beneath the photo.

"Michael Flynn with Jan and Lydia Wilkinson."

"*Lydia*? Who's this young broad? Where's Margaret?"
Sssshhhh!

Johnny turned to meet the stares of several others in the computer room who didn't appreciate his verbal commentary.

"Sorry." Johnny felt himself blush. He typed in the name Margaret Wilkinson and found the obituary.

She died from a heart attack four years ago.

After typing in "Flynn Corporation" and "Michael Flynn," the screen filled with numerous articles and photos of Michael.

Johnny scrolled through them.

You look so much like your mother, Bud.

He came upon a photo of Michael leaving what looked like a hospital. The cameraman had zoomed in on his expression, which was clearly one of anguish. Johnny read the caption.

Michael Flynn leaving Gypsum Ridge Hospital after visiting his long-time caretaker, Paula Strathmore, who was recently diagnosed with lung cancer.

"Cancer? No, not Paula!" He placed a hand to his mouth and checked the date of the article.

This was last month. Check the obituaries.

The Gypsum Ridge obituaries reported nothing about Paula's death. Relief flooded through him. *I have to visit you.*

Johnny resumed his search and stumbled upon article after article about Michael on the social pages, partying with supermodels and celebrities, hosting big fundraisers, and attending movie premiers. More articles told of Michael's DUIs, public drunkenness, and arrests for possession of narcotics.

"That's just great," Johnny muttered to himself. "You grew up to be an over-indulged bastard, huh, son?" He gazed at Michael's face and felt a lump form in his throat. "But I wasn't there to guide you, was I?"

Johnny turned his search to Maya. His heart soared when he read of her record-breaking athletic feats. He drank in every picture of her.

You look like both of us. You have my dark hair and green eyes and Dani's pretty features.

After the thick coverage of Maya's career-ending injury that killed her Olympic dreams, Johnny couldn't find any pictures, articles, or references about her. It was as if she had dropped off the face of the Earth. Johnny did notice after scrolling through the Flynn public files again that Maya still maintained her interest in Flynn Corporation.

Where are you, Petal? Are you okay?

Johnny glanced up at the clock and was shocked to see 4:30 staring back at him.

I've used up almost all of my time already? I'll take a break and come back after I gather my thoughts.

He got up, stretched his legs, and considered his next move. *I only have a few bucks to my name. How the fuck am I going to live on that for three days? If I call Auster now, my search ends.*

He rolled the decision over in his head as he walked toward the exit of the library. Head down and deep in thought, Johnny pushed the door open, took two steps, and ran head-first into someone carrying a stack of books.

"Oh, I'm so sorry!" Johnny tried to catch the books as they tumbled to the sidewalk.

"It's okay," a female voice responded.

Johnny picked up the books strewn on the ground and took a step toward the woman. "I'm really sorry about that."

"It's fine, really." The woman, curvy and smiling, swiped a wisp of black hair away from her face.

Johnny almost dropped the stack again when he realized who she was. *Gladys, the volunteer from the homeless shelter.*

She appeared older but still had the same glow and exuded the same warmth that had tamed Michael's teenage angst almost a decade ago.

Johnny handed her the books. "Here you go. Sorry. I'm preoccupied, I guess. I'm John, by the way."

"Gladys." She leaned forward and looked into Johnny's eyes. "Have we met before?"

"Sort of," Johnny said. "I helped out in the shelter a long time ago. You'd just started your nursing career."

"Oh, my. That was a while ago."

Johnny recalled how Gladys inspired Michael. *Maybe they've kept in touch.* "So, are you still a nurse?"

"Sure am." Gladys pointed behind Johnny. "Right over there at Thousand Wells Hospital."

"Bridget was in charge of the shelter when we volunteered. How is she?"

Gladys shifted her weight. "She passed away three years ago."

Great. Now I feel like an idiot. "I'm sorry, Gladys. I didn't know. I haven't been back in this area for a long time."

"It's okay. I took over after Bridget died. Sort of had to since no one else was willing."

"That's admirable." Johnny, still wondering if Gladys kept in touch with Michael, wanted to talk more. "Well, you're going to have to let me pay you back, since I threw your books everywhere."

"Oh, no, you don't have to—"

"I swear I'm not a weirdo stalker." Johnny held up a hand. "Swear."

"Anyone who volunteered at the shelter and was friends with Bridget can't be called a weirdo in my book."

"Well, it's kinda hot out," Johnny said. "And that juice bar between the pizza joint and Mexican food place sells a pretty mean smoothie."

"I know they do. I'm a regular there."

"Then it's settled."

Gladys pressed her lips together "I never do this, but okay. Let me drop off my books."

Johnny trotted across the square to the juice bar, ordered two large smoothies, and sat at a small table outside. The setting sun shone off of a window and he caught a glimpse of his own reflection. *I'm a stranger to myself.*

Gladys approached from the end of the square and Johnny could tell she was being cautious as she sat down opposite him.

"Two strawberries up!" the lady behind the counter shouted.

Johnny retrieved the smoothies. *Shit, ten more dollars—gone.* He set one in front of Gladys and had to keep himself from gulping his own down in three swigs.

"Thanks." Gladys took a sip.

The first three buttons of her white blouse were undone, and Johnny's gaze drifted down to the section of soft skin that led to the full breasts. *What the hell? This should be the last thing on my mind.* He quickly pulled his attention away from the area and his eyes met Gladys'. He felt himself turn red.

She shifted in her seat and adjusted her blouse. "So, what took you away from Thousand Wells, John?"

"I was in business, but I lost everything. Since then I've been...rebuilding. I guess that's as good a term as any."

"Do you have children?" Gladys asked.

"Grown and gone." Sadness flooded Johnny's body.

Gladys looked confused. "You don't look old enough to have grown children."

Johnny hadn't thought of that. "Well, I'm older than I look, and I was young when I had them." He changed the focus to her. "Are you married, Gladys?"

"Divorced, with a six-year-old daughter."

"Being a single parent isn't easy."

"Tell me about it. I have to work five or six days a week just to make it. Sometimes I feel sorry for myself but I try to keep it positive for my little Gina."

"Doesn't your ex send you anything to help?"

"He's already working on another family. He has a new girlfriend and a new son to support."

Johnny sneered. "Bastard."

Gladys sipped her smoothie and swept her hair behind an ear. "I'm sorry, John. Listen to me, blathering on about my problems. We're practically strangers. I feel silly."

"Don't feel silly. We're not strangers, Gladys. We have some history, even though it was a while ago." *And I had a different body.*

"That's true. Maybe that's why I feel so comfortable with you. I promise I'm not a total whiner."

"I can tell you're not." Then came an idea. "When I volunteered at the shelter, the Flynn family was there."

A wave of sorrow crossed Gladys' face. "What happened to them was so terrible. They were very kind. Michael still keeps in touch, though."

"Really?" Johnny sat up. "Does he still volunteer?"

"No. Last time he came by was about a year ago with an older man named Jan. Michael introduced him to me and said he was like a father to him."

Wilks. Still taking care of them—after all these years.

Gladys continued. "They made a generous donation on that day. Since then, Michael hasn't been back, but we keep in touch by email once in a while. He's donated a lot of money to help keep the shelter going. We're very grateful. I know he gets a lot of negative press, but Michael Flynn is a generous young man."

Warmth flooded through Johnny. *My Bud does have some character, after all. I guess I did something right.*

Gladys checked her watch. "Oh, my, I have to go get Gina. It was nice seeing you again, John."

Johnny thought about asking for her number as they stood up to leave, but he didn't have a phone. "Hope to see you again," was all he could think up.

"I'm a regular here *and* at the library, so I'm sure our paths will cross again. Thanks for the smoothie."

"You're welcome." Johnny tossed his empty cup. "I'd better get back to the library." He watched Gladys walk away and felt a cocktail of emotions run though him: guilt, hope, regret, uncertainty. He felt a familiar tightening down below.

Lust? What the fuck? I'm a middle-aged widower, not a goddamn sixteen-year old. What the hell is wrong with me?

Gladys reached the fountain and stopped to peer up at it. She turned back, locked eyes with Johnny, and smiled.

Oh, boy.

FIFTY-FOUR

Brickford got out of the car and surveyed the dilapidated building with the neon sign that read *Junebug's*. "The place looks pretty seedy."

"Sure does," Brady slipped on his shades.

They crossed the cracked asphalt that led to a door with peeling brown paint. Brickford pulled it open. Once inside, they stood for a moment as their eyes adjusted to the dim light.

When the room came into focus, Brickford smiled. "Shit."

The inside was a large open space that smelled citrusy-clean. The walls were freshly painted, the oak bar and tables polished so that they shone under the glow of the lamps.

"We're closed!" the guy wiping down the bar shouted.

Brickford checked his watch. "Sign says you open at 5:00. It's ten 'til."

"Yeah, which means we're *closed*."

Brickford stepped toward the bar. "We just want to ask you a couple of questions."

"That's what I figured. I can smell a cop from a mile away." He moved around the counter and mopped off a table.

Brickford stood across from him. "If you want us to come back later and question you in front of all your clientele, we will."

The guy stopped wiping. "What do you want?"

"We're looking for a guy named Bogart or Bogey." Brickford took out a little notepad. "Probably a nickname."

The bartender shrugged. "Not a clue."

"He's a regular here," Brady said. "He's not busted or anything. Just need to ask him a couple of questions."

"Like I said, not a clue."

Brickford took a step closer. "Heard he's a heavy-hitter in your late-night trade program."

The bar guy threw down the rag. "Still got nothin'. No Bogart, Bogie, Boogie, or any of that shit."

"Tall dude," Brickford said. "Black guy with green eyes."

The bartender's jaw dropped. "Humphries? *That's* who you're looking for? Don't know where you got the heavy-hitter part, but he's a regular, all right."

"Humphries? Got a first name?"

"John, Gene, Jack— somethin' like that. He ain't no criminal, though. Guy's pretty straight." He moved to another table. "Honestly, I think the dude comes here late to feel like a badass, but he's straight as an arrow—works for the county."

"Okay." Brickford scribbled down the information. "That's all we need. Thanks for your time."

Brady pushed open the door. "Damn!" He shielded his eyes from the bright sunlight.

"A bet's a bet," Brickford said, as they got in the car. "You're buying dinner."

"Shit, you'd rip off a poor rookie like that?"

"Stop your whining. I'll have a veggie sub with no chips. You know where to get it."

Brady flipped him off and started the car.

∞∞∞∞∞∞

At the station, Brickford combed through the database. "Got 'em! Samuel Humphries! He was in a car accident last year." Brickford scanned the report. "Not his fault." He spun the monitor around to face Brady. "Check it out."

Brady leaned forward and eyed the picture on the license. "Looks like him, all right. Where's he work?"

"Quartz County Refuse Department."

"He hauls trash?"

"Yeah, seems so. We'll visit him tomorrow." He leaned toward Brady. "In between calls, of course."

"Of course." Brady echoed. "You know your ass is busted if folks find out you're working the same eight-year-old case that got you sent down, right?"

"No one needs to know, rookie."

FIFTY-FIVE

Johnny was the last person out of the library at closing time. The information about Michael he'd found online tumbled through his thoughts. He mulled over what he'd learned through his conversation with Gladys. He even found the address where Michael lived in Gypsum Ridge.

Bud, I can hardly wait to shake your hand.

He couldn't find a thing on Maya.

Petal, are you okay? Auster said you're in Europe. Why?

The sun was down, and along with it went the sunny disposition surrounding Town Center Square. Businesses had locked up for the night, the protesters had bailed, and two homeless men had ducked under the yellow tape surrounding the fountain to bathe in the remaining water at the bottom of the concrete lake.

Johnny trotted down the street and pondered his options.

I can't risk contacting Auster. I'll have to live on the few bucks I have.

He came across a dollar store and, budgeting what little he had left, he bought men's body wash, deodorant, mouthwash, shampoo, and a shirt. He found a public restroom in Town Center Square and went inside. The acrid smell of urine saturated the little room, overpowering Johnny's senses as he looked for a clean place to set down his purchases.

He balanced the bag on top of the electric hand dryer and peeled off his white t-shirt. He used the body wash to launder the shirt in the sink, let it soak while he cleaned himself up as best he could, and swept on the deodorant. He pulled on the new t-shirt, then wrung out the wet one.

After several rounds of washing and gargling with the mouthwash, he stuffed everything back into the bag. "I almost feel human," Johnny murmured to himself as he pushed open the bathroom door and plodded across the square. *Now, let's see if I can find a way to run into Gladys again tomorrow. Maybe she knows something about Maya.*

Not wanting to stay outside all night, he made his way toward a 24-hour coffee shop on the other side of town that a librarian had recommended. He crossed the street leading away from the square, slowing as he approached the park next to the bus stop.

During the day, the park was crowded and busy. At night, the seven-acre space, enveloped in a dirty haze sent down by the orange street lights, gave off the air of being haunted. In the distance, a few homeless perched atop the playground equipment like soldiers standing guard. Johnny's insides churned.

I need to get the fuck past here, quick.

Fear made Johnny's skin crawl, literally. He glanced down at his forearm to see it roiling like something was moving under the flesh. Panic overtook him and he broke into a run, zipping past the park as fast as he could and hooking right at the corner. He saw the coffee shop's neon sign up ahead, stopped, and leaned over to catch his breath.

"Where ya going, jogging boy?"

A searing pain jolted through Johnny's head and sent him forward to the ground. He covered the back of his head and rolled over to see two guys, both wearing black knit caps. One of them brandished what appeared to be a broken tennis racket.

"Well, look what we have here." Racket-man eyed the bag. "Did a little shopping, huh? Bet you got some cash to cough up."

The other guy stepped forward and kicked Johnny in the ribs. "Empty your pockets!"

Johnny yelped in pain and curled into a ball. His vision fogged. A surge of energy coursed through him and he felt something beneath his clothes.

Then Johnny heard screaming. He looked up and saw his assailants covered in insects. *What the hell?*

Johnny glanced toward his own feet, where thick streams of flies, ants, and beetles, flooded from under his clothes onto his attackers. The men collapsed as the insects chewed and bit, ripping open the flesh on their faces and arms.

The other assailant struggled to his feet. He slapped away the insects and looked at Racket-man. "Holy shit! They're eating your fucking face!"

Johnny, still cradling his ribs, stared wide-eyed at the howling men. Taking several deep breaths, he felt the flow of insects slow. Awareness flooded him. *They respond to my emotions.*

Johnny focused on calming himself. He directed his attention toward the insects, then summoned them.

Come. Come back.

The swarms instantly ebbed away from their prey and drifted back to Johnny. He watched as the masses crawled beneath his clothing and disappeared.

Holy fuck, they're a part of me. I can control them.

"Come on!" Racket-man stumbled to his feet and mumbled, "Let's get out of here!"

"What the hell is that guy?" the other said, glaring back at Johnny as they staggered away.

A cop car, lights ablaze, rounded the corner and sped toward them. The siren blapped twice.

"Run!" Racket-Man said, pulling the other toward the park.

The police car skidded to a stop ten feet away from where Johnny lay.

"Freeze!" A cop threw the door open and chased after the muggers, disappearing behind the trees bordering the park.

The second cop climbed out of the car and cautiously approached Johnny. "You okay? What happened?"

"I was going to that coffee shop and they tried to mug me." Johnny glanced at his arms, still wrapped around his middle.

The cop reached down to help him up. "We'd better get you checked out."

"No!" Johnny panicked at the thought. "I don't need a doctor."

The other cop ran back. "They got away, Brick. I'm pretty sure one of them was Badouin."

Brick?

Johnny stared at the man who helped him up. *Dick Brickford?* He strained to get a better look.

I didn't even recognize you. You've lost weight.

"Nice going, slow poke," Brickford said to his partner. "I'm twenty years older than you and I can still outrun your ass." He turned back to Johnny. "You sure you're all right?"

"Yeah."

Brickford looked Johnny up and down. "Well, I'm going to have to take a statement from you. Why don't we go back to the station and I'll get you that cup of coffee."

"Okay." Johnny inhaled, recoiling in pain as he got to his feet.

"Looks like they got a rib," Brickford said. "What's your name?"

Shit.

Johnny hadn't considered that.

Jonathan Flynn is dead.

He thought of his father's favorite poem by Tennyson, and then looked toward the night sky as he answered.

"Fallow. My name is Johnny Fallow."

PART III
SPECIATION

FIFTY-SIX

A uster gazed along the serpentine wall that crested the tops of mountains and plunged into the valleys of China's rugged terrain. Tourists navigated around him, wrapped tightly in coats and taking pictures of the awe-inspiring landscape.

Boke Gal pointed to a distant mountain. "I've combed a thousand miles. The area east of here is clear." He glanced toward Auster. "The new Sentry, is he still verifying the truth?"

"Yes. It seems that humans need to revisit the life they've left before moving forward."

"I still think about the last time I saw my family before receiving the gift of light." Boke Gal's jet-black ponytail whipped in the wind. "It was difficult to resign myself to the fact that I would never teach my son to ride a horse, that his uncles would get that honor." He shook his head. "I don't expect you to understand. You're not human."

"No, I'm not," Auster said. "But I have felt the pull of kin. A preference, if you will, toward their success."

"Yet you've created armies for the sole purpose of wiping them out."

"On Earth, in human form, yes." Auster squared his shoulders. "You've lived for almost a thousand years. Can you say with certainty that you would be content to walk the Earth forever?"

"Not any more," Boke Gal answered. "I have witnessed the beauty created from wisdom and the destruction brought forth by ignorance."

"Humans are cyclical beasts," Auster said.

"True, I have seen many histories repeated." Boke Gal gazed across the vast expanse below. "I love my people. When I see a child racing across the steppe on a horse, my heart swells with pride. But I have watched my people dwindle down to a score of tribes, only a handful of which keep to our ancient traditions. I wonder how many generations will pass before I look down to see that I am the only one left of my kind."

Auster stared down at him. "Fewer than you think."

FIFTY-SEVEN

Johnny sat across from Brickford, sipping strong black coffee from a paper cup. His body ached, but he could feel it healing. He shifted in his seat.

"You sure you're all right?" Brickford took a swig from the mug on his desk. "We can still have you checked out."

"Not necessary." Johnny noticed the ring on Brickford's finger. "You're married, huh?"

"Yep. Married the same woman twice. Second time's a charm, I guess."

"Kids?"

"My girl's sixteen and my boy's six." Brickford paused. "And we have a little pain-in-the-ass furball named Louie who thinks he's one of the kids."

"Maddie's *sixteen*." Johnny winced. *Shit. Shouldn't have said that.*

Brickford's smile disappeared. His eyes narrowed. "How did you know my daughter's name?" He stared daggers at Johnny.

"You told me, a very long time ago. I don't expect you'd remember me."

Brickford crossed his arms. "Try me."

Shit. Johnny thought for a moment before electing to take a stab around the truth. "We met between eight and nine years ago. You were working a big case, the one that landed you here."

"The Flynn kidnapping?"

"That's it."

"And how did we meet?"

"You interviewed me. I worked for Owen Corp."

"Ah," Brickford said. "I did interview a lot of those folks. Don't remember a *Fallow* though, and I'd remember a name like that."

Johnny shrugged. "Maybe you wrote *clerk named John* in your little pad. That's what I was then, an entry-level, paper-passing, coffee-schlepping file guy. You asked me about Roderick Dennington, we talked about family for a bit, and you left."

"That makes sense." Brickford lifted his cup. "I don't see a ring on your finger."

"I was married then." Johnny glanced at the muddy, black liquid in his cup. "She died."

"I'm sorry." There was an uncomfortable pause. "So, what brings you to Thousand Wells?"

"I'm leaving the area and wanted to see some old friends before I make the move."

"And this is your welcome back, huh?"

"No shit." Johnny held up one finger. "I'm in town for half a day and I get mugged. My wallet and credit cards are gone, and if I call my new boss and tell him I lost the cash card he gave me *this morning,* I risk getting canned for being an irresponsible ass."

"Did they take your car keys?"

"No, I took the bus from Gypsum Ridge."

"The bus, huh?" Brickford eyed Johnny curiously and took out a notepad. "One of the guys who mugged you is named Marvin Badouin. He's sort of the big-wig drug dealer around here. Your assault is being added to the long list of crap he's done over the past few years."

"Great." Johnny slumped down in his chair.

"Okay, so you were walking down—"

Another cop burst through the door. "Hey, Brick, Humphries works the six-to-three shift tomorrow. We can duck over there and check out the Vander Broek barrel before breakfast."

Vander Broek barrel? Johnny stiffened.

Brickford leaned toward Johnny. "Can you hold on for a sec?"

"Sure."

Brickford got up and walked out of the office.

Johnny listened through the door.

"You sure you wanna risk going out of town again for a gun barrel, Brick?"

Brickford's response was clear. "That gun barrel left a three-year-old in a coma. I *know* it's the same one used to kill Vander Broek eight years ago. I gotta give it a shot."

A three-year-old kid? Johnny felt the blood drain from his face.

"Poor little fella," the other voice said. "It's awful to see a baby with all those tubes sticking out of him. All right, I'll be up before the damn roosters tomorrow."

"Great. Get outta here and I'll see ya then."

Brickford opened the door, rushed past Johnny, and sat behind his desk. "Sorry about that, Mr. Fallow. Let's get your statement so you can be on your way."

An hour later, Johnny left the police station. Not wanting to prolong their interaction, he refused Brickford's offer for a lift to the bus station.

Three years old. Did my actions really aid in a child being shot? Johnny's mind went haywire. *What if Brickford figures out that I killed Vander Broek? Would he go public with it? Would Michael and Maya find out?*

His thoughts drifted back to the mugging. *The insects attacked those thugs. They knew I was in trouble. How can I figure out why they behaved that way?*

∞∞∞∞∞∞∞

The following morning, Johnny took a bus to Thousand Wells University. After asking around, he finally found the entomology department and knocked on the office door of the Chair, Dr. Jeffrey Drendin.

"It's open."

Johnny cracked the door to find Drendin reading behind a desk piled so high with books and stacks of paper that the man was barely visible.

"Hello, Dr. Drendin. I'm John Fallow. May I have a minute?"

"Sure. What can I do for you?"

Johnny brought out a green foam board displaying bugs tacked down with pins. He set it atop one of the piles of papers.

Drendin chuckled as he stood up and regarded the collection. "Isn't that green stuff what you use to hold fake flowers?"

"Yeah," Johnny said. "I had limited resources. I was hoping you could give me some information about these insects."

The scientist eyed the specimens. "Where's the body?"

"Pardon me?"

"The body," Drendin repeated. "This is a murder investigation right? You're a cop?"

"I'm not a cop. Why do you ask?"

Drendin gestured toward the board. "They're decomposers."

"Decomposers?"

"Yeah." He pointed to some of the insects. "Blowflies, beetles, ants, maggots. Something dies, and they take over. They're nature's garbage men, if you will. They eat carcasses clean to the bone, and quicker than one might think."

Johnny stared at the board.

Drendin sat back down and folded his hands behind his head. "Cops love these little guys. They find a decomposed body, collect the bugs, forensic entomologists stick 'em in a blender, and voila, a DNA smoothie. John Doe now has a name and, if they're lucky, a perp's DNA will make it into the soup, too."

"Decomposers," Johnny repeated.

"Yep, every one of them." He took another look at Johnny's makeshift bugboard. "Where'd you find 'em?"

"You don't want to know."

Johnny thanked Drendin for his time and ambled out the door, his thoughts a jumbled mess.

I have decomposers coming out of me. Auster said he brought me back to life. Are these things eating me because I'm really dead?

Johnny dumped the bug board in the trash and clutched the rail as he descended the concrete steps of the building. Throngs of students sprawled on the north lawn in front of the science wing, studying, kissing, and soaking up the sun in between classes. His skin felt itchy as he plodded across the grass and eventually found a spot under a tree.

He dropped to his knees. "Decomposers," he said to himself. He lay back in the soft grass. *I haven't slept in twenty-four hours. I'll just close my eyes for a minute.* Within three breaths, he slipped into an uneasy sleep.

When he woke, Johnny was the only one left on the lawn and the sun had set.

"Oh, no."

He hauled ass and barely made the last bus heading downtown. He settled in for the ride, processing the information he'd learned since he woke the previous day.

Eight years have passed, Johnny thought. Maya's in Europe, Michael is divorcing himself from Flynn Corp, Paula is dying. "This is futile," he said aloud. *Everyone I left behind has moved on. And the kids won't believe it's me if I find them. What can I honestly hope to do here?*

Johnny closed his eyes. *I'm fucking starving. I should spend my last few bucks on a meal and call to Auster.*

It was dark when Johnny stepped off of the bus at Town Center Square. Enveloped in his thoughts, he trudged onward until he caught the scent of something delicious. The deep, savory aroma arrested his senses, bringing on a hunger unlike any he had experienced.

Meat. It smells fantastic.

His pace hastened as he followed the scent.

There!

He dashed down a street and turned left at an alley. Someone had dumped the leftovers from a large meal next to a dumpster.

Fuck, I'm starving and too broke to buy real food. I don't care if it's on the ground. I'm ravenous and it smells so good.

He checked to make sure no one was around then fell to his knees and shamelessly dug in, ripping pieces with his hands and stuffing them into his mouth to satiate his violent hunger. He chewed so quickly that he choked several times and his insides churned as he swallowed mouthful after mouthful. It was nearly gone when he finally had enough, then he sat back on his haunches and took a deep breath.

That was amazing.

The sudden smell of rotting garbage jolted him from his trance. He peered down at the remaining food.

No. It can't be.

A dead opossum, ripped to shreds and covered in a blanket of worms and ants, lay in front of him. Johnny had eaten much of it clean to the bone, but its head was still intact, the vacant eyes staring at him.

He raised his trembling hands to see them covered in blood.

No way. I didn't just...

He gagged, leaned over, and vomited next to what was left of the dead animal. Confused and panic-stricken, he stumbled to his feet and bolted toward Town Center Square. He ripped through the yellow tape surrounding the fountain and jumped into it, gagging more as he gulped the cloudy water.

After rinsing his mouth for a good five minutes, Johnny sat on the stone lip of the fountain.

I'm a monster.

He thought of his conversation with Brickford.

A three-year-old is in a coma because of me.

He thought of his kids, of Paula, of Dani.

I have nothing left. I am nothing.

In the distance, Johnny saw a cop approaching.

"You can't bathe there, fella," he called out as he got closer. "You shouldn't even be on the other side of that tape." The cop reached the fountain and his eyes zeroed in on Johnny's shirt, stained with opossum blood. "Are you all right?"

Johnny glanced down at himself and fought the urge to barf again. "I'm fine."

The cop looked Johnny up and down. "You're going to have to move on now."

"Yes, sir." Johnny stood up and plodded away from the square.

It's over.

Johnny thought back to the time under the jacarandas, remembering holding his father's hand as they walked through the purple pools on the green grass.

Come and get me, Auster.

FIFTY-EIGHT

Anisha Patel Corby lay over the side of William's hospital bed, her body weakened, her eyes swollen shut from crying. Frank sat beside her with Katie on his lap. Anjali and Ben flanked William's other side.

The curtains were drawn, the room dim. The sucking of the ventilator and blip of the heart monitor cut through the thick silence.

A nurse slipped in to take William's vitals, startling everyone from their trances.

Ben got up, went to the window, and parted the curtains. The light cut through the space like a knife.

Anisha adjusted the sheets around the little boy after the nurse finished. She looked across the bed at her sister. "I'd do anything…" She paused when she felt a stitch in her side. Focusing on the unborn sleeping inside of her, she tried to calm herself. *Breathe.* She placed a hand on her swollen belly, and carefully sat back down.

"Ani, are you all right?" Anjali looked worried.

"I'm fine."

"Are you in pain?" Frank placed a hand on her back..

"Of course. "Anisha took one of William's hands into both of hers. "My baby is clinging to life. I want to break through the wall that keeps him unconscious. I want William to wake up."

Frank swept a tear from his cheek. "Me, too, Ani." He stood and kissed his son's head. "Come on, big guy, we need you."

FIFTY-NINE

Auster materialized in an outdoor shopping area. Yellow caution tape surrounded a large stone fountain.

Jonathan Flynn sat cross-legged at its base. "Welcome to Town Center Square," he said as Auster approached.

"An interesting structure." Auster gazed at the stone shaman at the base of the waterfall.

"That's Thousand Wells. He protected this area at one time." Flynn gestured toward the small group of Native American women ducking under the tape to leave flowers at the shaman's feet. "They're hoping he'll return to help the city."

Auster shook his head. "Gods and magic—humans' way of diverting blame away from themselves throughout time. Only action, a change in human behavior, can save this place."

Flynn gazed up at the fountain. "My parents used to bring me here when I was a boy. I'd stand here, just staring up at this fountain for as long as they would let me. I *loved* the smell of it. It was so unique to me. Even today, when I pass by a water feature, I catch that chlorinated water smell and my mind takes me right back here."

Auster tapped into Johnny's memory, then scanned the stone monolith. "The structure has weathered."

"They're tearing it down soon."

"Everything has a life span."

Flynn stood up. "So it seems. I needed to see it one more time."

"I'm surprised you called so soon. Those before you have taken much longer to resign to their posts."

"You were right. Nothing is the same." Flynn locked gazes with Auster. "What *am* I exactly? Why do decomposers come out of me?"

"Come out of you? I don't understand."

Flynn told Auster about the insects in the car with Gingham, about the mugging incident, and his visit to the university.

"You were able to *control* the insects' behavior?"

"Yes. When I focused and called them back, they returned to me."

"Interesting."

"So I'm *made* of bugs?"

"They were used to rebuild you," Auster said. "You drew in the insects' life energy and bodies to stay alive, and then I melded you with a human to shape your current appearance."

"Right." Flynn looked down at himself. "The thirty-four year-old motorcyclist."

"Correct. But you seemed to have done more than absorb the insects' energy and tissue. The insects and the human contributor have both melded with you on a cellular level. The insects could even sustain you in such a way that you may not need to build new bodies."

"New bodies?"

"Yes."

"Am I even *alive*?"

"Of course. Make no mistake about your biological state." Auster gestured toward Flynn's chest. "Your heart pumps and blood runs through your veins. Your systems function the same way they would if they were made of human tissue. You will need rest. You will need to eat and drink, although your dietary urges may be slightly different."

Flynn appeared sickened by the thought. "I've noticed. So, what happens now?"

"If you are ready to accept your duty as Sentry, you come with me. I open your aperture, test it to make sure you are able to read my signature. If you show that you're worthy, I will bestow upon you the ability to wield light."

"My life is over, anyway," Flynn said.

"It was the moment you took your last breath in the Pacific."

"Good morning, John." A voice called from behind them.

Flynn spun on his heels. "Good morning, Gladys."

Oh, my. Auster peered at the woman. *Another one. This area is teeming with their kind.*

Flynn cleared his throat. "Nice to see you again. You're off to an early start."

"My shift starts at six today, and I wanted to drop by and visit my little friend for a while. Send him some healing thoughts."

"Your little friend?"

"Yeah. William, the three-year-old little boy who got shot two days ago, is a family friend. It's been all over the news."

Flynn appeared to weaken at hearing this. "Yeah, I heard about it. How is he? Any change?"

"No," she answered. "But he *will* wake up." She toed the ground. "He has to." Her attention then went to Auster, her smile fading a little as she regarded him.

She senses me. Very astute.

"Oh, where are my manners?" Flynn said. "Gladys, this is my...boss, Auster." He turned to Auster. "This is Gladys."

Auster held out a hand. "Pleasure to make your acquaintance."

Gladys shook it. "Thank you. Nice to meet you, too, Auster." She faced Flynn again. "Well, I'd better be on my way."

"All right, take care." Flynn watched Gladys walk away.

Auster smiled. "Your choice in friends is interesting."

"Why? Do you know her?"

"Not exactly."

He will understand when I open his aperture.

Flynn appeared to grow impatient. "What do you mean? Either you knew her before I introduced her, or you didn't."

"*Know* is not the term I would use. You'll understand later." Auster held out a hand. "Now, close your eyes. We're about to fly very, very fast."

SIXTY

Dick Brickford gripped his coffee cup as he and Jason Brady arrived at the Quartz County Waste Industries service yard at 5:20 a.m. They sat in the car while they finished their breakfast sandwiches.

"You look wiped. Kids keep ya up?" Brady asked.

"Naw, just got to bed later than I wanted. This new car situation's beginning to be a pain in the ass. I spent three hours researching cars online with Maddie. Every time we got close to picking one, she or Helen would change their minds."

"It's a woman's prerogative—"

"Yeah, yeah." Brickford waved a hand. "Don't even bother to finish."

"Just take her to the lot and get it done," Brady said. "She'll test drive something, fall in love with it, and *boom*, you're signing papers and everyone's happy."

"That may be an idea. I think I'll take them over to the used car place in the next couple of days."

"You won't regret it, Brick. Trust me."

They finished their food and downed the rest of their coffee.

"Who's the head honcho here again?" Brady asked as he cracked the door open.

"Manager's name is Dusty Harwood. I spoke to him yesterday and he confirmed that Humphries starts at six."

They entered the building and were directed to Harwood's office. Brickford knocked.

"Come in."

Brickford opened the door. A man with slate-gray hair glowered at them from behind a small desk. "You must be the cops."

"Yes, we are."

On the wall behind Harwood hung a large, framed picture. The man in the photo stood on a dock wearing an old fishing hat, a huge grin plastered across his face as he hefted a giant bass in both arms. A small metal inscription attached to the bottom of the frame read:

Catch of the day
Corbreath County Bass Fishing Competition

Brickford pointed up at the photo. "Whoa, check him out. I haven't been up to Corbreath in some time. You use spinner bait to catch that guy?"

Harwood's sour disposition changed immediately. "Nope. That somebitch was caught midday."

"Ah, so you ambushed him close to the shoreline?"

"Sure as shit did." Harwood cracked a smile. "Fished a jig-n-pig rig under a fallen tree."

"That'll do it." Brickford eyed the picture. "What's that, about ten pounds?"

"Ten pounds, seven ounces. You know your bass."

"I do, and that's a helluva catch." Brickford gave an approving nod.

"Thank you." Harwood's grin matched the one in the picture.

"I'm Dick Brickford. We spoke yesterday."

"Dusty Harwood." He stood up and they shook hands. "Look, um, between us, is there anything I should be concerned about here?"

"Naw," Brickford said. "It's just a routine thing." He pulled out his little note pad and clicked his pen. "How long has Humphries been with the county?"

"About twenty years, I think. He's a hard worker, always on time. Haven't had one complaint about him."

"Well, that's real good to know," Brickford leaned in toward Harwood. "Hey, would you mind if we talk to him here in your office, you know, so it doesn't draw attention and all?"

"Sure, what the hell," Harwood said. "Oh, there he is now."

Samuel Humphries sauntered through the front door. He greeted several other workers then turned toward the locker room.

"Sam!" Harwood called out.

Humphries stopped and glanced over, the smile on his face vanishing when he saw Brickford and Brady.

"Would you come in here a sec?" Harwood turned to Brickford. "He's all yours." He checked his watch. "His shift starts in fifteen."

"We shouldn't be long." Brickford held the door open as Humphries walked into the office.

"Good morning, Mr. Humphries. I'm Dick Brickford and this is Jason Brady. We're with the Thousand Wells Police Department and were hoping you'd answer a few questions for us."

Humphries shrugged. "Okay. What's up?"

"Have a seat." Brickford moved around and sat behind Harwood's desk. "Did you sell a gun a year or so ago?"

"Nope." Humphries sat down. "I'm a lover, not a fighter."

"Hmm," Brady said. "A guy we talked to several days back said he bought a gun off you at Junebug's about a year ago. Said you wanted to get rid of it."

Humphries looked offended. "Don't deal in guns. This is where I earn my money."

"Do you own a gun?" Brickford asked.

"Several, all registered. I live in Thousand Wells. You own a gun here or people rob your ass—or worse. In case you haven't noticed, there ain't no shaman here to protect us anymore."

"You ever piece a gun together?" Brady asked. "Rebuild one from old parts?"

"Nope."

"You're a regular at Junebug's, right?" Brickford looked at his notepad. "The guy who runs the place says you are."

"Sure. I chill there to watch a game or have a beer. Lots of guys from here hit Junee's."

"Ever heard of a guy named Theodore Jessup?"

"Nope."

Brickford let the silence settle in.

Humphries gestured toward the door. "Is that it? I gotta clock in and get going."

"Yeah, I think it is." Brickford stood up. "Thanks for your time, Mr. Humphries."

∞∞∞∞∞∞

"That was a horrendous waste of time!" Brady shouted as they walked out the door. "I got my black ass out of bed at four in the morning for this shit?"

Brickford turned to see Humphries smiling after them. "Good job, Brady. He heard you."

They marched to the car and got in.

When both doors slammed shut, Brady turned to Brickford. "Brotha's lying like a muthafucka."

"Totally," Brickford said. "Did you get what I got?"

"Whenever he was telling the truth, he had diarrhea of the mouth, went on and on. And when he was lying, it was just—"

"Nope," they said in unison.

"You're a quick learner, rookie." Brickford scooped up the empty fast-food bags and balled them up. "Pull up to the side there so I can throw this away. It's making the car smell like grease."

Brady drove around to the side of the building and Brickford hopped out to toss the trash. Some of the trucks were already pulling out of the side exit on the way to their routes.

Brickford walked up to the dumpster and tossed the garbage inside. He froze when he heard a voice, angry and sharp, then peered between the dumpster and the building to see Humphries holding a wispy little blonde guy by the collar.

"Tell me!" Humphries spat.

"I didn't say anything, Bogart! I swear."

"Then why did the goddamn cops show up?"

The guy squirmed. "I swear, I didn't say nothin' 'bout Rancid to nobody."

"Don't say the fucking *name*, you idiot. Ever." Humphries let go of the guy's collar and pushed him. "A month after you come aboard, the cops come sniffin' around."

"I haven't told a soul. I swear on my mother's grave."

Humphries jabbed his index finger an inch from his face. "I'll be pissing on yours if a cop comes poking around my ass again." He spun around and marched away.

Brickford made sure he was clear before returning to the car. He threw the door open and slid onto the seat.

"What the hell?" Brady said. "You look like you've seen a ghost."

"Ever heard of Rancid?"

∞∞∞∞∞∞

"Nothing." Brady held up both hands. "I've searched for two hours and there's no match on the word rancid anywhere."

"Shit," Brickford said. "There's gotta be something. Did you check the web?"

"There's a bunch of rock bands that use *rancid* in their name. Let me check it again." Brady typed in the word. "Yep, that and the definition of the word, which is, having a disagreeable odor or taste of decomposing oils or fats; rank. Repugnant and nasty are synonyms."

"Okay, so rancid describes rotten trash," Brickford said. "Maybe something's going down at the facility or at the landfill."

"Shit, I don't know," Brady tapped his pencil against his desk. "Guys get their trucks, go out and pick up the trash, take it to the landfill—"

"Unless they're recyclables," Brickford interjected. He took out his notepad. "Recyclables go to the material recovery facility five miles away."

"That's it." Brady punched the desk.

"What?" Brickford said.

"How many thousands of pounds of recyclables are taken to that facility every day?"

"Look it up!" Brickford sat forward as Brady typed away.

"Okay." Brady's finger ran along the text as he read it. "It says here that the average household generates about a pound-and-a-half of recyclables every day." He glanced up at Brickford. "That's a lot of material."

"That could yield a decent sum if it were recycled privately."

"True," Brady rubbed his chin. "If Humphries and the others had a system for separating out the stuff they could get cash for and processed it at different locations throughout their shifts…"

"I hear ya. Bulk like that could yield a bit of a supplement for those guys." Brady scratched his head. "Would that even be considered stealing?"

"Don't know, but they could lose their jobs, I'm pretty sure." Brickford shrugged and exhaled. "Well, that ends that mystery. I still think Humphries sold Jessup the gun, though."

"Me, too. But everything's getting a bit convoluted. This guy's connected to Jessup, who used a gun with a barrel that was used eight years ago..." Brady shook his head. "It's sounds kinda out there."

"Yeah." Brickford slapped his thighs. "I'm starting to feel like I'm barking up a tree out in nowhere."

Their radio went off. "All units, we have a two-eleven at the corner of Main and Thousand Wells Avenue. Suspects are on foot heading east."

Brickford picked up the radio. "Brickford here, we're on it."

"Guess our secret research time is over." Brady pulled out the car keys.

"Shit, you're probably right, rookie." Brickford got up. "Over for good. I'm chasing my tail on this."

SIXTY-ONE

Johnny hunched on his knees atop a summit overlooking the city lights of Thousand Wells, his face beaten and swollen. A plastic gallon jug lay empty beside him. He breathed in and out, fighting the urge to puke.

"I'll blacken your other eye if you vomit again." Auster stood above him, bare-chested and bleeding from two gaping wounds in his abdomen. "This process is not pleasant for me, either."

Johnny clenched his fist. "This is fucking insane. I have to eat your fucking flesh to *open an aperture*?"

"Many of the things you are about to experience will be firsts." Auster leaned down, snatched up his T-shirt, and slipped it on.

Johnny gazed up at the waxing moon, his head reeling. "Everything's so intense—what I see, what I hear. My senses are out of control."

"That's expected. Your aperture was just opened. You're able to see all life energy now. The sense of overwhelm will diminish as you adjust."

Johnny stood on wobbly legs. "So, this is how I will see every living thing from now on? Through this *haze* of energy?"

"Yes, but it will get easier over time. You will be able to filter energy the same way you filter the innumerable things you see when you walk down the street."

"This is the light you were talking about?"

"No. Wielding light is a power that involves an additional application. Right now your ability is the same as that of a Hand. You are able to read life energy and track my source signature, which will be tested tomorrow."

Johnny touched his swollen face and winced. "How many Sentries are there?"

"There are many around the world."

"How do you choose them?"

"Each had an energy source unlike other humans. Each was unique in life. Throughout history, my Sentries have risen to the top of their society, as you did."

Johnny paced back and forth. "In case you hadn't noticed. I wasn't exactly at the top of society the night I drove off that cliff."

"Did you not control every moment leading to your own demise?"

Johnny thought for a moment. "I suppose I did. So, you want me to kill your descendants with this *life* you've given me?"

"Not want, *expect*. And if you are made Sentry, you will have the ability to wield light, which you will use to create Hands to assist you."

"In killing innocents—women, children."

"Some are, yes," Auster said evenly. "You are only to dispose of those with my signature. All others are spared."

"I can't kill kids. There's no way."

"You already have," Auster said. "Why do you think you were chosen?"

"I've killed people, but not innocent women and kids."

Auster slowly shook his head. "That's incorrect. You are responsible for the demise of many innocents."

"Bullshit!" Johnny spat. "I should just kill myself again."

"I suspected that you may consider that option," Auster answered. "To ensure you don't take your own life again, I've sent some of your life source to each of your children. You are unable to die unless both of your children perish first."

"You sent my *life source* to my kids?"

"A small portion," Auster replied. "The effect is positive. Additional life source improves both mental and physical abilities."

"I'm going to outlive both my kids." Johnny turned his face to the night sky. "I can't think of anything crueler than making someone outlive their children."

"You will adjust. The others have."

Johnny crossed his arms. "If I'm not *deemed worthy*, as you say, you'll kill me, right? So I'll just fail your little test and that will be that."

Auster smiled at this. "Do you honestly believe that petulant behavior will be an effective ruse? Granted, it will be annoying and you will be punished, but my Sentries and I are able to see right through it."

"How do you judge, then?"

"It is customary that I and three of my Sentries deem you worthy of joining us. You will spend time with each Sentry and then return to me to be given the gift of light—or destroyed."

"And when does all of this start?"

"Now. Your first visit will be with Torphis."

"Torphis? Where is he from?"

"He resides in Europe."

Auster took hold of Johnny's hand. "Since you are not able to change states, I must take you. It is best if you sleep through this." Auster raised a hand above Johnny's head and sent forth a pulse of yellow light.

Johnny collapsed.

SIXTY-TWO

Brickford trudged through the front door at dusk. Hank ran into the entry with a leash in hand. "Dad, wanna take Louie for a walk with me and Maddie?"

"Sure, pal. Let me change out of my work clothes."

Brickford marched down the hall toward the bedroom, stopping at Helen's little office. "Hey, miss author pants."

Helen spun her chair around. "Hi, handsome. Traffic was a bitch today, huh?"

"Awful. Crawled the whole way home. Thank God we moved here from Gypsum, though, else I'd be on the road another hour."

"I like it better here, anyway." Helen pushed away from the desk. "Jasper Hills is just as nice, and far less pretentious. How was crime fighting today?"

"A typical Thousand Wells day—robberies, knifings, domestic violence, vandalism. The usual."

"Too bad," Helen said. "It used to be such a nice place."

"I remember." Brickford walked in, pecked Helen on the cheek, and glanced at the computer screen. "How about you? Getting the great American novel written?"

"Don't know about that, but I managed to squeeze out another chapter. It's rough, but my critique group will kick its ass into shape."

"That's great, baby." He jerked his thumb back toward the door. "I'm going with the kids to take Louie for a walk."

"Oh, good. The little turkey needs it. He's been lazing around the house all day. He's like a twenty-pound, breathing rug."

"I wish I had his life." Brickford walked toward the door. "Sleep all day, get petted, eat treats."

"He *is* spoiled," Helen said. "You want to jump online with Maddie and look for cars when you guys get back?"

Brickford sucked in a breath. *Please make this work.* "Actually, I was thinking maybe tomorrow we could take her over to the used car dealer and have her test drive a few." He held his breath, waiting for a response.

"Good idea. I'm in." Helen spun back around to face the computer.

Yes! Thanks, Brady.

In the bedroom, Brickford changed into shorts and tennis shoes and headed for the front door. "Okay, kids. Let's go!"

"Louie, walk!" Hank yelled.

The black terrier mix with a severe underbite bounded into the room, yelping and jumping up on Maddie and Hank.

"Chill out, Louie!" Maddie laughed as she hooked the leash onto his collar.

Brickford trailed behind the kids as the little dog pulled Hank out the front door. He exhaled deeply, plodding along the sidewalk of the quiet neighborhood. The evening breeze had kicked up and the setting sun reflected pink off the distant clouds.

"This is a good way to end the day." Brickford patted Hank on the back.

Hank smiled at the wiggly-tailed mutt. "Louie sure likes it."

"It's like he has some internal clock or something," Maddie said. "He starts bugging us at this time every day."

"Hey," Brickford said to Hank. "I met a guy today who caught a big one up at Corbreath recently. Made me want to take another fishing trip up there. Would you like that?"

"Heck, yeah! I'll catch another big one!" Hank jumped up and down.

"Okay, I'll ask your mom about it when we get back." Brickford turned to Maddie. "What about you, kid?"

"No gooey guts for me, thanks." Maddie's curly hair bounced in the breeze. "Plus, I've got practice weeknights, and, you know, friend stuff."

"That's what I figured." He put an arm around her. "Hey, we're gonna take you over to the car dealership to drive a few tomorrow. See if we can pick one out."

"Yay! That's awesome, Daddy!" She hugged him. "I'm still voting for a convertible."

A neighbor getting out of her car waved at them. "Hello."

"Hi." Hank waved back then turned to Brickford. "Watch, Dad, I'll bet Louie's gonna poop now."

Right on cue, Louie stopped, arched his back, and laid a big turd on the lady's lawn right in front of her.

Maddie pulled a bag from the holder on the leash and held it up. "We'll pick it up. He likes to poop in front of people."

The lady laughed. "It's like they know, huh?"

"Yep," Hank said as Maddie tied off the bag.

They rounded the corner to the next block. The sun was about to drop below view, taking with it the heat of the day and ushering in one of those delicious California evenings portrayed in magazines.

Brickford took the leash. "This is pretty nice. The sun's going down. It's getting cooler. I should join you guys more often."

"Yes, you should," Maddie said.

"Before you know it, you'll be away at college." Brickford leaned in toward Maddie. "Unless you want to live at home, which would be great!"

"Yeah, stay home, sis!" Hank reached for the leash. "Here, Dad, I'll take him."

Maddie jogged to a trash bin on the street, opened it, peeked inside, and tossed in the bag. "Whew, even though it's empty, that trash can is drug-deal rank!"

"It's *what*?" Brickford asked.

"Drug deal rank." Maddie gave Brickford the 'you're so out of it' look. "Come on, Daddy, you're a cop. You know what I'm saying."

"No, I really don't."

"It's like, how things are passed around at school now. If someone's going to cheat on a test, they hit the bathroom, put the answers in the trash, and cover it up with a bag filled with something gross. Then they go to the bathroom during the test and pull the answers out."

"Wow, cheating's come a long way from whispers and note-passing," Brickford said.

"Yeah, but there's more than just test answers going around, Dad." Maddie kicked a rock in her path. "Kids hide cigarettes, beer, and stuff like that in the trash, too. The worse the trash smells, the worse the offense underneath."

"Hence the term *drug-deal rank*." Brickford glanced back at the trash container.

"Yep." Maddie pointed behind her. "No one would ever think a trash can that smells like *that* would have something valuable hidden in it."

Brickford stopped.

Maddie continued. "But at school, there aren't bags of dog poop, just rotten food to cover the contraband." She spun around. "What, Daddy?"

Holy shit. Samuel Humphries isn't recycling at all.

SIXTY-THREE

Johnny opened his eyes to see to a vaulted ceiling. He sat up, letting his gaze drift across the cream-colored walls of a large suite adorned with rich, colorful tapestries. On the left side of the room, thick burgundy curtains had been pulled away from glass double doors, allowing sunlight to bathe the space in a warm, buttery glow.

He swung his legs over the side of the bed. The stone tiles felt cool beneath his bare feet as he crossed the room and swung the doors open.

A breeze carried in the scent of lavender as Johnny stepped onto a balcony of a horseshoe-shaped building that appeared to be more of a hotel than an estate. The view overlooked rolling green hills that spanned as far as he could see.

"Good morning."

Johnny turned toward the voice to face a tall, lean man with jet-black hair and bright blue eyes. "Torphis?"

"I am." He spoke slowly, his voice deep and silky with a thick, English accent.

"Did you turn to dust and fly here like you did in the cave?"

"We don't turn to dust." Torphis held out his hand and it melted into floating particles. "The light enables us to change states. You're familiar? Solid, liquid, gas?"

"I know the states of matter."

"Most of the human form is water, so you can think of it as more as a mist." Torphis brought the fog up close to Johnny. "Go ahead, run your hand through it."

Johnny swiped through the mist and then rubbed his fingers together. "I don't feel anything. Wouldn't my hand be wet since it's mostly water?"

"It is the same as us passing each other on the street. All of the material that makes up my hand went around yours." Torphis materialized his hand, took a step back, and analyzed Johnny. "Your energy is unique, part human, part insect."

"I'm told. My aperture is open but I can only read life energy as a glow, and I can read Auster's signature."

"You will be able to discern much more after you're made Sentry. I cannot explain the experience adequately. It would be like trying to describe the taste of a strawberry to someone who has never eaten fruit."

Johnny leaned forward on the railing. "Is this your home?"

"Yes. It's about a thousand acres, as you would say." Torphis pointed to the far end. "The entire west wing is fully functional on its own. It's used to shelter battered women and children." He pointed beyond the green hills. "About a third of the land is used to grow organic crops to be given to the poor. There is an animal sanctuary here, as well."

Johnny felt confused. "You are a Sentry for Auster, right?"

"That is correct."

"So, you kill innocent people on a regular basis."

Torphis looked at Johnny. "I do, which is what I did in my life before Auster."

Johnny waved a hand toward the estate grounds. "So this altruistic front is bullshit."

"No, others are receiving help."

"But you would kill them if they had Auster's signature."

"Yes, and that has happened. Speaking of which, let's see if you are able to read Auster's energy." He took Johnny's arm. "Close your eyes."

Johnny did as he was told then felt a whoosh and a pull. He dared to crack one eye open and saw the green blur of the countryside far below. When he opened both eyes, they were standing on the edge of a busy city street.

Johnny looked around. "I know this place. We're in Piccadilly Circus."

"Right you are. People from all over the world visit London, so we're bound to encounter Auster's signature here. Let's walk."

Johnny marveled at the energy he was able to sense as they tooled through the city. People, animals, even plants seemed to burst with it. It felt like countless vibrations coming from all directions.

They passed an outdoor pub and Johnny felt a familiar twinge. He spotted a man exiting a gift shop. He nodded toward the man. "He's one of Auster's relatives, isn't he?"

"Yes." Torphis said.

"So you have to kill him?"

"Yes. Not here, of course. Public places are not wise."

Johnny faced Torphis. "What if he has children? My wife was murdered. I know what it's like to look into the faces of your children, knowing she'll never return."

"You caused the death of your wife by murdering innocents yourself, yes?"

Johnny had no answer.

"You are the bad guy, new Sentry, don't forget that. Your concern is misplaced." He turned away. "Let's proceed."

Johnny took one final look at the doomed man before catching up with Torphis. "Do you believe these charities you set up undo the murdering of innocents?"

"I've never believed that. I help others because I am able. I will do the work of a Sentry regardless, so why not provide help where I can?"

"How long have you been a Sentry?"

"Over three-hundred-and-sixty years."

"What were you when you were alive, you know, the first time?"

"Before Auster brought me back, I was a religious man who dedicated his life to the church. I believed Satan was tightening his grip on humanity and had deemed our village to be a source of evil. This was announced and people panicked. Then came the accusations."

"Accusations?"

Torphis nodded once. "Witchcraft."

Johnny stared. "You were part of the witch trials?"

"Yes."

"I remember studying that in college," Johnny said. "About torturing women to get confessions. I had to take breaks from it because it made me sick."

"During my short tenure, more innocents were killed in England than in the previous one hundred years," Torphis explained.

"How did you die?"

"Illness. My death was more merciful than any sentence I had given to the innocent men and women I tortured."

Johnny felt another twinge. He glanced up at a tour bus passing by and pointed out two more of Auster's descendants riding on the top tier.

"Good enough," Torphis said. "Let's visit a place closer to home." They turned a corner and stood behind a row of buildings. "Close your eyes."

∞∞∞∞∞∞∞

They landed on the grass just outside a little village in the countryside and strolled along a cobblestone street lined by traditional buildings built of timber and brick.

"How about a pint?" Torphis tilted his head toward a small doorway at the end of the block.

They entered the pub and took a table by the window.

A gray-haired man with ruddy cheeks approached. "Pleasure to see you again, sir. Will it be the usual?"

"Yes, thank you," Torphis said.

"And you, sir?"

"Your house ale would be fine."

"All right, then."

The man returned a few minutes later and placed the ales on the wooden table. "There ye go."

Johnny waited for the man to be out of earshot before he asked, "Did Auster choose you because of what you did in life?"

"Partly. At first, I thought Auster bringing me back was God rewarding me for my good work in dispelling evil. I proudly did Auster's bidding, destroying those whom he'd asked me to kill. When Auster showed me the truth, everything changed."

"What do you mean?"

"It would be better if you see for yourself. Finish your pint and we'll return home."

Ten minutes later, Johnny stood on the balcony of his room at Torphis' sprawling estate.

Torphis excused himself for a short time before returning with a tray bearing a small glass filled with red, bubbly liquid. He set down the tray and held up the glass. "Drink. It's my signature."

Johnny thought of how he'd acquired the ability to read Auster's signature. "It's your blood, isn't it?"

"That and a bit of tissue. Soda water has been added to make it more palatable."

Johnny swallowed hard and regarded the glass. "I don't have a choice, do I?"

"No. It is a connection that all Sentries have. I don't expect you to understand now, but you will appreciate it later. Take it."

Johnny cringed at the thought, took the glass, then belted the liquid back in one gulp. He gagged.

Torphis held up one finger. "You know not to throw it up."

Johnny forced the liquid down. "I take it I'll be able to read your descendants now?"

"Auster said you're a fast learner. There is more to it, though. Sentries who are connected are able to communicate thoughts, even memories. You asked how Auster revealed the truth about my life. Discussing this will not adequately communicate it. You must see it for yourself." Torphis raised a hand.

The blinding light forced Johnny to shut his eyes. He felt weightless at first and then as though he was spinning and falling. *What's going on? Am I moving?* Then all went still.

Johnny opened his eyes and found himself standing in a small house, which was little more than a room with a dirt floor and a tiny soot-blackened fireplace. He glanced around, confused and nauseous, and then the door burst open.

Two men marched in, both seeming unaware of Johnny's presence. Their appearance was odd, their clothing costume like—high-crowned hats, long hair over broad linen collars, hip-length capes, breeches, and bucket-top boots. The man closest to Johnny had a short beard and light hair, the other wore a longer beard and dark, curly hair that spilled down his back.

Where in the hell am I?

The short-bearded man spoke.

"I believe we are winning our fight against evil, Auster."

*Auster? It looks nothing like him. Wait...*Johnny stopped using his eyes and read the signatures.

It's Torphis and Auster, in different bodies. This must be hundreds of years ago.

Torphis continued. "Those three men were undoubtedly doing the work of Satan."

Auster turned to Torphis, appearing confused. "You believe we are fighting evil?"

"Of course," Torphis replied. "What else would we be doing?"

"What do you believe constitutes evil?" Auster asked.

"People who turn away from God and are guided by Satan."

Auster instantly turned to mist, scooped up Torphis, and yanked him out the door.

Light blinded Johnny as he was pulled into another home—this time in a bedroom where an old, withered woman aided in childbirth.

Auster and Torphis stood silently in the doorway, watching the mother scream in pain. The baby's head crowned.

Johnny thought of the birth of his own children.

The midwife placed her hand under the baby's head and shifted its shoulders. The infant slipped out of the woman's womb.

"It's a girl, Mum." the midwife said. She held up the babe, but there was no cry. The child was blue.

Johnny knew what that meant. *The baby's not breathing.*

The midwife turned the infant upside down and smacked her bottom. She smiled as air filled the baby's lungs. The shrill mewing of a newborn rang forth, her tiny, rapid breaths turning her a healthy pink.

Johnny felt a twist of angst. *I know that cry very well.*

Auster turned to Torphis. "That child did not take a breath on her own. That woman," he pointed to the midwife, "performed an action to cause the child to pull air into her lungs. If she hadn't done that, the child would not have lived. Would you call this witchcraft?"

"Of course not." Torphis answered.

"The midwife brought forth life from death, which, according to you, is the sign of a witch." Auster turned to mist again and swept Torphis into the air.

Johnny felt the pulling sensation and closed his eyes, then found himself outdoors, where women chanted in a circle.

Auster pointed to the women. "They are attempting to bring forth healing energy."

Johnny followed them into a hut where women pressed herbs against the fevered faces of the ill. Auster then led Torphis into another hut where a woman served the dying, giving them tonic mixtures to help ease the pain and holding their hands as they took what sounded like their last, rasping breaths.

"These women, all healers, were deemed 'witches' by the tenets of your faith." Auster began to change states. He grabbed Torphis by the arm. "Now see what you did to them."

Johnny felt the pull again as Auster turned to mist. A moment later, the three stood in a small chamber where the same midwife who aided the birthing was strapped down, bare-chested. Both withered breasts and her soft belly bled from puncture wounds. Two men, wrapped in hooded capes, flanked her, one held a red-hot poker.

What's this? Johnny couldn't believe his eyes. *What's going on?*

The inquisitor leaned close to her ear. "Admit to witchcraft! Admit you are Satan's concubine."

The woman gasped for air. "No. I'm not."

The torturer pressed the burning end of the poker to a bleeding breast. Her screams were blood-curdling. He pulled the iron away, taking flesh with it.

Monsters. Johnny covered his eyes. *They're fucking monsters.*

The woman's head lolled to one side and she passed out. The torturers revived her then took the iron to the other breast.

"Say you are one with Satan."

The screams shook the room. "Stop! Please. Anything. I'll say anything."

"Admit you do the work of Satan." The torturer brought the hot poker to her face.

The woman, barely conscious, whispered, "Yes, I do. I do the work of Satan."

The torturer threw the poker into the fire.

"The witch finally speaks the truth." The inquisitor turned to the other torturer. "Take her to the dungeon. She will hang tomorrow."

A flash landed Johnny in another torture room where one of the women from the chanting circle was being held down as a man took a sharp instrument to her hand. Her screams echoed off the stone walls.

Johnny glanced across the room to see Torphis with a horrified look on his face.

Torphis turned to Auster. "I didn't know these women were the accused."

Another flash. Another healer was bound to a chair beside a murky pond. The torturer pulled red hot pincers from a bonfire and held them close to the woman's face. "Shall I use these, or do you want to try to swim?"

"No, no." She shuddered and cried, "Swim!"

The inquisitor tossed the pincers aside. "Toss her in. If the water rejects her, she's a witch."

Two men lifted the chair, carried the crying woman out, and threw her, face first into the water.

Johnny watched in horror as the woman screamed and fought against her restraints. The chair sank below the surface. The woman, choking and gasping for breath, went down with it.

Johnny pointed to Torphis. "You did this!" But no one heard him.

Torphis, face pale and sick, turned to Auster. "Please stop. Don't show me any more." He hung his head. "I see the truth."

Auster turned to mist, there was another flash, and then Johnny found himself back in reality, standing beside Torphis on the balcony of his estate.

It took a moment for Johnny to calibrate his thoughts. "Did that really happen?"

"It did," Torphis answered. "You witnessed, first hand, my life's work as a human."

"I don't know what to say." Johnny wouldn't even look at Torphis. "I'm stunned."

"I was a learned man," Torphis said. "Yet I was enveloped in ignorance. I thought I was doing God's work, but if *God* is a benevolent force, then *God* was in that woman when she slapped the babe's bottom to call forth its breath. *God* was in the women chanting together, sending forth healing thoughts. *God* was in the woman pressing warm herbs onto the sick."

"Why show you the truth?" Johnny asked. "Why didn't Auster let you believe you were doing God's work and tell you those with his signature are witches? You would still kill for him."

"Auster doesn't tolerate ignorance and self-delusion." Torphis scanned the landscape. "Make no mistake, he is unwavering. He will kill without remorse. He will do what he believes is necessary without hesitation. Auster will not, however, stand for his Hands and Sentries to reside in a self-aggrandizing state, believing they were chosen because of some quality that makes them superior to ordinary humans."

Johnny couldn't shake what he'd just seen. "Auster must know that showing you the truth would hurt you."

"Auster is well-aware of the effects of enlightenment on his Sentries." Torphis exhaled a shaky breath. "Sometimes I think he's punishing us, keeping us alive for centuries to remind us of our deeds. It's like living in hell, only the hell is in your head. You have the entire world as your playground, more money than you can ever spend, and abundant health for eternity, yet you cannot escape your thoughts. It is the perfect torture."

"So you've come to accept doing Auster's bidding?"

"Yes. I kill who he tells me to, knowing I bring ugliness to the world. When I can, I use my resources to enable humans to help each other." He leaned in closer. "I do not deserve the peace that death brings."

"So, for eternity you will walk the Earth in sadness because of choices you made hundreds of years ago?"

Torphis drilled his eyes into Johnny's. "I do not believe in forgiveness, in excusing one's actions by hiding behind a book or citing some declaration. We are accountable. We should carry every one of our mistakes like weights. Learning to deal with the burden of our deeds makes us stronger, reminds us that we are flawed. It keeps us from committing more atrocities. I oversaw the brutal torture and deaths of hundreds—all innocent. I *deserve* to walk the Earth for many lifetimes, sick to my stomach knowing that."

Johnny thought of his own life, of those he had killed. *Was it really necessary to murder them, or am I a monster, too?*

Torphis faced Johnny once more. "As a Sentry, you must acknowledge who you were. You will not be given the gift of light if you do not take responsibility for your actions." He turned to mist and blew away.

Johnny lay down but couldn't sleep, much less keep a thought in his head. *Torphis tortured people. Auster kills without remorse. Was I a deliverer of horror to the world, too?*

He tossed and turned for a while, but eventually exhaustion overtook him and he fell into a deep sleep.

∞∞∞∞∞∞

"It is time for you to move on."

Johnny sat up, disoriented. It took a minute to remember where he was.

Torphis stood above him. "I have gauged you long enough. It is now time for you to visit another Sentry. I am sending you to Fokazi. He resides in Africa." He stepped forward. "You'll need to sleep through the trip." He raised a hand and sent forth the light.

Johnny blacked out.

SIXTY-FOUR

Dick Brickford marched through the double doors of the Gypsum Ridge Police Station and strode by the front counter without stopping.

"Excuse me!" the receptionist barked, chasing after Brickford as he continued toward Captain Thomas Keesler's office door. "You can't go in there."

Brickford turned and faced her. "You must be new."

She stopped in her tracks and inspected Brickford's face. Her expression changed as recognition set in.

Brickford flung the door open and went inside.

Keesler's eyes widened when Brickford approached his desk. "Brick?"

Brickford slammed the door. "I need you to put together a team to track all Quartz County Waste Industries trucks that service Gypsum Ridge, specifically along routes 237 and 238, which run along Gypsum Ridge Highway down the coast."

"Why?"

"I have reason to believe a trafficking ring of some kind is running through Gypsum Ridge using waste disposal trucks."

Keesler sat back. "Look, Brick, I know we go back, but I can't justify using a bunch of manpower just because you have a hunch."

"Hunch, my ass, it's twenty years of paying attention." Brickford stepped forward and stood above Keesler from the opposite side of the desk.

"You're way out of your jurisdiction on this, Brick." Keesler shifted in his seat. "I mean, Gypsum isn't your territory. If anyone got word that you were behind a massive search around here… you know, based on what happened before, I don't think—"

"No, *you* look, prick!" Brickford slammed both fists on the desk and leaned forward. "When all the shit with Flynn went down eight years ago, I, along with Trillson, Gingham, Burnham and Capra faced a shitstorm for the misinformation that led to the fuck-up. And all the while you had your nose straight up admin's ass. Everyone was sent down, except for you. I find that very ironic."

Keesler's Adam's apple bobbed up and down as he swallowed.

Brickford leaned forward, inches from his face. "I didn't say a fucking thing when I found out that you served up Dennington, knowing full well that he had been partying overseas for months and couldn't have taken part in the kidnapping. I also kept my mouth shut when your files on Dennington went missing."

Keesler pulled off his glasses.

"You let us all take the fall and continued to suck ass until you got promoted. Congrats, *Captain*, you get to sit in the big-boy chair. Now, get a fucking team together or I'll start talking. It will only take a few conversations before it's your turn to know what it's like to be on the receiving end of a true ass-fucking."

SIXTY-FIVE

Johnny stirred, feeling dizzy and sick. *Where am I?* He ran his fingers through his hair and looked around the space—another sizable room, clean and decorated with a few ornate vases.

He rose to meet the dark-skinned, bald man who stood before him.

"Welcome. I am Fokazi. Come, let us talk." His bright, loosely fitting clothing swished around his strongly-built frame as he led Johnny to an outside terrace where a small table was set with a pitcher of ice water and two glasses.

Johnny stepped outside and shielded his eyes from the harsh sunlight. "That's intense."

Fokazi opened a sunshade next to the table. He poured water into each glass. "Your energy is different because of the insects. It's very interesting. Can you feel them?"

"I've *seen* them. They come out of me when I'm threatened."

"*Really?* That's very interesting. It's like your body is changing form, and you're not even a Sentry yet." Fokazi leaned forward, eyebrows raised.

"Yes. My body turns into them."

"At any given time?"

"No. They appear when I feel intense emotion."

"Excellent." Fokazi smiled. "I am sure that will come in handy some day. How did you like your visit with Torphis?"

"It was a lot to take in."

Fokazi stirred the ice with his finger. "Torphis is quite the tortured soul. The embodiment of shame, is he not?"

"He seems to be."

Fokazi gazed over the balcony at the sea, his smile fading. "Understandably so. When Auster showed Torphis the truth behind his actions, Torphis was devastated. He refused to use his father's name from that point on, said he wasn't worthy of carrying it. He asked Auster to give him a new name."

"So Auster came up with Torphis?"

"In Auster's language, Torphis translates to 'one who sees darkness in light.'"

"Where is Auster from?"

Fokazi's smile returned. "You wouldn't believe me if I told you."

"Try me."

"Not now, new Sentry. All questions will be answered in time."

"Right." Johnny gazed around. "Where are we?"

"You are in KwaZulu-Natal in South Africa. This region was once known as the Kingdom of Zulu. It's beautiful, don't you think?"

"Yes, it is." Johnny glanced around. "I've traveled to the northern part of the continent with my wife and father."

"Egypt?" Fokazi gave him a knowing smile.

"Pretty predicable, huh?"

"Of course, the pyramids are one of the wonders of the world. But to me, this place is just as magnificent."

"You were born here?"

"I was, and I died a warrior's death here."

"How?"

"I perished during the Battle of Isandlwana on the 22nd of January, 1879, a famous battle where the Zulu pushed back the British army." Fokazi leaned back and stared upward as he remembered. "I was young and fast, so they placed me in the right horn."

"I don't know what that means," Johnny said.

"I will make the history lesson brief," Fokazi said. "You've heard the name Shaka Zulu, yes?"

"Yes."

"He was ruler before I was born. He is known to have developed a fighting formation called the 'bull horn', representing the horns and chest of the buffalo. The young, fast juniors like me were the 'horns.' That said, I think you'd be better served witnessing the account yourself."

"You mean pull me back in time again?" Johnny shuddered as he recalled what he had seen with Torphis.

Fokazi got up. "Torphis took you through his history. Allow me to show you mine." He excused himself. A few minutes later, he returned with a small glass of red liquid. He handed it to Johnny. "Drink."

Johnny eyed the cloudy fluid. "Your signature?"

"Consider it a gift. In a sense, we will be brothers, if Auster and all three of us deem you worthy."

Johnny took the glass, shot back the liquid, wincing in disgust.

Fokazi raised a hand. "Now, see how I became what I am."

A flash of light sent Johnny swirling into oblivion. The pull felt stronger than before. Johnny gritted his teeth and clinched his fists, trying to stay centered. When the feeling was almost too much to bear, all went still.

Johnny opened his eyes and startled at the sound of gunfire and screaming. *This must be the battle. I'm right in the middle of it.* Thousands of men swarmed around him. Once again they seemed unaware of his presence. He smelled gunpowder and turned to see white men in uniform—red coats, black dress pants, and tea-colored pith helmets, all charging forward.

They must be the British.

The Zulu warriors, bare-chested with cow tails worn around their upper arms and calves, carried no firearms. Their armory consisted of large oval shields made of colored patterns of cowhide and wooden spears with iron points.

The combination of rage, fury, fear, ferocity—the desire to kill, was so intense Johnny had to hold the sides of his head. *I've never felt anything like this. Only war can bring on such negative energy.*

The Zulu had surrounded the British, their spears launched time after time with such accuracy that most claimed the life of the targeted soldier. One Zulu—tall and sinewy, skin glistening with sweat, stood out from the masses. Although the man looked different from the one who sent him into this trance, Johnny knew who it was. *Fokazi.*

Fokazi raced across the field, hurled his spear and impaled a British soldier in the chest, then deftly retrieved his weapon to advance on another. His speed was unmatched. His precision and force claimed enemy after enemy. A British soldier raised his rifle and Fokazi countered with another javelin-style throw of his stabbing spear. The rifle shot careened to the sky as the soldier collapsed.

Fokazi pulled the shaft from the soldier's chest, and at that moment, the sky grew darker. The shots and battle cries quieted along the battlefield. Warriors and soldiers glanced upward, their faces horror-stricken.

Fokazi yelled something in Zulu to the others, but somehow Johnny understood it. "The sun is turning black!"

Johnny glanced up to see a shadow creeping across the midday sun. *An eclipse.*

Time seemed to stand still as the darkness coated the sky. When the shadow's movement reached a total eclipse, a collective gasp rippled across the battlefield. For a moment, the fighting ceased. Silence swept across the land like wind.

"What does it mean?" Johnny heard Fokazi ask.

Whispers flitted across the field, sending waves of fear and bewilderment.

Then, slowly, the shadow broke away from center.

Stirrings led to grumbles as the sky turned brighter, and then gunfire pierced the silence, instigating the resurgence of combat.

Johnny peeled his gaze away from the eclipse to see Fokazi leading a group of men into the battle.

Another flash yanked Johnny away from the field. He sucked in a breath as he felt himself drop and take in the scent of damp earth and sweat. He looked around. *I'm in a tent.*

Two teenage boys were on the opposite side of the tent adjusting their British uniforms, drums at their feet. The muffled sounds of war echoed in the distance.

Johnny was shocked at how young they looked. *They're only kids. What are they doing here?*

The older of the two boys glanced through the parted fabric that led to the outside. "You ready?" he asked the other.

The younger boy nodded and bent down to retrieve his drum.

Screams erupted from outside. The boys looked at each other in panic.

"What do we do?" the younger said.

"I don't—"

Three Zulu warriors plundered through the opening, led by Fokazi. The older boy scrambled toward the entrance to the tent. A Zulu blocked his path and in one quick move, bludgeoned him with a large ball at the end of a wooden weapon.

The younger boy shrieked and backed up.

Fokazi seized him by the throat and, with one blow, caved in his head with a similar weapon.

"No!" Johnny shouted. "They're only kids, for God's sake. And they're not even armed!"

But the warriors walked right through him.

Johnny followed them outside. The Zulu stepped over the lifeless soldiers they'd just ambushed.

Fokazi raised the unconscious boy and used a hook to hang him on the side of the tent by his clothing. He then took out a short metal blade.

Johnny watched in horror as Fokazi plunged the blade into the boy's abdomen just below the sternum and sliced the child all the way down to his pelvic bone, laying him open like a fish.

Johnny gagged as the boy's insides spilled down the side of the tent to the ground.

Children. Fokazi slaughtered children.

The boy's body shuddered a few times as the life force slipped away, and then another Zulu hooked the older boy to the tent and ripped him apart.

Fokazi glanced at the other two warriors and jerked his head toward the opposite side of the camp, and the three moved on without looking back.

Johnny could barely catch his breath when he was yanked into another vortex that landed him on the battlefield again.

Fokazi, holding a blood-stained shield, darted across the combat zone with the other Zulu in the horn. A gun blast pierced the air and the warrior beside Fokazi collapsed. Fokazi launched forward and thrust his spear into the soldier who fired the shot, then ran back to see if his comrade was still alive.

Then came another blast.

Fokazi dropped to his knees with his hands covering his abdomen. He peered down at the hole in his middle. Bleeding profusely, he touched his headband, murmured something Johnny couldn't hear, and crumpled to the ground.

Death wasn't instant. Johnny watched for what felt like hours as Fokazi moaned and slithered on the ground. Men fought around him as though he were dead. Finally, as the sun set in the western sky, Fokazi closed his eyes for the last time.

A strange mist appeared, drifting across the battlefield. It stopped above Fokazi's body, hovering like a cloud. Johnny recognized the signature.

Auster.

The mist covered the body, then emitted a pulsing glow. The light faded and the fog hung in the air above Fokazi, but he did not move.

A warrior several feet away uttered a weak cry.

Johnny gaped at the man, who moaned and writhed in pain in a pool of his own blood, his left arm severed at the elbow.

Auster, still in particle form, drifted over to the dying warrior. He scooped him up, placed him on top of Fokazi's body, and sent light into both of them.

Johnny watched as the armless warrior stopped moving. Auster pulled away the dead man and tossed him to the side.

Fokazi's fingers moved. He opened his eyes.

Auster brought him back from the dead using someone else's energy, just as he did with me.

Auster materialized. This time he was very tall with dark hair and olive skin. "Get up," he said in Fokazi's native tongue.

"I thought I was a dead man," Fokazi said to Auster.

"You were. I brought you back."

Fokazi stood, his eyes widening as another cloud approached. Within moments, a man and two women stood on each side of Auster.

Johnny stared at the people flanking Auster. *They're Sentries.*

"Who are you?" Fokazi asked. "What is happening?"

"You'll find out soon," Auster said. "You must follow us."

"My people need me."

"They have won the battle—today," Auster replied. "You cannot help them anymore. You belong to me now."

Fokazi looked offended. "I belong to no man."

"*I'm* not a man." Auster turned to particle form, lifted Fokazi, and shot across the battlefield. The Sentries followed.

A flash of light sent Johnny to another place. He opened his eyes in a quiet room where a woman held a newborn infant. She smiled and nuzzled the nursing baby.

An older woman entered the room with a pail of water. She leaned over and touched the baby's forehead. "He would have been so proud of this beautiful child."

The new mother's smile faded as she regarded her newborn. "Yes, Fokazi would have been very proud." She held up the baby. "He sees her. I know he does."

Then Johnny noticed the mist in the corner of the room. The two signatures were clear. *Auster and Fokazi.*

The scene faded, then Johnny felt a whoosh and a pull.

"That's enough for you to see," Fokazi said.

It took a moment for Johnny to realize that he was back in the present. His mouth was cotton-dry and it felt as though he'd just staggered off a spin ride at the carnival. "I need a minute to organize my thoughts."

Fokazi laced his fingers. "Take all the time you need."

With a trembling hand, Johnny reached for the pitcher on the table, filled his glass with water, gulped it down, and refilled it. "You killed unarmed children."

Fokazi glared at Johnny. "Yes. It is something I am forced to live with every day. My dreams are haunted by it."

"And the baby was your daughter?"

Fokazi ripped his gaze away. "I had been married shortly before the battle, too soon to even know my bride was with child. I regret not being able to cradle my daughter in my arms, but I could not risk returning to my village in human form at that time. My daughter lived to be ninety-four years old. I had the honor of meeting her in person throughout her life."

Johnny thought about meeting his own children again. "You did? How? When?"

"The first time was when she was eight years old. From that point on, I kept watch over her, visiting her village in different bodies to avoid suspicion. The last time I saw her was when she was on her deathbed. I came in as a healer and held her hand. I wanted so much to tell her who I was, to tell her that I'd loved her since the day she came into this world, but I couldn't. She died believing her father never knew her."

Johnny thought of Michael and Maya. *Fokazi's right. Trying to explain who I am would only cause pain. They would never believe I'm their father.* "Did your daughter have children?"

"Yes. She had four children, and I now have over seventy original descendants, many of whom still reside here. One of the small pleasures I enjoy is watching them flourish."

"Were you accepting of Auster making you a Sentry?"

"Not at first." Fokazi looked at Johnny. "I was much younger than you are and far less angry. I spent time with three other Sentries, and by the end of my education, I accepted what I had to do." He grimaced. "You, from what I am told, do not seem to be accepting at all."

"I'm not keen on killing innocents because Auster tells me to," Johnny snapped.

"I see. So, future Sentry, Auster would not have brought you back unless you were a killer. Who did you kill and why?"

Johnny resigned himself to telling the truth. "The first time I killed someone I was eighteen. I did it because he had killed my mother."

"A good enough reason. I would have done the same."

Johnny remembered that Auster owned all of his memories and, just in case Fokazi spoke with Auster, Johnny wanted to make sure he wouldn't be called a liar. "Well, he didn't exactly kill her, but his actions led to her death."

"How? Please explain."

"When I was a kid, my mother was one of the first women in the area to be promoted to manager of a department store. It was a really big deal at the time and, from what my father said, many men—and women—resented her for it. Her subordinates were purposely late. They'd defy her authority and sabotage visits from the regional managers to make her look bad."

"A difficult position to be in," Fokazi said.

"She fought back, fired a few people. She could have fired the entire staff, but she only let go people who really harassed her. One of them, a guy named Gene Housen, was enraged over being canned, so he cooked up a scheme to get back at my mom. With the help of some employees my mom didn't fire, he stole a bunch of money from the safe and doctored the accounting books to make it look like my mom had embezzled it."

"And so your mother ended up losing her job."

"Yeah." Johnny took a sip of water. "It was a big scandal. They called the police in, escorted her out in handcuffs, and filed charges against her. It was a mess. The local news rag milked it for all it was worth, printing pictures of her every day until the charges were finally dropped. The whole thing wrecked my mom. She couldn't get another job. She started drinking, and everything began to unravel from there."

Fokazi sat back. "Unravel how?"

"It took years, but the drinking eventually killed her. My father sent her to recovery programs, counseling, doctors, but he couldn't help her. The public humiliation was too much. She died of cirrhosis of the liver."

"I don't know how you could have exacted revenge for that. Who did you kill?"

"I tracked down the fucker who started it all, Gene Housen. He was living in a golf resort retirement community. I told him I was a reporter doing a story on influential people in the city and, of course, he was glad to sit down with me. He got a little uncomfortable when I started asking about my mom. I showed him the photo I took of her on her deathbed and revealed who I really was. I put a bullet in him five seconds later."

"So you killed the man because he started the chain of events leading to your mother's death?"

"Yes."

Fokazi shifted in his seat. "Based on the story you just told, there were many factors that steered your mother toward death, the primary of those being her own choices."

Johnny felt his face redden. "Those people killed my mother's spirit. Her body followed years later. To me, that's murder."

"Forgive me, but you said yourself that your father loved her very much. You did as well. That kind of love nourishes the spirit, does it not? A man who refuses food ends up dying from starvation, but isn't it really suicide?"

"Enough!" Johnny clenched his fists.

"You anger easily, new Sentry." Fokazi crossed his arms. That won't serve you. I am only sharing my thoughts and pointing out the flaws in your logic for your own good." He waved a hand. "Forgive me if I offended you."

Johnny shrugged.

"As a Sentry, you must accept who you are. A man does himself no favors by pulling the wool over his own eyes. You've killed others as well, am I correct?"

"Yes, all for business." Johnny eyed Fokazi. "Make no mistake. Business *is* war and businessmen *are* murderers. Businessmen killed my father, too. He wasted away because a corporation decided that the cost of lawsuits from dying employees and their families would be less than the cost required to provide a safe working environment in the first place."

"Death for profit," Fokazi said.

"Exactly. I swore after I buried my mother that I would never be victimized by businessmen. I swore that *I* would be the force to be reckoned with. "

"By *force*, you mean you would kill whoever got in your way."

Johnny crossed his arms. "I'm sensing that you don't deem me *worthy* of being a Sentry."

"I do not have to like you, hothead," Fokazi said. "I use my knowledge to determine whether or not you will make a good Sentry."

"Have there been bad Sentries?"

"There have been, but only a few and Auster has destroyed them. And there is one Sentry who has gone missing."

"Missing?"

"Yes. Kothra cannot be found."

Johnny thought for a moment. "Auster said he owns all of our memories. He knows where we are all of the time."

"Only when you think of the past *before* he brought you back."

"So the Sentry who has disappeared *never* thinks of the past?"

"Apparently not. Kothra is older than most of us, with over a thousand years of memories to draw on at this point. Even so, Kothra had a family in life, and never thinking of the time before Auster—"

"Takes a hell of lot of discipline," Johnny finished.

"Yes, it does. We Sentries find solace in each other's company. If one is destroyed, it is very difficult on the others. Kothra's departure took place forty-six years ago. This has not been easy for the other Sentries, especially Torphis. He and Kothra had become close friends."

"Why did Auster destroy the others?"

"Defiance. Do as you are told, new Sentry. Acknowledge what you are, and you will continue to exist."

The following morning, Fokazi woke Johnny from a sound sleep. "I have had some stewed meat, amandumbe, and amasi prepared for you."

Johnny sat up. "I only recognize the stewed meat."

"Amandumbe is like a sweet potato. Amasi is milk, Zulus drink it in fermented form, so don't expect what you buy at American supermarkets. Eat and then I will send you on your way to meet Boke Gal. Your trip will be better on a full stomach."

"Where am I going?" Johnny asked.

"To Mongolia." Fokazi's gaze met Johnny's "I must warn you, new Sentry, that the Mongol is not as friendly as Torphis or I."

"Great. Looking forward to that." Johnny stood and walked out to the terrace.

SIXTY-SIX

Anisha Patel Corby opened her eyes. Groggy and disoriented, she let her gaze drift across the dark place. Slowly, the unfamiliar became familiar.

A clean, white room.

A small bathroom.

One couch against a closed-draped window.

An empty bed beside hers.

Pain ripped through her lower abdomen. She moaned and shifted on the mattress, trying to ease the ache, then discovered Ben sitting by her side.

"Oh." The memories flooded back. Anisha cradled her now-empty womb and let the tears come again. "I shouldn't be in this bed. It's not necessary."

"Sshhhhhh," Ben said. "It is, Ani. You lost a lot of blood and had a fever. You know the drill. You'll be kept overnight. Quiet now, you need to rest."

"What time is it? Where's Frank?"

"He's having dinner with Katie in William's room. They'll be back soon."

"The baby," Anisha sobbed. "I lost the baby."

Ben took Anisha's hand. "I know, honey, and I'm so very sorry."

"I felt her go. Yesterday, I felt her slipping away. Remember? I told you something was wrong."

Ben closed his eyes. "Yes, I remember."

Anisha looked up at her friend. "You felt it, too, didn't you? You felt her fading."

A tear slipped down Ben's cheek. "Yes, I did. Such a helpless feeling. There was nothing you could do."

"Mother said—"

"Don't do this, Ani." Ben leaned forward. "Not now."

Anisha covered her eyes. "Mother said that I'm a carnal, worldly woman. That my husband married used goods and I'll reap what I sow."

"That's bullshit and you know it. Please don't give her words power. Being a virgin when you marry doesn't make you a good wife and mother. The way you treat your husband and children does. How many times throughout your childhood did she go on about how she despised your father and loathed being your mother? How many?"

Anisha shrugged. "Too many to count."

"Stop this nonsense. There's no place for her here."

Anisha glanced down the bed, longing for the familiar flutter in her tummy that was no longer there. "My baby's gone."

"I know, sweetie. It's the strain. The amount of stress you and Frank are under right now is unfathomable. Your poor little body just couldn't take it. Please don't punish yourself any more."

Anisha's eyes met Ben's. "Why do you think, during times like these, *she* always floods my mind?" She turned both palms up. "My baby is in a coma and I just miscarried, for God's sake, yet there she is, in my conscience, telling me that it's my fault because I'm a bad person. It's like a poison that's inundates me when I hurt."

Ben looked her in the eyes. "Our mothers are the first to define who we are. What they say when we're young is our complete truth."

Anisha plopped her head back on the pillow and stared at the ceiling. "Yes, but I'm an adult now. I'm a doctor. I'm a mother myself, Ben. She shouldn't be able to do this to me anymore."

"Sorry, honey." Ben kissed her cheek. "Starting at four years old, you were trapped in a room with an angry beast who filled your head with ugly for hours. You'll always struggle with feeling worthy of joy."

Anisha closed her eyes as she remembered. "I used to pretend I was somewhere else, someone else, when she raged at me."

"Could you imagine doing that to Katie?"

Realization hit Anisha like a hammer. "No, never in a million years."

Ben stood up, went to the window, and parted the curtains. The setting sun bathed the room in an orange glow. "There are all kinds of monsters in the world, Ani. Yours has no place here."

Anisha inhaled a ragged breath.

"Feelings follow thought, *mon amie.*" Ben returned to her side. "Banish the beast from your mind if you want to heal. You have a husband who loves you and two children who need you now more than ever."

"As always, my dearest friend, you're right." Anisha wiped away a tear with the back of her hand. "I feel her grip fading as I say these words." She hugged her middle. "Oh, how I long to hold this baby, and my little William."

"You need to heal now." Ben nestled up, wrapped his arms around her, and rocked back and forth. "No monsters allowed."

SIXTY-SEVEN

It's fucking freezing.

Johnny cringed as his muscles, taut and pulling in different directions, told him he'd been sleeping for a long time. He drew in a shallow breath of icy air. Based on the smell and feel of where he lay, he knew he was on hard ground. A chill ran through him and he wrapped his arms around himself.

He opened his eyes a crack and got the ankle-level view of what appeared to be a large yurt. A mattress draped with a blood-colored blanket sat at the edge of the space. The wax from a single lit candle pooled on a short wooden table with two seat pillows placed on either side. A rug woven of dyed wool lay right beside him.

Johnny tried to stretch, but his stiff body protested. *Damn, couldn't they have at least dropped me two feet over on the rug?*

"Sit up."

Johnny glanced up to see a stone-faced man standing above him, his dark eyes devoid of emotion. The muscles of his caramel-skinned frame bulged beneath his wool shirt, and a leather thong tied back his long black hair.

"Are you a baboon, or do you speak the English language?" The man kicked Johnny in the ribs.

"Arrgh." Johnny curled into a fetal position.

"I said, sit up!" The man seized Johnny's arm, pulled him to a sitting position, and stepped back. "I am Boke Gal." He eyed Johnny with disdain. "Your energy looks like a swarm."

"I've been told."

"Can you feel them?"

"A little." Johnny cradled his ribs. "There's a constant stirring."

"Humph." Boke Gal turned and knelt down to retrieve a small wooden bowl from the table. Next to the bowl lay a hunting knife, dripping with blood. He thrust the bowl at Johnny. "You know what to do."

Fearing he may be kicked again, Johnny moved the bowl toward his lips, pausing when he saw it wasn't liquid, but blood and tissue mixed together into a goopy sludge.

Boke Gal noticed Johnny's hesitation. "I didn't flavor or dilute it for your culinary pleasure as the others do. You're lucky you're receiving my signature at all." He sneered at him. "You seem weak, and I loathe having to take a knife to myself for you. Consume it before I change my mind."

Johnny tipped the bowl back and swallowed the lumpy substance. He tried not to taste it, but it was impossible. The smell of iron permeated his senses. He felt the rubbery texture and his eyes rolled back. He struggled against the urge to spit it out. He swallowed, took a breath, and opened his eyes, still fighting the urge to gag.

Boke Gal's stare drilled into him. "You've met two of us," he said. "I am the third and last. What have you learned?"

"They showed me their pasts." Johnny thought about what he'd seen. "Showed me why Auster chose them."

Boke Gal gritted his teeth. "That's all you took from those meetings? Do you think this is a game of historical show and tell? You think we're sharing because we want to be your friends?"

Johnny didn't know how to respond. He quickly recalled his time with Torphis. "After Torphis showed me his past life, he said to be a Sentry you must acknowledge what you have done."

Boke Gal crossed his arms. "And Fokazi?"

"He said to be a Sentry, you must accept who you are."

Boke Gal exhaled. "You're not an idiot, that's a start." He knelt beside Johnny. "I will now take you back eight hundred years." He raised a hand. "Steady yourself."

The flash sent Johnny backward. His head slammed against the cold ground and he felt as though he was being pulled from his body. He experienced the same spinning sensation as before and closed his eyes, pushing down from his diaphragm the way his father told him fighters pilots did to fight passing out during intense g-force turns. He took a few gasping breaths, fighting the urge to scream. Then it all stopped.

His eyes snapped open and movement fluttered by. Johnny realized he wasn't on the ground but on horseback behind a Mongol warrior.

The signature read immediately. *Boke Gal.*

As with the other Sentries, the man he rode behind had a different body from the man he'd met in the hut.

How many bodies has he had in the past eight hundred years?

In life, Boke Gal was smaller-framed, his arms scarred. When he turned his head, Johnny saw his face was scarred as well. His pointed iron helmet had a horsetail plume. Leather panels hung from inside the helmet to cover his neck and ears. His bright-colored, leather armor was coated with some kind of lacquer. he clutched a circular leather shield with one hand and held the reins with the other.

The strongly-built horse, slightly smaller and stockier than those Johnny was familiar with, charged on, frothing at the mouth, his brown flanks gleaming with sweat. Johnny noticed a white kidney-shaped marking beneath the horse's left eye as it jerked its massive head.

Boke Gal gripped the reins. "Gan Vachir, *züün!*"

The horse swerved left. Johnny became aware of other warriors riding alongside them. They shouted back and forth in Mongolian and Johnny was once again surprised that he was able to understand. Most of the dialogue was single words: *up, there, four, behind.*

Johnny pulled his gaze away from the warriors and saw that the Mongols had nearly finished sacking a village. Huts were ablaze. A few old women and children fled for their lives. Some Mongols were off their horses, pulling the young women into the few domiciles that weren't on fire. Three remaining men of the village stood fast, holding weapons.

"*Dumda!*" Boke Gal shouted to the others.

Middle, Johnny registered.

He called down to his horse. "Gan Vachir, *udaan.*"

The horse slowed. Boke Gal dropped the reins and drew a bow and arrow. He pulled back the bow, took aim, and sent the arrow into the chest of the villager in the middle of the threesome. Shouts followed, more arrows flew, and the last men fell.

Boke Gal rode with the other warriors to the edge of the village and dismounted. He walked into one of the remaining huts, followed by several other Mongols. Inside the hut were two young women, holding fast to each other, cowering against the wall.

Oh no, Johnny covered his mouth. *They're not going to—*

Boke Gal smiled as he approached them, took one by the hair, and pulled her to the ground.

"No!" Johnny yelled. "They're practically children!"

No one heard him. He wasn't really there.

Johnny watched in horror as Boke Gal held the woman down with one hand, ripped away her clothes with the other and lowered himself.

"Don't do it!" Johnny yelled at the top of his lungs.

The young woman screamed in pain as Boke Gal raped her.

Her pleas continued through every harrowing moment.

When Boke Gal finished, he stood, pointed to the pool of blood beneath the woman, and laughed. Then another Mongol took her and the cries began again.

Johnny dropped to his knees, trembling with rage. The scene flickered in and out, then a sudden flash of light yanked him back to the present.

Boke Gal stood at the far side of the yurt, eyes as wide as silver dollars, while insects flooded from Johnny's body toward him. "Call them off!" he barked. "Call them back or I'll send the signal for you to be destroyed."

Johnny calmed himself and the insects receded, flowing back to Johnny and disappearing into his body.

Boke Gal stepped forward. "What kind of abomination are you?" He sneered as he took a seat.

Johnny felt anger bubble up again. "*You're* the abomination. What the fuck was that supposed to teach me? That you can rape women?"

For the first time, Boke Gal pulled his stare away from Johnny. "I'm showing you the truth. What I was in life and why Auster chose me. Now still yourself while I show you the rest. If you change form again, I will inform Auster that you are unfit."

A flash of light sent Johnny to another battlefield. This time he was afoot. An older version of Boke Gal lay with an arrow through his chest. His horse, Gan Vachir, stood over him, as though trying to protect him from being trampled as the other Mongols thundered by. The horse, crazed and frantic, whinnied and reared continuously when Boke Gal stopped moving.

In the distance, Johnny saw the cloud approaching.

Auster.

The cloud hovered above Boke Gal. Auster bathed the body in a beam of light, and the arrow rose from the dead man's chest.

Boke Gal coughed then sat up.

In particle form, Auster spoke. "The others saw you die.

Mount your horse and follow me."

Boke Gal looked at the warriors riding away in the distance, then back at the cloud above him. "Did the gods send you?"

"No. Follow me. You have fulfilled your duty here. You know they will not accept you back."

Boke Gal watched the Mongols ride out of sight and turned to his horse. "Gan Vachir!"

Gan Vachir nuzzled Boke Gal as he stepped around to mount. "Your loyalty is greater than any of theirs." He jumped into the saddle.

Auster swirled upward and shot toward the mountains. Boke Gal yelled a command and the horse followed at top speed.

A flash brought Johnny back to the yurt.

"There were thousands of us for Auster to choose from. Now you know why he chose me," Boke Gal said.

Johnny thought of the horrific acts of Torphis and Fokazi. "Auster chooses people who not only kill but are cruel?"

"Not exactly." Boke Gal glanced away. "It's more than that. Auster considers many factors when assessing who to bring back."

Still sickened by what he'd seen, Johnny pressed on his wrenching gut as he spoke. "Torphis was tormented when he saw the truth."

Boke Gal locked eyes with Johnny. "Enlightenment has sent almost every Sentry into a state of constant anguish. Some lost their minds. Torphis suffers, and yet he sleeps in a warm room on a feather bed. He deprives himself of nothing."

"So you *do* regret what you did?"

"Every day." Boke Gal stared past Johnny, remembering. "In life, I thought women were weaker. I thought I was entitled to them as a prize when taking their village. I am no better than Torphis or any other Sentry. Wait until you see your own life's truth. You are no better, either, bug man."

Johnny couldn't believe what he was hearing. *I'm not like*

these men. Nothing Auster could show me in my life compares to what these monsters have done. He glanced around the tiny yurt, cold with meager accommodations. A chill ran through him and he hunched forward, balling up to keep warm. "Torphis said Sentries have more money than they could ever spend."

"This is true."

"And you live here?"

"Living in luxury doesn't...suit me. Now get up," Boke Gal snapped. "I must see if you can read the signatures."

Johnny rose, still tight and freezing. Boke Gal strode forward and pulled away the brightly colored door panel. "Outside." He pointed down. "Step over the threshold, not on it. It is our custom."

Johnny squinted as his eyes met the outside light. Avoiding the threshold, he plodded outside to see a vast steppe that stretched all the way to the mountains. Just east was a small settlement, and ten paces away from the yurt stood a pair of saddled Mongol horses.

Boke Gal gestured toward the horses. "Come, let's ride." He paused. "You *do* know how?"

"When I was a child, I rode with my father."

"Then you will remember." Boke Gal marched forward, grabbed the saddle of the closest horse, whose brown coat shone under the cool sun. The horse stood about fourteen hands high and looked as though it were made of steel.

Johnny examined the beast then stopped when he saw the eyes—ghost-like, glowing silver almonds. Below the left eye was a kidney-shaped, white marking.

Johnny felt his jaw drop as recognition set in.

This can't be the same horse Boke Gal rode eight hundred years ago.

Boke Gal answered Johnny's unspoken question. "Gan Vachir has been with me through the ages. When he died, I made him my first Hand. The first Hand a Sentry brings back shares a special bond with his creator." He patted the horse's rump. "I don't know why his eyes turned color when I brought him back. It's never happened with a human subject."

Johnny regarded the heaving beast, whose silver eyes bore into him. He took a step and the horse whinnied and bared his teeth.

"Gan Vachir doesn't like you."

"Does he like anyone besides you?"

Boke Gal gazed up at him. "No." He chuckled, gave the horse another swift pat on the side, then climbed into the saddle.

Johnny gingerly moved around to the second horse and gauged his energy—calm and docile. The horse's dark brown coat twitched and glistened as Johnny stroked the trimmed mane and gazed into large, cocoa-colored eyes that seemed to be evaluating his ability as a rider. He patted the horse's side, slid his foot into the stirrup, stepped up, and swung his other leg over the saddle.

"Ha!" Boke Gal called out.

Gan Vachir bolted forward and the two stormed into the tall grass.

Johnny's horse stood, as though waiting for instructions.

Unsure of what to do, Johnny mimicked the command and his stallion shot into a full run. The speed took him by surprise. He held on for dear life as the stallion charged forward, eventually catching up with Gan Vachir.

They raced side-by-side along the steppe past the settlement then began an upward climb. Fifty yards up, the ground began to level. Boke Gal held out his arm and slowed his horse to a stop.

Johnny halted beside him and stared in awe at the activity taking place in the distance before them. Throngs of people dressed in bright clothing surrounded a stadium of green grass. Jewel-toned flags whipped back and forth high above their heads.

Though he heard nothing, Johnny felt the energy of the crowd as horses raced across the green field.

Boke Gal shouted over the stallions' huffing and pawing.

"You are looking at Mongolia's capital, Ulaanbaatar. They're in the midst of celebrating Naadam, our most important holiday, the seeds of which were planted back when I walked the Earth as a man. I have sired many offspring since Auster brought me back, but here is where the last of my true descendants live. When they are gone, all that was truly me will go with them."

Johnny pondered this. "The children you've created since then mean nothing?"

"They are different. You will see. They will not be like the children you created when you were human."

"How so?"

"They will be the descendants of a Sentry. Auster opened your mind, correct?"

"Yes." Johnny recalled the process: searing pain, the glowing light, consuming Auster's raw tissue, and then the awakening of all of his senses. "I'm still getting used to the intensity."

"The descendants one creates after becoming a Sentry share a small portion of this gift."

"They can see energy?"

"Yes, it's a mere fraction of what we perceive, but they do have the ability to read. Most of them don't know what they're sensing. Some will think they are psychic, others will think they see ghosts." Boke Gal huffed. "Try to explain the concept of ghosts to Auster."

"Do our descendants pose a threat?" Johnny asked.

"Quite the opposite. Many enter into professions where their intuition is put to good use. They often end up as healers and public servants. It's quite interesting." He turned to face the stadium. "You will know when you encounter one. Come, let's watch the games." Boke Gal jerked the reins and Gan Vachir shot down the hill.

Johnny urged his horse on and chased after them. By the time he reached the event, Boke Gal was already off his horse.

Boke Gal tied Gan Vachir to one of the posts outside of the

festivities. Johnny slid off the saddle and did the same.

Boke Gal turned to him. "Do you feel prepared to take on the conquest that will be thrust upon you?"

"Killing innocents?" Johnny snarled. "Look, I've killed before, but what Auster wants me to do is sickening."

"If we didn't kill them, things would be much worse. As a Sentry, you must accept what you must do."

"What's worse than killing throngs of innocent people?"

Boke Gal didn't answer. Instead, he threaded through the crowd to get a good view of the upcoming horse race.

Johnny followed, awkwardly bumping into people as he tried to keep up.

They eventually reached the front row and Johnny was hit with the smell of turned soil where the horses had plodded by. At the far end of the stadium, a race had started. The spectators roared and cheered.

Boke Gal smiled as riders passed. "The boy on the far end is one of mine, untouched and true." He faced Johnny. "You don't seem to understand your role, new Sentry. Let me make it clear. If Auster has to eliminate all life on the planet in order to obtain his goal, he will. As a Sentry, you must accept your task and your impact on the world. By destroying Auster's descendants, we are actually preserving the rest of all life on Earth." Boke Gal beamed at the boy. "I want *him* to live."

"Killing a million people is a service?" Johnny ran a hand through his hair. "That's pure evil."

"Would you call the ants that blanket and consume dying animals *evil?* Would you consider their actions to be malicious and cruel?"

"No," Johnny answered. "They're just trying to survive. That's not the same thing as what Auster is doing."

"Yes, it is."

"So Auster is doing this so he can survive?"

At this, Boke Gal broke out laughing.

Johnny felt insulted. "I don't understand what's so funny."

"Were you not told about a Sentry's immortality?"

Johnny thought for a moment. "Auster told me I can't die until my kids die first."

Boke Gal turned up both palms. "The same is true for Auster."

Johnny gaped at him. "Auster's trying to *die*?"

"If *dying* is leaving Earth, then yes."

Johnny was dumbstruck. "Why?"

"The sources of Auster's life force are calling him back. His departure is inevitable. As his Sentries, we help him go, or watch the Earth be demolished with light so intense that it will tear a hole in the universe. You can call what we do *evil* if you wish, but it is a necessary evil if you want life on Earth to continue."

All life on Earth, gone? Johnny's mind throbbed from both the intensity of the life force around him and what Boke Gal had just told him. *Kill a million or everyone dies.*

"How long has Auster been trying to leave?"

"Several thousand years."

"What?" Johnny squinted as horses raced by, sending dirt clods into the crowd.

"It's the truth. So you see the reason for the urgency. Come, survey my people and tell me what you read."

They meandered through the crowd. Johnny squinted at the glow that emanated from every living thing. A woman passed by and Johnny gazed at her then at Boke Gal. "One of yours?"

"Among many."

A tall man walked by, a camera clutched in his hand. Johnny recognized the signature and turned to Boke Gal. "That man. Is he from Fokazi?"

"Yes."

They spent several hours combing the crowds, where Johnny successfully found descendants from each Sentry he'd met.

There are none from Auster. Johnny exhaled. *I actually feel relieved at this. Would Auster really end life on Earth if his descendants are not all killed?*

Boke Gal turned to Johnny. "I am satisfied with your ability to read life source. It's time to send you back."

"But I haven't identified anyone with Auster's signature."

At this, Boke Gal crossed his arms. "Because there are none here with his signature. I've made sure of that."

Thoughts swirled through Johnny's head as they returned to Boke Gal's yurt and fed and watered the horses. As the sun set, the air took on a distinct chill. They went inside.

Boke Gal paced back and forth. "Auster has destroyed two Sentries in the last three hundred years. I fear he may be growing impatient. Adding one more Sentry may ease the tension."

"Fokazi said that one Sentry disappeared."

"Yes, Kothra. No Hand or Sentry has ever been able to flee Auster before, and it has affected him in a way I haven't felt before. The others and I share the concern that Auster will grow weary and choose to vacate Earth by demolishing it."

"Why did Kothra disappear?"

"Not much progress had been made in Kothra's regions for some time. Auster destroys anyone who do not show results."

"Progress," Johnny said under his breath. "So what happens now since you're the last Sentry I visit?"

"You return home and it is determined whether or not you're worthy. If you are not, Auster will destroy you. But, if you are worthy, Auster will give you the ability to wield light. This involves a ceremony in which Auster sends a universal command that draws all Sentries together in one place. This event is very rare."

Johnny shuddered at the thought. "And if he decides to kill me, he'll have to kill my kids first?"

"Yes."

For the first time, Johnny hoped he would be deemed worthy. "Is the process of receiving light similar to opening an aperture?"

"No," Boke Gal said. "It is unlike anything you could imagine. When Auster bestows the light upon you, he shows you his true form."

"His true form?"

"You will see, *if* you are chosen. Now, for the last time, you will sleep during your journey back home. If you become a Sentry, the next time you travel will be with the wind, as we do." Boke Gal raised a hand

"Wait," Johnny said.

Boke Gal lowered his arm. "What?"

"All Sentries come to this event?"

"Yes. All of us. The creation of a new Sentry is a rare occasion. The last one occurred over one hundred years ago."

Johnny thought. "If Kothra comes to this gathering, since all Sentries are pulled to it, what would happen then?"

"Kothra will not come," Boke Gal said. "Auster has tried the summoning command many times, but Kothra has been able to completely separate from us."

"He must be very powerful to do that."

"Yes. Kothra has walked the Earth for over a thousand years and is one of the most wise and dominant Sentries." Boke Gal gazed away. "I cannot describe the sense of loss." He raised his hand toward Johnny again.

"And I never said that Kothra was a *he*."

SIXTY-EIGHT

Inside Gypsum Ridge Hospital, Maya Flynn fought hard to keep from crying. *Not now. This isn't about you.*

She sat opposite Michael at the bedside where Paula lay sleeping. Cancer had transformed the once-robust Irish woman into little more than a ghost. Her cheeks were drawn, her hair brittle and white, her skin paper-thin and as pale as the sheet covering her frail form.

Maya fought the urge to break down. She bit her lip and squeezed her eyes closed as tight as she could. *Of all the people in the world, why does Paula have to suffer like this? It's not fair.*

"We love you." Tears welled in Michael's eyes.

Maya held Paula's hand. "I hope you know how much you mean to us."

They sat for a while. The blips and wheezes of the medical equipment that kept Paula's body alive echoed in the little room.

Finally, Maya felt the hand in hers squeeze. "Paula?"

The old woman slowly opened her eyes, her gaze meeting theirs. "Oh… my sweet loves." She gasped for breath every few words. "How long…have you been here?"

"A little while," Michael said. "How are you feeling?"

"Not so...bad," Paula shifted in the bed, but her labored breathing forced her to pause during every sentence, and the obvious pain impeded each small move.

"Here." Maya slipped her arm around Paula, fluffed the pillow beneath her head, and helped her scoot up.

"Ah, thank you, love." Paula attempted a smile. "My, look how long..." She stopped and labored to breathe. "Your hair... like your father's."

Maya stroked her brunette ponytail. "Yeah, it grows fast."

Paula nodded. "How's the world traveler? Is my girl enjoying...work?"

Maya inhaled. "Yeah, it's definitely been eye-opening lately." She gazed down. "Certain parts are rewarding."

"I know," Paula said. "I'll bet you've... learned a lot more... about how the world works."

"Exactly." Maya smiled. "You've always understood things. But I guess that's it, isn't it? Learning the truth about life is part of growing up?"

"It is. Don't let...parts you don't like get to you, love." Paula kissed Maya's hand. "Do the best you can...let go of the rest." Her attention went to Michael. "And you...handsome lad, still set on letting go of the business?"

"I think it's best," Michael said. "Wilks has been very helpful in all of this. I don't think he wants me to give up my portion, but he's showing support."

Maya stiffened and stared out the window. *Don't say anything to Mikey about that. Not now.* "You'd be fine," she managed to whisper. "Give yourself more credit, Mikey."

The nurse bustled in to check vitals and change IVs. Paula appeared to struggle while being poked and prodded, but it was obvious the process drained her of what little energy she had. The nurse left and Paula settled down in the bed, struggling to keep her eyes open.

"We should let you rest." Maya leaned over and gave her a peck on the cheek.

"Yes…love." Paula gasped between words. "I'll be up to visiting… after I have a nap."

Michael and Maya walked down the silent corridor. Sick with grief, Maya avoided meeting the gazes of passersby. Once outside, she shielded her eyes from the harsh sunlight as they plodded toward their cars.

"I'm glad you came to visit," Michael said.

Maya hooked her arm around his. "Me, too."

"When do you fly back across the pond?"

"Tonight." Maya thought about her job and let out a sigh. "Wish I didn't have to go."

"Me, too." Michael looked down at his feet. "Doctors said she doesn't have much time."

Maya swept away a tear. "She's the only family we have left, Mikey."

"I'll never be ready." Michael turned to Maya. "Sis, what are we gonna do?"

Maya covered her face and wept as Michael pulled her into a tight embrace.

SIXTY-NINE

Johnny woke lying face down on asphalt. He lifted his head and brushed away the gravel stuck to his cheek.

I'm in an alley. Fuck, this can't be good.

Unlike the other trance-like slumbers between visits with the Sentries, Johnny had dreamt. In the dream, he was in a filthy bathroom needing to pee, but every toilet overflowed with brown sludge.

Disgusting. So fucking disgusting.

He roused and got to his knees, realizing the overwhelming desire to piss was real this time. He stood and stumbled to a wall to empty his bladder.

Something rustled behind him. Johnny finished, zipped up, and turned around to see Auster materializing. "The present locale doesn't lend itself to a positive outcome. What did the others say?"

Auster's bright eyes drilled into Johnny. "You must be deemed worthy by all three Sentries. You were not. The decision was split."

Fear rippled down Johnny's spine. "So you've come to destroy me?"

"Yes, but you were rooted here, so I'm waiting for word from the others that your descendants are gone. Then you will be destroyed."

"NO FUCKING WAY!" Johnny rushed toward Auster. "Don't you *dare* hurt my kids! Who said I wasn't worthy?"

"That is not disclosed."

Johnny gritted his teeth. "Then let them face me. I want each of them to tell me why I'm not worthy due to their goddamn vote. After what they've shown me, the things they did in their lives, they're going to say *I'm* not good enough to be their equal?"

Auster stared. "It is not about comparing your past deeds to theirs. The factors to determine a potential Sentry are—"

"I find it interesting that the pitfalls of each of your Sentries' lives involved a dogma that led to their evil deeds, yet you're unwavering regarding the rules in this mysterious Sentry selection process. You cling to your ways like they're ordained."

"This has been the process for thousands of years,"

"It hasn't been perfect by any means," Johnny said. "You've destroyed Sentries you felt weren't cutting it. And one Sentry even dropped off the face of the Earth. I know about Kothra."

To Johnny's surprise, Auster smiled. "You're cognitive and reasoning abilities are strong." He shifted his weight. "Although this process has been effective, nothing is perfect."

"Then bring the other Sentries here to face me. It's the least you can do before killing innocent children."

"Your offspring are no longer children and both are far from innocent, but your points are taken." Auster closed his eyes, paused for a few seconds. "I have called to the *dayyani*."

"*Dayyani*?"

"Yes." Auster opened his eyes. "The *dayyani* are the three Sentries chosen to determine your worthiness. They will be here momentarily. I normally wouldn't allow this, but there was quite a schism with regard to your merit, which is another reason why your request is being granted."

"A schism, huh? Sentries don't usually argue over a candidate's worthiness?"

"It's never happened before. Usually each Sentry sends their decision to me and it stands. If a candidate is destroyed, it has no emotional effect on the *dayyani*, regardless of their determination. This time they communicated amongst themselves before contacting me. Each has a strong leaning."

Johnny thought hard about the previous few days. *Which one—or ones—said no?*

A change in the wind drew their attention toward a massive cloud of fog in the distance. The cloudy mass rolled toward them, swelling and pulsing forward until it reached the yellow streetlights. Then the forms within began to take shape.

Seconds later, Torphis, Fokazi, and Boke Gal stood beside Auster.

Johnny stepped forward. "So, one or more of you don't think I'm worthy to exist beside you? Who is it?" He pointed at Torphis. "You believe I haven't taken responsibility for my actions." He gestured toward Fokazi. "You think I'm a hothead." He nodded toward Boke Gal. "And you think I'm insolent and don't give a fuck about the future."

Fokazi turned to the others. "At least he listened."

"I'm surprised," Boke Gal added.

Johnny stepped forward. "Which of you is it?"

Torphis crossed his arms. "Your sense of entitlement isn't helping you right now. That information is only—"

"You were on your way to kill my kids! MY KIDS!" Johnny felt his body change. He gritted his teeth, trying to fight what he knew was happening, but the rage was too strong. The skin on his hands melted into countless black flies, mosquitoes, and beetles. The process continued all the way to his elbows in a matter of seconds, then the swarm bolted toward Torphis.

Auster raised a hand and sent forth a bolt of light, sending Johnny airborne and slammed into the side of a building.

Torphis appeared to be in shock. "The insects within him *attack* when he's enraged." He turned to Auster. "What do you make of this?"

Auster turned to Boke Gal. "Is this similar to the incident you reported?"

"Yes." Boke Gal glared at Johnny in disdain. "He was in trance, wasn't even aware it was happening."

"I must say I'm fascinated," Fokazi said. "You are a unique specimen, hothead. But your temper can prove to be disastrous, as you can see."

Johnny rose to his feet. "What do I have to do to prove I'm worthy?"

"It's not like an examination you have to pass," Auster said. "There are innumerable intricacies that make up an individual's psyche, temperament, and will."

"This process has worked for thousands of years," Boke Gal said. "What would you suggest in its place?"

Johnny turned to Auster. "Show me my past. Show me the truth as you did with them. All three of them lost subjectivity when you did that. Maybe if I show you that I'm able to do it, too, whoever thought me unworthy will change his mind. You said you're able to see through lies, so I won't be able to fake it."

Torphis faced Auster. "I'd be willing to witness this, but can it be done? He cannot wield light."

"I can send him enough light to perform the task without making him Sentry." Auster turned to Boke Gal and Fokazi. "Would you be disposed to seeing his past?"

Each gave a short nod.

Auster reached into his pocket, took out a hunting knife, and stepped toward Johnny. "I own all of your memories, but each of the Sentries will need your signature to access your history. I think you know what that entails." He held out the blade. "You must give flesh if you wish to share your signature. Carve deep as I and the others did."

With a trembling hand, Johnny took the dagger. As fear gripped him, insects spilled from Johnny's pant legs and pooled beneath him on the dark asphalt. They vibrated and hissed as Johnny lifted his shirt.

"Is he even human?" Boke Gal asked.

"More or less," Auster responded.

"This was your request. Get on with it," Fokazi ordered.

Johnny wiped sweat from his brow. The stench of dead rodents and rotting trash in the alley dominated his newly-acquired sense of smell.

"Perhaps now you understand what we went through to allow you to see us," Boke Gal snapped. "Be a man and cut."

Johnny placed the tip of the blade on his stomach. He sucked in a deep breath, then hesitated.

"Your children will perish if you do not proceed," Torphis said.

Johnny met Torphis' gaze.

"Do it quickly," Fokazi added. "One circular motion, two seconds, and it will be done."

Johnny exhaled. "Michael, Maya," he whispered. He clenched his teeth and screamed as he pushed the knife through the fat layer. He reached the tougher layer of muscle, paused to gasp, then continued and made a small circular motion. Blood spilled forth from the gaping wound. He held the blade as steady as he could and drew out the jagged edge covered with his flesh.

He dropped to his knees, supporting his weight with one hand as he held the offering toward Auster. "Please say it's enough."

Auster took the knife and examined it. "It will do."

Johnny winced as each Sentry took a pinch of dripping meat, shoved it into his mouth, and swallowed without hesitation.

Auster raised a hand and sent forth a thin ray of light toward Johnny's middle. A moment later, a small divot in smooth skin had replaced the open gash. Auster directed the beam at Johnny's forehead.

Johnny tasted metal and felt the now familiar sensation of being pulled from his own body. He blacked out for a second, and then, as if in a dream, he floated above the alley. He saw himself lying on the ground and the three Sentries standing above him. Then he felt like he was falling. He opened his eyes and was back on the ground, looking up at Auster and the Sentries.

"Stand," Auster commanded, "and see your truth."

A whirlwind pulled Johnny out of the alley. He opened his eyes to behold a sea of green. It took a few seconds to focus, and then he realized he was looking at a golf course from the balcony of a home. He lifted his hands away from the wooden railing, and turned around to see himself, a much younger self, seated at a bistro table on the patio, embroiled in conversation with an older man.

The man appeared distressed. The few strands of gray left on his head were combed over a scalp freckled with age spots and glistening with sweat. Johnny's young face was taut, jaw squared, teeth gritted as he held up a photo and showed it to the man.

We're at Gene Housen's house. He was my first kill.

The conversation grew heated. Johnny watched himself pull out a gun.

Housen held up both hands. "Wait, don't!"

Young Johnny fired. Housen's head bucked back and bits of his skull blew over the railing and onto the golf course.

I didn't remember it being that brutal.

Housen slumped forward as Johnny's blood-covered, younger self disappeared though the sliding glass door.

Auster and his Sentries hovered in particle form above the far end of the balcony. Johnny turned up both palms. *This shows me nothing. I already told Fokazi this story. That bastard killed my mom, broke my dad's heart, and left me half-orphaned. He deserved what he got. I didn't kill kids, rape innocents, or torture anyone. How can Auster even compare me to the Sentries?*

"Grandpa?"

Who's that? Johnny caught his breath.

The small voice called again from inside the house. "Grandpa, where are you?"

There's a child inside.

A heartbeat later, a tow-headed boy carrying a plastic fire truck stepped through the sliding glass door.

He walked onto the patio. "Grandpa?"

The boy toddled forward and shook the old man's hand, causing the body to slouch down more.

Oh, no. Johnny's stomach turned to lead.

The child's eyes widened in horror when he looked down and saw he was standing in an expanding pool of his grandfather's blood. He stepped back, leaving child-sized bloody footprints on the white concrete patio.

What did I do?

Another flash landed Johnny in an office where a woman sat opposite a well-dressed man at a massive oak desk. A glance at the bookcases and walls covered with framed university degrees made it easy to figure out where he was.

A lawyer's office. I don't remember this. Why is Auster bringing me here?

"I can't believe the court is just going to let the child suffer," the woman said.

The lawyer shifted in his seat. "The court is enforcing what is stated in Gene Housen's will."

The woman pointed to the document in front of the lawyer. "Circumstances have changed since that thing was drafted. That's been proven."

"It has, but the court will back a signed document over all else. I'm sure, as a case worker, you've seen the occasions when the law falls short."

"More than you'd care to know."

The lawyer sifted through the pages. "Mr. Housen's will is clear. The only person entitled to his estate is his son."

"His *son* is a fall-down drunk. Gene and Mary raised Steven since the age of two."

"But they never had legal custody and Mary died a year before Gene." The lawyer leaned back in his chair. "Look, I wish there was something I could do, but there isn't."

"This is total bullshit." The woman stood. "Steven Housen has been in foster care for the past four years. The kid's smart. He could read when he was three years old. Since he found his grandfather murdered, he's been bounced from home to home five times. He's changed schools eight times and been suspended more times than I can count. And he's only nine!"

"Perhaps we should attempt to contact the boy's father again."

"He's gone with daddy's money. He doesn't care about Steven."

Another flash sent Johnny to a living room of a filthy home. Two broken chairs and a dirty sofa flanked a rickety coffee table covered with plates of half-eaten food, trash, and drug paraphernalia. Johnny eyed the living space, the entirety of which could be seen from where he was standing.

A trailer home. Who lives here?

The door rattled open and a disheveled young man stumbled in. Full-sleeve tattoos did little to hide his clearly visible track marks. His once-white sleeveless shirt was yellowed and torn. He fell onto the sofa, which barely gave under his thin frame.

The man inspected the clutter on the table, then gritted his teeth when he lifted a mirror caked in dust. "Bitch!" he spat as he hucked the mirror across the room.

An instant later, a reed-thin woman with a swollen belly traipsed into the room, clasping the hand of a toddler. Both were as grimy as the living space.

"Where the fuck were you?" She tried to slam the flimsy door, but the latch bashed against the distorted frame. "How am I supposed to work with the fucking kid around?"

"I was busy." The man waved a hand at the table. "Where's the stuff? You use it all? You're fucking pregnant."

"Like you give a shit." The woman let go of the child's hand. "It's bad enough fucking Johns don't go for pregnant bitches. Try getting a trick with a kid standing there. I had to pay Tina to take her to get ice cream so I could bring home thirty bucks!" She scoffed. "Fucking waste of time."

Johnny eyed the little one dressed in rags, her blonde hair greasy and matted with tangles. Tears had streaked her dirty face, leaving the only signs of a pink complexion.

Who are these animals?

"Did you score anything?" the woman sneered. "Even a fucking dollar for food?"

The man shrugged. "Not today. I'm working on it."

"Like hell you are! Why don't you be a fucking MAN and support your kid, Steve?" The woman marched over to the table and, in one swipe, sent everything on it flying.

Steve? This is Steven Housen?

The toddler cried and covered her eyes as plates crashed to the floor. The woman tried to slap Steven, but he deflected the blow and pushed her to the ground.

"Fucking whore!" he spat as he plodded toward the door.

Flash. The white light landed Johnny in a convenience store. It appeared to be empty, but he saw a sea of police cars parked outside, lights blazing.

A megaphone bleated, followed by a tinny voice. "We know you're in there, Housen. Don't make this any harder. Come out and raise your hands so we can see them."

Johnny walked to the next aisle to see Steven curled in a ball on the floor, covered in blood, a gun in his hand.

What the fuck did he do?

Steven lolled his head back, his bloodshot eyes fixed on the fluorescent lights above. He took a deep breath, stood, and stumbled toward the door. The cops had weapons drawn, some crouched behind their cars. Others could be seen atop the neighboring buildings.

Steven Housen strode out into the open and scanned the area, eyes stopping on each police car.

"Drop the weapon," the cop holding the megaphone commanded.

Steven looked down at the gun, closed his eyes, and sighed. For the briefest moment, there was complete silence. Then he raised the gun and took aim at the closest cop car.

"NO!" Johnny shouted.

An explosion of police gunfire sent Steven back three feet and flat on his back.

The cops charged forward.

One kicked the gun away. "Cop-killing son of a bitch!"

Two others crouched next to Steven.

One took out his walkie talkie. "MacAllan here. We got 'em. He's dead."

"Roger that."

MacAllan pressed the talk button. "You at Housen's place?"

"Yeah," the voice paused. "It's brutal. The pregnant wife and kid are dead. Both shot in the head."

Johnny felt sick. *Oh, no. I caused the chain of events that led to all this death.* He covered his face with his hands. *I never knew.*

The other cop leaned over and hollered into the walkie talkie, "What about Nellis? Is he gonna make it?"

"Docs say he'll pull through." A long pause followed. "When he wakes up, he's gonna be—"

"I know." MacAllan glanced at Steven's body. "No one I know has gotten over losing a partner. It's over now. See you back at the station."

"Roger."

MacAllan clipped the walkie talkie to his belt and turned to his own partner. "Baptism by fire, huh, rookie? It's a pretty fucked up way to end your first month."

"Such ugliness," the newbie responded, almost to himself. "How could things go so wrong? Where did it start?"

"With me," Johnny said. "It started with me."

The rookie glanced at MacAllan. "How do you get used to it?"

"You don't, if you're human."

The young cop took off his cap and placed it over his heart. Johnny noticed tears welling in his eyes. His eyes. His face. Recognition set in.

Is that...it can't be...

Johnny couldn't believe who he was staring at.

Brickford! A young Dick Brickford.

SEVENTY

B rickford leaned against his car, ashing a cigarette as he waited in the parking lot of Quartz County Waste Industries. Beside him was the manager, Dusty Harwood. Both men watched as a truck pulled into the lot.

Harwood checked his watch. "Four o'clock, right on the nose."

"Fucker's punctual." Brickford said.

"Always."

Samuel Humphries pulled through the drive and into the back parking lot. Brickford and Harwood followed. Humphries parked the truck and got out, glancing around in confusion at the empty lot.

"Afternoon, Mr. Humphries," Brickford said.

Humphries looked at Harwood. "I'm not early, am I? Where are all the trucks?"

"Around the side." Harwood took the keys from Humphries and jumped into the truck to pull it around.

Brickford pointed toward the side lot. "Follow me."

Brickford led Humphries across the lot and behind the building. When they turned the corner, Humphries froze.

Police cars had blocked in the side lot, where sixteen waste disposal trucks lined the side wall. Behind each truck sat its driver, on the ground, in cuffs. White bags were still being pulled out of the beds and inventoried.

Humphries spun around to bolt, but several officers stood beside Brickford.

Brickford faced Humphries. "Looks like routes 237 and 238 were hauling more than trash, huh?"

"Fuck you, pig." Humphries jerked his shoulders as a cop snapped the cuffs behind his back.

Brickford raised his eyebrows. "Project Rancid, indeed."

∞∞∞∞∞∞

"Heroin, meth, pot, guns, cash—you name it, those Project Rancid motherfuckers were moving it." Brady shook the report in front of Brickford. "Damn, Brick. You rocked 'em to the core. Gypsum Ridge has gotta give you props for this."

"Yeah, right." Brickford turned on his computer, clicked over to the local news, then turned the screen so that both he and Brady could see it.

"That's it," Brady said, eyeing the thumbnail picture of a reporter in front of the line of trash trucks. "Press play."

Brickford clicked on the frozen frame and the reporter sprang to life.

> "Gypsum Ridge Police busted a massive drug ring today that resulted in over twenty arrests. The traffickers were using garbage trucks to move drugs and money through all of Quartz County from Gypsum Ridge to Thousand Wells. Gypsum Ridge police Captain Thomas Keesler credits his team for bringing in the bad guys."

The shot cut to Keesler in front of a sea of microphones.

Keesler smiled as he leaned forward and looked at the cameras.

"Finding the perpetrators of this crime took a lot of hard work, but with the correct leads and the amazing diligence of the men and women here at the Gypsum Ridge Police Department, we've made Quartz County a safer place to live."

Someone in the audience asked, "It's amazing that you were able to bust this ring so effectively and quickly. Tell me, what hunch led you to take such aggressive action in this case?"

Keesler grinned. "Hunch? I don't think so. It's years of paying attention."

Brickford burst into laughter.

Brady gaped at the screen in disbelief. "That weaselly motherfucker. He didn't even mention you. It's like you don't exist."

Brickford took a swig of coffee then said, "Welcome to the real world of police work, rookie."

Brady looked shocked. "You're not going to do anything?"

"Nah," Brickford blew out smoke. "The real cops at Gypsum Ridge know the truth, and I learned the truth about that gun barrel. That's all that matters to me."

SEVENTY-ONE

Johnny struggled to catch his breath. "I can't believe it. That little boy...his wife, the toddler, the cop—all dead because of things I set into play when I killed Gene Housen."

"Humans don't realize the true effects of their actions." Auster's stare bored a hole through Johnny. "The ripple caused by Housen's murder wasn't the only one you caused." He raised a hand. "Time to see more."

∞∞∞∞∞∞∞

Flash. Johnny found himself amidst a throng of people dressed in black. Organ music wafted through the dimly-lit space. A shiny, black coffin rested on the podium.

Whose funeral is this?

A pastor appeared at a podium to the left of the coffin and began the service, in Dutch. Like the time spent with the Sentries, Johnny understood everything. Then he heard the name of the deceased.

Dirk Janssen. The guy who took my clients and almost destroyed my business when I first started out—until I sent Ming after him.

Johnny sat through the somber event, after which the man's wife began the procession to pay last respects before the coffin was closed. The attractive, middle-aged woman heaved deep sobs.

She stopped to set a white rose on his chest, leaned forward, and placed her hands on each side of his face. "Dirk, I love you forever. Forever." She kissed his lips then collapsed. Family members helped her up and escorted her back to her seat.

Flash. A house. Dirk Janssen's widow stood by a teenage boy and girl as all of their belongings were hauled out the front door and into a giant truck.

Oh, no. Johnny placed his hand to his forehead. *Not again.*

The scenes that followed rolled at full speed.

The widow and teens in a small, ratty apartment.

Medics pulling a white sheet over the widow's body. The kids huddled in a corner, eyes red and swollen.

The teen boy on a street corner selling drugs.

The teen girl, now a young woman, at the kitchen table of another seedy apartment, one eye blackened. A man lounged in the living room, watching TV, a glass of clear liquid in his hand.

More lives I destroyed. Johnny trembled. *I never knew.*

Flash. This time the transfer seemed to take longer, pulling Johnny into another whirlwind. He opened his eyes to find himself in a conference room. Each seat around the long table was occupied. Each person wore a somber expression. Conversation was minimal, the air thick with tension. He recognized the men at the head of the table.

Hector and Roderick Dennington at an Owen Corp. meeting.

Hector stood. The old man appeared worn and tired. "Good morning to all of you." He paused and took a deep breath. "I am aware that rumors have been circulating, so I'll pay you the courtesy of being brief and to the point. You've seen the annual reports. It is clear that our business is going in a less-than-profitable direction. "

Dead silence.

Johnny felt the apprehension as the employees waited to hear the rest.

Hector glanced at his son and placed a hand on his shoulder. "After twenty-seven years and four months, we feel it is time for the Owen Corporation to close its doors. It is best to do it while we're still in a position to receive top dollar should another corporation wish to take over our share of the market."

"Flynn Corp?" a woman asked.

"Yes," Hector answered.

Everyone at the table groaned.

"The guy's an animal," one man said.

"How many businesses has Flynn shut down?" another asked.

"A lot," Roderick Dennington answered, his face stone-rigid. "I'd rather have it be anyone but that monster."

"But things do not end here," Hector said. "Keep your eye on the news. Schuyler Vander Broek and I may have come up with a plan to keep Flynn at bay."

That plan must have been Dennington moving to the board of directors of Vander Broek. It actually worked, until I had Dennington killed at Vander Broek's Diamond Celebration.

Johnny closed his eyes as Dennington discussed the logistics of the business shutting down. Several at the table dabbed tears away.

What happened next was like a hundred lives whirling before Johnny's eyes, flashing in and out like a 1920s flicker show. Every fragment seemed an eternity that ripped Johnny's insides apart.

One moment, an elderly janitor mopped the Owen Corp headquarters floor. The next moment, the same man, thin and with tattered clothes, lay on a bus stop bench covered in an old, filthy navy blanket.

Flash. A family celebrating a holiday dinner one moment, then the same family clustered around a shopping cart filled with their belongings a moment later.

*How could?—When I discussed closing down Owen Corp to Wilks, I was pissed. It was more like a game. I never meant to hurt innocent people. I never realized...*Johnny's heart lurched as he watched the frightened eyes of the children who clung to the cart while the family pushed it forward to seek refuge in a public park as the sun went down.

More scenes unreeled before him.

A woman was diagnosed with cancer and said she couldn't afford to treat it.

A man signed divorce papers then went home and overdosed.

A single mother, face streaked with tears, patted her daughter's hand. They sat at a table in the same homeless shelter where Johnny's family had volunteered years ago. He spotted Gladys carrying two trays of food to them.

Johnny placed a hand on his chest. *Gladys. The light in the darkness. The only sign of hope.*

The woman averted her eyes as Gladys set the trays of food in front of her. "Thank you."

"No problem." Gladys pulled the flower from her own hair and clipped in onto the little girl's ponytail.

The little girl smiled. "Thank you."

More flashes followed

A middle-aged man in a suit driving drunk. Johnny recognized him from the Owen Corp. board meeting. He ran a red light and plowed into a sedan full of people.

Funerals. Children in foster homes.

Flash. Flash. Hundreds of them. Each life seemed more tragic than the last. Johnny's body reeled back in shock from the images. He couldn't breathe. He couldn't think. He couldn't believe...

I did this. I did all of this.

Then everything went black. It was like he was floating in some in-between space, soundless, bereft of light. He became aware of the echo of his own breath, then another scene unfolded in front of him.

A large, elegant ballroom, tables draped with expensive linens and the ceiling sparkling with festive lights.

Johnny knew where he was. *The Vander Broek Diamond Celebration.* He watched a play-by-play of the massacre he had orchestrated with Ming.

Dennington, one of Johnny's identified targets, fell backward when shot in the head and chest.

His wife screamed and threw herself onto his blood-soaked body. "Call a doctor, please! Call an ambulance!"

Another scene. This one showed a beautiful woman walking in a mall parking lot.

Dani! Johnny covered his mouth with both hands.

An old van screeched to a halt in front of her. Two men pulled open the side door, grabbed her, and dragged her into the van.

"Dani!" Johnny dropped to his knees.

Flash. Danielle bound to a chair.

A man punched her in the face. "You will die in front of your evil husband so he will never forget," he said in a Dutch accent.

"No! Please," Danielle begged. "I have children."

The man sneered. "So did the people your husband killed. Blood for blood." He punched her again, this time square in the jaw. She sagged, unconscious.

"No! You motherfucker!" Johnny sobbed.

Flash. Danielle, face swollen and bloody, tied to a post on the pier of the old factory district.

"No, I can't watch this again."

Johnny saw his former self get out of the car, recognize Danielle, and call her name.

No, not again.

He witnessed himself getting shot, then covered his mouth as the other assassin put a gun to Danielle's head.

"No, please, no."

Pow. The gun snapped back in the assassin's hand. Blood sprayed. Danielle's body went limp. Johnny watched one of the gunmen shoot him again, then he watched himself crawl toward Danielle. The memory was too much.

My beautiful wife.

All went black again. Johnny felt suspended, weightless, yet broken.

Light filtered through the darkness. Johnny was back in the alley with Auster and the three Sentries. His chest felt tight. A pool of insects swirled beneath him.

He trembled, watching the bugs move in circles as though disoriented. "I killed so many. The horror I brought to the world. The ugliness."

"You seem intelligent," Torphis said. "You've never realized your impact before this?"

"No." Johnny rested back on his knees. "It was like a chess game. I thought the people I killed would have killed me. The businesses I absorbed would have done the same to me. I never thought about…"

"All of the innocents," Fokazi finished.

"There are so many of them." Johnny lifted his aching head to address Boke Gal. "I understand why you sleep on the cold ground." He looked at Torphis. "I understand why you live in a state of constant torment." He eyed Fokazi. "I understand why your dreams are haunted."

The Sentries looked at one another, their surprise evident.

Johnny closed his eyes and took a ragged breath. "I deserve to be destroyed. I can't deal with—live with—what I just saw." He scanned the pool of ants, earwigs, and centipedes undulating beneath him, then stared into the night sky, soul heavy and feeling as though he'd been gutted like Fokazi's drummer boy.

I killed out of greed and anger. I caused Danielle's death. I ruined the lives of so many innocents. He pressed off the ground. As he stood, the insects retreated back into his body.

Johnny addressed Auster. "I was as much a monster as any Sentry. I have no right to make demands and deserve no mercy.

I'll do what you want—if you find me worthy. I acknowledge what I've done in life, I accept what I am, and I understand who I will become." Johnny thought of the burden he would take on. "All life on the planet is at risk. It's the least I can do."

Torphis turned to the others. "Perhaps we should discuss his candidacy once more—privately."

Boke Gal crossed his arms. "Yes."

The three Sentries faced each other, closed their eyes, and appeared to fall into a deep, hypnotic state. Boke Gal furrowed his brow, Fokazi nodded, Torphis tipped his head as though considering a point. Finally, all three roused from their trances.

Boke Gal stepped forward and spoke to Auster. "We believe his disposition has shifted and he will walk in truth. He is awake. We deem him worthy."

Auster turned to the Sentries. "I will send for the others. See to your regions until we all gather."

The three Sentries bowed, turned to mist, and disappeared into the night sky.

"Your transformation will take place at daybreak tomorrow. For now, there's something I must do. You may as well be present since you will carry out the same task many times in years to come."

Auster reached forward and took hold of Johnny's arm. "Close your eyes."

SEVENTY-TWO

Michael Flynn adjusted his ball cap as he sat on the balcony of his estate overlooking the Pacific. "Only a few more days, Wilks."

Wilks stroked his white beard. "You're sure you want to do this, son? It's a big step. Your father sacrificed a lot for this company, and he'd probably hate to see you divorce yourself from its interests."

"I wasn't a baby when my father died, Wilks. I learned enough about him to know he would want me to follow my own dreams and pave my own way, like he did." Michael paused. "Like Maya did. Hold on a sec." Michael got up and dashed in the house, returning a minute later with a bottle and two glasses. "I bought this for the occasion."

Wilks leaned forward and read the label. "Ah, single malt, small batch. A good choice."

"I'm learning," Michael poured a dram for each of them.

Wilks raised the glass to his nose. "Although I feel a bit sad, I want you to know that I'm proud of you. It takes courage to break such a powerful mold and carve your own destiny."

Michael smiled. "Thanks, Wilks. You've been like a father to me."

"It's been an honor," Wilks said. "It's nice of Maya to come back for the occasion."

"It is. From Europe and back twice in a week can be a butt-kicker. Michael raised his glass. "Let's toast."

Wilks held up his scotch. "To…"

"Freedom."

"To freedom." Wilks smiled.

SEVENTY-THREE

Johnny's world blurred for a moment, then he found himself standing in front of a swing set and monkey bars. He glanced around. "This is Thousand Wells Park."

"Yes," Auster said. "Our task is up ahead."

Johnny followed Auster along the winding sidewalk that carved through the green grass. In broad daylight, the park seemed like any other—mothers watching their children play, joggers passing by, and people picnicking on the lawn. But Johnny's new ability to read energy told a different truth.

I feel sorrow, angst, anger.

In the distance, he caught sight of a group of homeless men and women, clustered together in pools of shade under the trees. Johnny felt their eyes on him as he and Auster passed.

Thoughts of the mugging resurfaced. The insects stirred inside of Johnny, as though his body was priming itself for battle. He forced the memory from his mind to keep them from emerging.

Auster stopped in front of a man crumpled against a tree. The man looked emaciated, ribs protruding through thin skin as he drew in shallow, rapid breaths. Large patches of hair were missing, the bald spots were covered in scabs.

Johnny recoiled at the smell—rotten, like meat left out for days. "What's wrong with him?"

"This is a Hand whose life force is slipping away. The body he's using is deteriorating and must be renewed."

Johnny stepped away from the pathetic creature. "Renewed how?"

"By absorbing the energy that has left another."

Johnny looked around at the people in the park. "You have to kill someone to do that, right? You're just going to—"

"No," Auster interrupted. "Sometimes killing is required. However, it is most efficient to pull energy from one who has expired naturally. Auster turned toward the man. "Up, Hasler. We're going to the hospital."

"You said my body would last twenty years." Hasler got to his feet and stumbled forward.

"The one you absorbed was ill," Auster said. "Did you use narcotics?"

"Didn't do no drugs." Hasler glanced at Johnny. "You ain't a Hand, are ya?"

"No."

Hasler looked him up and down. "What's inside of you? It's weird."

"Decomposers."

Hasler waved Johnny off. "You're fuckin' with me."

Sick and injured people packed the Thousand Wells emergency room. Several people gave Hasler a disconcerted stare as he took a seat in the crowded waiting area.

Auster turned to Johnny. "I will find a suitable body. We will need access to all parts of the hospital, so give me a moment." In an instant, he was gone.

Johnny scanned the room, feeling each person's unique energy. *Auster was right. I can already discern subtle differences.*

A minute later, Auster returned with two key cards. He handed one to Johnny. "I will search the area for one who will be expiring soon. Meet me in the morgue." A second later, he sifted through the door as mist.

Johnny walked around to the front entrance of the hospital and ducked past the information desk. He eventually found the morgue and waited. Auster arrived minutes later, dragging Hasler behind him. "Did you get him all the way here without anyone seeing you?"

"No." Auster closed the door. "Several hospital employees will wake up with headaches shortly so we must move quickly." He opened one of the cadaver drawers and shoved Hasler in, then opened another drawer and turned to Johnny. "In!"

Knowing he had no choice, Johnny stepped up to the drawer and lowered himself into it. A surge of anxiety washed over him as Auster slid it shut. He closed his eyes and tried to relax, his breath echoing in the small space. He heard voices and what sounded like a gurney being pushed into the room. A thought sent another wave of panic through him. *What if they find me?*

He held his breath as the voices came closer.

"Here, put him in this one."

The sound of a drawer sliding open was followed by the thuds of a body being dumped into it.

"Whoa, sorry there, guy."

"He's dead, dude. He can't feel it."

"Yeah, but still."

The drawer clicked shut.

"One more hour, then it's cerveza time."

"I hear ya, partner. Now let's get out of here."

Johnny listened as the rattle of the gurney wheels crossed the floor and faded away.

Whew, that was close. For a moment, it was almost peaceful, then Johnny was jerked into reality when Auster pulled his drawer open.

Johnny squinted against fluorescent lights and got to his feet. Then he turned around. "What the fuck?" he shouted.

Hasler stood bare-assed naked in front of an open drawer containing a body.

"Watch closely. This can only be done shortly after the body dies, before the energy slips away."

Auster gripped Hasler by the neck with one hand and held the other above the corpse. Light radiated into the dead body and it began to quiver.

Johnny moved forward to get a closer look.

Auster continued to send forth light until the skin began to bubble, then he lifted Hasler off the ground and smashed him on top of the cadaver. Hasler squirmed and squealed as his body appeared to melt into the dead man's.

Auster turned to Johnny. "The light transfers the life force. I'm moving the energy that is leaving the deceased into Hasler. The energy will renew his tissue as well."

"Doesn't this hinder nature's process?" Johnny asked.

"What we do would be like taking a shovelful of wet sand from the ocean shore. The impression in the smooth surface lasts only moments before the breaking surf fills it with the sand around it. The universe immediately compensates."

Hasler had stopped writhing in Auster's grip.

"Is he passed out?" Johnny asked.

"Yes, the process is very painful. I am told it feels like being burned alive. But it is necessary. Hasler will wake with renewed flesh. His appearance will now resemble that of his benefactor."

That's a plus.

Auster peeled Hasler off the body and stood him up. He turned to Johnny. "Toss him his clothes."

Johnny grimaced at the melted remains of the cadaver. "You're just going to leave the dead guy like that?"

"Humans have a propensity to deny the existence of what they do not understand. Trust me. This will be explained away."

Auster pushed the drawer closed. "I will get Hasler back to the park so his body can settle."

"What should I do?" Johnny asked.

"Occupy yourself as you see fit." Auster took hold of Hasler and headed toward the door. "An hour before sunrise tomorrow, call for me. You will receive the light at daybreak."

SEVENTY-FOUR

Tomorrow at sunrise. Johnny tried to keep his thoughts straight as he exited the hospital.

The warm sun felt good on his back as he rounded the corner and headed toward Town Center Square. The energy Johnny felt around him was amazing, like a thousand rays of light. Some people radiated powerful life forces, others were weak, some positive, others negative.

It's difficult to focus on a single thought.

"John!"

Startled, Johnny saw Gladys walking toward him. "Hey." He noticed the purple flower in her hair and warmth washed though him like a sip of scotch.

"Where are you out and about to today, John?"

"Just finishing up some last-minute errands before a long business trip I'm taking tomorrow. How about you?"

"I'm going to visit my little buddy in the ICU."

The boy in Brickford's case. The three-year-old who was shot by the junkie—with my gun barrel.

"How is he?"

Gladys' smile faded away. "They can't seem to stabilize him. I'm really worried. He needs all of our prayers right now." She paused. "Why don't you come visit him with me?"

"Me?" Johnny recoiled at the thought.

"Sure, why not? He needs all the support he can get."

Johnny looked back toward the hospital. *I deserve to see what I've done.* "Okay, Gladys, let's go."

As they entered the intensive care ward, a lump formed in Johnny's throat.

"This way. His room is at the end of the hall."

Johnny drew in a shallow breath as he looked ahead. A couple and child stood outside. The man was hand-in-hand with his wife, a pretty Indian woman. Both looked familiar.

"This can't be," Johnny said aloud.

Gladys turned toward him. "What?"

Johnny couldn't believe his eyes. *That's Dr. Patel. And she's married to Frank Corby. Please tell me the three-year-old who was shot using my gun barrel isn't their son?*

Johnny wanted to scream at the top of his lungs. He wanted to undo his entire life and live it over.

Frank stepped forward. "Hi, Gladys." He faced Johnny. "Have we met?"

"Yes, a very long time ago." Johnny's mind went back to the first time he saw Danielle. He fought to keep his voice steady. "I met my wife at your high school graduation party."

"Wow." Frank touched his forehead. "That *was* a long time ago. We appreciate your visit…"

"John." Johnny held out his hand and they shook.

Frank gestured toward his family. "This is my wife, Anisha, and my daughter, Katie."

Johnny's eyes met Anisha's. "Hi."

"Hello." She gave Johnny a curious stare.

A nurse exited the boy's room. "He's ready for you."

Frank walked into the room. Anisha and little Katie followed.

Gladys took Johnny's hand. "Come on."

The sucking sound of the ventilator echoed in the dimly lit room. Johnny put a hand to his mouth as he observed the tiny boy, lying still, IVs stuck in each arm and a respirator tube down his throat.

Anisha leaned forward and smoothed William's hair then kissed his forehead.

Gladys approached the bed. "Hi, William. It's Auntie Gladys again. How are you, buddy?" She took his hand. "You look better today. Pretty soon you're going to get right up and play catch with Daddy, right?"

Johnny scanned the life-support system keeping the child alive, the faint blip on the heart monitor, the drip from the bags to the IVs. The aperture Auster opened in Johnny made it clear.

The boy's energy is slipping away.

A nurse entered the room, her expression stern, no-nonsense. "I'm sorry, but there are too many visitors in here," she whispered, her voice raspy.

"We'll go," Gladys said, taking Johnny's arm.

"Thanks for stopping by," Frank said.

"He's in my thoughts," Johnny said. "You all are."

Numbness flooded Johnny as he and Gladys left the hospital and plodded down the sidewalk toward Town Center Square.

The ripple from my actions continues. I deserve anything Auster does to me.

Gladys reached into her purse, pulled out a pair of sunglasses, and slipped them on. "I know we only visited for a few seconds, but I believe he hears us and knows we're there."

"I do, too," Johnny said. *But his life force is dwindling.*

Gladys pointed to the fountain as it came into view. "Are you going to the protest tomorrow?"

"What protest?"

"Practically the whole city will be up at sunrise tomorrow to block the fountain so it won't get torn down."

"Really? They're tearing it down tomorrow?"

"They're gonna to *try* to. But with a couple thousand people in the way, I'm not sure if they'll succeed."

How ironic, Johnny thought. *A major symbol of my childhood is being destroyed the same day I become a Sentry.*

"I'm going to grab a coffee and then I'm due at the shelter. Feel like joining me?" She flashed Johnny a sweet smile.

"That sounds perfect," Johnny said. A thought came to mind. *Perhaps my last day here should be put to good use.* "If it's okay, I'll go to the shelter with you. Maybe they can use a dishwasher or something."

"That would be fantastic. We always need help."

"Okay, then. Coffee it is, and then helping." Johnny extended his elbow.

Gladys blushed then hooked her arm in his.

SEVENTY-FIVE

Maya Flynn checked her watch. *8:30 p.m.* She let one of her six-inch heels slip off her foot and dangle from her toes as she sipped coffee and glanced across the city at the Eiffel Tower.

Mulling over the information she'd gathered earlier that day, she took out a small journal and scribbled a few notes—a trick she learned from watching a police officer almost a decade ago.

She reread what she'd just written. I'll handle this later, she thought. *Just let tonight go smoothly so I can get home. I can hardly wait to see you, Mikey. There's so much we need to talk about. So much you need to know.*

Her phone rang. "Yes."

"The meeting will take place as planned. Eleven o'clock, after the dedication dinner. They'll be meeting at Café L'eau."

"His attendance is certain?" Maya asked.

"Affirmative," the voice answered.

"Then confirm mine as well."

"Will do."

"The job must be finished tonight. I have to be in California for an event."

"Understood."

"Good." Maya ended the call, tucked the phone into her clutch, and took a few minutes to finish her espresso. She swiped away a long, brunette strand that had come loose from her chignon, and then got up and sauntered toward the door, sensing the stares of several men in the café following her.

Before reaching the busy sidewalk, her attention fell on a small table where an Asian man sat alone. He puffed on a cigarette, the smoke curling up beside his scarred face. Their eyes locked briefly, then he pulled his gaze away, phone pressed against his ear.

Maya drew in a shallow breath, the little hairs on the back of her neck standing up, and then slid on her sunglasses and strode toward the Parisian sunset.

SEVENTY-SIX

Johnny was surprised to see Auster waiting for him when he walked out of the homeless shelter before sunrise. "I didn't call for you, did I?"

"Your mind dwelled in the past most of last night."

"Yeah." Johnny thought again of Dani, the kids, Paula, and the life he left behind.

"Come," Auster said. "It's time. They're waiting for you."

Johnny sucked in a ragged breath and shuddered. The insects, reacting to the fear that inundated his body, solidified. He scratched at the bumps forming under his skin. "I feel like I'm going to my own execution."

"In a sense, you are," Auster said. "But you are also attending your own rebirth. Everyone you will see in a few moments has gone through the same thing."

Johnny averted his eyes and asked the question he'd been toiling over. "Will it hurt?"

Auster took Johnny's arm. "Unlike anything you have known before."

Great. Johnny's mouth went dry. "All right. Let's do this."

Johnny felt a *whoosh* as he was lifted off the ground. He closed his eyes and counted silently. *One thousand one, one thousand two...*When he reached one thousand four, he crashed to the ground. His eyes snapped open just as his face hit the dirt. "Shit!"

He got to his feet and saw that he was standing on top of a mesa just outside Thousand Wells. A throng of individuals surrounded him. Their energy felt powerful and different. Johnny couldn't tell how many there were. *A hundred? Two hundred?*

Johnny scanned the crowd in disbelief. *Their collective life force radiates so intensely that I can see colors, like a rainbow of energy branching out in all directions.*

Standing closest to him were Torphis, Fokazi, and Boke Gal. Next to the Mongol stood a tall woman, lean and strong, with jade eyes and ivory skin. Auburn hair spilled down to her waist. She nodded briefly when she and Johnny locked gazes. Beside her, a blond man, equally pale, with a stocky build and blue eyes whispered something to the woman, then smiled at Johnny.

They're from everywhere—men and women, of all shapes and sizes, from all corners of the globe.

A large man with dark skin and dreadlocks chuckled. "Your face says it all, new Sentry."

The sun threatened to peek above the horizon, casting a light-orange halo in the paling sky.

Johnny felt a wave of trepidation shudder through him as Auster stepped closer and stopped an inch away from him. "New Sentry, state your name."

"John Fallow."

Whispers of his name rippled through the crowd.

Auster continued. "John Fallow, will you accept the light?"

Johnny glanced one more time toward the city. "Yes, I will."

Auster raised both arms. "Let a Sentry be born!"

"Let a Sentry be born." The crowd chanted.

"Now, John Fallow, see me." Auster melted into an iridescent beam that looked as if it were made of silver and diamonds. He shot into the sky, fracturing the new morning light and sending millions of prisms across the heavens as he coursed upward.

A mixture of awe and fear filled Johnny. *What is he?*

In the sky, Auster's form shifted into what looked like a blade, glistening like ice and charging high up into the clouds. Light spilled from the innumerable facets as it twisted in the air, pulsing like a heartbeat.

Something stirred in the heavens. The silver blade changed direction and descended, plummeting back to Earth to create a silver arc that extended into space. The tip of the blade hurtled toward him.

Holy fuck.

The blade plunged through Johnny's chest, sending an electric current through him that felt as though every cell of his body was being boiled. He convulsed as the blade jerked him upward and a sphere of light exploded around him. Johnny felt like he was on fire. Suspended several feet off the ground and paralyzed by pain, he opened his eyes to see swarms of insects encased in the light sphere with him. The deafening hum and crackling ricocheted in the space.

In the orb of floating heat, the pain intensified—sharp, burning—surging through him like jolts of electricity. He glanced down at his body to see his skin was translucent, revealing the sea of insects that cloaked every inch of his skeleton.

His entire life passed before his eyes—childhood, marriage, business, fatherhood, death.

He felt an intense pull upward. Seconds passed. Warm turned to cool, light faded to black, cacophony to silence. Johnny peered around. He saw the Earth below him, a blue marble with swirling white clouds. *I'm in space?* Then he felt a severe drop and was in his body again, still impaled on the silver, pulsing blade.

The inferno orb exploded, sending sparks of fire hundreds of feet into the sky. Like a sword being pulled from a stone, the silver ray retracted, whipping back into the heavens.

Johnny's limp form dropped to the ground. Feeling broken and unable to move, he watched the silver blade twist in the sky like a funnel, then, in the blink of an eye, it was gone. Johnny struggled to draw in a breath before slipping into unconsciousness.

∞∞∞∞∞∞

Johnny opened his eyes. The sun had risen in the sky, the warmth baking his sore muscles.

How long did that last?

He bent his elbow. The reaction in his muscles felt strange. He sat up and looked at his hands, acknowledging the response of his body to the minutest detail.

I have direct control of every system, every cell.

Auster looked down at him. "The new Sentry is awake."

A rumble of conversation erupted in the crowd.

Johnny stared at Auster, whose energy now looked more like glistening particles that radiated light.

"You will adjust to having the eyes of a Sentry. Get up."

Johnny got to his feet and met the gazes of the sea of Sentries.

"Change," Auster said.

Johnny knew what he meant.

Turn to mist, like they do.

Johnny held up an arm, spread his fingers, and focused. Before his eyes, his hand disintegrated, but not into particles like the others, into millions of tiny insects.

The crowd's gasp splintered into a wave of whispers.

The insects hovered, mimicking the shape of Johnny's hand. He made a swirling motion with his wrist and the insects burst outward, creating what looked like a small firework at the end of his arm.

"Entirely now," Torphis said.

Feeling stronger than he ever had before, Johnny glanced down at his feet and focused, calling on each cell. Beginning at his toes, his feet transformed into whirling swarms. He ran the same command up his entire body, and like a paint roller running up a wall, his form disintegrated into a buzzing, hissing cloud.

This feels strange. I feel every nuance of my being. My emotions are present but less chaotic.

"Change back," Auster said.

Johnny drew the insects back. He stood breathless before the large group.

Auster called to the witnesses. "Behold your new comrade, John Fallow."

"Welcome," they chanted in unison. "We will walk the Earth together."

Auster turned to Johnny. "It is now time to exchange signatures with the other Sentries."

Recalling what that required, Johnny gaped at the mass of people, feeling his eyes widen. "I'm going to have to eat—"

Laughter erupted in the crowd.

"It will not be the same as before," Auster said. "Slicing and eating flesh is not necessary among Sentries. You transform and exchange in particle form. You will see once the process has begun." He raised both arms and called to the other Sentries. "Take to the air."

At once, hundreds of Sentries turned to mist and rose in a giant haze that covered the mesa. Johnny changed form and ascended toward the clouds as a swarm of insects.

The mist charged him, particles intermingling with his.

Inhale, someone communicated. *Take in our signatures.*

Johnny opened his senses and drifted through the mist, taking in the unique essence of each Sentry—spice, leather, musk, fermented, floral, metallic, woodsy, briny, acidic, sweet, talcum. One by one, each Sentry changed signatures with Johnny before drifting out of sight.

After several minutes, only Auster and the three *Dayyani* who had deemed Johnny worthy remained. They transformed back and the four stood before him atop the mesa.

"You are one with us," Fokazi said. "Once Sentries exchange signatures, there is no longer a need for words."

Respond if you understand me, new Sentry, Johnny felt Fokazi ask.

Somehow, this method of communication felt natural. *I can,* Johnny sent back.

Fokazi nodded to Auster.

"Good," Auster said. "Regarding your assignment, you will oversee the progress in North America, beginning immediately. I will now apprise you of all the Hands in the area, as well as the Sentries who border you." Auster sent the information.

Johnny put a hand to his forehead. "Volumes worth of information absorbed in moments. Pretty amazing."

"Many things will be new to you," Auster said. "Which is why it is customary that one Sentry stay as council until you feel ready to take on your responsibility alone. Which of the three *Dayyani* would you like to stay?"

Johnny thought of his three visits. "Torphis," he answered.

Torphis stepped forward. "You will first establish residency somewhere and acquire a computer. Then I will show you how Sentries monitor progress in their regions."

"It is time for me to leave you, new Sentry," Boke Gal said. "Until we meet again." He bowed slightly, turned to mist, and shot through the morning sky.

Fokazi stepped forward. *Keep that hothead in check.* Then he rose and drifted away.

Auster turned to mist. "I will monitor your progress and we'll speak again after one lunar cycle." A moment later, he was gone.

Torphis turned to Johnny. "The sun is up. What do you wish to do on your first day as Sentry?"

"I have several things in mind, but the first order of business is right down there." Johnny pointed to the city. "The fountain."

Johnny and Torphis changed form and shot toward Thousand Wells.

Cop cars with lights ablaze surrounded the coil of people blocking the fountain. The police had managed to corral the crowd and clear the path for the demolition equipment. The media had descended as well, with reporters and cameras jostling to get the best shot.

Surviving members of Thousand Wells' tribe had assembled around the stone structure. A hundred bouquets rested at the feet of the likeness of their shaman.

The crowd must have heard them coming, because all faces were upturned as Johnny and Torphis swept down from the sky.

"What the hell is *that*?" he heard someone scream.

Targeting a bulldozer that was approaching the fountain, Johnny sent forth a stream of insects. The driver screamed and covered his face as rivers of flies and beetles plunged through the vents and under the hood, clogging the engine, eating through the electrical system. The machine let out a few blurps and gasps before all power cut out.

Johnny turned his attention to the next machine, and the next. Within minutes, all of the demolition vehicles were nothing more than huge, metal shells. Dumbfounded workers sat in disbelief.

The crowd split in all directions when a swirl of mist encircled the fountain. The bouquets of flowers shot high into the sky and rained down into the crowd as the twister sandblasted away the stains left by time.

Nice, Torphis.

Johnny glided down and lifted a flower from the ground. He carried it to the fountain, the stone now clean and polished, and placed the bloom at the feet of Thousand Wells. "Restore this place," he commanded.

Everyone in the crowd glanced around, as though searching for the source of the voice.

We're done here, Johnny communicated to Torphis. *Let's go. Time to save a little boy.*

SEVENTY-SEVEN

In Thousand Wells Hospital, Johnny entered William Rakesh Corby's room through the window. Torphis followed.

"*This* is the boy?" Torphis gazed at the child, a look of surprise on his face.

"Yes, why?' Johnny asked.

"Can't you read the sig...oh, you wouldn't be able to." Torphis continued to smile placidly at the sleeping child, like he cared about him.

Realization flooded Johnny. *There was only one Sentry who wasn't there.* "He's Kothra's descendant, isn't he?"

Torphis nodded. "Yes."

Johnny scanned the little body, sensing each break in energy that caused the life force to drain away. "No modern medicine can help him. He has hours at best."

"Only the light can save him," Torphis said. "You must take energy from another, as you saw Auster do."

"I don't want to do that. There has to be another way."

"You can draw from the light source itself, but doing this would result in the boy being different from other humans."

"Fine. I'll do whatever it takes. I have to save him." Johnny focused on the light, the new energy that Auster gave him access to, and placed his hand above the boy.

A white, glistening ray spilled from Johnny's hand and into the boy's chest. Johnny felt the light connect the breaks in the boy's energy. The boy grew stronger each moment he was bathed in light.

It's working.

He held the stream steady until he felt it, the spark that turned to...life—sustainable on its own.

The boy exhaled a long breath.

Johnny let the light fade and pulled his hand back. "It's done." He turned to Torphis. "I did it. He's going to live."

"Yes," Torphis said. "But you should know that since the child has been rebuilt with light that has never been attached to a life source before now, he will be what we call *kashurra*."

Johnny thought for a moment. "I remember Boke Gal saying the descendants of Sentries are different, more perceptive."

"*Kashurra* are different from the descendants of Sentries. Descendants are the relatives of Sentries, they are highly perceptive because their apertures are open. *Kashurra* are connected to light and are even more evolved." Torphis returned his attention to William. "So much so that he will not be able to reproduce with other humans."

"What?" Johnny looked at the boy. "*Kashurra*, as you call them, are sterile?"

"He is not sterile. Unlike using your human form to mate and create a child, you have rebuilt the boy with the light you wield, the source. His body is not like a descendant or Hand. This child will have to grow up and mate with someone whose structure is similar to his, or his seed will not take."

Johnny couldn't believe it. "So William is now another *species*?"

"Yes, he is." Torphis answered.

"Are there more like him?" Johnny stared at the sleeping boy.

"Yes," Torphis moved closer to the child. "They are rare and spread throughout the world. Yet, somehow, they manage to find each other and reproduce. Their impact in the human world is staggering. You would be shocked to learn who in your history were *kashurra*." He leaned down to look closely at William's face. "I'm curious to see what he will do, being both a *kashurra* and a descendant of Kothra."

"What's going on?"

Johnny turned to see Ben standing in the doorway.

Ben, the nurse who took care of me after I was shot. Johnny read his energy. *Whose signature is that? You've got to be kidding me. Ben's a descendant of Torphis.*

Ben marched in. "You shouldn't be here." He stopped at the foot of the bed, a look of astonishment washing over his face as he stared at William. "There's been a shift. I can feel it."

"Yes," Johnny said.

Ben peeled his gaze away from the boy and approached Johnny. "We've met before, haven't we?"

"A long time ago," Johnny answered

Ben's attention went to Torphis. "And who are you? There's something—"

Torphis smiled. "You feel a connection, don't you?"

Ben nodded.

"We are distant relatives."

To Johnny's amazement, Ben didn't seem surprised. He simply nodded. "I can sense it. What is your name?"

"Torphis." He took a step forward and held out his hand. "You're a healer, aren't you?"

"Yes." Ben shook hands with him.

"That's good." Torphis released his grip and gazed away as if in thought.

Anisha busted into the room. "Ben! Something's changed. I felt William—" She stopped. "What—?"

Johnny held up his hands. "Just here to help."

Anisha walked to her son's bedside. "He's…better."

"He's going to live," Johnny said.

Anisha bent down and cradled William's face in her hands. "Yes, he is." A laugh escaped, and then she kissed the boy's forehead. "He really, really is." She looked up at Johnny. "I met you the other day. You were with Gladys."

"Yes."

Torphis moved to the opposite side of the bed, his expression a mixture of surprise and joy. He gazed into Anisha's eyes. "You even look like her."

"Like who?" Anisha stood up, keeping one hand on William's arm.

"An old friend of mine," Torphis said.

Kothra.

Torphis walked toward the door. "Come, new Sentry. We're done here."

"Yes." Johnny smiled at Anisha. "William will wake up soon."

Anisha stroked William's cheek and brushed away a tear. "Why do I feel I should be thanking you?"

"No need."

They left the room and headed down the hall. Once outside, they turned to mist and swarm and disappeared into the sky.

SEVENTY-EIGHT

Johnny sent his thoughts to Torphis as they flew in particle form above the clouds.

If it's all right with you, there are a few things I'd like to handle privately.

I am here as a guide, Torphis answered. *Do what you must and then find a place to settle and call to me.* He peeled away in a different direction.

Johnny headed toward Gypsum Ridge.

∞∞∞∞∞∞

The wing of Gypsum Ridge Hospital that Johnny walked through was silent. Passersby wore placid smiles, some were genuine, others seemed painted on. He gauged the energy. It was as he expected.

Very weak. Everywhere.

He tiptoed into one of the rooms. The frail woman in bed couldn't have weighed more than seventy pounds. Her white hair was thin enough to show her scalp. Tubes fed life fluids into both arms. An oxygen mask covered her mouth.

Johnny stood beside the bed. His heart sank as he watched her take labored, shallow breaths. He gently took her hand in his. "Hello, Paula."

Too weak to move, Paula's eyes shifted to Johnny. "Who are... you?"

Johnny leaned closer. "It's me. Paula. The man who would get huffy when you made fun of American football."

Paula looked at Johnny. "The eyes...*your* eyes...It's really you, Mr. Flynn." She had to stop to take a few rapid breaths. "Why do you look...different?"

"It's a long story."

Paula squeezed Johnny's hand. "You...went...away."

"A mistake I will pay for many times over." Johnny looked up at the monitors. "Do the kids visit you?"

"Yes. Michael more...Maya...yesterday..." She gasped. "I try to smile...but—"

"I know." Johnny kissed her hand. "I miss the way we were."

Paula closed her eyes and a tear trickled down the side of her face. "I do, too. But now... my life...is pain from the moment I open my eyes."

Johnny gauged the energy. *She's suffering.*

"Mr. Flynn. If ya ever...really cared ...one bit about this old Irish lady," she paused to gasp, "pray... it's over soon."

Johnny closed his eyes and listened to her labored breathing, then he leaned forward and spoke into her ear. "I love you like family, Paula. You've always been loyal and true."

"I love...you, too, Mr. Flynn...and Mrs. Flynn...and...the children."

A tear slipped down Johnny's cheek as he raised a hand to the machines, sent forth the light, and watched the readings on monitors begin to fall.

Paula, sensing the change, turned her eyes toward Johnny and saw the ray coming from his hand.

She closed her eyes and whispered, "Thank you."

SEVENTY-NINE

Johnny entered the twenty-four hour coffee shop in Thousand Wells. News reports of the anomalous events at the fountain blared from the television behind the counter as he took a seat and ordered coffee and pie.

"Thought you'd be out of town by now, Fallow."

Johnny twisted on the stool. "Dick Brickford."

Brickford held up his cup. "That's me. Pulling a double today." He took a sip of coffee. "What do ya think of all the shit that went down this morning at the fountain?"

"Would you be pissed if I said I thought it was great?"

"Hell, no! It *was* great." Brickford took another sip. "Fucking weird, though. Out of the blue, a tornado filled with bugs comes down and blows the equipment to shit. Fucking thing even sandblasted the statue, and yet not *one* person was even hurt."

"It's amazing, all right." Johnny smiled as the waitress brought his coffee and pie.

Brickford stared at the TV. "Rumor's goin' 'round that Thousand Wells himself came back once again to save the city."

"Interesting," Johnny said.

"Well, I can't think of a better explanation for it." Brickford swigged his coffee. "PD had an emergency meeting with the Mayor today. Cheap fucker's gonna restore Town Center Square to its "original splendor" as he put it. He knows if he doesn't, they won't re-elect his ass."

"That's good news," Johnny said.

"Wanna hear more good news, Fallow? Today there wasn't one call in for violent crime, drugs, or prostitution. Only cats in trees and old ladies losing their keys."

"Unbelievable."

"In Thousand Wells? I'd call it damn near impossible."

Johnny sensing Brickford's guard was down, thought he'd risk bringing up the subject. "Did you find out anything about the gun that shot the kid?"

Brickford looked at him sideways. "You have a good memory, Fallow. As a matter of fact, I do know where the gun came from."

Johnny waited. "Well?"

Brickford raised an eyebrow. "Why do you give a fuck?"

"I'm from Gypsum Ridge. I followed the case." Johnny shrugged. "I won't say shit about what you tell me."

"Wouldn't matter if you told or not," Brickford said. "There's not a shred of proof to back up my theory. But I pretty much know who did it."

"Who?"

"Jonathan Flynn pulled the trigger on old Vander Broek."

Johnny took a bite of his pie and, with a full mouth, said. "How do you figure?"

"Flynn blamed Vander Broek for his wife's murder. I have lots of shit to prove why I think so, but I was pulled off the kidnapping case before I could get all of my facts together."

Johnny thought of Danielle. "It was a terrible thing."

Brickford stared at the black liquid in his cup for a moment. "The outcome of the kidnapping, yeah, it was terrible. But I feel there were other things in play that caused me to get sent down."

"Such as?"

"Well," Brickford took another gulp of coffee. "I'll tell you one thing. Everyone tightened up as tight as a frog's ass when I started digging into Vander Broek's past. When I learned that there's no requirement to forward foreign records of any kind over here when someone immigrates, I pushed to send Gingham and Capra overseas to check out Vander Broek's Dutch records." He lifted both hands in the air. "Boy, I was met with serious hostility on that one."

"By whom?"

"Vander Broek Corp, of course."

"Figures," Johnny said.

"Yeah, but, believe it or not, it wasn't Vander Broek's protests that got me pulled off the case. It was Flynn's partner, Jan Wilkinson."

"Wilkinson? Why?"

"He was a mess. The guy blamed me for everything and wouldn't shut up about it. Kept saying Mrs. Flynn would be alive if I had done my job. Apparently he has friends in high places who felt compelled to assuage his grief."

"That's a shame," Johnny said.

"Yeah, the irony is I would have gotten Wilkinson the answers he demanded if he would have shut the hell up." Brickford waved a hand. "Fuck it, it's all water under the bridge now."

"Yeah," Johnny said. "I guess so."

"But the truth behind those murders is in those Dutch records, I just know it." Brickford sighed. "I swear I'm gonna vacation there someday, just to check it out for myself and get closure."

Johnny nodded. "I don't blame you." He finished his pie and coffee and got up. "It was nice seeing you again, Brickford."

"Same here, Fallow. So, are you sticking around town, after all, or what?"

"Unsure right now."

"Okay. I guess I'll see ya when I see ya."

Johnny left the coffee shop, changed into swarm, and rose into the sky.

He sent a message to Auster. *How do I cross the globe the way you and the Sentries do?*

When you received the light, I sent you outside of Earth's atmosphere for a time. You have knowledge of the world inside of you. Focus on the place and you will go there.

Johnny focused.

Europe. The Netherlands.

Johnny gauged the trip, felt the pull, and the swarm shot through the sky. He was shocked at the effortlessness of his ability. *I'm traveling faster than a plane.*

Calm swept over him, like his autonomous cells knew what do, which gave his mind some down time. Johnny calmed himself and settled in for the trip.

EIGHTY

Johnny sat in front of his new computer in the small apartment he'd leased the day he returned from the Netherlands. His thoughts whirled, tossing around the information he'd acquired from delving into the Dutch archives.

I can't believe how calm I am. The old me would be exploding right now. Mind focused and goal clear, Johnny logged on and found the business news. He scanned the headlines.

"Found it." He read the report.

> Michael Flynn, who sold his remaining shares of Flynn Corp to co-owner Jan Wilkinson yesterday, will be recognized in a Flynn Corp celebration tomorrow night at the Gypsum Grand Prince Hotel ballroom. Former Olympian, Miracle Maya Flynn is also reported to be attending to honor her brother.
>
> Wilkinson, who now owns the majority of Flynn Corp shares, is in a position to merge with Vander Broek Corporation, a move analysts have been speculating on for months.

Johnny's eyes drilled into the photo accompanying the story. He read the caption aloud. "Jan Wilkinson with Michael and Maya Flynn in front of the Thousand Wells Homeless Shelter."

Johnny shut down the computer and sat back. *I will see my children tomorrow. They won't know it's me, but I'll see them, and that will have to do.*

He gazed around at his new apartment. *Clean, carpets look new, still smells like paint.* Then he thought of his old home. "I don't need much now," he said aloud. *Furniture is ordered. It will be nice to sleep in a bed. But what to do before tomorrow?*

Recalling what Torphis said about his own philanthropic efforts, a plan formed. *I help others because I am able. I will do the work of a Sentry regardless, so why not provide help where I can?*

"True." Johnny stood, scooped up his keys, and headed out the door. Minutes later, he walked into the homeless shelter.

An elderly man hobbled up. "Yes?"

"I'm a volunteer. Came over to put in a few hours." He looked past the man into the building. "Gladys wouldn't happen to be here, would she?"

The man smiled. "That angel is always here. She's in the back right now." He leaned forward and added in a whisper, "She's helping someone who's having a nervous breakdown."

"Oh."

"Come on in," the man said. "Looks like you'll have KP duty. Lots of dishes need cleanin'. I'm Freddie, by the way."

"Hi, Freddie. I'm John." He walked into the kitchen and snatched an apron off a hook. "If you don't mind, tell Gladys I'm here. I'd like to say hi."

"Will do, sonny. Happy dishwashing."

"Yeah." Johnny looked at the dirty dishes stacked shoulder high next to the sink and sighed. "Well, a journey of a thousand miles…" He pulled on some rubber gloves and got to work.

After an hour passed, Johnny looked at his progress. "I actually made a dent."

"Hi, John."

Johnny spun around to see Gladys in the doorway. "Hey."

She stepped forward, a broad smile on her face, a pink flower in her hair. "Freddie said you came by to help."

Johnny read her energy and froze. *Unbelievable. Gladys is a descendant of a Sentry.*

He thought of the many Sentries he'd exchanged signatures with that morning. *Because of that, I know who her ancestor is. Looks like I'll be making a trip overseas to meet another Sentry in person.*

"John?" Gladys looked worried. "You okay?"

"Yeah, great." Johnny held up his sudsy arms. "Putting in a few hours. Seems I'll be staying in Thousand Wells for now."

"That's great news. I'm going home for dinner. It's only a few blocks away. Hungry?"

"Lead the way." He grabbed a towel and dried off.

Gladys let out a "Thank Goodness!" as they trotted down the porch steps onto the sidewalk. "I needed to get out of there!"

"Me, too." Johnny took her arm as they rounded the corner. "I honestly don't know how you do it. What was going on with that guy?"

"His name is Dale. He lost his job about a decade ago when the company he worked for went out of business. He couldn't find steady work afterward. They moved around a lot. His son got into some bad stuff and ended up getting shot and killed."

"What? That's terrible." Johnny's thoughts drifted to Danielle.

"After losing his son, Dale's marriage crumbled and his wife took their daughter away. He lost his apartment because work was unsteady and all he had to subsist on was the tiny pension from the company he worked for, Owen, I think it was called."

It was as though Johnny's mood was doused in mud. *Owen Corp. I shut them down. I caused this.* He recalled what Torphis had told him. *You are the bad guy.*

"So you're sticking around," Gladys said. "Is that *good* news?"

"In a way it's good news. Granted, I'll be traveling a lot." He thought about the following day. "And I'm actually going to see my children for the first time in eight years."

"Wow, I'll bet you're nervous, huh?"

"Terrified is more like it. They won't even recognize me. But I need to see them, Gladys. I have to talk to them."

"It takes courage to do what you're doing, John."

Johnny thought about seeing Michael and Maya. "I don't even know what I'm going to say. I can't just waltz up and start talking."

"Don't beat yourself up. You're their father. Just enjoy being in their presence again. They'll feel it, I promise."

"You're right," Johnny said. He turned to her. "Did they teach you all this in homeless shelter training?"

"Not exactly, smartass." She smiled. "Although, I do have training in crisis management, much of what I know I learned from being on the job for years." She pointed to a small apartment up ahead. "Well, this is it."

They slowly strolled toward her front door.

Gladys sighed deeply. "Okay, I'll admit it. I have no idea why, but there's something about you, John. I just like being around you."

"I feel the same way. Your kindness has been like cool water in the middle of the desert. I hope you know how inspirational you are."

Gladys blushed as she turned the key in the door and pushed it open. "It's funny, I can tell you've been through a lot, and yet you pulled through it. I kind of think of you as my strongman."

Johnny stared at her.

"What?" she asked.

He pulled her to him and kissed her. She held his face and kissed back, open-mouthed and hungry.

Johnny swept her up in his arms and carried her through the door, down the hall, finally making it to the bedroom. They fumbled though the unbuckling and stripping off of clothes then fell onto the bed.

Johnny's mouth glided down her silky soft skin, exploring her body. He paused to lick and kiss here and there. He caressed her full, round breasts. She reached down and felt him.

I'm so hard I'm going to explode.

For a fleeting moment, Johnny thought of the insects. *Am I going to shoot bugs inside of her?*

"Take me." Her voice was sultry. "Make love to me, John."

He pressed inside of her. She arched her back and moaned, which aroused him even more. She reached around and pushed him in deeper.

Johnny was electrified. The passion was different than when he was human. Each cell of his body responded to hers, each cell registered the need, the pleasure, the hunger. It was unbridled, animal, pure. He clutched a pillow and stole a quick glance at his hand to make sure it wasn't dissolving into a sea of insects.

"Yes!" Gladys chanted as the rhythmic sound of the headboard thumped against the wall.

Johnny moaned as his passion reached its peak. Gladys reached around and pushed him deeper inside, crying out in climax. Then they collapsed in an embrace.

Johnny leaned over and kissed her. "You're amazing." He brought her close.

"I had no idea," she said between breaths. "If you had told me at breakfast that I would be here with you…" She kissed him. "Not that I'm complaining."

Johnny nuzzled her neck. "I didn't expect it, either, but I'm certainly not sending out any protests."

She turned on her side and put her hand against his cheek. "We should have dinner, but I want you again." She glanced at the clock. "I have to pick up Gina in two hours."

"Two hours, huh?" Johnny ran a hand over the curves of her body. "Dinner is overrated."

EIGHTY-ONE

Johnny arrived at the Gypsum Grand Prince Hotel at 8:00 p.m. He straightened his jacket, feeling poised and ready.

He was met with a cool stare from the door attendant. "Are you on the guest list, sir?"

"Of course."

"Your name?"

"Lauritz Herrick." He waited as the man scanned the list, the *new* list that had been updated the day before.

"Ah, here it is." He checked off the name. "Have a lovely evening, sir."

"Thank you." The massive ballroom was enveloped in a creamy glow from the crystal chandeliers. Johnny stood in the doorway for a moment, allowing the dull hum of hundreds of quiet conversations wash over him. He sauntered inside and wove through the room.

These events don't change. Some faces are familiar, others not.

He spotted Wilks in the distance, hobnobbing beside his young wife, a whiskey glass clutched in his hand. Johnny could tell he'd had a few by the pink tinge in his cheeks.

He approached. "Good evening, Mr. Wilkinson."

Wilks smiled. "And a good evening to you, too. Please forgive me for having to ask your name again if we've met."

"We have," Johnny said. "I'm Lauritz Herrick."

The smile melted from Wilks' face.

Johnny motioned toward a door. "Would you care to speak in private?"

Wilks turned to his wife. "Excuse me for a moment, darling."

Wilks led Johnny through an adjacent ballroom and into a conference room with a handful of undressed tables and chairs stacked along the far wall.

Johnny let the door close behind him. "You look older in person than you do in the social pages, Wilks."

Wilks stiffened. "Who are you and what do you want?"

"I'm Lauritz Herrick." Johnny raised a finger. "No. Wait. That's impossible isn't it? Herrick's been dead for over fifty years. He died in the Netherlands at age sixteen when vandals set fire to the shack where he hung out with his friends." Johnny took a step forward. "That fire also killed one other kid from his orphanage, Jan Wilkinson. But you already know all of this, don't you, Josef Vander Broek?"

A trickle of sweat ran down the side of Wilks' face. In almost a whisper, he repeated, "Who are you?"

Johnny gazed into the air. "He was going to tell me about you. At the wedding, moments before I blew your father's head off, the old fuck said, 'I want to tell you about my son.' If I had let him, maybe I would still be—"

Johnny locked gazes with Wilks. "How did you do it? How did you keep the fact that Schuyler Vander Broek was your father a secret for over half a century?"

"Silence has a price, and you're about to pay it."

Two men in suits entered the room.

Johnny regarded them coolly for a moment before turning back to Wilks. "Your own father agreed to your charade?"

Wilks crossed his arms. "Schuyler and I never got along. I watched as he got kicked around by his competition back home. At age fourteen, I tried to give advice on how to keep business and earn respect, but he dismissed my ideas. 'The ludicrous rantings of a petulant child,' I believe were his words." Wilks chuckled.

"So you quit?" Johnny asked.

"No. When I was fifteen, I started to handle our business the way it should have been. Profits soared, but Schuyler didn't like the way I dealt with competitors who took from us. My father was a wise businessman, but he lacked the guts to do what was necessary. When I was sixteen, I took care of two men who threatened to shut us down."

"You killed them," Johnny said.

"No. I killed everyone they loved."

Johnny thought of Dani. "So all the stories of Schuyler Vander Broek's ruthlessness, how he hurt the relatives of his competition…" Johnny's eyes drilled into Wilks. "It was you."

"What I did saved my father's company and made him a legend, whether he acknowledged it or not. After that incident, Schuyler told me he wanted to separate himself with everything having to do with me. I changed my name and left the country. Schuyler agreed to remain silent as long as I kept my distance and respected the code."

"What code?"

"Those in our bloodline are *never* to be touched."

Johnny paced back and forth. "The fire that killed those orphan boys sure came at a convenient time. You have something to do with that?"

Wilks tipped his head. "I might have. They were human trash. No one kicked up a fuss about it." He reached beneath his jacket and pulled out a Ruger. Steely-eyed and red-faced, he said. "Now, for the last fucking time, who are you?"

"I'll give you a hint. You attended my daughter's princess party and dressed up as a frog."

Wilks rolled his eyes. "You're not suggesting that you're Jonathan Flynn." He laughed. "You're insane if you think anyone would believe you."

"Ask me anything, Wilks. Anything. How about the flat tire in Rome that almost got us killed? Or the time Margaret packed your lunch in your suitcase and your yogurt exploded on the way to Toronto? My shirt was tight as hell on you and you went commando because you wouldn't wear another man's *undergarments*."

Wilkinson's face lost all color. "How could you know all of that?"

"You tell me."

Two more people walked in the door. A broadly built young man with blond hair and a svelte woman with jet-black hair. Both had Johnny's piercing green eyes.

There they are.

A lump formed in Johnny's throat. *How I wish I could run over there and hug you both.*

Michael looked at Johnny then at Wilks. "What the hell's going on, Wilks?"

Maya glared at Johnny. "Who are you?"

"He's suggesting that he's your father," Wilks barked. "Which is ridiculous."

"What? The guy's a nut job!" Michael yelled. "Get him out of here."

"What kind of psycho are you?" Maya shouted at Johnny.

Johnny stepped toward Wilks. "Why did you kill Danielle?"

Wilks shook his head. "I didn't—"

"Cut the bullshit! I just returned from the Netherlands." Johnny tried to keep his voice steady. "I spent a lot of time researching. Turns out, everyone involved in Dani's shooting has history tracing back to you. I have the documents to prove it."

Michael marched forward. "Wilks, what in the hell is he talking about?"

"He's lying!" Wilks said through gritted teeth.

"The hell I am! Get 'em where they *live*, right? *You* coined that term. You taught me how to fight dirty." Johnny trembled with anger. "Why did you kill her?"

"You motherfucker!" Michael launched himself at Wilks, but the two bodyguards grabbed him by the arms and held him.

"Knock it off, you little twit," Wilks barked toward Michael. "All you care about is getting drunk and fucking. And *you*," he nodded toward Maya, "are some James Bond imitation. Please, you think I didn't know you were investigating me, Miss Flynn?"

Maya pulled a .38 from her purse and pointed it at Wilks. "I always sensed something was off with you. This Vander Broek merger you're planning just seemed a little too perfect. Now drop the weapon."

"Not yet, princess," Wilks called behind him. "Guards!"

The men holding Michael pushed him aside and each pulled a .45 from their side holsters.

"Drop it! Hands up," one said to Maya.

Maya placed the gun on the floor and raised her hands.

Wilks smirked at Michael and Maya. "You both may as well hear the truth since this *robber*," he jerked his head in the direction of Johnny, "is going to kill you both tonight."

"You better not touch them." Johnny felt his skin ripple.

Wilks raised the gun and took a step toward Johnny. "The truth is, one of the men Jonathan Flynn murdered at Vander Broek's Diamond Celebration was my cousin's son. I held him when he was a baby. Flynn killed my blood."

"You killed *Dani*!" Johnny seethed with anger. "She loved you like family!"

"*Flynn* killed her," Wilks answered back smoothly. "He crossed the line. He killed my blood. You must repay blood with blood." He waved a hand. "It doesn't make a difference now."

"All these years you acted like you really cared." Michael looked like the wind had been knocked out of him.

"I did, in a way," Wilks said. "But I knew you were never going to be a businessman, so it was best to have you move aside."

"You're a monster," Maya said. "Everything you touch bleeds."

"Only those who get in my way." Wilks redirected his attention to Johnny. "Did you honestly plan on going out there and telling the world you're Jonathan Flynn? No one would believe you. Look at yourself." Wilks chuckled. "You're no one. You're a weirdo with a story."

"A story that will bring you down," Johnny said.

"I don't think so." Wilks steadied the gun. "The question of the moment is, should I shoot you in the head and kill you instantly or in the stomach and let you die in excruciating pain?"

Johnny's entire body vibrated with anger. Tiny insects flowed from beneath his pant legs onto the ground.

"But, just in case you are who you say you are," Wilks held up his free hand. "Elliot!"

A shot rang out.

Maya collapsed.

"SIS!"

Wilks sneered at Johnny. "For my father. Blood for blood."

Rage colored everything red. Johnny focused. *I call on you, every one of you.*

The insects gathered in every tissue, every cell in Johnny's body. A singular force, with one purpose, churning, building.

Now.

Johnny exploded into an angry swarm. Millions of flies, ants, and beetles rose in a swirling vortex, and shot straight at Wilks.

It only took seconds for the hissing killers to completely cover Wilks's body. He fell to the ground, screaming and flailing as the thick blanket of creatures devoured him. Skin split, revealing fat and muscle that were quickly covered with more ravenous assailants. Another massive swarm hurled toward the guards. One fired into the air as the cloud covered both of them and tore into their flesh.

It took less than a minute before the microscopic assassins had devoured the flesh of their victims, leaving clean, dry bones. The mass then pooled together, reforming Johnny.

Petal! Johnny ran to Maya.

Leaning over her, Michael spat, "Don't touch my sister! Get the fuck away, you freak!"

Johnny gauged Maya's energy. "She's dying!" He looked at Michael. "I gotta get her out of here."

"You're not touching my sister, you fucking freak." Michael scanned the room, looking as though he was jolted from a trance as he saw the carnage. "Holy shit!" He leaned away from Johnny. "What the fuck are you?"

Johnny held out his arms. "Give her to me."

"Go fuck yourself." He stood up and pushed Johnny away then ran toward the gun on the floor.

Johnny raised an arm. "I'm sorry to have to do this, Bud." He shot forth light, hitting Michael in the back. "Sleep for a while."

Michael fell to the ground. Johnny turned to swarm and scooped up Maya. He took one last look at his son, out cold, then rocketed toward the door.

Once outside, Johnny hurtled Maya away from the coast, toward the desert of Thousand Wells.

Help me, Torphis. I have to save my daughter.

You know what to do. You saved the boy.

I can't afford to do this wrong.

You won't. You wield light. You give life force.

The new moon in the sky left the open desert landscape inky black. When Johnny felt they were far enough out, he descended on a small area beside a cluster of boulders. He swooped down and laid Maya in the cool sand.

He raised his hand above her chest and sent forth a ray of light. "Live, Petal."

Maya began to glow. The light intensified. She gasped for breath.

Good.

Then her skin began to ripple.

"That's too much!" a voice called out.

Johnny pulled back the light. He turned to see Torphis hovering above. "Oh, no. What have I done?" He leaned down and stroked Maya's face. "She's breathing. Is she going to be—"

"You've saved her," Torphis said.

Johnny sat back on his knees. "Thank God." He regarded her again. "I used source light to mend her. She's *kashurra* now, isn't she?"

"No, new Sentry," Torphis said. "Your feelings for her are blinding you. You didn't need to draw from the source, you drew life energy from another to bring her back."

"What?" Johnny looked around. "From who?"

"Read her."

Johnny focused on Maya's energy. "NO!" He leaned over and swept her off the ground.

Torphis sent down a beam of light, revealing a baby rattlesnake, half-pipped from its leathery egg, coiled and hissing next to the mushy, bubbling pulp that used to be its siblings.

Johnny looked at his daughter. "She absorbed life energy from snakes?"

"Yes. Life energy is life energy. The casing is irrelevant."

"Bullshit!" Johnny held up an arm and his hand turn to swarm. "Auster used insects to heal me. Look what the fuck happened."

"It's not the same," Torphis said. "You had no body. Auster used insect flesh to create your form." He gestured toward Maya. "She is fully intact. Her energy may register as different, but what you did was the equivalent of patching a hole. It's nothing like what Auster did with you."

Johnny held Maya close. "All right. Let's get her back to my apartment so she can rest."

EIGHTY-TWO

Maya Flynn woke in a haze. She felt the thin sheet covering her. *Hospital again.* Something felt different. *No, wait.* The room came into focus. *This looks like a bedroom.* She inhaled a cautious breath, expecting the rip of pain that comes with being sewn up. There was none. She dared to move. *It doesn't hurt. Wasn't I shot?*

"You're awake."

She startled at the deep voice. "Shit! You scared me." She pressed her hand against her chest, heart fluttering.

"I'm sorry." The thin, blond man at the foot of the bed laced his fingers together and hung his head.

Realization set in. "You're the guy from the party. Where am I? Where's Michael?"

"You're at my apartment. Michael is home."

"Your apartment?" Maya sat up. "I remember being shot." She inspected her stomach. "But I'm not injured."

"You've been healed. You'll be fine."

"I've been *healed*?" The memories flooded back. "If I recall, you tried to convince Wilks that you were my father. Now you're saying that the gunshot that went into my gut is *healed*, just like that?" Fear set in, bringing with it a clammy, cold feeling.

It was as if the man sensed Maya's trepidation. "No need to panic. I pretended to be Jonathan Flynn to get a confession out of Wilkinson. I didn't mean to upset you. As for the healing part, all I can tell you is that I have a gift." He smiled. "You understand the concept, don't you, *Miracle Maya*?"

Maya was stunned by what she just heard. *How does he know?* She thought for a moment. *Ah, he's an agent, too. Where do they find us?*

"Well your *gift* certainly is useful," she said.

"I'm glad it worked." The man smiled at her.

Maya recalled the event of the previous night. "What happened with that bastard Wilks? Did he really kill my mother?"

The man appeared visibly upset at this. "He did, Maya."

"Please tell me he didn't get away."

The man shook his head. "Wilkinson is dead."

"Did you kill him?"

"Yes."

Maya nodded. "Good. And Michael is okay?"

At this, the man squirmed at bit. "I did have to knock him out. He wouldn't let me close to you." He held both hands up. "Believe me, hurting him is the last thing I wanted to do, but if I didn't get you out of there right away you would have died. I promise that Michael is fine now. I checked on him myself an hour ago."

"Who are you?"

"I'm John Fallow."

"Fallow, I'm glad you were sent for backup, but I wasn't on assignment. So who sent you?"

John paused for a second, then smiled. "Actually, *I* was the one on assignment. Our paths crossed is all. Who sent me is not important. I'm just glad you're safe and Wilkinson is gone. I'll bet you are, too after what you learned."

"I always knew he wasn't who he portrayed himself to be. I started investigating Wilkinson as soon as I joined the force. Maya looked down at herself. "I'm a filthy mess. It looks like I rolled around in dirt."

"You were healed outdoors," John said. "Why don't we get you some clothes, a meal, and then talk more."

"Fair enough." Maya flung the sheet off and swung her legs over the side of the bed. "I'm staying at the Oceanside Resort in Gypsum."

∞∞∞∞∞∞

The table where Maya and John had brunch at the Oceanside Resort overlooked the Pacific. The ocean breeze that swept in through the open windows was a welcome tonic. Maya breathed in deeply, holding her phone six inches away from her head as Michael yelled at her.

"I'm fine, Mikey," Maya insisted. "The guy works for the same people I do. He's sitting right here."

John shifted in his seat as Michael blathered on.

Frowning, Maya leaned toward John. "Mikey says a *swarm-like thing* disintegrated Wilks and his thugs into bones. Is that true?" She held the phone out toward John.

John leaned forward and spoke. "New weapon. Sorry, can't say more."

"Holy shit. They're issuing that type of stuff?" Maya shook her head.

"Not to everyone," John answered.

Maya pulled the phone back. "There, satisfied? Look, I'm fine. I'll come see you when we're done here. Love you, bye." Maya ended the call.

"Is he okay?" John asked.

"He's still pissed that you hit him, but he'll get over it." Maya shifted on her chair. "I must say, even after a shower and food, this is still hard to get my head around."

"I realize that. I don't know what to say. How are you feeling? Did the healing take effect?"

"Yeah. Lunch helped." She eyed John's empty plate. "Steak tartare and a chocolate sundae is a strange Sunday brunch."

John observed his empty plates. "Strange, but oh, so, good."

Maya laughed.

"I crave weird stuff," John said. "Won't deny it." He looked out at the ocean. "Will you tell Michael that I'm sorry I knocked him out?"

"Yeah, he'll be touchy about it for a while, though." Maya said. "Thanks, John, for saving me. And for the truth about Wilks. I was a few steps behind you on that one, but what you revealed was quite a shock."

"No need for thanks." John put his elbows on the table. "I'd like to follow up in the weeks to come. To make sure the healing is complete and handle any details that may arise from the Wilkinson departure."

"Sure." Maya lifted her coffee cup. "That's a great idea. I'll give you my number."

∞∞∞∞∞∞

After saying goodbye to Maya, Johnny called to Torphis.

Ready to begin your work, new Sentry? Torphis asked.

Yes, I'm done here. I'd like to start somewhere far away. I need to distance myself from the west coast for a while.

New York will be a good place to start, Torphis replied. *Meet me in Central Park.*

Okay. See you shortly. Johnny turned to swarm and shot into the sky.

EIGHTY-THREE

William Rakesh Corby held up the empty container. "Mommy, can I have more pudding?"

Anisha smiled. "You ate that one already?"

"Yep. I'm hungry."

Anisha smiled at Frank, seated on the other side of the hospital bed, then walked to the door. "Ben, can you get William another pudding?"

Ben poked his head in the door. "Someone's getting his appetite back."

William grinned and thrust the cup into the air again.

"You got it, kid. One pudding coming up!"

"Me, too!" Katie chirped.

"Two coming up!" Ben patted the door frame and left.

Anisha walked to William's side and planted a kiss on his forehead. "We should be going home soon. And then we'll have a proper three-year-old birthday party for you. How does that sound?"

"Great!" William leaned toward Frank. "I'll get lots of presents, huh, Daddy?"

"Yes, pal. Lots." Frank stroked the boy's hair. "And I'm amazed at how well you speak now."

Ben trotted into the room a minute later. "Two puddings for the Corby kids!" He tossed one to Katie, who caught it in mid-air. "Nice catch. And for William." He put the pudding on the tray.

"Thanks, Ben." William picked up the container and stared at it. "What is *Thiamine hydrochloride*?"

Anisha froze. "William, did you just *read* that?"

"Yes." William pointed to the label on the back of the pudding. "*Thiamine hydrochloride*." He peeled back the top seal and said to himself, "H*ydro* means water."

Anisha felt the little hairs on her arm prickle up as she locked eyes with Ben. *What did those men do to my child?*

EIGHTY-FOUR

Johnny stood in the bedroom doorway, waiting for the family to arrive home from dinner. *Just the mother and children.*

He heard the fumbling at the lock, then the door sprang open and two children bounded through, laughing.

"Let's go there again!" the little girl called out to her parents as they followed her inside.

"Yeah!" the younger brother chanted.

"Yes, it was fun," the mother said, closing the door behind her. "I think we can probably talk Daddy into taking us again. What do you say, Daddy?"

The father raised his hands. "Well, I think we can arrange—" He froze when he saw Johnny enter the room. "Who are you?"

Johnny didn't wait for the others to react. He raised his hands and sent forth the swarms from his fingers, blanketing the mother and children.

It only took seconds for the insects to devour the flesh and leave the bones clean. Not even a drop of blood remained. Johnny turned to swarm and, avoiding the stunned look on the father's face, flew out the window.

For a fleeting second, Johnny allowed the thoughts in. His heart sank when he recalled losing Dani and not being able to see his own children reach adulthood.

I do this to others now. This is what I've become.

He would visit three more households that night.

So many people, all innocent. I'm sick every day. The work is endless. How do the other Sentries do this for centuries?

Two things had kept Johnny sane. The first was the unlikely friendship he'd begun with Maya. They spoke on the phone several times and even managed to meet in New York for lunch.

The second was Gladys. He thought of her often. Fighting to push what he'd just done from his mind, Johnny got back to his hotel and called her. "Hey, it's me."

"Oh, John, it's so good to hear your voice." Johnny could practically see her smile.

"It's good to hear yours, too. I'm coming back to Thousand Wells soon. I really want to see you."

"Oh, good. I can hardly wait to see you, too."

EIGHTY-FIVE

Johnny returned to Thousand Wells one month after killing Wilks.

Your first assignment as Sentry is a success, Auster reported. *I am pleased.*

Success. Johnny's feelings told him otherwise. Waves of anger, frustration, guilt, and grief surged though him.

I've murdered innocents. I take orders from a creature. Am I a monster, or am I really saving life on Earth?

Johnny slowed as he approached his apartment, noticing something on his doorstep. He moved closer and stopped in his tracks when the object became clear.

A bouquet of wildflowers.

He turned in a full circle, trying to see if anyone was watching him, but there was no one. He rushed to the door, leaned down, and scooped them up.

Who left these here?

He trudged into his apartment and dumped the flowers and two month's worth of mail onto the counter top. A honey-colored envelope, slightly larger than all of the others, caught his eye.

He read the return address, "Pratapgarth, India." He searched for the name of the sender but found none. He tore it open to find a hand-written letter on single piece of parchment.

New Sentry,

If you wish to alter your path, you must understand yourself. Gaze within and ask what makes you who you really are. When you obey your true self, the universe will fall into place and no force, no matter how strong you perceive it to be, can overpower you. I no longer kill. You do not have to, either. Seek me. I will show you.

There was no signature. Johnny let go of the letter and let it drift to the floor.

Kothra.

The ring of Johnny's phone startled him out of his trance. A wave of relief flooded him when he saw the caller. *Maya.* He put the phone to his ear. "Hi, Maya."

"Hi, John. How was New Jersey?"

He paused. "Could have been better. How about you?"

"I'm finishing up a job in Prague right now. I'm heading to India tomorrow."

Johnny glanced down at the letter. "India? You're kidding? I'm going there as well. Tomorrow, as a matter of fact."

"What? We *have* to meet up. Email me your itinerary and we'll make it work."

"I will." Johnny smiled. "I look forward to seein' ya, kid."

"Okay, John. See you soon."

Johnny ended the call, tossed the phone on the counter, and picked up the letter to reread it. Then the doorbell rang.

Johnny stiffened. *Who could possibly know I'm here?* He crossed the entry and pulled the door open.

"Hi, John." Gladys stood on the landing, wearing a tentative smile.

"Gladys, I was just about to call—" Johnny froze.

Her energy.

He read her energy, stopping at her center, which glowed like a lit fireplace.

"You're pregnant."

She nodded, eyes welling with tears. "Yes, how did you know?"

Johnny wrapped his arms around her and picked her up. "I just knew. You've made my decade, Gladys."

EIGHTY-SIX

Maya woke up in a pool of sweat. She pressed a hand against her forehead. *Another nightmare.*

It took a moment for her to orient herself and remember where she was. *Still in Prague.* She shivered. *Why can't I get warm?* She glanced at the thermostat. *Seventy-four degrees.*

"A shower will do it," she said as she sprang off the bed and hustled into the bathroom. She pushed the bath curtain aside, turned on the hot water, and waited.

After a minute, steam enveloped the room.

Maya inhaled and smiled. "Much better."

She peeled off her camisole and, right before she stepped into the shower, caught a glimpse of her back in the mirror. The skin looked odd, almost gray. Maya reached back and touched it, then pulled her hand back in panic.

What the fuck? It feels scaly.

She spun around and leaned forward to get a close look at her face in the mirror.

Yellow, reptilian eyes stared back.

Oh, my god, what's happening to me?

EIGHTY-SEVEN

Johnny drank in the warmth of India as he wound through the crowded streets toward the little restaurant where Maya said she would meet him.

He wondered how Kothra would know where to find him. *The fact that she knows I exist at all stumps me. She was able to find me in Thousand Wells, so I guess I'll just wait and avoid thinking about the past so Auster doesn't know where I am.*

In the distance, Johnny spotted Maya standing with a man. *Who's the guy?*

Maya hopped up when she saw him. "John!"

He reached her and gave her a hug. "There's my pal." He held her shoulders as he scanned her life source.

It's still a little different, but she looks fine.

Maya turned her attention to a man standing a few feet away. "Where are my manners? John, this is my associate, Ming. Ming, this is my old friend, John Fallow."

Johnny did his best to hide the feeling of shock as he stared at the face of the Asian man with a faded, jagged scar on his left cheek. *No fucking way.*

Ming stepped forward, cigarette in hand. He offered the other. "Old friend, huh? Pleased to meet you."

Johnny laughed aloud as he shook it. "Same." He twitched his finger toward the cigarette. "Bum a smoke?"

Ming paused, raised an eyebrow, and pulled out the pack. "Sure."

"Thanks." Johnny lit up, took a long drag, and blew the smoke into the air. He watched it curl up and travel in a thin wisp down the busy thoroughfare.

"The heat feels great," Maya said. "Let's go grab something to eat."

"Lead the way," Johnny said.

In the distance, he caught sight of a dark beauty with raven-black hair that fell to her waist. She stared at him as she sat at a small café table. Even from afar, Johnny could feel the difference in her energy.

Kothra.

She rose, a blossom amidst the busy throng, her crimson sari billowing in the breeze.

She smiled.

ACKNOWLEDGMENTS

It takes a village to birth a book. Words can never adequately express my deepest gratitude to those who have supported me throughout this process. Your wisdom, friendship, encouragement, and constant belief in me has been both inspirational and empowering.

My deepest thanks to Ed Aluzas, Carol J. Amato, Marian Attkisson, Steve Attkisson, Marissa Brake, Maria Cisneros Toth, Melissa Crown, Maria De Maci, Julie Fredericksen, Annie Hodson, Alanna Kilty Heck, Rilla Jaggia, Stephanie Jefferson, Lynn Kelley, Leah Leonard, Judith McAllister, Patricia O'Brien, Nancy O'Connor, Melissa Salazar, Kathy Sant, and Joanna Woods.

And thank you Jeff, Charlie, Lily, Max, Quin, Chloe, Henry Ralph, Dewey, and Freddie for being there through thick and thin. Jeff, the book cover rocks!

ABOUT THE AUTHOR

C. Sonberg Larson has been writing stories since the age of seven.

Larson lives in Southern California and, when not writing, can be found hiking, swimming, biking, running, gardening, cooking, and dog-walking.